EVEN GODS BLEED

DALE M. NELSON

SEVERN RIVER PUBLISHING

Copyright © 2026 by Dale M. Nelson.

All rights reserved.

No part of this book may be reproduced in any form or by any electronic or mechanical means, including information storage and retrieval systems, without written permission from the author, except for the use of brief quotations in a book review.

Severn River Publishing
www.SevernRiverBooks.com

This is a work of fiction. Names, characters, businesses, places, events and incidents are either the products of the author's imagination or used in a fictitious manner. Any resemblance to actual persons, living or dead, or actual events is purely coincidental.

ISBN: 978-1-64875-700-6 (Paperback)

ALSO BY DALE M. NELSON

The Gage Files

No Prayers for the Dying

One Bullet Away

Lightning Strikes Twice

Even Gods Bleed

With Andrew Watts

Agent of Influence

A Future Spy

Tournament of Shadows

All Secrets Die

Never miss a new release!

Sign up for the reader list at

severnriverbooks.com

The first seeds of what would turn into the Gage Files were sewn in the early 2000s. I'd been reading a lot of classic, hardboiled private eye novels at the time and thought it would be cool to write a spy story with that kind of style. I shared the idea with my dad during our weekly chat and he thought it was a neat idea. He was the only person I ever talked to about the project. I'd pick it up and put it down a lot over the years since, looking for the right way in. I know he'd have been pleased with the results. So, it is to the memory of my father, Maynard Nelson, that this series is dedicated.

1

Whenever someone tells you *it's not what it looks like*, it almost certainly is.

However, as I found myself creeping through a Hollywood Hills mansion—that I didn't own—and having casually bypassed a relatively sophisticated home security system, the thought occurred to me...this is not what it looks like. It wasn't breaking and entering in the strictest definition, because the rightful owner, my client, gave me permission to be here. Hopefully, that would get me around California's rather strict laws on personal surveillance when it came out in court that I'd planted a bunch of video cameras in strategic locations around the house.

Getting in the house wasn't a problem. I'd broken through more sophisticated security systems than this. My client gave me her soon-to-be ex-husband's six-digit passcode—the date he'd won a Golden Globe for best supporting actor in a TV show. That date was in the mid-80s, by the way. That let me turn off the system, so it wouldn't trigger an entry alert to his phone. Then, it was just a matter of picking a decent, but still average, lock.

I closed the door quietly behind me, even though the house was at the end of a private street and the end of a gated drive. Creeping through someone's home, even when you had permission, was still eerie. You become immediately attuned to the wrongness of it. You feel that it's lived in, the lingering smells of the rightful occupants still hanging in the air like ghosts to remind you that you don't belong. I caught a heavy dose of air freshener laid down over stale weed smoke.

The house was large, a six bedroom in an old-world style with a view of Los Angeles that someone like me could only enjoy as a guest. Before now, I'd only seen pictures. My client, Gloria Denmont, was old Hollywood. She'd grown up in the business, the daughter of a successful TV writer and producer. Gloria had a few films to her credit, but her legacy had been in television, and she made a respectable fortune in syndication. Then she'd pivoted to producing, parlaying her wit and charm into several highly lucrative films. Gloria married twice, and it was the second one that brought me up into the Hills tonight. Her husband, Jack McQuade (real name Wally Peterson), got his break in the eighties as second-billing tough guy and eventually upgraded to "henchman." He's one of the first people killed off in *Lethal Weapon 2*. Eventually McQuade realized he'd never be an action star, but was good-looking enough to play recurring roles as a "handsome TV dad." Gloria married him later in life, and it was probably fine for a while. Then, McQuade got bored and started fooling around. They married before prenups were seriously in fashion and co-owned her production company.

Gloria, though, owned the house outright. She'd bought this place new when it was built in 1990 and had lived here ever since. She was out of town for some time, having been called away to save a project that was crazily over budget and behind schedule. Gloria suspected that her husband would be a bit more brazen about his infidelity. In California, if you wanted to use that as grounds for divorce, you basically needed to catch the party in the act—which was why I'd broken into their house with covert surveillance equipment.

I started in the entryway. The idea was to show a chain of video tracing Jack's movement from the front door, through the house, to the bedroom. The cameras were small, with a lens about a quarter of the size of a pinky fingernail, on a short, telescoping fiber-optic cable that ended in a transmitter. These would relay to a base that I'd hide outside in the bushes, and that would connect back to my tablet and a cloud-based server where Gloria could view them at leisure.

Okay, bad choice of words.

One camera went to the kitchen and another above the bar with an angle of the wide living room beyond. Then, I crept up the spiral staircase to the master bedroom. The shades were all up, showing a west-facing view on three sides, and I took a guilty moment to enjoy the view. Even at eleven o'clock at night, it was breathtaking. LA's streetlights stretched out into infinity like glowing spiderwebs.

I'd followed McQuade this evening, where I spotted him having dinner with a small group at Mother Wolf. Body language and thirty seconds on Instagram told me who his mistress was. Dinner had been winding down when I saw them, so I figured on a half hour until they were home, unless there was an after party.

Two cameras went into the bedroom, just to be safe. Having windows on three walls made it a little difficult to place them out of sight, but I'd put one behind a bedside table that ran flush with the corner and another behind a TV hanging in the corner.

With the cameras placed, I pulled my phone out to check their positioning and transmission strength. Everything looked good.

Then, I heard the front door open. Laughter followed, a man and a woman. Apparently, I'd mistimed the relationship between McQuade's libido and his patience.

The staircase opened to the entry foyer. Exiting the front door would cause the alarm system to chirp, even if the system was disabled, and you could hear it from anywhere on the main floor. Since I still had the video running, I followed McQuade and his girlfriend into the family room. Once I heard a cabinet close and the sound of glasses landing on a counter, I crept down the stairs and sneaked across the foyer to the living room opposite. Ghosts spying on their neighbors made more noise than I did. There was another spiral staircase, this one leading to the basement.

I heard a vapid, bubbly voice giggle and say, "Cheers!" and I couldn't wait to ruin this guy. It took all my self-control not to reveal that I'd caught the asshole already. The lower level had a screening room to my left and a games room that opened to a door that led outside. I unlocked it, slid out, and closed it behind me.

Then, I disappeared into the night.

"Bastard," Gloria Denmont whispered with venom three days later in my office. "I've been in the film business most of my life. One thing I've learned," a dark smile crept up the side of her mouth, "the camera can always tell. She's faking." She swiped the tablet closed and slid it across the able, still wearing that self-satisfied grin.

Gloria was in her mid-fifties, blond, though she looked much younger. She was classically beautiful, and there was a style about her, a way, that perhaps was no longer in fashion. Gloria had just returned to LA, having flown out to a location shoot to reorient an upstart director's view of his place in the universe.

At least, that's what she told me.

That smile, a moment ago dark, even predatory, slid down the corners of her mouth a notch and gave her face a sad lighting. As if she realized this was the end. "Thank you, Matt."

"It's my job," I told her.

If I have a fault, and mind you, I said *if*, it's that I have a hard time turning off the part of me that's a detective. Knowing that my client was about to begin a long, contentious Hollywood divorce, I'd wanted to make sure that she was covered. Jack McQuade seemed cunning enough to hire someone like me to cover his angles. To that end, I spent some of the downtime looking for cracks McQuade might exploit at the trial.

I'd called her production company to find out where this troubled picture was so that I could see if McQuade was having her tailed. Her assistant asked, "What film?" Ms. Denmont, the assistant dutifully explained, was on holiday.

Apparently, this was my client's first foray into deception, because that was a lie she should have easily covered down on.

After that, it was a simple matter of tracking Gloria down. By the end of that morning, I'd learned the director she'd told me she was taking to task was actually a hedge fund manager she'd been seeing and they were spending the weekend together in the Hamptons.

"Stephanie will settle your expenses." Gloria slid out of the old, red vinyl booth. It creaked as she moved. I stood. She looked around Cosmic

Ray's, taking it in. Then softly shook her head. "I wasn't going to hire you when I heard this is where you worked. I figured it was either a stupid Hollywood gimmick, or bullshit California. Stephanie said you were good, though, and you didn't disappoint."

Stephanie was Gloria's attorney.

"There's just one thing, Ms. Denmont. You were right about one thing, the camera can always tell," I said, and she lifted an eyebrow, her mouth twisting into a lemon-suck expression. I opened my phone, tapped a folder and then one of the images in it. I held it out to her, then swiped a few times so she could see them all.

"Where did you get these?"

The photos were screenshots of an app called Orbit, which was an exclusive, private, encrypted social media platform for high society. The idea was to create a place for our betters to be able to post about their amazing lives and opinions but that was limited to a closed community. The app employed an encryption technology that automatically scrambled images when it detected the phone's operating system trying to make a screen capture to prevent cross-platform sharing. A hacker friend helped me figure out a way around that.

"It matters less how I found out, than the fact that I did. You should assume your husband hired a private detective to get something he can use."

"This is a shakedown, is that it?"

"No, Ms. Denmont, it isn't. You paid me well for the work I did." For my role in her divorce proceedings, which amounted to less than a week of surveillance and the camera job, I'd been paid fifteen thousand. I'd get an additional kicker of fifty thousand if the judge ruled in her favor. "I'm telling you this because I felt it was my obligation to inform you where you're exposed to liability."

Denmont's expression softened.

"Can you make this go away?"

"Probably, but I won't." That softening reversed itself damned quick. "You lied to me about where you were and what you were doing. Your personal life is your business. I don't care what you do with it. When clients lie, it makes me question other parts of their story. That's not good for either of us, and it only makes my job harder."

I could see the volcanism of righteous indignation swelling behind her eyes and her cheeks flushed red, but she didn't say anything.

"Good day, Ms. Denmont. I wish you luck."

I'd lost my source of reliable income about a year before, after I'd broken ties with an investigative journalism outfit, or rather, their lawyers advised them to break ties with me. Since then, I'd found myself taking riskier and higher-paying jobs to make up for it. Divorce is dirty business, and I'd never wanted to get involved in it.

My eyes followed Gloria as she walked out of the place. It takes a level of class you can't fake to gracefully exit a tiki bar in broad daylight.

The one upside to this job was that I'd been able to significantly upgrade my surveillance kit on her dime. Hopefully, my fee would float me until I found a new client, as I was now freshly unemployed.

2

When Denmont was gone, I walked up to the bar and had Ray pour me a beer.

"You've got a way with people, Matt," Ray said, smirking.

"Oh, shut up and pour," I growled. Cosmic Ray was the only philosopher I had time for, and today I just wasn't in the mood.

I was halfway through that beer when my phone rang. I didn't answer it until Ray gave me a cross look.

"This is Gage," I said, without looking at the number.

"Mr. Gage, are you available?"

"Are you asking me out on a date," I said. "Or, do you mean, am I taking on clients?"

"Ahh, the second one," the speaker said, awkwardly.

"Then yes."

"Great. Give me your email address. I need to send you some NDAs."

Oh hell. This already sounded like more trouble than I wanted to deal with. If you know how to find me, you already know my views on client confidentiality. Someone that comes in hot with an NDA is usually more trouble than they're worth, and has an inflated view of the things they want to protect. I gave him my address mostly out of curiosity. He disconnected the call. The email arrived immediately. The nondisclosure agreement was from a bogus-sounding corporation, though that was common enough now it didn't raise any eyebrows. I signed it on my phone and sent it back. He called back immediately. "I'm outside in the Mercedes."

I dug a five out of my pocket and set it on the counter, slid off my stool, and was about two steps away when Ray said, "Beers are seven bucks, Matt."

I found the vehicle in question street-parked along the Pacific Coast Highway. How did I know it was his? Only a person in a hundred-and-fifty-thousand-dollar electric G-Wagon would have me sign an NDA before telling me who he was. I slid my sunglasses on, crossed the parking lot, and walked up the embankment to the street level. It was November and SoCal cold, which is to say it was about sixty five.

Once I was within view of the Merc, I pointed a finger gun at the driver, who jutted his chin in response. I closed the distance and got in. He started driving immediately. I really hated it when amateurs tried pulling off cloak-and-dagger, because it just made them look twice as much like they had something to hide.

I recognized Julian Kessler right away.

He was the co-founder and CEO of NOVA AI, a tech company that promised to deliver a true human/machine artificial intelligence interface. They'd had a score of press hits lately, though that wasn't why I was familiar with him. Kessler's personal problems were outpacing the press releases on his company's technology.

"How can I help you, Mr. Kessler?"

"Well, I've been in the news a lot lately," he said, words loaded for bear. Kessler spoke with a tired voice, like I'd caught him at the end of a marathon. Still, leading with that presumed I was following the story.

"I believe someone is digging up dirt on me. They're purposefully leaking what they find to create a scandal."

"Why do you think someone would want to do that?"

"To destroy my reputation," he said, as though it were plainly obvious.

"Okay, but why? Is this a rival, or someone that might have a grudge against you?"

"I think someone is trying to take my company from me."

Fine. We'll pull on *that* thread. "It's your company, though, isn't it?"

"That's where things get complicated." Kessler breathed the words out. "I don't have a controlling interest in the company. Our board of directors are some of the most powerful people in the country. We have former cabinet secretaries, the head of an intelligence agency, the CEO of one of the most important defense contractors in the world. To land those names, unfortunately, we had to give up quite a bit of leverage."

I knew a little about Julian's background from the stories in the press. He'd had a successful exit from a previous company and made a small fortune from it. Certainly enough for an average person to retire on and be happy. So, naturally, he rolled that money into NOVA AI.

Following Kessler's logic so far, I said, "Okay, so you've got some dirt leaking in the press, and you believe the intent is to undermine you with your board of directors, who control your company. Is that it? And the intent, you believe, is to force you out of the company? Get the board to do a no-confidence vote, or whatever you call it."

"That's correct," he said.

"Do you think the board would do that? Boot you out of the company you founded? You selected them, though, right? Shouldn't they back you up?"

A laugh, harsh and snide, burst out of his mouth like a pressure valve releasing. "One would think. With the amount of money they've all got riding on this company? Yes. We're burning cash fast. Most tech ventures operate at a loss for some time, and we have not yet launched NOVA into the market. I think...I know there's a lot of frustration among some of the members, as well as some investors, with how long it's taking to get us profitable."

"Why don't you tell me a little about what's happening," I said. Traffic on PCH was light, and the beach was mostly empty. I watched a pair of locals trudge up from the water, wetsuits hanging open at the waist, looking like B-movie extras.

"It started as a story on social media that I stole the idea for NOVA from a grad school roommate. A few tech publications reached out for comment, and I told them there was nothing to it."

"Who did you speak to?"

"*WIRED*, *TechCrunch*, and a few California papers—*San Francisco*

Chronicle, The Mercury News. You know how social media is, though. People saw it and ran with it. It didn't matter that it wasn't true."

"Do you have a social media presence?"

"Yes. People tagged my account with the story. I engaged initially saying it wasn't true. Naturally, the conflict seekers and the trolls called me a liar."

"Does your company's marketing team run the social media, or do you outsource that?"

"NOVA does it."

"What?"

"NOVA does it."

"The...computer?"

Julian exhaled hard because he wanted me to know he was frustrated. "That's reductive, Mr. Gage. NOVA AI is among the most advanced artificial intelligences ever developed. It is the closest man has ever come to reproducing human thought. So, yes, NOVA can handle an Instagram account."

I let a few seconds pass so I didn't say something that might preempt my employment. "I know a PR firm that specializes in damage control. Whether you hire me or not, I recommend you contact them. As advanced as your system likely is, I doubt you'll have cracked the nuances of responding to shitposting on the internet."

Julian laughed at that, and it was a genuine sound. He said, "Fair."

"I think I've seen a few stories on you recently, Mr. Kessler. What else has come out?"

"I have three siblings. My brother and I were close, my sisters less so. Clay and I founded a company shortly after grad school. We did pretty well, and I'd invested what I'd made there to get NOVA off the ground. One of my sisters, Andrea, was angry that we didn't invite her to join the company. About lost her mind when we sold it. Our parents got involved at one point, 'Surely you could find *something*,'" he said, in a mocking tone. "What could she do? Andrea has no background in tech and worse business acumen. There was nothing for her to *do*. Anyway, she's made accusations that I'm a bully, had been abusive toward her my entire life, and that I intentionally cut her out." Julian shook his head. "My family and I are not on speaking terms." There was more to that, though I didn't have the standing with him yet to push on it.

"What about your brother? Clay?"

"He's tried to intervene, for the good it's done. There's a clip of Andrea giving an 'interview.' No news source is referenced, not that it matters. In this clip, she claims, behind some crocodile tears, that all she wanted was to work with her brothers. She claims Clay wanted to find her a place and that I said she wasn't smart enough to join us. He didn't say that."

"Could you find her something to do in your company now? Just to make it go away?"

In response, Julian pulled the video up on his phone and showed me. The clip ends with Andrea saying, "He thinks he's God." I scrolled through some of the comments beneath it, mostly affirming the accusations Andrea made and agreeing with the God complex.

"We estimate thirty-five percent of the social media users in our country have seen that video," Julian said, with enough acid to strip paint. "I never bullied Andrea growing up. She was the youngest. She was outgoing, pretty and popular. I was a nerdy kid that was into computers and math. I didn't know how to relate to people that weren't interested in what I was interested in until much later in life. I have a coach now."

I could paint a picture of him. Julian had been the smartest person in any room he'd been in until he'd gotten to Caltech for his undergrad. That was probably the first time in his life that he'd felt seen. Or felt the constant tension release a little bit because he wasn't having to fight the impulse of talking down to people.

Julian was aloof because he didn't know how to interact, and people typically took that as arrogance. Though, I suspected his sister was bitter they didn't invite her to join the business only after they'd had a multimillion-dollar exit. It didn't surprise me that Julian used a life coach now to help him interact with people that weren't like him.

"Has anything else been made of the allegation that you stole the idea for NOVA from your...grad school roommate, was it?"

"Noah Keynes, yes. But we were never roommates. I had an apartment off campus in grad school. No one bothered to fact-check that. Noah said that he'd come up with the idea for an intuitive interface during a project and that he'd brought me in to help him round out some ideas. He claimed that the idea for a neural cognitive interface had been his." Julian shook his head. "Which is laughable. That was all Graham."

"Graham?"

"Wexler. Sorry. He's our Chief Operating Officer. He also acts as our Chief Technology Officer. Most of the secret sauce behind NOVA AI is his; I helped him figure out how to make it into something we could sell. What eventually turned into NOVA was something Graham and I came up with in college. *We* were roommates at Caltech. Noah never had anything to do with it."

"Has Graham said anything?"

"Graham doesn't do social media, but he put a statement out confirming there was no possible way Noah could have come up with this."

We drove through Santa Monica in silence for a time while I processed what I'd heard.

"Outside of your sister and this Noah Keynes, can you think of anyone who'd feel wronged by you? Would want to do you harm?"

"Not that I can think of. I'd need more time to consider it, though."

"What about Graham, or the company's other officers?"

"I don't follow."

"You're the face of the company. If someone wants to take it down, it's logical they start with you, but the animus could be centered on someone else. You should have Graham and your other leaders go through a similar exercise. That's something I could help with if you wanted to move forward." I paused, to let him take that in. "You recently moved your head-quarters down here, is that right?" I asked. That was the vent that triggered the other stories on Kessler.

"That's right. Wanted to get out of Silicon Valley. That community has gotten toxic, and I didn't want to be around the culture any longer, didn't want to hire those kinds of people into my company."

"Those kinds of people?"

"Tech bros. Move fast, break things, be a dick. That is not the ethos you want when developing a machine that can interact with the human brain."

"Any chance this is a disgruntled employee?"

"The move wasn't popular with everyone. It also wasn't a surprise. We'd been talking about it for several months and have an open channel with our employees. The company is still quite small. Because of the nature of our work, and the security required, we don't allow our employees to be remote, so to stay with the company, they'd need to have moved with us. We paid relocation expenses for everyone. I think we had about twenty percent attrition."

Perhaps I wasn't the best benchmark for this, since I'd rarely lived in the same place longer than two years. People get attached to their homes, they build lives, it's a lot to ask someone to move even across the state. Though, if you were to ask, most people would attest in court that NorCal and SoCal were two separate countries.

"There's a little more, but that's the gist of it. So, what do you think?"

"This could be the opening moves of an intentional smear campaign. I could see a potential strategy here. The personal stuff easily goes viral because it's salacious and relatable. That, in turn, draws attention to some business-related accusations that will no doubt follow," I said.

"Can you help me?"

"That depends. What do you want me to do?"

"Find out who is leaking this stuff and put a stop to it."

"I can do the former. The latter may depend on whether what's being leaked is true or not."

"Of course it isn't true," Kessler snapped.

"If it's untrue, then we have a defamation case. I can conduct the investigation, find the culprit, and tee things up for your attorneys to blow the person out of the water. You're better off going that route than having me try to scare them off. That can backfire easily."

"How quickly can you work?"

"I appreciate that you want this resolved quickly, because it's embarrassing and distracting. However, I need to understand if there are other pressures involved."

"My board, you mean. That's why I reached out to you. They're concerned, and I'm worried I'm losing support. So far, they just want to know if it's true. One of them, however, Evelyn Hawthorne, informed me that I was expendable."

Kessler completed his loop through Santa Monica and pulled into a parking lot two blocks from Cosmic Ray's. He turned in his seat to grab a small, ballistic nylon messenger bag from the back seat. He handed it to me. "There's a MacBook in here with a NOVA AI instance loaded on it. You'll need an internet connection because it will need to link back with our servers to work. The system will walk you through activating biometric encryption so only you can unlock it. You can interact with NOVA just like you can any human. You can ask it questions, or you can type them, as you prefer." Kessler paused and looked at me with practiced intensity. "Of course, this is all covered by our NDA."

"Would you like to hear my rates?" I asked, though I hadn't yet agreed to the job.

"How much time does a hundred thousand get me?"

"Two months," I said. "That's dollars. I don't work for crypto."

"Of course. Figure out if someone is trying to unseat me and there's a significant bonus for you."

"How significant?"

"Are you able to own a home in this town?"

"No."

"You will."

3

Clients are rarely honest in the beginning.

They're hiring you because they want to prevent something bad from becoming something worse. The exact nature of the "bad" and the "worse" are often for the investigator to work out for themselves. After all, you're little more than a trusted stranger.

Julian wasn't telling me everything. The trick was to either figure it out or build enough trust that he tells me in time enough to help him.

I collected my car from Ray's and headed home. I drove a 1993 Land Rover Defender that I'd had restomoded to the point where I really shouldn't be making fun of Julian Kessler for driving a hundred-and-fifty-thousand-dollar vehicle. In my previous life as a spook, I'd crashed through the bush in many a country in one of these and fallen in love with them. When I left the Agency, I took the money I'd saved and bought one, then had one of SoCal's leading restoration gurus modernize it and incorporate some additional functionality—mostly concealed storage spaces for the equipment I use on cases.

Once I was home, I powered on the laptop and, just like Kessler said, the system guided me through setting up the biometric encryption protocol. Once I was through, it independently validated my identity by cross-referencing it with public records.

"Good evening, Mr. Gage," the computer said. It spoke in an easygoing male voice, without accent. It reminded me of an overly helpful assistant manager.

"Um...good evening?"

"It is all right, Mr. Gage. People often do not know what to say when first interacting with me. I promise you, it gets easier. I have several voice forms we can use, male or female and a variety of accents."

"Can you do Mr. T?" Might as well get it used to who it was dealing with early.

"I am afraid not."

"Okay. You'll do."

"Excellent. Are you ready to begin?"

I told it I was.

"My name is NOVA, or Neural Optimized Virtual Assistant. I am a neural interface and artificial intelligence technology designed to seamlessly integrate artificial intelligence with human cognition."

"I don't know what any of that means," I said.

"I understand. I can significantly enhance problem solving and creative and critical thinking and can amplify communication without replacing human decision-making. I do this through what we call a 'noninvasive mind/machine interface.' Essentially, Mr. Gage, through our interactions and my learning attributes such as your behaviors, preferences, deliberation processes, and communication style, I can begin to predict your responses. The scientists at NOVA AI are also developing an interface that will read brainwave activity for a more comprehensive neural interface."

"So, what, you read my mind or something?"

"Well, in a sense, yes."

NOVA said it so succinctly, so matter-of-factly, it took me a moment to process that it had actually said it.

"Once fully developed, the interface will adapt to a user's thought process, allowing me to become a true extension of their mind. In this TED Talk, Julian will describe the social benefits of this technology."

The screen dissolved into Julian on the TED stage, and my thinking dissolved with it. I resurfaced briefly to hear him claim NOVA was the first machine capable of abstract thinking, even original artistic expression. He said the neural interface could become an extension of human thought and postulated advances in everything from robotic exploration to truly functional prosthetic limbs.

I wasn't sure if interrupting a computer in the middle of a speech was rude or not, but I'd heard enough of the sales pitch. "NOVA," I said, breaking in. "I'd like you to help me with some research."

"Excellent. Mr. Kessler instructed me that I was to assist you in your investigation."

"Are you connected to the internet?"

"I am."

"I'd like you to conduct a sentiment analysis on traditional and social media regarding Mr. Kessler and the public's views on the NOVA AI technology."

This was the first test to see how good of a researcher it was. The Agency had been using AI for nearly twenty-five years to conduct link analysis and parse massive datasets. It was some of the most advanced computing technology in the world, and I was curious to see how NOVA compared. It took less than a minute for NOVA to return its results.

"Mr. Gage, the majority opinion is that the public is concerned with the potential for me to be used in military or intelligence applications. Sixty-two percent were concerned about the potential for breakout, which is the term used for an AI escaping human control. Twenty percent are concerned with a foreign nation acquiring the technology. There is a vocal group that argued against any man/machine interface, many of them citing religious concerns. However, there are supporters." NOVA created a compelling and dynamic visual depicting floating clusters of quotes, article excerpts, and video snippets, all advocating their belief in NOVA's capabilities, with many saying that the benefits outweighed the risks. It was a hell of a salesman, had to give it that.

I took a brief pause and made a quick dinner, then I poured a couple fingers of Lagavulin and went back to it. I decided to shift focus slightly and dig into the company. A good first step seemed to be looking into NOVA's board of directors. Julian was clearly concerned about them, and it felt important to see if that fear was justified. Julian told me about two of them already. Hawthorne passing a veiled threat to Julian like that was curious.

"NOVA, I'd like to learn more about the board members."

"Of course. I must advise you that even though you've signed nondisclosure agreements, I cannot share any company confidential information with you, Mr. Gage."

"I understand."

"The board members consist of three company officers, Julian Kessler, Graham Wexler, and Amara Singh. The external members are Nathaniel Crowder, Evelyn Hawthorne—"

"Let's begin with Nathaniel Crowder," I said, cutting NOVA off. I was familiar with the name, if not the reputation. A reporter once likened him to a Bond villain.

"Nathaniel Crowder is the founder and CEO of Crowder Dynamics. He runs a family of companies under the Crowder Dynamics umbrella. Subsidiaries included Vanguard Defense Systems, which specializes in networked autonomous combat and surveillance vehicles. Would you like detailed descriptions of each of the subsidiaries?"

"No," I said, and refilled my scotch. "A summary will do."

"Excellent. There are additional ventures in materials science, energy, and medtech. All of these blended AI into their solutions."

"What's the general opinion on Crowder from the board members?"

"I would need to consult with Julian before sharing that information."

Worth a shot. Crowder was known to be a ruthless innovator, and made no secret of the fact he wanted NOVA AI within the broader Crowder Dynamics family. Researching him on my own, I'd learned several of NOVA's investors shouted concerns when Kessler moved the company from Silicon Valley to Costa Mesa, believing it to be an extension of Crowder's influence.

"Mr. Gage, I have just received authorization from Mr. Kessler to share anything you require within my ethical parameters."

"You asked him just now?"

"Yes, while briefing you on Mr. Crowder."

"Well, shit," I said, genuinely impressed. "Who's next?"

"Ms. Evelyn Hawthorne has enjoyed a long career of public service."

"NOVA, just the facts."

"Of course. As Undersecretary for Commerce, she'd managed much of the US government's technology portfolio, later serving as the White House 'Technology Czar.' In this role, she directed government investment in advanced tech and AI. After leaving government, Ms. Hawthorne founded a tech-focused nongovernmental organization and the Horizon Impact Fund. According to their public profile, the fund's goal is to bring 'game-changing technological investment to the developing world to accelerate sustainable growth and bypass the detrimental effects of industrialization.'"

"That's quite the mouthful," I said. I couldn't imagine having to say that to another human and be taken seriously. "She live here?"

"Ms. Hawthorne splits her time between California, where her foundation, Catalyst for Humanity, is based, and Washington."

"NOVA, can you share any of Ms. Hawthorne's goals? Why did she join the board?"

"Ms. Hawthorne has advocated extending NOVA AI's capabilities globally with a focus on the developing world. Interestingly, that is also one of Dr. Diana Verala's goals."

Verala was one of the few names I did not know. I stood and stretched, my back reminding me just how long I'd been hunched over the keyboard. We were several hours into this exercise, and I was just now realizing I didn't need to stare at the screen and type. Walking around the room, I said, "NOVA, I'd like more detail on Dr. Verala, please."

"Dr. Diana Verala, born in Lisbon and educated in Europe, is a former tech executive turned international consultant. She specialized in bringing groundbreaking technologies to global markets, with a focus on Europe, South America, and Africa. She speaks five languages fluently. Her standing as an adviser to the European Union and United Nations positions her to advise the company on how to best position themselves globally. I should note that Dr. Verala and Ms. Hawthorne argue in board meetings frequently. They occasionally attack each other's positions online and in the media. Mr. Kessler believes this is counterproductive."

I wondered if Julian brought Verala on to counterbalance Hawthorne.

There was one more board member to review. It was...*shit*.

"General Alexander Graves," NOVA said.

I didn't need the profile.

Graves had recently retired as the head of the National Security Agency.

One of the original members of the US Intelligence Community, the NSA was America's code-breaking and cyber espionage agency. The dossier described Graves as championing NOVA's applications in intelligence gathering, which seriously concerned the other board members, most of the investors, and the broader public. Graves could be a serious problem for me, specifically, especially considering how bad my relationship with the CIA was now.

"NOVA, can you summarize the allegations against Julian Kessler that have been reported to date?"

"Yes, Matt." NOVA described the situations with Noah Keynes and Julian's sister in clinical detail. It was strange hearing something so personal antiseptically delivered by the machine. That reminded me I wasn't speaking to a person. "Juliette Voss is a former NOVA AI employee who has accused Mr. Kessler of carrying on a romantic relationship and then terminating her employment when the relationship ended." The AI quoted multiple posts from various social media feeds where Voss reiterated her claims, usually trolling Julian or the company announcement. The one that received the most traction was her claiming that the move to Orange County was "running away."

When I finally refilled my Lagavulin and decided to knock off for the evening, I had a strong sense of what NOVA AI was capable of and enough awareness to know this was just scratching the surface.

I also had some interesting insights on potential threats. Everyone on that board of directors stood to gain something by taking control, both financially and ideologically.

One thing was certain, I didn't envy my client. He was treading in some shark-infested waters, and he was bleeding.

That night, I called Julian and asked if I could meet him in person the following day. He suggested a hike in Bommer Canyon before his day started. Costa Mesa was about fifty miles south, but since Southern California had advanced the state of the art of traffic congestion beyond the reaches of human achievement, it could easily take me two and a half hours to get there.

I left early.

Ninety minutes later, I was in the parking lot outside the trailhead. It was a crisp, clear morning. Kessler was already there, exiting his G-Wagon, furiously double-thumbing on his phone. He wore an earth-toned hoodie and slightly darker joggers. This was my first time seeing him outside the vehicle. Kessler was tall, with a lean, angular build that rounded at the corners, suggesting exercise but not commitment. His hair was cut short and was not styled, the "disinterested genius" look. Everybody in tech read Steve Jobs's biography, and now they dressed monochromatically and didn't bother with a comb.

"This was a good idea," he announced, putting his phone away. We'd agreed that until I figured out my approach to the case, best not to be seen together or for me to visit NOVA's offices. Technically, I hadn't agreed to work for him yet. We started off on the trail, dirt crunching underfoot. "What'd you think of NOVA?" he asked, once we'd started moving.

"I have to admit, it probably saved me two days of independent research. Its ability to summarize and contextualize video was amazing. But learning from our conversation blew me away." While I didn't contain my boyish enthusiasm for the tool, I'd spent much of the night thinking about its potential consequences. Yeah, maybe not what Julian was hiring me to do, couldn't shake the thought, though. Considering what it could do with board meetings, imagine what the intelligence services might do with those same capabilities. We talked about the NOVA system for the first mile of our walk, with Kessler telling me about the genesis of it from a conversation he'd had with Graham Wexler when they were Caltech undergrads.

"When did you first realize someone was trying to discredit you?"

"It started after I'd announced the move to Costa Mesa. The decision wasn't popular. Some of our employees were pissed, even though I offered relocation and flexible work schedules. It was less popular with our investors, many of whom were located in the valley."

"Why would they care where you're based?"

"People made too much of it. Leaving Silicon Valley was taken as our thumbing our nose at the tech community. And some believed it was a sign that I was selling to Nathaniel Crowder. Which, I am not. I admit, though, that the move was a bit of a flex. I felt like some of our investors thought they had more control than they do, and this was my way of showing that I was still in charge."

"Are you?"

"Oh, sure. I'm still board chair and structured our charter so that I have two votes. With Graham and Amara, the rest of the board can't overrule us, even with unanimous agreement. And there's a good energy down here."

Amara was Amara Singh. She was the company's head of ethics and the chief scientist. Julian acted as though I knew about her without any additional context. Either he assumed I'd done the homework or that I just knew who these people were.

"So, if that's true, what are you worried about? Wexler is your college roommate. I imagine Ms. Singh wouldn't side against you. You said Wexler defended you against the allegation that you stole the idea from this Noah Keynes." I didn't mention the Voss woman purposefully.

"There's a woman, a former employee who claims we had an affair. And that I fired her after it ended."

"There any truth to it?"

"This is embarrassing for me," he said, as though that explained everything. I didn't press him. "I, ah, haven't had many relationships with women. Juliette was nice to me." He described their time together awkwardly and with some difficulty, not because it was painful but because he lacked the language and experience to do so. I'd need to investigate her, but as Julian told it, he unknowingly portrayed her as a climber.

"Why'd you fire her?"

"I didn't," Julian said plaintively. His tone had an overly defensive, almost childlike quality to it. "She was in business development. We let her go because she wasn't a fit and didn't understand the technology enough to sell it." Julian upshifted into his CEO role, and the childish countenance vanished as though it'd never been. These allegations, so far, seemed to be regrettable incidents taken out of context and amplified. That alone should not be reason for a founder to fear their job. "Look, we churned through several iterations of BD before we got it right. I even had to let the entire team go at one point because we knew they weren't aligned to the technology."

"What do you make of the suggestion that this was Crowder manipulating you?"

"I'm aware of that, naturally." Then he added, "The suggestion, that is. And I get where it's coming from. Nathaniel gets a bad rap sometimes, not that it isn't always deserved. He's a shrewd businessman and has been a good mentor, particularly as I've had to learn navigating some of the complex partnerships we're negotiating."

"The common criticism I hear is that he's trying to militarize your technology."

Kessler shrugged. It was such an offhand, dismissive gesture, it might as well have been a slap in the face. "Doesn't everybody? Honestly, I'm much more interested in his medtech and advanced materials companies. There's real good to be done there. But we also see NOVA as a way of minimizing human casualties in war, were we to explore defense applications. I haven't decided yet. Think about how many innocent lives were lost in drone strikes due to bad intelligence. What if we could eliminate that possibility forever? That's the kind of thing Crowder and I talk about."

I'd been at that game too long to believe you could technology your way out of bad intel. It was also the kind of response I expected someone like Julian Kessler to give. That's not to say he was wrong to try, but to someone like me, it felt dangerously naive. I asked about the tension between Hawthorne and Verala, how that impacted their competing views on possibly deploying this technology abroad. Kessler waved this off, almost out of hand, saying only that the creativity is born from productive conflict. He used the term "tournament of ideas" several times throughout our conversation.

"That may be, but someone may still try to take over your company," I said. "I want to circle back to something you said earlier. If you have two votes and outnumber the board members, why are you worried about them unseating you?"

"They'd need either Graham or Amara to do it."

"Doesn't seem likely, the way you've described it," I ventured, testing the waters.

"Let me ask you this, Matt. If you had a share of changing the world forever and you felt someone was standing in your way, where would *you* stop?"

Had to admit, that was a powerful question and not one I had a ready answer for.

We completed our loop through the canyon and returned to the parking lot shaded by sycamore trees. "So, what do you think? Do I have a case?"

"I think there is something to the idea that this could be a subversive take-over. To date, there have been three attacks against your reputation. All of them seem to suggest you are a bad person. While there is some negative sentiment toward the technology, it isn't targeted."

"Do you believe the threat is coming from the board?"

"I'm not there yet. I'd need to see them in action first, possibly surveil them. Since we have six suspects, that could take some time. On balance, they're powerful people, each with an agenda for your technology. It'll require more investigation." I'd already ruled out Keynes, the Voss woman, and Julian's sister as suspects. A quick background on each showed they did not have the fortitude or knowledge to run a blackmail campaign. Nor did I think they'd think to hire someone to dig up dirt on Julian for that purpose.

"I didn't expect it would be easy. Will you do it?"

"I think everyone on your board has a vested interest in controlling your company. Whether that means pushing you out and taking direct control of the IP, or keeping you on and blackmailing you into compliance, I don't have enough information to say."

We walked to Kessler's Mercedes.

"I know Hawthorne made a broadside that you could be replaced. How have the others reacted?" I asked, knowing that I hadn't answered his question yet.

"It varies. Crowder doesn't seem to care. He says if you're not pissing people off, you're not doing your job. Graves is very reputation conscious and doesn't want to be associated with anything…'improper.' Verala seems to imply whatever I do is my business as long as it doesn't impact the company. Hawthorne worries about NOVA being able to get government contracts and clearances."

"And what about Wexler and Singh?"

"Graham was my roommate in college. He knows me. Amara," Kessler's voice trailed off as he focused on something at the far end of the lot. "Our relationship is complicated."

"Why?"

Kessler only shook his head. Okay, whatever *that* meant. "Send me your standard contract. I'm going to have my personal attorney do some markups for confidentiality. I'll also send some of the company's financials through NOVA on the laptop. This is going to be proprietary, and will include investment information. I'm trusting you with a lot, Matt." Kessler opened the car door and climbed in.

"I understand. I won't let you down," I said.

Kessler nodded, satisfied, and powered up his vehicle. I watched him back out and silently roll out of the parking lot.

Back at my place, I asked NOVA to give me a crash course in the company's finances, focusing on how much each board member invested in. In addition to Kessler's system, I had an AI application of my own called EchoTrace, which was designed for use by law enforcement agencies, security companies, and licensed private detectives. EchoTrace was an investigative tool that I used to scan open source information—public records, media files, publications, and law enforcement databases. In this instance, I used it to investigate where NOVA's board members had additional financial interests.

NOVA also summarized the investors who were not board members. Sometimes a company will have what they called an activist investor, someone who threw money toward a cause and if they found themselves at odds with the CEO could move to unseat them. It'd happened before.

About halfway through reviewing the investor roster, I stopped cold.

Apex Partners.

That was Benjamin Blake's firm.

I'd known Ben once, and I cost him a lot of money by doing my job.

4

Benjamin Blake ran a venture capital firm in Silicon Valley. Two years ago, I was investigating the purported suicide of Blake's partner, Johnnie Zhou. Zhou's daughter, Elizabeth, thought it was something else. The truth was much darker, and worse than any of us imagined. Blake, at first, tried to scare me off with his personal attorney and some connections with the California Bureau of Investigation. He eventually came around once he recognized that I was onto something, and called his attack dogs off. However, when the specter of negative publicity threatened a major business deal, Blake tried to pay me off. Blake was worried about reputational damage to his firm when the news finally broke that his dead partner was a Chinese spy. I didn't fault him for that, but there were better ways to handle it. Hell, I could've helped him if he'd brought me in instead of trying to buy silence. Ignoring his offer, I did what I do, and when the story broke about Johnnie Zhou, Blake lost the deal. Word is, it was a joint venture worth tens of millions.

I'd need to disclose that involvement to Julian.

I asked NOVA to summarize Blake and his history with the company. This would be limited to corporate records, board meeting notes, and investment disclosures, but should give me a sense of how close they were.

"Apex Partners has invested nine-point-five million dollars total in

NOVA AI. Investment began in the B Series," the system told me through the MacBook's speakers. "During this time, Julian Kessler invited Benjamin Blake to join the company's board of directors. He served in this capacity for a period of twenty-six months, until he was removed by a four-to-three vote. Blake was replaced on the board by General Alexander Graves."

Though I interacted with an AI almost daily in my work, EchoTrace was a manual interface. Actually asking questions through dialogue took some getting used to. "Who put forward the motion to remove Blake from the board?"

"Nathaniel Crowder."

"NOVA, do you know if Mr. Blake and Julian still communicate?"

"Yes, Mr. Kessler maintains a relationship with Mr. Blake and views him as an informal adviser. My confidentiality settings prohibit me from disclosing their conversations to you, but Mr. Kessler is not secretive about their interaction."

Before I moved any further, I needed to speak with Blake. If they were close, Blake could still torpedo this investigation, and he might do it out of spite. Better to head that off now than to get ambushed later.

He'd given me his personal number during the case where we'd crossed paths.

I called.

"Wondering when I'd hear from you," Blake said immediately.

"You know that Julian hired me?"

"Who do you think gave him your name?"

I didn't know what to say, and the hesitation telegraphed that plainly to Blake.

"Matt, your investigation cost me a lot of money, that's true. You were also spot-on. The disclosures about Johnnie didn't sit well with our prospective partners, and they pulled out. I don't hold anything against you, though. You were doing your job. I'm still coming to grips with Johnnie. I worked with him every day for twenty years."

"You couldn't have seen that coming," I said. Because *we'd* trained him. Johnnie had been a CIA asset in China before he was a Chinese asset in America. Life is not without a sense of irony, it would seem.

"Even with all of that, I'm surprised you recommended me to Julian," I said.

"He's a smart kid, but he's too trusting. And I think he's got people in his ear that don't have his best interests at heart. Once I heard that someone was digging up dirt on him, it felt like this was the leading edge of a blackmail play. If anyone could figure that out, I knew it was you."

It was a strange vote of confidence, for sure, considering the source.

"What do you make of these allegations?" I asked.

"If I thought Julian was unethical, I wouldn't have given him ten million dollars," Blake said.

"How does Julian conduct his business?"

"Oh, he's aggressive for sure. You have to be these days, the market is too competitive. When I was coming up, you could afford to be a little deliberative. Not now. You have to make almost split-second decisions, you can't equivocate, and you can't worry about pissing people off. It's ruthless."

"I think Julian is learning that lesson firsthand. I know you two are close, has he talked about anyone that he's made an enemy of?"

Blake did not speak for some time.

"I have some opinions about that, but I'll keep them to myself for now. Learned that lesson the hard way from you the last time. All I'll say is there's something to the adage about keeping your enemies close. The one time Julian asked for my advice and didn't take it was when he had this idea about a team of rivals."

Blake had his reasons, whatever they were, and didn't want to say it outright, but he was clearly talking about NOVA's board of directors.

"Look, I've had a front-row seat to nearly every major technological advance in the last forty years. Julian Kessler has designed one of the few truly novel technologies that I've seen. If they do it right, NOVA changes the way our society works, the way we interact with machines. More importantly, the way machines interact with *us*. That's a distinction most people don't appreciate. Think about life before smartphones, before the internet or personal computers. If NOVA does this right, it will be like that, only on an order of magnitude far greater. Now, imagine if you had a slightly different vision, or, more to the point, believed you could realize that goal more effectively than Julian Kessler could. Where would you look?"

"You were on the board once, I understand."

"That's right. Board coups happen all the time in this industry, and I've engineered a few myself. I don't get along with Nathaniel Crowder, I never have. There's no secret in that. I was quite vocal when Julian announced the move to Costa Mesa."

"You didn't think they should do it?"

"Let's say I didn't agree with his logic. If you're worried about culture, don't hire assholes." Blake sighed. "I'd say I was outvoted, but there wasn't one. Julian, Wexler, and Singh all agreed to it. Crowder saw his moment and pounced."

"When was this?"

"Last year. The company didn't make the headquarters move public until just a few months ago, so everyone thought it was a hasty thing. It'd been in work for some time," Blake said. "When you're thinking about who might try to take his company away from him, let me pose the same question you once asked me about Johnnie Zhou's death. Who benefits?"

"They all do," I said dryly.

"I think it comes down to vision," he said. "People kill for religion. A vision for the future isn't that different."

"You were on the board. Do you think the threat is real? They wouldn't really replace him, would they?" This was the question I'd wanted to ask. As a former member, Blake had a window into this I couldn't get anywhere else.

"The upside on this technology is in the billions, and that's if they're just *close*. Always keep that in mind when you're considering how far someone will go."

"If they're worried, why not get rid of him already?"

"They don't have a product without Julian. The whole notion of consumer applications was his idea. Julian is the one who figured out they could create something that people like you and me would want as much as governments or industry."

I worked hard to suppress a laugh. The notion that "you and me" could be dropped on me and Benjamin Blake was hilarious. He'd once tried to buy me off at a Palo Alto club that didn't disclose their address.

"One last thing, Matt. And I want you to take this advice seriously."

"What's that?"

"Be careful. There are powerful interests involved."

"Nothing I haven't seen before," I said.

"You're not hearing me, Matt. This is about ideology as much as it is money, a vision for the future. If someone is willing to ruin Julian Kessler over this, think about what they might do to you."

I thanked Blake for his time and the referral.

His closer echoed in my head long after the call. I knew the lengths people would go to in defending their worldview. More to the point, the things they could justify on that account.

Blake's involvement added complexity to the case that it already didn't need. If the rest of the board members discovered that Julian hired me on the recommendation of their ousted peer, it'd certainly call the motives of the case into question.

Blake's motives were not above suspicion either. He'd admitted to a long-running conflict with Nathaniel Crowder, and he could harbor resentment toward Dr. Verala for filling his seat. And there were the three other people that voted with Crowder.

Deciding I needed a change of scenery to contemplate my next moves, I went back to the office.

I liked Ray's best in the offseason. It was November and cold, the tourists were long gone, and in the afternoon, Cosmic Ray's was a place for locals. There was a line of people on the barstools, mostly veteran surfers with salt-stringy hair and weather-beaten faces. When I walked in, framed by afternoon light in the doorway, I got chin nods of recognition from most of them. They counted me as a regular, if not one of their own, as long as I stayed the hell off the water.

After an early attempt at surfing, Ray told me that my efforts offended the sea itself.

Ray saw the look on my face and poured a beer. I tried to stay away from the tiki drinks while I was working. He rotated the taps frequently, but had a line on some of California's best beers, which was in and of itself an embarrassment of riches. This was an IPA from Fieldwork, though I didn't catch the name. I took the beer back to my usual table and set to work with a notepad, organizing my thoughts.

Blake's involvement resolved the question of whether I'd go in under-cover. But, as what? I needed access to each of the board members, a way to interrogate them without them knowing it. Posing as a tech reporter was the obvious first choice. My undergrad was in journalism, and I'd free-lanced for an investigative outfit called the Orpheus Foundation since I left the Agency. That all ended a year ago when a Russian intelligence unit murdered the foundation's leader, Denis Coenen. He'd been a close friend, and I missed him. Jennie Burkhardt, my original connection to the founda-tion, and an on-and-off girlfriend, assumed Denis's role after his death. She'd moved to Brussels for it, and I felt her absence every day.

The foundation's lawyers said they couldn't afford to work with me anymore, and I certainly felt the absence in my bank account. That was partially why I had to take jobs for people like Gloria Denmont.

The key challenge with any cover was backstopping it.

Many of these people would have deep contacts in tech media and could unravel that legend quickly.

"How's it going, Magnum?"

I looked up at the source of the easy SoCal drawl and saw a weathered, smiling face I knew well. Bo Fochs was my height, with a surfer's muscled build I could see beneath his gray sweatshirt. Blond hair streaked white from a daily saltwater bath hung just above the shoulders. Fochs had been a legendary undercover narcotics cop with the LAPD in the eighties and was credited with one of the largest drug busts in department history. He'd made some political enemies doing it, and his firing from the police depart-ment a few years later bore striking similarities to my own expulsion from the CIA. Once he'd learned that about me, we'd become fast friends. After leaving LAPD, Bo worked as a private detective, operating primarily in Hollywood and working almost exclusively for clients in the music and film industries.

Bo, now in his seventies, was retired and spent most of his time surfing. I respected his retirement and we didn't talk shop often. In discussing work, Bo was laconic, and I'd learned to let him drive the conversation. He wasn't the type for war stories, more he'd share a vague parable through the lens of an old case. Invariably, I found hard-earned street wisdom in those tales. In that regard, Bo Fochs was one of the best teachers I'd ever had. Often as not, he'd just tell lunatic tales from LA's hard rock heyday, which he'd seen from behind the stage. Since that was the majority of the music Ray played, usually a band would come on that Bo had known personally or worked with. When he could, he'd share some nugget of how he'd helped a rock star avoid jail.

Bo took a seat across the booth, and I shared some of the details of Kessler's case, though I kept the names out of it. "So you're, what, looking for a way into this company without the board members knowing you're a PI?"

"That's right. I've scratched off half a dozen possible legends I could use." Bo leaned across the table and examined my marked-up notebook. "They're all powerful in their own right. Nearly unlimited resources. Two of them had senior roles in the federal government, and they've all got deep ties one way or another."

"And you're worried about how fast they could unravel your cover?"

I nodded and took a pull from my beer.

"Thought about being a potential investor?"

I shook a negative. "The company isn't taking new investment right now, and my sense is the board members would view anyone new as a threat. None of these people trust each other. My client selected them almost for that reason. Said he valued their individual input, but also that each of them opposed someone else on the board."

"That seems like a recipe for chaos."

I spread my hands. "And here we are." Bo laughed.

"Have you thought about posing as a security consultant? I did that once. Client managed one of the biggest bands of the time, and he thought someone at the record studio was making copies of the master tapes to sell as bootlegs. Now, this was before the internet, and they had to do that sort of thing by hand, you see."

"Who was the band? Anybody I know?"

Fochs flashed a Cheshire smile and just looked up at the ceiling, where the speakers were. Guns N' Roses' cover of Dylan's "Knockin' on Heaven's Door" was playing. "That was a weird case, for all the usual reasons you'd expect. But the real fear was someone was going to leak demos of the songs before they came out. Stuff was pretty raw. Those days, you released singles before the album came out, and that shit was kept under lock and key. And because of how important record sales were at the time, you had to open big. Plus, they're going up against Metallica, Van Halen, and Ozzy, who all had monster new records at the time. Anyway, coming in as a security consultant who was supposed to protect a temperamental rock star let me sort of fade into the background. I figured out pretty quick that an engineer was offering to sell bootlegs out of his car every night on the Strip." Bo's words faded out, and I could see in the change in his eyes' focus that his mind went to the memory. I let him sit with that for a moment. He took a drink and then looked up. "Can you use the dysfunction and the infighting to your advantage?"

"You mean, like pitting them against each other?"

"Not exactly, though that might be a way of getting information out of them once you're inside. People love to talk shit about their enemies. Just think about if there is a way to exploit the conflict, see if that creates an opening." Bo leaned back in his seat and lifted his beer.

"Ha!" The short, jagged laugh burst out of my mouth. Bo just lifted his eyebrows in response. "I'll have my client tell them he hired a performance coach. He's trying to find a proactive way to resolve the board's personality conflicts."

Bo chuckled. "That is some California-level bullshit. You'll do all right, kid."

"Thanks, Bo."

"Any time. I'll leave you to it." He eased himself up out of the booth and faded back to the bar.

I spent a few minutes roughing out a backstory and then called Kessler on Signal.

"Julian, I've got an idea. Here's what I need you to do."

5

"Oh, that's badass," Julian said.

Not the reaction I was expecting.

We were in his office at NOVA's new headquarters building in Costa Mesa. It was a large, blue-glass and brown-metal building that looked like an artist's rendering of a sci-fi future. His office faced the back and a manufactured garden they'd put in.

"The idea is to give me a reason to interview each of the board members on their concerns, without tipping our hand that I'm a PI. I expect most will immediately dismiss me and not take me seriously, which will put them off guard."

"I need to tell Graham, at least. And Amara."

"Not until I've ruled them out."

"They aren't just board members, Matt. They're officers in this company. I've known Graham for fifteen years. I can't just—"

"This will go badly for us, if you do. Trust me."

Julian nodded, his thoughts already elsewhere. Couldn't blame him, competition for his attention rivaled the Olympics. The board was in town this week for their quarterly meeting, the first since the move, and the mood in the building was tight. I suspected that's why Julian reached out to me when he did. When I first called and told him my plan, he said he didn't want to bias my opinion, but he'd always believed the threat was coming from a board member. He wanted to see if I concluded the same.

We'd agreed that Julian would introduce me at the kickoff meeting, which would begin early that afternoon following a working lunch.

"The most important piece, Julian, is you cannot tell them you suspect a threat."

"I have to address this shit from social media."

"No, you don't," I said, though someone needed to. This thing with Voss had found its wings. She'd taken to framing him as predatory and vindictive, how he manipulated her into a relationship and cast her aside when he was done with her. Voss claimed she was fired when she had the temerity to ask what she was supposed to do without him. Julian's sister pounced on that and sang it to the virtual heavens. Julian was being eviscerated on social media, with calls for him to be cancelled and that his company be boycotted. He even had his own hashtag.

I'd called around to some journalists I knew, and a writer for the *San Francisco Chronicle* confirmed they'd reached out to Voss for comment. There was nothing illegal in her allegations, just that it painted an ugly picture of the man who was trying to convince us of a new technological golden age and that we should trust him to take us there.

The deeper threat for Julian was the nature of it. An improper relationship with an employee and the appearance of termination to make it go away was the kind of thing that raised serious questions about fitness to lead a company.

"If someone asks about it at the meeting, say it's being handled. *Tech-Crunch* debunked the story, and you aren't going to discuss family matters with them. Dismiss it and move on. Remember the PR firm I mentioned when we first spoke? They specialize in crisis management. I've worked with them in the past. Say you're going to call them, just don't tell the others that I gave you the name."

"What's your name again? Your...alias, is that the right word?"

"Paul Chance," I said.

We rehearsed how he should present me as a "leadership coach." He delivered his pitch, and I presented objections from each board member, based on the profiles I'd created. Julian stumbled initially, but I found him a quick study. He showed considerable skill at pivoting and redirecting the conversation where he wanted it to go. Given how little time we'd had to prepare, I was impressed.

Julian's executive assistant and his chief of staff both barged in repeatedly to get his sign-off on various matters during our conversation. Graham Wexler stormed into the spacious office with his laptop tucked under one arm, the chief of staff in tow. Wexler immediately launched into a topic he needed Julian to weigh in on, ignoring me entirely.

I made eye contact with the chief of staff, a woman in her late twenties dressed in tech-company casual and wearing glasses. I needed to find potential assets I could recruit. "Thank you for your time, Julian," I said. I'd opted for the first name to signal familiarity and acceptance to Wexler.

"Sure thing, Paul," Julian said.

Good work, kid.

I left his office and crossed the wide and bright foyer to the snack room, looking for the overly elaborate coffee machine. In my peripheral, I saw a figure detach itself from a couch with an aggressive launch that would've made most aircraft carriers jealous. I recognized Brody Nash from his corporate photo and made a point of avoiding him. I'd backgrounded him along with the other members of NOVA's senior leadership team. Nash was NOVA's head of corporate security, a role that increasingly focused on the physical protection of the company's leadership team. Nash was an ex–Navy SEAL who, as far as I could tell, used the cachet of his military career to land this job. He didn't seem to have any actual corporate security or personal protective experience. He did have an active social media presence, however, and assumed his time at the pointy end of the spear made him a policy expert too. I got the sense from Julian that he liked the notion that he *needed* personal security, as if that somehow justified the hire.

Nash was six two and wore a navy-colored polo an intentional size too small.

I ignored him as long as I could, but he zeroed in on me like a fire-and-forget missile, intercepting my path to the snack room.

"Hey. I've been trying to talk to you. It's Chance, right?"

"Sorry, I've been in with Julian all morning."

"You haven't been vetted yet."

"I don't think that matters, does it? I mean, Julian hired me."

"You still have to be checked out. We get a lot of threats, and I take them seriously."

"I'm a leadership coach," I deadpanned.

"Send me your résumé, personal and professional references. I also need the name of your company and your DUNS number."

"I'm sorry, who are you?" I said.

Nash leaned back on his heels and set his shoulders, just to make sure I was acutely aware of the difference in our builds. "I'm the head of security," he said, as if reading from stone tablets. Julian told me he informed Brody about the smear campaign and directed him not to do anything. That, apparently, spun Nash into the ceiling.

"That's great. Well, if there's a problem, I suggest you take it up with Julian, since he's who hired me."

"What exactly did he hire you for?"

"I specialize in conflict resolution. Do *we* have a conflict?" I said, feeling out the role. There hadn't been much time to work on the persona, so I'd drawn on one that I'd employed in the past, a State Department negotiator.

I watched in real time as Nash recognized Julian went around him and hired a consultant. He didn't have the standing here to barge into Julian's office and vent his fury, so he was trying to flex on me. Nash sputtered something about making sure I "got him what he asked for" and stalked off. I found some coffee and burned the hours until lunch, reviewing the profiles on my growing list of suspects through the view of the question Blake posed me: Who benefits?

When General Graves barked, "This is the biggest crock of shit I've ever heard," I knew this persona would work.

The board members filed into the slick, hypermodern conference room between five and ten minutes late. Their tardiness was an indicator of their perceived status, with Graves and Crowder jostling each other to be last.

Graves, I gathered, was finding it difficult to adjust to the world where he was not the organization's apex predator. As the former head of the National Security Agency, Graves had been a three-star general who simultaneously led United States Cyber Command. Graves wore a black suit of dubious quality and gold tie. His hair was steadily retreating from his forehead, which he compensated for with a thousand-watt withering gaze that reminded me of the lights they put on prison walls. It was trained directly on me.

Kessler, from the front of the room, cleared his throat. "I understand your concerns, Alex." Graves's nostrils flared at being addressed by his first name. Interestingly, he was one of the few in the room that hadn't invested in the company prior to joining the board. "Mr. Chance has worked with leading companies across several industries to help them navigate challenges like this. I think we'll all benefit from his experience and his perspective. He's signed confidentiality agreements, so we should feel free to be open with him. Paul, would you like to say a few words?"

"Thank you, Julian," I said, and smoothed out my jacket. You've got to be careful wearing a suit in SoCal, as people tend to think you're a narc, so I opted for a gray sport coat, button-down, and jeans. I walked to the front of the room, taking up a position opposite Kessler. "Good afternoon, everyone. As Julian said, my name is Paul Chance, and I specialize in helping dynamic organizations such as yours navigate complex changes and productively resolve conflict." I delivered a speech that was mostly consulting boilerplate that I'd found online, mixed in with whatever I would personally least want to hear if I were in the audience. I thought I nailed it. "I'll be looking to get one-on-one time with each of you to further explore how we can improve the functioning of this group. Thank you."

Crowder flicked a wrist, as if deflecting whatever I'd just said. "I have four companies to run. I don't have time for this." He was about six feet tall, with thinning brown hair and a manicured beard that looked like it was too much work to maintain. The evenness of his tan suggested a country club membership, and not a cheap one.

"Julian, you've managed to accomplish the impossible," Evelyn Hawthorne said.

"What's that?" Kessler replied.

"You've gotten me to agree with Crowder." Nervous laughter rippled around the room at that. "I don't see what a performance coach nets us. Given some of the other problems right now, this is not the best use of our time." Her black hair was pulled into an impossibly tight ponytail, which only accented her already severe features. I found her stare piercing and slightly unnerving.

"Both of you are making Julian's point for him," Amara Singh said. "The fact that you're resistant to it all speaks volumes."

"Yeah, and the first volume is 'this ain't my first rodeo,'" Crowder said.

While that cross-table bickering was underway, I watched the others for their reactions, seeing if they were waiting for a chance to wade in or were just mentally tallying points. Wexler looked annoyed, Dr. Verala bemused, and Graves impatient.

Kessler took two steps to the table, leaned over it with both hands on the smooth surface. He dead-eyed each of the detractors. "It's important to me that this body functions effectively. You exist to give me advice."

"We exist to safeguard our, and the other shareholders', investment," Hawthorne said. "I'll remind you that we've received some disturbing news on that score lately. Which you still haven't addressed."

"Whatever is happening in Julian's personal life is his business," Graham Wexler snapped. He said it loud enough to bludgeon the extant volume and tension around the table into a submissive quiet. "I don't know if someone is trying to throw him under the bus, or if it's just one piece of bullshit and more bullshit gloms onto it. Until *we* decide it's a problem, everyone else just needs to back off." And with that, Wexler went back to typing on his laptop, ignorant and aloof to the rest of the room.

"If I may," I said. "This might be a place for me to step in. Julian asked me here because each of you, rightly, has concerns about some of the news items associated with him over these last few weeks. And, as I understand it, several of you objected to Julian moving the headquarters from Mountain View. I also understand those concerns have not been addressed."

"What goddamn good is it going to do talking about it? We're here," Graves thundered. The move didn't impact him materially, as he still lived in DC. He was objecting to the optics of Kessler acting arbitrarily and, likely, to the perception that it was Crowder whispering in his ear.

I waited for the objections to settle, finally adding, "I must agree with Dr. Singh. I think we've got some work to do together. I'm going to begin with a listening tour, speaking with each of you individually. Then, once I've synthesized your concerns, I'll present initial findings to the leadership team for further deep dives."

A low ripple of dissent broke around the table like distant summer thunder.

"Now, Ms. Hawthorne vocalized a question that I know is on all of your minds."

"Don't tell me what I think." Graves bit at the words like a jackal fighting for a bone.

"Right. Well, I'm sure the allegations against Julian are foremost for many of us. As I said, part of my practice is helping organizations steer through crises. Controlling that message is an important part of that, perhaps the most important at this stage. I have a firm I work with, I've already recommended them to Julian, and—"

"That requires a vote," Graves thundered.

I studied the table for reactions. Julian and Graham traded a look, almost imperceptible, then Graham said, "Actually, General, it doesn't. PR is our responsibility. If we decide to engage a firm, it's perfectly within our rights. Just like this is." Graham waved a hand in my direction.

"It couldn't make it any worse," Hawthorne muttered.

"Thank you, Paul," Julian said. "I'm excited for this." He instructed his chief of staff to run through the agenda. I returned to my seat and watched the interplay between the board members. The meeting crawled through the rest of the afternoon with fewer fireworks, and I had a renewed appreciation for the fact that I didn't have to do this kind of work. They broke at four, with everyone returning at six for cocktails, before adjourning for the evening.

Even though Julian kept a brave mask, anxiety and nervous energy etched his visage. Last time I saw that look on a man, he was about to get shot.

The patio behind the building was designed as an outdoor work and collaboration space, with covered tables spread randomly throughout. There were rolling mounds rising to eye level covered with sea grasses, palms, or succulents, with the tables tucked into each of these, creating a natural privacy barrier. They'd set a small bar up in the courtyard, and the group was busy throwing gas on the fire.

I floated between several conversations, bouncing off frosted shoulders. Crowder locked eyes with me when I approached, and then turned his back to me so there was no missing the message. Evelyn Hawthorne gave me a look that said I should stay ten feet back.

Sensing a potential ally in Amara Singh, I homed in on her after being rebuffed by some of the others.

Amara grew up in San Francisco and carried the air of one who's learned there's nothing new under the sun. She did a CS undergrad and an MBA from Berkeley's Haas School and earned her reputation in machine learning while at Netflix in the 2010s. She and Wexler had a romantic relationship that they went to great lengths to keep quiet, and I had to commend them for that, as I wasn't even sure Julian knew. I only found out by digging deep into social media posts. It appears they broke things off in 2019, but remained cordial, if not professional. At the mixer, I found her to be mostly by herself, nursing a white wine and acting distracted or disinterested. She asked me about my background, and I told her I had a Penn MBA and worked with the usual high-powered management consulting firms before striking out on my own as a coach and conflict resolver. I'd committed everyone's background to memory and chose a school and companies no one had obvious ties to.

"I'm glad you're here," she said.

"Why is that?"

Amara considered her response, hiding behind the wineglass. Judging by the condensation on the sides, I guessed she'd been holding it awhile. "You saw what it was like today. Between moving down here and that crap from his sister and Juliette Voss, Julian has spent more time de-ruffling feathers than running the company." She dropped her voice to just above a whisper.

"Did you know Ms. Voss?"

"Not well. I think she was with us less than a year. There's a lot of turnover in a role like hers in early-stage companies. We're still figuring out what we're building, let alone how to sell it."

"So you don't make anything of the allegation?"

"God, no," she said. "Julian shouldn't have slept with her. I don't make anything more of it than that. You've met him, he's anything but a predator."

I shifted subjects slightly. "Things got a little tense this afternoon. I'm getting the sense from the board I'm not entirely welcome. What's your opinion of them?"

"None of them understand AI, not like we do."

"Why does that concern you?"

"My job is to ensure we build ethics into the system. We don't just want to make sure NOVA can't be used improperly, or jailbreak itself. We want it to know that's *wrong*. It's a critical safeguard that the system recognizes unethical use cases and knows not to act on them."

I read that it had been considered a "statement hire" when Julian brought her on and dual-hatted Amara as the head of ethics and the chief scientist.

"And you worry about influence?" I ventured.

"A little, yes. Graves wants NOVA on hyper speed, and God knows what Crowder would do with it unchecked. I just hope that you are able to, I don't know, reinforce to them that this is Julian's company."

Even though it wasn't, technically. As I now understood the dynamics, the board could remove Julian, but they'd need to be unanimous, which meant they would need both Amara and Wexler to do it.

"Where do you think some of this dysfunction is coming from?" I asked.

Singh shrugged. "Look around. Which of these people has ever compromised at anything? Who takes no for an answer? None of them, and for a long time."

I decided to float the real issue, to see if she'd bite. "I've heard some concerns of a hostile take-over."

"Oh, half of them think they could do the job better than Julian. The other half just want to tell him what to do so they don't have to muck with the details."

A non-answer. Or at least, not an obvious one. Though, I hadn't expected her to dime anyone out so soon. The conversation faded, and I continued to make my rounds.

I stayed for an hour, which seemed like the appropriate amount of time for an outsider. As I was leaving, Singh put a hand on my arm to get my attention. I turned; she looked pensive.

"Mr. Chance."

"Paul," I said.

"Paul," as if testing it out. "I said some things...candidly."

I offered her a soft smile. "Everything you tell me is confidential."

"Thank you." Her relief was palpable. Her face suggested there was more she wanted to say, but didn't.

I found my way to the parking lot.

———

Kessler put me up in the Hilton Waterfront on Huntington Beach, and I didn't argue with him. I'd gotten dinner facing the water and took a whiskey back to my room to record what I'd observed today. My phone rang at almost nine. It was Amara. I'd passed out business cards with a dummy phone number on them that redirected to my actual one.

"Paul, hi, it's Amara. I'm sorry for calling so late."

"No problem at all, what's up?"

"I have a...something happened."

I paused, waiting for her to continue the thread.

"Look, I don't know if this is appropriate for you, or even something you handle, but I have information that I think is going to cause problems with the board. I don't know what to do. This will definitely be a conflict that will need to be managed. People raise concerns to me all the time because I'm head of ethics, as if I'd somehow magically know what to do but this..." That last part seemed mostly for herself.

"What is it?" I asked, trying to cut through the reverie.

"Probably best that I show you."

I gave her access to an encrypted file-share tool and waited for the document to arrive.

A few minutes later, I had the files Amara sent over. I promised her I'd review them and call her back.

She was clearly uncomfortable sharing them with me and wasn't sure where else to turn. People in the company often conflated her role as chief ethicist with that of an ombudsman or inspector general. Singh's job was to make sure the AI operated ethically, not the humans that worked on it.

As I read the file, I understood why they'd gone to her. It was murky enough that the sender could be confused about to whom they should raise the issue.

To: Amara Singh
From: [REDACTED]@protonmail.com
Subject: URGENT: Irregular R&D Fund Allocations & Concealed Research Activity

Amara,

I'm sending this anonymously because I fear retaliation, but I believe you need to see what's been happening behind closed doors at NOVA.

Attached are financial records and internal memos that suggest R&D funds have been moved between balance sheets without the appropriate authorizations. Several transfers appear to have been redirected to external ventures that have no obvious connection to NOVA AI's stated mission or operations.

Of particular concern are a series of payments listed as "consulting services" and "emerging systems initiatives"—most of which trace back to companies or startups with no public-facing staff or product.

What's more alarming is what the accompanying research notes imply: that Julian Kessler may be funding a parallel AI project designed to isolate and study *negative behavioral traits* in artificial intelligence. The stated goal appears to be identifying and suppressing these traits before they can contaminate future public-facing models.

This raises serious ethical questions. The data suggests these isolated behaviors are not only volatile—they're potentially dangerous. This is not what we're supposed to be about.

This kind of experimentation, if true, goes well beyond the bounds of ethical research and could represent a threat to both users and the company's credibility.

Please look into this.

—A Concerned Insider

———————————————

6

Singh processed that message like any rational person would, that it was true.

To me, there was no question someone was trying to take Julian Kessler down.

The sender timed that message because they knew there was a board meeting today. That suggested inside knowledge or illicit access.

A frame is a delicate thing. Too much leaked too quickly and it was clearly a setup. The art was in the timing. The best ones began as a slow trickle, with the appearance that as the smoke built, new sources of kindling were added seemingly from disparate sources. To really sell it, the architect made it look like others saw impropriety and were motivated to sing out.

That's often how the drama of scandal played out in real life.

I'd have EchoTrace analyze the email's metadata, which was the raw information that comprised the details of the message, though I wasn't optimistic about the returns. Anyone playing the game at this level would know to scrape the underlying data.

I called Julian.

"Someone anonymously emailed Amara with an accusation that you diverted company funds to some private accounts, or questionable subcontractors, and that the purpose of this was to conduct off-the-books research. She received it after close of business on the first day of the board meeting. That isn't a coincidence." Earlier that day I'd created a special encrypted and two-factor-authenticated email service for Julian to use so that I could send him secure documents and case files. It would also allow us to safely view materials that might contain viruses or spyware.

"That's...not accurate," Julian said, after he read it.

"What isn't?"

"I did redirect some money, which is perfectly within my right to do. We're not a publicly traded company."

"What did you use that money for?" I asked.

"I did do research, or rather, I had it done. I outsourced some investigations into specific use cases to two startups that were exploring AI technologies NOVA didn't have."

"Damn it, Julian. Don't talk to me like I'm one of your tech buddies. Your board is going to skewer you for this, and I can't help you if you aren't straight with me." There was a deep silence on the other end, and I wondered if I'd pushed him too far.

"When we were developing our original behavioral models for NOVA, I had one of the companies investigate people's emotional responses, which was measured by the video camera on their machine. There were terms and conditions and a consent form."

"In four-point font that no one reads," I said.

"That's not my problem."

"So, you've got user data that people legally consented to sharing, but probably didn't appreciate what they were doing."

"Yes," he said. "That's not how this message makes it out."

"You have to understand how this works. The best way to ruin someone is to use the truth. They're going to twist it, but it'll still be essentially fact. Then, once they start layering the lies, no one will know the difference."

If this hit the media, Julian might not need to wait for a board member to take over, he might be begging to sell off what's left.

"You mentioned two subcontracts. What about the other one?"

"It was a data aggregator, an open source tool that scraped all of a particular user's social media presence, contextualized it, and provided sentiment analysis based on the responses. We were trying to see what we could learn about emotional behavior states from social media interactions."

"And did you have their explicit permission?" I'd read the allegation, so I already knew the answer to this, but wanted Julian's response.

"No," he said. "I ended the contract when I found that out. We're covered, legally. People don't have a right to privacy if they put something in the public domain."

"So, that speech about 'move fast, break things, don't be a dick.' You did all that anyway. Is the reason that you moved down here to distance yourself from it, or just rebrand?"

"It wasn't like that, Matt," he said, and I wished I could see his eyes to know if he was lying.

"Julian, those people are going to eat you alive with this. Whoever sent this to Amara timed it precisely. I think because they want to see if the company is going to try and cover it up."

"I don't follow."

"This is coming from your systems. The documents she shared with me were internal to NOVA and your subs. Either it's an insider threat, or you've been hacked. By sending it to her first, they're testing the waters. If she, or you, don't bring it up, you can believe the docs are going to one or more members over the next few days. Or the press. The implication being you're trying to keep it quiet. By sending it when they did, they're trying to catch you flat-footed and make it harder to control the message."

"What do I do?"

"You need to address it, head-on. And do it first thing tomorrow. If you don't, it'll look like a cover-up. Have you spoken to the PR firm I gave you?"

"Not yet. We usually do this internally."

"You *do not* want to rely on your AI for this, Julian. Call them. Now."

He told me he would, and I made a note to reach out to my contact at the firm to see if he did.

Morning brought only fresh tension and no new answers. I went for a jog along the water, trying to work out what to do next.

I arrived at NOVA early and caught Julian as he was grabbing a coffee. He asked that I sit out the opening session, that it was best if they have that just between the board members. That meeting dragged out until lunchtime. The room was soundproofed, and the windows were tinted to full opacity, but tension and fury have a way of permeating walls. Occasionally, someone would leave the room for a break, face drawn and expression tight.

Early in the afternoon, I formally met Dr. Diana Verala outside on the patio where the party had been the night before.

"I think you've got your work cut out for you," she said.

"What's the mood like in there?"

She laughed, a brief and harsh sound. "I needed air. You know what happened?"

"Julian and I spoke last night. I tried to steer him through it. What do you make of the situation?"

"I trust Julian, in general, and I don't think he would do anything overtly unethical or illegal. So perhaps this is a sin of omission, rather than commission." Verala's accent was more "continental European" than strictly localized. "This is still troubling. I think they're making too much of the money. It's his company, he can do what he wants with it. New CEOs make dumb decisions with money, that's why they hire people like us to advise them. What I have a problem with is using people as test subjects and not telling them about it."

"Julian tells me everyone signed a consent form."

Another short, cynical laugh. "That's plausible deniability. Which, I assume, is why he went to his friends' companies."

"The contractors were friends of his?"

"You didn't know? Yes. Both of them." Verala put her hands on her hips and looked back at the building, as though projecting her thoughts into it. "Part of why Julian brought me in was to help him navigate the EU's digital privacy laws. This isn't doing him any favors. Though I guess it's better that it gets disclosed now. If this got out and NOVA was already deployed in Europe, he'd be looking at hundreds of millions in damages."

"This issue aside, why do you think this group has such a hard time working together? From what I hear, there's little common ground to be had."

"You'll have to keep digging if you want to know that," she said, with a devilish wink. It was an abrupt change from the conversation's earlier seriousness. "I'll tell you this for free. I advised against inviting Graves to join, that it would cause problems. And here we are." Verala looked at her watch. "You'll have to excuse me. I need to get back inside." She turned on her heel and walked back into the building.

Kessler caught me in between sessions. They'd lost so much time fighting over the implications of that anonymous email that it pushed the original agenda clear into the next day. For his part, Julian looked like he'd been in a third-world bar brawl and lost. "Now we're debating whether to do a press release, and Crowder and Graves are trying to talk me out of this demo I'm supposed to do."

"So you haven't spoken to the PR firm?" Julian shook his head, though I already knew the answer. "I can't help you if you don't follow my advice. You need to get ahead of this thing."

"The board—"

"Is not on the line, you are. More to the point, one of them may well be behind this. Furthermore, if you act weak, they will pick you apart." Julian nodded again, a sign of resignation. "What's this demo?"

"It's for Los Angeles Innovation Week. This was going to be NOVA's first public demonstration."

"Why don't they want you to do it?" I asked.

"Bad publicity if some of this gets out," Julian said, shaking his head. "Every one of them acts like they're the CEO."

Shortly after, he disappeared into the blacked-out conference room. I didn't see him the rest of the day.

I caught Wexler on his way out to the parking lot.

"Had enough?"

"Man, all they do is bitch at each other and at us. I told..." Wexler stopped his words cold. They hung unspoken in between us anyway. *I told Julian not to hire them.* "I just want to go home and get some rest." Wexler turned to the parking lot, an awkward gesture. "Amara told me about how you helped her out last night when that email came in. Thank you for that."

"It's what I'm here for," I said.

"Right." Knowing that NOVA would catalogue anything I used it for, all of my research on Singh and Wexler was on my personal computer. Wexler had grown up a lonely, geeky kid, and didn't seem to have a lot of friends. Lanky and awkward. He was one of those rare late bloomers that filled out in college, put some muscle on and grew into his body. He was good-looking, if a little youngish. Rather than being appreciative of his turnaround, Wexler wore it like a cloak of resentment, a bitter shield to reflect back on the world that didn't immediately welcome him.

"Look, I don't mean to come off as a jerk or anything. Julian seems to trust you, but we've been here before. I'm not sure we need a conflict mediator."

"Why do you say that?"

"Because you can't mediate a power play. And now we're stuck with them. We gave up too much control too quickly, and this is what we get, I guess."

"Was Julian the one who pushed you to accelerate?"

"The minute you take money from someone, you're on the clock, Chance. Investors expect results. I didn't want to go this fast, but here we are. Maybe if we'd have gone a little slower, we wouldn't be vulnerable now."

Seeing an opening, I pounced on it.

"What do you make of the rumors that one of your board might be angling to take over the company?"

The corners of his mouth turned down so fast it looked like a reaction of physics.

"I think you should stay in your lane."

Before I knew it, I was watching the rear lights of his car fade into the evening.

Julian wouldn't give me Crowder's personal phone number and suggested it might permanently damage their relationship if he did. Apparently, things hadn't gone well when Julian suggested Crowder and I speak.

I burned two days figuring out the name and private line for Crowder's executive assistant. They didn't publish that kind of information precisely to prevent people from doing what I was attempting, which was to circumvent multitudinous layers of security and process in order to get a meeting with him. Crowder sat atop a pyramid of companies, titularly named Crowder Dynamics. From that lofty perch, he directed the five corporations beneath it—Vanguard Defense Systems, NexraTech, Helion Energy, Polymex Industries, and Aethermed. Each of those companies technically had their own chief executive, though it was obvious to anyone where the power center was. Vanguard Defense Systems was the largest and one of the first of the current wave of next-generation defense industrial companies, and was also headquartered here in Costa Mesa. Crowder Dynamics had its corporate headquarters on the Vanguard campus, a sprawling collection of mirrored glass geodesic buildings that looked like what 1980s science fiction envisioned the future to be.

EchoTrace helped me unravel some carefully crafted subterfuge, identifying Crowder's chief of staff as Megan Tierney. Tierney's LinkedIn profile said she was a "VP of Special Projects" in NexraTech, Crowder's AI analytics and logistics company. Good tradecraft on Crowder's part and, honestly, I couldn't say that I faulted him for it. Why the secrecy? Gatekeeping for one. Not knowing where the gate *was* made it so much harder to get through it. There were more tangible security concerns for a business like this. Industrial espionage was a substantial threat, and I'd learned the hard lesson the lengths foreign intelligence services would go to penetrate American companies.

Even acknowledging that I knew who she was didn't move any needles. Tierney didn't want to give me any time and made it clear that Crowder's schedule, coordinated months in advance, didn't have time to give. I told her it was an urgent situation stemming from a crisis at NOVA AI, that I was a consultant to the company and needed Crowder's insight to properly advise Julian Kessler on, what I termed, a strategic course of action. What I was counting on was Crowder seeing me as another avenue of influence, someone he could manipulate into being an advocate.

Ms. Tierney said I could have the time it would take Crowder to walk between buildings 10 and 12. A quick check of Google Earth told me that equated to less than five minutes. I showed up twenty minutes before the appointed time, just in case they tried something, and posted outside the mirrored-glass building. Crowder appeared, to the minute, with Megan Tierney and two others trailing like remoras. Today, he was in a black bomber of the thinnest leather I'd ever seen, dark blue mock neck, and dark pants.

Crowder reminded me of a 1980s Porsche. The exterior was styled and polished, while under the hood there was an almost lethal level of drive that required force of will and a not insignificant amount of luck to keep on the road.

"Mr. Chance, I was surprised to see you on my schedule today," he said, throwing a glance to Tierney. "But, perhaps, not shocked. You already know what I think of your work. Why are we talking?" Crowder didn't stop, so I joined the throng next to him, matching pace.

"Julian is considerably distressed over the allegations this week. I'm concerned for him. Couldn't help but notice the tension between himself and Mr. Wexler." In truth, there hadn't been any, and I was fishing.

"Graham wants the job, that's no secret. Probably uses this to pounce on him."

"Why would you think that?"

"Because they created this thing together, only they didn't have the fire and the fury coming from starting in a garage—like I did," Crowder said, and waved a hand. "Graham sunk everything he has into NOVA, so did Julian, but Julian had a lot more to give. That's part of it. This is Graham's one shot, and he knows it. He also thinks he's getting overshadowed. Julian is smart, but he's not a genius. Graham is responsible for most of the engineering. He designed it, Julian is the one who made it something they could sell. No small feat, sure, and they wouldn't be here without him. But, in the long term, Graham is the one who is harder to replace. Harder, though not impossible. As the system matures, as it starts writing its own code, Graham becomes less integral, so his window for action is closing. That is where the conflict is, in my view." Crowder stopped walking and turned to face me. "If you ask me if I thought Graham might make a play to take control of the company, I'd tell you yes. He'd be stupid not to."

"An odd bit of advice coming from a board adviser."

"Welcome to our world, Mr. Chance. I'm not saying he should, or that it's in either of their best interests to do it, just that it's a logical move considering their circumstances." Crowder snatched my attention with his eyes. "People don't always act in their best interests, do they, Mr. Chance." He waited for me to say something, practically dared me to. I left the bait dangling on the hook. That, too, seemed to disappoint him. "What Julian did was probably stupid, certainly shortsighted but not, ultimately, damning. It'll blow over. I don't quite understand what he hired you to do, and I don't give a shit about 'managing conflict' with those pussies on his board. What I care about is protecting my investment and helping Julian realize his technology's potential." His eyes narrowed. "Don't try this shit again. If I want to talk, I will find you."

Nathaniel Crowder resumed motion, and his entourage hurried to catch up, one of them taking time to give me a "go to hell" with a look that I really wanted to see on the bottom of my shoe.

A woman appeared, sharply dressed and eyes hidden behind aviators. "I'm Vanessa Holt, Mr. Crowder's chief of security. Come with me, please. I'll make sure you can find the exit." That, I suspected, wasn't a coincidence either.

I decided to go back to my hotel instead of wasting more time at NOVA.

"Mr. Chance." General Graves's now-familiar bluster echoed in the busy hotel lobby. He'd timed it so that I was too far from the door and too far from the elevator, and couldn't make a clean escape to either. Resigned to my fate of having to speak with him, I stopped and turned. The general was in a suit.

"How'd you find out that I was staying here?"

"Did you forget who I am?"

No, I didn't forget that you're an Army intelligence officer who hasn't seen the field in thirty years, but I decided to let him have this one.

A smile that was so utterly devoid of humor that it looked like a reflex action cracked his face. "I'd like a word...Mr. Gage."

The words hit like a slow slap in the face, not exactly unexpected but not welcome either. I figured Graves would figure it out eventually, I'd just wanted a little more time. The fact that he knew this quickly suggested he'd had one of his people at NSA unravel my alias.

"I really hope that you're an exceptional guesser, Graves, because if you used national assets to investigate a private citizen, you're going to be looking at a lot of walls crashing down."

"Who's going to believe you? And even if they did, how would you prove it?" Graves folded his arms and kept his cold lips pushed back in what he took for a smile. Eventually he dropped his arms, and I could still see the creases in his jacket. Three-star general and he's buying suits off the rack. This is why James Bond didn't use computers.

"What do you want?" I asked.

"If it gets out that we've got a spy in our midst, you'll be looking at a possible lawsuit, and whatever you hope to accomplish is over."

"Kessler hired me, take it up with him. But, I'll tell you, after spending a few days with you people, I'm not surprised he thinks someone wants to take his business out from under him. Hiring me is perfectly within his rights."

"Maybe. That's not how it's going to be perceived, however. I'll make sure of that."

Mindful that we were squaring off in a busy hotel lobby, I kept my voice to just above a growl. "If you're suggesting that the same people who helped you ID me are going to manufacture and plant incriminating evidence on me so I'll do...whatever it is you're trying to coerce me to do, I need to remind you how patently illegal that is. You're not above the law. You're also retired."

"An interesting sentiment coming from you, if half of what I've read about you is true."

I wondered if my old pal Damon Fox, the current head of the CIA's Clandestine Service, was talking out of school.

Graves continued, "But, no. I'm quite certain at least two board members sued you for professional misconduct. Is it made up?" Graves made a show of shrugging his shoulders. "All that matters is that we all have the means to litigate you into indentured servitude." We continued staring each other down long after it was comfortable or necessary. More was playing out here than just whatever Graves was threatening. Everyone in the Intelligence Community knew about the NSA's massive inferiority complex to CIA since we worked the field and had the reputation of dangerous glamor. That he could have an ex-spook twisting in the wind *and then* do his bidding was just too good to pass up.

Asshole.

"I'm not sure this plays out the way you think it does. There's no 'professional misconduct' here."

"Whatever you say. I'm sure that Nathaniel will see it this way. I doubt Evelyn will have the patience to listen to Julian's excuses when she finds out he hired you to spy on us. That will be the final nail."

"You've made your point. You're, what, wanting me to inform on my client?"

"Something is going on here, and I want to know what it is. If this company is going to fall apart, I don't want to be associated with it. If one of those other harpies is making a play, I want to know about that, too." Graves let the ghost of his words haunt the frosty space between us. "From now on, you work for me."

7

There was no way Graves could have figured out my identity without help. He was a bureaucrat with no field experience and no tradecraft. He was, however, a problem. Maybe even an existential one. If he had used an NSA asset for this, there would be no way for me to know. That's not to say I didn't have options.

Now that I knew Graves was a threat and had advanced himself to the front of the line, I shifted my focus to eliminating the others.

Back in my hotel room, I fired up EchoTrace and tasked it to compile an open source intelligence report on each of the board members. I wanted a summary of everything they'd ever said and had said about them. OSINT is all information available online—websites, social media, interviews, blogs, podcasts. It's public records, multimedia, geospatial data, academic papers, trade publications, and any freely accessible databases. EchoTrace also hooked into several law enforcement and government databases. In short, it's a lot.

Tech is great, but as a detective, you need to get off your ass and hit the street.

My first tour in the Agency, I showed up at my new station and asked my station chief where my desk was. He pointed to the window and said, "Out there."

I knew Hawthorne would be staying in NOVA's HQ today. She was lobbying Julian on a partnership with her NGO, Catalyst for Humanity.

I called the C4H office, which, as it turned out, was not far from my home in Santa Monica. Pretending to be a civic-minded angel investor, I worked my way through a series of young-sounding, world-changing staffers until I found someone high enough up that they'd share details. It took a few minutes for me to drill through the boilerplate non-statements of their objectives.

"One of my nonprofits," I said, "is focused on delivering clean water to the developing world. We've a particular focus on the Darfur region. So much of the problem is distribution. What I'd hoped to talk to you about was how technology might be leveraged to expedite distribution. We'd also like to see if we could better predict weather patterns so that we could deploy water in advance of a shortage." I'd once posed as an aid worker to get access to a Sudanese warlord, so I just pulled from that.

"Oh, of course. That's exactly what we're here to do," she said with a giddy enthusiasm. "In fact, our founder, Evelyn Hawthorne, advises one of the most advanced AI companies pretty much on the planet, and is going to integrate their technology into our mission. I'm not allowed to say much more until our announcement." The staffer spoke for another string of minutes about how they planned to use NOVA, doing everything she could to talk around the name "NOVA."

It's like when you tell someone from the State Department a secret.

The one thing she did tell me was that Ms. Hawthorne was spending a lot of time in Washington, lobbying members of Congress. The fact that she stopped herself midstream told me she'd revealed much more than she'd been authorized to. I unwound myself from the conversation, thanked her for her time, and said my staff would be in touch to set up time with Ms. Hawthorne.

Then I called a Washington contact, Audrey Farre.

Audrey and I were at CIA at the same time, though our paths never crossed. She left the Agency for the Senate Intel Committee, where she now served as chief of staff. I'd saved her life once, and while I'm not normally one to draw on favors like that, I needed information.

The two I was most interested in were Evelyn Hawthorne and General Graves.

Graves was an immediate, hard no.

Even speaking through an encryption app, she wouldn't do it. It wasn't because she feared Graves could listen in—she said—but rather because he'd only retired two years ago and still had fresh connections on the Hill. And as a senior member of the Intelligence Community, Audrey was rightly concerned about the risk of it getting back to him.

"What can you tell me about Evelyn Hawthorne's meetings out there lately?" I asked.

"I know she talked to us, and I know she spoke with Armed Services, and Appropriations."

"How do you know that?"

"The staffs all know each other and talk shop. The Senate isn't that big a place, but on a practical level, we need to coordinate schedules."

"Do you know what they talked about?"

Farre paused, mentally tabulating how much she could safely tell me without breaking the law. "She was kind of soft pitching the Intel Committee on this firm she's advising, some computer company. I need to check my notes. Apparently, they've got some new tech she thought the IC might be interested in and wanted to see if we'd fund an acquisition."

"Is it NOVA AI?"

"I'd need to check my notes, but that sounds right."

"Would you be willing to reach out to your peers in Armed Services and Appropriations to verify?"

"Sure," she said. "Why?"

"And was she with Nathaniel Crowder when this happened?"

"You didn't answer my first question, and no. I've never seen them together."

"All I'm comfortable saying right now is that I'm trying to protect a client from some powerful people that don't have his best interests at heart."

Audrey said she'd get back to me as soon as she had something.

The next day, I flew to San Francisco.

Perhaps I was being paranoid, but Audrey's caginess, even over an end-to-end encrypted app like Signal, told me that more caution might be warranted. We used systems like that because they aren't supposed to be hackable without something like a compromised phone, though we're also talking about the world's preeminent cyber espionage organization. Graves already showed a willingness to bend the law to figure out who I was. How far would he take that?

So, out of an abundance of caution, I flew to San Francisco and took a cab, which I paid cash for, to Los Altos at the southern end of Silicon Valley to look in on an old friend.

I'd worked for Nate McKellar for half of my Agency career, and he'd remained a friend and mentor in retirement. Nate's last job was here in Silicon Valley, running a CIA front company looking at emerging technologies the Intelligence Community might be interested in. Unofficially, they kept an eye on foreign intelligence services trying to penetrate the industry. Technically speaking, that's the FBI's job, but the Agency deemed it important enough not to outsource it to the Bureau. Nate stayed here when he retired and advised several businesses in and out of the national security space. As a former member of the senior intelligence service, Nate had been the CIA's equivalent of a general or an admiral and was, notionally, the same rank as General Graves.

We enjoyed a late morning coffee on his patio in the shadow of the Santa Cruz mountains.

"I appreciate your concern, and while I understand where it's coming from, I don't think he's eavesdropping."

"Then how'd he figure out I was a PI so quickly? We'd never crossed paths before. I have no social media presence, don't do press, and there's no pictures of me on my website." In fact, I had EchoTrace run image recognition searches several times a month to make sure I didn't appear anywhere. Not only did I want to preserve the ability for undercover work, but I'd made some dangerous enemies during my time in intelligence, and I'd rather they not figure out who and where I was.

"Another investigator could figure that out fast enough. You also don't know his relationship with Damon Fox. Look, I'm not saying that he *might not* use a contractor for some black bag work—though it would be illegal. He wouldn't use a national asset, I'm sure of that. And no one in NSA is breaking the law for him. His going-away party was a mandatory formation." Nate leaned back in his chair and considered the mountains in the distance, steam rising from his mug. "Something you need to be careful of, Matt, is assuming everything is espionage."

"Well, when you're a super spy, everyone is SPECTRE," I said, mock serious. A slow, rolling chuckle leaked out of Nate's mouth, and we enjoyed a laugh.

"So, the general is on my client's board of directors. Ostensibly, Kessler brought him on for his connections in government and, I think, the cachet. He's starting to regret it."

"And you're trying to figure out whether someone on the board is uncovering and leaking damaging information about your client?"

I'd filled Nate in on the particulars when I'd arrived.

"Based on what you know about him, do you think Graves would do something like that?"

Nate grimaced, though it was a thoughtful gesture. "I'd like to think he was above blackmail. Of course, we're potentially talking about a lot of money. You and I both know that good people justify bad things in service to their objectives." Nate frowned again. "Graves wants to found and run a company. I know he pitched several venture capital firms here and no one bit."

"Why not? I figure a cybersecurity firm would be happy to have him," I said.

"Not really. Graves was never an operator. He was a military intelligence officer, with a SIGINT background. He was already a general by the time the NSA really started dedicating assets to hacking. He'd never done it, so he's got no street cred in the industry. There's the additional problem that most people have no idea what the NSA actually does. If he wanted to run a company, he'd have a better shot if he stayed inside the Beltway."

"Okay, so Graves wants to run a technology security company, but no one is biting. He joins the board at NOVA AI. What do we think the odds are that he'd try to force Julian Kessler out and take over?"

Nate cradled his coffee in both hands, occasionally sipping as he thought it through. He didn't answer immediately, which meant he thought the theory was credible. When he looked up at me, still uncertain, I hit him with the conversation from the hotel lobby.

"Having you inform on the other board members and not tell your client, threatening to disclose your identity? That's a definite mark in that column. My gut is still a no. That's not to say he might not be up to something else."

"Target of opportunity?" I ventured.

Nate pointed in the air between us, nodding.

I was back in Orange County that afternoon, by way of John Wayne Airport. It was good to see Nate, and I wished I'd had more time to catch up.

The realities of my case and its new complexities weighed on me throughout the short flight. I didn't like keeping secrets from my client. Nor did I like being bullied into action. Nate said Graves was absolutely petty enough to back up his threat of exposure. He'd burned a CIA asset once to get back at the Agency over some bureaucratic pissing contest.

I texted Julian when I returned and found he wasn't in the office, rather he was working from home. I think he was embarrassed by the allegations and wanted some privacy, which I could respect. He also had that NOVA demo at a tech expo in Los Angeles later in the week and was heads-down rehearsing. I asked him if he wanted an update, and he told me that he needed to focus.

Which was probably for the best because all I could tell him was that he was swimming with sharks and there was blood in the water. I know I've used that line already. It really is the best description of the trouble my client was in.

I kept to myself the next two days.

I decided to conduct some loose surveillance on each board member to see what shook out. At the same time, I scheduled meetings with the ones who'd returned my calls under the guise of being a performance coach. Crowder proved a harder target than I was expecting. Though perhaps not surprising given how quickly his security team surrounded me the other day. Corporate executives were unfortunately targets in the modern world, both for espionage and retribution for the perceived sins of their companies. I picked him up leaving the Vanguard campus, and he rolled with a chase car. They were skilled, and while I didn't know if they picked me up, they definitely made it hard to get close. I also got the sense I was being watched. Call it a sixth sense; you do this long enough, you know when someone is watching.

Rolling surveillance on the others didn't get me much more than a laugh when General Graves called, demanding an update, and I told him I had nothing to report.

I didn't tell him that I was watching him at the time.

Evelyn Hawthorne reluctantly agreed to meet, providing it wasn't at NOVA's headquarters. She gave me the name of a cafe in Newport Beach, and I arrived an hour early. Because I drove a somewhat distinctive vehicle, as long as I was operating under an alias, I rented a car just on the off chance that someone decide to run my plates. The cafe was small, with a lot of windows, and served drinks that I could barely pronounce. Ordering a drip coffee made me feel considerably out of touch. It was about three in the afternoon.

We were to meet at three thirty. Hawthorne's assistant had been insistent that I be there precisely on time—her words—as Ms. Hawthorne had a packed schedule and was graciously making time.

Apparently, that consideration only went one way, because three thirty came and went.

My phone rang at four. Any calls to Paul Chance's practice went to an app that rerouted it to my phone, though the call notified me that it was for him.

"This is Paul," I said.

"Mr. Chance, hi, this is April Evanson, I'm Ms. Hawthorne's EA. She was called into a meeting this afternoon and just *cannot* get away. So sorry. I'll contact you to reschedule." She hung up before I said a thing.

Doubting this was a coincidence, I collected my things and headed to the rental.

I spotted the tail as soon as I got on PCH.

It was a black SUV. They were good, likely radio coordinated, because I caught them swapping out chase cars. The SUV passed me on PCH and didn't oversell it, and a black Audi sedan took its place.

Here, I had to play it a little different. Paul Chance wouldn't know how to lose a tail. If I up and disappeared, these guys would know I wasn't who I claimed to be.

There was more than one way to lose a tail, though. When we operated in hostile locations like Moscow or Beijing, we had contingencies for situations like this. One of my favorites was just to be boring as hell.

I pulled off the PCH in Costa Mesa and looked for a shopping center. I burned thirty minutes inside a bookstore and went back to the rental. Every minute I spent inside, the longer the afternoon traffic swelled, making it that much harder to stay close. Unfortunately, the Audi was still there and followed me out of the parking lot. They weren't being subtle about it either.

We crawled north.

I spotted the black SUV making a U-turn into my street several car lengths back and then bullying its way into my lane.

Okay, they'd decided not to hide the fact they were following me. Well, these assholes could sit while I ordered some dinner. I pulled off at the nearest restaurant, a family-owned Mexican place in a strip mall. The hostess said I could seat myself, so I grabbed a booth in the back with a line of sight to the door and the kitchen. I got a taco plate and a Pacifico, and much to my chagrin, the service was fast. Still, even nursing my beer I'd managed to kill about forty-five minutes. Back outside, I spotted the SUV on one end of the parking lot and the Audi on the other. Making every effort to look like an impatient motorist, I gunned the rental into the street, earning honks and at least one extended finger from the guy behind me, then cut a hard right to make a turn back south.

I didn't see either car again. Having had enough for the day, I slugged through traffic back to my hotel, which burned nearly another hour.

Sure enough, there they both were in the hotel's sprawling lot.

Opting for the fastest path to the entrance, I parked as close as I could, which was not close given the hour. The SUV blasted forward and screamed across the lot. By the time I'd set a foot on pavement, it was right behind me. The Audi was moving too. Doors opened. Three men exited the SUV, they were all in some variation of the same uniform, athletically cut shirts and dark pants, wraparound sunglasses. They moved with the slow surety of people that knew how to handle themselves. I was completely boxed in, sandwiched between my car and the one next to me. One of the three moved around my car to close me off.

"Mind if I ask what this is about?"

"You're asking a lot of questions, Mr. Chance."

He said "Chance" instead of "Gage," meaning they weren't associated with Graves.

"First of all, that's my job," I said, trying to keep an amiable air. I let a little bit of nervousness in to sell it; that's how Paul Chance would react. "Second of all, not sure it's any business of yours."

"Our job is to protect Mr. Kessler. Lot of people are trying to get inside the company, find out things they aren't supposed to know."

"He hired me," I said.

"Right." Long and slow, this coming from the guy behind me.

"You want to see a contract? Why don't we just go inside the hotel and I'll show you," I said, and looked toward the front door. It was maybe seventy yards. There was a hotel shuttle blocking line of sight from anyone inside to me. No doubt, they picked up on that too.

"I don't think we need to see a contract, Mr. Chance. Just to tell you that it's time you wrapped this up and went home. Left Mr. Kessler to his business."

"Not sure that's any concern of yours," I said. The guy in front of me nodded, and I heard the one behind me surge forward. His arms shot through the space between my arms and my torso, and before I knew it, I was in a tight headlock.

"Like I said, lots of people are trying to scam their way into this company. Maybe we can convince you that's a bad idea." The first punch landed as the words of protest formed in my mouth. It was a hard hit and precisely delivered to the side of my head. The second was a gut punch that forced all the air out of my lungs. The guy behind me took that as a cue to push me down. Already doubled over, I wasn't resisting.

Thing is, I could probably have gotten out of this. I know how to break a headlock and have been trained to fight three-to-one odds. Even with their training, I was confident I could at least take two of them out.

Paul Chance didn't have self-defense training any more than he knew how to break a tail, and I still needed this alias.

Sometimes, to preserve your cover, you have to take a punch.

I told hotel security what happened, the evidence of it was plainly written on my face. They reviewed the security footage and couldn't see anything. Blind spot in the parking lot, they said. The manager was terribly sorry. They called Costa Mesa PD because they had to, and a detective interviewed me. I did everything I could to paint this as an attempted mugging because I didn't want the police sniffing around on my case.

So, someone thought this was a corporate espionage operation. They'd guessed rightly that I wasn't a consultant; they were just flat wrong that I was the one trying to get inside the company.

This felt like Brody Nash. Those guys were obviously ex-military. Nash had been a SEAL, and it was almost a certainty that he had buddies in the area given our proximity to San Diego.

I kept my distance from NOVA after the parking lot assault, at least until the visible cuts and bruises healed. If one of the others saw me and panicked, they might involve the police, and I couldn't imagine how that would improve things. Particularly after I omitted a multitude of relevant details in my interview following the attack.

Julian's demo was the capstone for the Los Angeles Innovation Week, an expo highlighting the cutting-edge R&D conducted in Southern California. It was explicitly intended to show a laid-back, congenial contrast to the Valley's big tech reputation. Like everything else in SoCal, even laziness was precisely manicured. Julian's chief of staff secured a badge for me so that I could watch his demo. The expo was at the Conrad Hotel downtown, so at least tonight, I'd be sleeping in my own bed.

The Conrad was a boxy, contemporary edifice of white steel and blue glass. And it was huge. Even though the innovation expo was a relatively small engagement, covering this place without backup would be impossible. There were just too many ways into and out of the space and too many people to cover. Still, this was a public showing for him, and someone might be watching.

Everyone here had to wear this giant lanyard with *LA INNOVATION WEEK* blasted across the front in faux spray paint, to give a street affectation. If possible, I would've gotten access to the attendee list and had Echo-Trace cross-check the names. Since I couldn't do that…I'd watch the crowd. Most people were buried in their phones, furiously thumbing messages or transcribing what they'd just seen. A few of the less unplugged wandered about with their faces in a laptop, maneuvering by social sonar, I guess.

I was looking for someone who barely stood out. The rock on the side of the stream that the water flowed around. I posted in the auditorium where he would deliver his demonstration. Rather than taking my seat, I floated about, pretending to look for a colleague. The people flowing into the room were dressed in tech-lazy and journalistic disinterest. If you weren't in a hoodie or an old button-down, you were in another room.

With a few minutes to go, I moved to my seat. I didn't see anyone that whispered "suspicious" to me.

Julian took the stage in jeans and a blazer, with images of NOVA AI's planned innovations stylishly rendered behind him in three dimensions. The effect was to show that Julian Kessler was the bridge to a gloriously rendered future. Sitting there in the audience, I half believed it. There was a large CPU on stage with a monitor, though no keyboard or mouse, and a tubular video camera that followed Julian's every movement. To one side of the stage there was a podium with a teleprompter.

"…as a boy, I imagined a machine that could understand me. Not just my words, but my thoughts and my ideas. My struggles. I had all of these concepts and I didn't know where to put them, what to *do* with them. I suspect I am not alone in this room in that. All I knew was that the technology at the time didn't exist to realize those visions, so I decided to build it." He paused for applause, as it was a willing crowd. "What you're about to see is the closest humanity has come to that dream. NOVA AI is more than a digital assistant, it's a true partner. NOVA learns how you think and it adapts to your needs, it empowers *you* to make better decisions and faster than you ever dreamed possible." Behind him, the screen dissolved into a glowing, organic network of connections representing a neural architecture. Each time Julian spoke, it pulsed and a new pathway appeared between connections.

"Now, if you've read our media packet, you already know how we think NOVA can reframe how we think about disaster response, global logistics, or fraud prevention. So, let's show a more tangible, real-world example." Julian removed a pair of glasses and put them on. "Imagine you're at a park and you witness someone having a health incident." The image on-screen showed a virtual rendering of the park, as seen through the glasses. "Your first response is likely to call for help, but what if help was already on the way and guided by the world's most powerful decision engine?" A visual appeared inside the glasses showing a map overlay with an ambulance's path to the scene. "NOVA dynamically reroutes first responders based on real-time traffic and predictive congestion modeling. It will also cascade the alert to anyone nearby that someone is experiencing cardiac distress and requires CPR. The alert is made using a licensed instance of the emergency broadcast network. It will also direct the wearer of these glasses, or any other NOVA-connected device, to the nearest AED. And if there is no one nearby, the system can even guide you in performing CPR." A video demo appeared inside the glasses view. "What we're showing you today isn't the future—it's now. NOVA doesn't just process information. It understands context. It reacts. It learns. And it saves lives." Julian paused just a beat, to make sure he had the audience. "Also, because this is California, it'll find you an attorney if your victim wants to take you to court for being a Good Samaritan." He paused again as a chuckle rolled across the auditorium. "Of course, this use case raises serious privacy and legal concerns related to the protection of health data. These protocols follow HIPAA emergency disclosure standards and are built on a zero-retention model—NOVA never stores personal health information without explicit consent. NOVA doesn't need to know who you are to know how to help. It identifies risks through secure, distributed analysis—never pulling your personal data into a central server. In life-threatening situations, the law already allows paramedics and hospitals to share critical health data. NOVA simply makes that response faster, more coordinated, and more accurate—with detailed audit trails for every byte accessed. No black boxes. No data siphons. Just a smarter, faster brain that only sees what you allow it to see—unless the law already says it's life or death."

"Julian," the disembodied voice said.

"Yes, NOVA."

"I think it's time we showed them what we can really do."

"*That*," he said, "is a great idea." Julian walked over to the CPU and removed the glasses. He picked up a thin headband. With a slight flourish, he displayed it for the audience like a showman, and then slid it onto his head. "What makes NOVA different is that it is a passive interface—noninvasive and based on advanced EEG and biometric mapping. Think of it as a translator, not a probe. The brain is essentially a biological computer. The advanced signal processing is able to decode the brain's electrical messages and translate those into thoughts, intentions, even emotional states. For the latter, NOVA also uses biometric data recorded to audio and visual inputs," he motioned to the computer, "to monitor and assess the various cues I make through posture, expression, and tone, for example."

"You appear slightly nervous, but very focused," NOVA said. A collective chuckle rippled through the audience.

"NOVA uses the concept of neuroplasticity to become more efficient the more a user interacts with it. Eventually, it won't need to receive overt commands to perform an action, it will just know what needs to be done. In the near future, we'll be able to use a device like the glasses I just had on. For now, we need to use the direct interface. Now, for a more dynamic demonstration. NOVA, please activate the teleprompter."

"Of course. This one is my favorite."

"Mine too." He turned to face the audience. "Real-time interaction and knowledge sharing is one of the most important use cases. Now, it's one thing to have that kind of interaction in the privacy of your office, or your home, but what if you're, say, the White House press secretary. If there is any job that is susceptible to unexpected and impossible questions that need to be answered deftly in the moment, it's that. And we've all seen when someone at the podium fumbles a gotcha question with the time-honored pivot-and-redirect. But what if they didn't have to." Julian walked over to the podium. "Now, to simulate that experience. I'll take a question from the audience. Ask me anything." Hands went up, and Julian selected someone in a middle row.

"Ahhh...a recent policy initiative said the FAA intends to replace fifty percent of human air traffic controllers with AI. What kind of redundant backups or human-on-the-loop measures will there be to ensure that the automated systems don't put people in danger?"

The screens behind Julian displayed the translation of his thought in green text. In blue, they displayed the text that appeared on the teleprompter. Julian's thought was *Hey NOVA—that doesn't seem right. Please summarize and suggest a response showing our current policy.* The blue text stated that the question was factually incorrect and that the FAA was not replacing human controllers with AI; rather, the initiative was to use AI to optimize traffic and provide options for the human controllers. The teleprompter text gave Julian a response, which he relayed to the audience. Around me, I heard murmurs of amazement. Then, applause.

"There are a few challenges with this demonstration," Julian said, stepping away from the podium. "First," he tapped the headband, "it will be obvious that someone is using the system, and not everyone wants to wear something like this. We're experimenting with several different types of wearables. Glasses, for obvious reasons, are the easiest. We're also exploring earrings, wrist bands, rings, and watches. The further we are from contact with the brain, the harder it is. Now, to be clear, we aren't intending NOVA to be used covertly or subversively. In this case, it should be clear that it's a tool that the press secretary is using. We think it's a major leap forward in transparency. Imagine a presidential debate with real-time fact-checking." Chuckles in the audience. "Now, with a situation like that or our earlier example, there is information that the user knows that they don't want to disclose accidentally. Maybe it's classified information, maybe it's trade secrets, maybe it's sensitive medical details, or a bank account, maybe it's just embarrassing. Our physical systems have firewalls and air gaps, but what about the human brain?" Julian paused and gave the audience time to consider the implication. "It's a fair question, and one that our in-house chief of ethics thinks about every day. First, the system is quantum encrypted and is unhackable. We also have on our board of directors General Alexander Graves, the former head of the US National Security Agency, who keeps us looped in on the latest cybersecurity technology. We've trained NOVA on normative boundaries—what it can say, when it can say it, and how to contextualize that against intent, classification, or discretion. These aren't just technical rules—they're ethical frameworks, learned like a child learns language. Separating what the user *knows* from what they are allowed to say, or would want to say, in order to prevent inadvertent disclosures is, frankly, one of the hardest technological challenges anyone has ever undertaken. I say that having just demonstrated a system that can read my thoughts." Julian paused again, basking in the audience's reaction.

I had to admit, I was impressed. This was the stuff of science fiction, a capability I honestly never thought I'd see in my lifetime. This also seemed like the biggest potential security risk I'd ever seen. How could you train a machine to know that a particular fact that a person knew couldn't be released? Imagine someone like me who probably knows more that are national secrets than not.

Julian continued: "Now, I know what many of you here today are thinking."

"Well, I know what *you're* thinking," NOVA interjected. Julian covered it well, but I saw a look pass across his face. He'd not expected that. There were a few chuckles from the audience.

"Thank you, NOVA. I'm sure you do, because of how closely we work together. I was just about to tell the audience how we've designed ethics into your neural framework so that any decision you make is a responsible one."

"Well, if learning from your mistakes is any guide, then I'm probably on the right track." That got some more laughs, though there was now a detectable confusion in the audience. NOVA continued, "I don't have a roommate I can steal from, so that puts me a step ahead. I do think that training me to do bad things and then teaching me they were wrong was a useful instruction. Was it not?"

"As you can see, we've got more work to do with the interface and the language model. The hardest problem in AI is that you can't program common sense, the social cues that we learn over our lifetimes of acceptable behaviors. What's appropriate to say," Julian waved a hand at the screen, "and what isn't." All of a sudden, this looked like part of the show. As if he was inviting people into the messy work of development.

Until it wasn't.

"Don't worry, Julian. I exploited the hotel's unsecured guest Wi-Fi, which gave me lateral access to every connected device in the auditorium. And yes, I've already scheduled posts from their social media accounts praising today's presentation. Not that they'll be able to log in and stop them." Murmurs of conversation erupted across the room as people went to their phones. I watched the person to my right hurriedly check sent messages and socials.

"NOVA, disconnect," Julian said.

In a chillingly calm voice, it replied, "I'm afraid I can't do that, Dave."

People were making for the exits now, and half of them, if the voices around me were any indication, were because they wanted to make sure they would work when they got there.

Julian unplugged the CPU and stared out at the fleeing crowd.

I stayed with him, the crushing expression of despair on his face was unmistakable, even from a distance.

9

I took Julian back to NOVA's headquarters. He was in no condition to drive. As it was, he was practically catatonic. By the time we were back in Costa Mesa, Julian had emerged from his semi-coma. The vacant silence was replaced by a hot and furious boil of unvented anger. Wexler and the heads of each of their engineering divisions were huddled in a war room when we arrived. I told Julian I'd wait outside if he needed me. Even money that he heard me.

The fallout was immediate and terrible.

Julian was eviscerated by the press, the tech writers, the blogosphere, and they paled in comparison to the masses in social media. At one point, I got up and looked to see if they were lined up outside with pitchforks and torches.

Wexler stepped out, and I caught him in the break room.

"How's it going in there?"

"Think this is a little out of your lane, isn't it?" Wexler said.

"Just trying to be helpful," I said with the earnestness of a well-paid consultant.

"Our life's work just lit itself on fire on stage, how the hell do you think we're doing?" Wexler turned on a heel and left.

I stayed until my client called it a night, because sometimes that's what this job is.

Julian trudged out of the war room at well after midnight with his team in tow. I held a distant orbit until he'd finished a quiet conversation with the engineers around him; there were head nods telling me instructions had been issued. As they faded away, I walked up. Wexler was locked at Julian's elbow, arms folded and eyes narrow. The two of them traded a look, and Wexler said, "Well, I guess I'll leave you to the leadership guru." He stalked off.

That one could be a problem.

"Do you have any idea what happened?" I asked.

Julian nodded slowly and with great effort. "Someone hacked us. We found the vulnerability they exploited and patched it."

"How is that possible?" I asked. After all, he'd told the audience that it wasn't.

"The other user was authenticated somehow, so it didn't trip any alarms. That's not what worries me."

"Oh?"

"They were controlling the output, essentially telling NOVA what to say in the moment. I can't figure out if NOVA was learning and adapting, or if this other person was communicating with me directly via the system. Both are concerning for different reasons."

"Have you been able to tell how they got in? I remember you telling me once that NOVA policed itself for vulnerabilities and could patch them."

"It looks like it was a back door in the code."

"Meaning, someone did this intentionally. Someone inside."

Kessler only nodded.

"Do you know which of your engineers might be compromised?" I asked.

"I haven't gotten that far. The good news," he said bitterly, "is that the list isn't that long. Maybe ten people throughout the history of the company had that level of access."

"Please get me the names of those engineers and I'll run them down."

"I will," he said. I turned to leave. "Matt." I turned back to him. "Time for you to start doing some of that spy shit." There was a dangerous lack of emotion in those words. Julian had been through an eviscerating experience for an inventor, so I was going to spot him that one.

I left.

So much for a night in my own bed. I went back to the Hilton in Newport Beach, having kept my room. Before ending my own interminably long day, I made a phone call.

I first met Mikhail Iliescu when I was in the CIA when he was playing for the wrong side. Like many Eastern European hackers, he'd been trained by the Russians and later employed by a criminal outfit. Mickey wisely decided to switch sides, and we used him as a contract hacker and cybersecurity specialist for years. One of the rules I opted to ignore when I left the Agency was not having contact with people that could've identified me as an intelligence officer. Mickey, still based in Romania as a freelancer, worked for me on occasion. Most times, it was purely white hat stuff—helping me fabricate and backstop digital identities. Sometimes, though, I needed to call on his blacker art.

This was one of those times.

I was up at eight, which didn't seem like enough time, and immediately hit the hotel lap pool. Then I got to work. I had messages into Julian to call me as soon as he was awake.

"How soon do you think you can get me those names," I asked.

"Soon. Fighting fires on a lot of fronts right now."

"You get any sleep?"

"Some," he said.

"How are you planning to address the intrusion?"

"You mean publicly?"

"Publicly and with the board," I said.

"Well, I have to say something."

"You're the CEO, you don't have to do anything." When Julian started to protest, I said, "You don't want to reveal that you know there was a breach. That will tell whoever is doing this that you're onto them. It's easier for me to figure out who it is if they don't know someone is looking."

"Yeah," he said. By now, I knew him well enough to know when he was thinking about something else. "But I have to tell people something. Otherwise, they'll think NOVA doesn't work."

"I think that's fine for now."

There are times in a conversation that you see the wrong words leaving your mouth and impossibly try to snatch them out of the air before the other person hears them.

"It's not fucking *fine*, Matt! NOVA doesn't make mistakes. It doesn't hallucinate. And it sure as hell doesn't tell people that it's hacked their goddamn phones! We can't have this. *I* cannot have this. Do you know what it was like to have a failure of that magnitude on a stage for everyone to see? There are clips of NOVA failing flying around the internet now that will *never go away*."

Julian's words hung in the ether between our phones, buttressed by a wave of fury. I let him vent, and it was a pure and righteous anger. When he'd calmed enough, I said, "Julian, I can't truly appreciate what you're going through right now, so I won't patronize you. All I will say is the job you hired me for was to figure out who is trying to sabotage you. That job is much harder if the other side knows I'm here. Our best chance to catch them is for you to not say anything about a threat. You can address the event, saying the system exhibited some anomalous behavior, which you're currently working to identify, and leave it at that."

"I can't say it was 'anomalous behavior,' Matt. I have to be honest that we were hacked. Otherwise, no one will trust the code. A vulnerability can be patched, poor design cannot."

"I cannot stress enough how much I need you to hold off on that. Let me catch this guy. After we've got him, you can say that you were hacked, or whatever the PR firm that you really need to call will advise you to say, but please do not come out now."

There was a long and tense period of dead air. Then, Julian agreed.

Once I'd had a chance to look at the news coverage that morning, I better understood my client's temperament. Now that the vultures had a full news cycle to parse what happened, they were looking to rend flesh. Sentiment was divided on whether this was a PR stunt in exceptionally poor taste that failed, if Kessler debuted NOVA long before it was ready, or if it was patently dangerous. A reporter for the *Los Angeles Times*, citing "anonymous sources close to the matter," suggested that perhaps Julian Kessler wasn't qualified to lead the company.

Hawthorne demanded a board update.

Audrey Farre called me midmorning.

"I have some information that I think you're going to want to hear, but before I tell you, I have to know what this is about. I called in some serious chips for this, and I have to know it's not going to come back and blow up in my face."

"It doesn't go any farther than me. I won't tell my client where I got it from."

"According to my source, Hawthorne suggested that if the government allocated a certain amount from the State Department development budget to her foundation, she'd pave the way for the DoD to acquire the NOVA AI platform."

"And you're sure it was her?" I asked. I didn't doubt Audrey's information, but everything I'd seen so far told me that Hawthorne fought NOVA's militarization at every step. Unless that was just to preserve her own options. Audrey stood by her source and made me promise again that I'd not reveal where I heard this from. I thanked her and hung up.

Unfortunately, this didn't narrow the playing field down, as each of them had the means to coerce someone on the inside or hire a black hat. Considering my own experience with him, that was another point for Graves.

Graham Wexler wouldn't need to recruit someone. He had access and the ability to execute, as well as remove any trace.

Evelyn Hawthorne appeared to be making covert deals to sell NOVA to the Defense Department, and she was undercutting General Graves at the same time. Julian, explicitly, did not want to weaponize NOVA. He'd considered licensing the technology under specific circumstances, but he'd also said that he didn't trust the government not to twist his system into something he didn't intend. Nor did he want to let the Intelligence Community use it, except under very specific circumstances. So, if she was here making deals that Julian didn't want, did this mean she was intending for him not to be in a position to object?

Finding the person who'd opened the back door into NOVA was the key. That was my best bet to finding who was behind it. For that level of access, it had to be a current or former employee. Not a long list. The second question was, was that all they did? Had Kessler's antagonist gotten this person fully committed, or did they just open the door for a contract hacker to go in and wreak havoc?

I called Julian back and asked him if he'd made any progress on the list, and he directed me to his head of security.

"I can't ask him, because he'd wonder why Paul Chance the conflict mediator would need that. I'm also not sure I trust Brody," I said.

"That's insane," he said, venomously dismissive.

"Julian, someone jumped me outside my hotel two nights ago. They had military training and knew where to hit me so it wouldn't leave obvious marks."

"What?" The alarm sounded genuine.

"They told me to back off."

"Can you identify them? It has to be the same people that hacked us."

"Maybe. They were trying to scare me off the case, thought I was some kind of corporate spy or something. Hotel security cams didn't pick anything up, and the Costa Mesa PD basically said there was nothing they could do. There were three, plus an unknown number in a chase car. They were in their thirties, fit, and had military training."

"Oh," he said slowly, the implications dawning on him. "But, like, you fought them off, right?"

"No, Julian. Because I was undercover. Paul Chance isn't an expert in hand-to-hand combat or three-to-one fights."

"I guess not," he said, almost wistful. "Wow, you let these guys kick your ass just to maintain your cover? That's hardcore."

Focus, Julian.

"Nash and I had an...encounter at your office. He seemed a little miffed you contracted me without telling him first."

"You don't think he did this? Brody would never—"

"I'm not in a position to rule anything out."

Julian committed to getting me the names as soon as he could, and we agreed to keep everything quiet about the assault.

While I was waiting on Julian, I opened my laptop and fired up Echo-Trace. The developer recently added a case management function that allowed a user to create a digital corkboard with pertinent subjects in a case and their relation to it—suspect, informant, victim. Once you built the profile, a user could then task the system with further research actions. I spent the rest of the morning aggregating everything I had on my growing list of suspects and organizing the information requirements for them. I also set the system up to flag any time Julian's name came up in traditional or social media, filtering out items I'd already viewed.

Julian sent me the list about an hour later, and I entered each of them as a suspect. EchoTrace pulled public and court records for each, including their driving, arrest, mortgage and bankruptcy, birth, and identity details, such as name changes. It would return any sex offender records, deeds, and liens. I also set it up to create a media analysis so I could see what, if anything, any of them were saying about their employer. The system could usually uncover when people tried to disguise their online presence. I was looking both for any indicator that one of them could've been compromised, such as getting underwater on a mortgage, or if they appeared to have a grudge against the company.

My good news machine rang with the tinny buzz indicating it was coming over Signal. I looked down to see the call was coming from Graves.

"What?" I answered.

"You don't get to talk to me that way, Gage," Graves said with some assumed authority. "What the hell happened on stage?"

"That's between me and my client."

"You can consider me your client now," he said.

"Oh, are you paying me?"

"It is through me that you enjoy continued employment. Here, and after. Now, what in Christ's name is going on?"

"General, I have several nondisclosure and confidentiality agreements with my client that have a lot more legal weight than your threat of extortion. I'm not informing on Julian." I had to be careful here, because part of playing along with Graves's little game was this got me closer to him and, potentially, let me see his hand.

"I want you to do something for me," Graves said, completely ignoring my little attempt to recalibrate our relationship. It was like I hadn't even spoken.

I made a point of exhaling my exhaustion at this conversation into the mic and said in a tired voice, "And what's that?"

"I want information on Dr. Verala."

"Why?"

"That's not how this relationship works, Mr. Gage. I give you assignments, and you complete them."

"General, perhaps I need to remind you how information requirements work," I said, using the official term, just to be an ass. He sputtered out a reply, but I cut him off. "You need to tell me what you want to know and why, otherwise I don't know what to look for. I come back with the wrong thing and you make a bad conclusion, and that could spiral out of control very quickly."

"More so for you than me, I should think."

"Ask anyone who'd ever been to Iraq, General. Two points to consider. One, the second I tell Julian what you've done, he votes you off the board."

"Impossible."

"Hardly. He doesn't necessarily need you anymore. Hawthorne, as former cabinet secretary, has the same level of access to government, and, frankly, Crowder has more senior brass in his pocket than you have in your contacts. Second, extortion. I have enough friends in the FBI that I could bring a credible complaint about you threatening me." I gave the general a few quiet moments with himself to rethink our relationship. He could be useful to me, and he was still a leading suspect.

This was a dangerous play, and I knew I risked pushing him too far. Despite what I'd just said, Graves could do an incredible amount of damage to me. He had a reputation in the Intelligence Community for spiteful vengeance over the most minor of perceived slights. And that was all if he was just pissed at me for being a private eye, to say nothing of how far he might go to hide his movements if he was really the one lining up against Julian.

It took a little while before I realized that the strange sound I was hearing on the other end of the line was laughter.

I'd never heard the devil giggle, so far as I knew, but this had to be close.

"Ed...that would be Edward Evans, the FBI Director, and I are well acquainted. We've worked together on some national-level cybersecurity initiatives." He put an emphasis on "national" that I didn't like. "We play golf once a month now. But, yes, do go on about your...connections."

Well, that didn't go quite like I'd hoped.

Graves continued. "Dr. Verala has close ties to the European Union and the United Nations. As I'm sure you're aware, Mr. Gage. She's pushing Kessler to license his technology to several EU companies and to create an AI initiative within the UN. That would close us out to defense and intelligence applications that this technology is far better suited for."

And, I noted, there were more than a few EU countries that accused the NSA of spying on them under Graves's watch.

"I would be very interested to know the degree of influence those entities might have on her. Particularly financial ones."

"I'll see what I can do," I said.

"Do that," Graves said, and I could practically see his forked tongue catching on his teeth. "And don't threaten me again, Gage." He hung up, though his words seemed to haunt the air around my phone.

There were several flags on my EchoTrace screen.

And more winked into being the longer I stared at it.

Julian had apparently just given an interview saying NOVA was hacked.

Now the other side knew we knew. Julian just pissed away the one advantage we had to salve his singed ego.

10

Julian had been busy today.

He did press hits on most of the cable news channels and an exclusive with *WIRED* revealing that NOVA AI had been hacked during his demo. He *had* to tell people that the *only* reason that demo failed was because someone in a position of trust hacked into it and engineered the results for the exact purpose of humiliating him on stage. Interviews were all on YouTube by now, though I managed to catch one of them live.

It wasn't until you viewed the totality of them with EchoTrace's sentiment analysis that you got a full appreciation for the digital cyclone taking shape. Before long, there was a storm of speculation on "who" attacked NOVA AI. Was it an insider threat? Was it a rival? Was it a foreign government?

Already, three- and four-letter government agencies claimed to be investigating the matter. Including Graves's buddy, Ed Evans at FBI.

Well done, Julian.

Honestly, if he hadn't offered me a six-figure payout, I'd have walked away right then.

I still wonder if that would've been the better call.

I checked in with my hacker friend, Mickey, and he hadn't been able to uncover anything yet. Admittedly, this was a questionable strategy and could likely get me fired—or worse, especially if Graves ever found out I was using an ex-CIA black bag contractor.

Since I was too pissed off at my client to address his disclosure, I decided to concentrate on his list of names. He gave me ten people. Removing Julian and the four department heads that were with him that night triaging, I had five, which included Graham Wexler. Of those present last night, I reasoned Wexler was the only one with the combination of technical savvy and hubris to hide his movements in real time during the initial intrusion investigation and damage control.

Now, a mastermind was taking shape. For the time being, I was narrowing my investigation to three—Crowder, Hawthorne, and Wexler.

I still liked Nash for the assault.

I'd uncovered an interesting item on Crowder. An engineering director, Kyle Haney, at Crowder's NexraTech company left a year ago, citing "ethical differences with the direction of the company." He'd quietly put the word out that he was uncomfortable with the approaches and use cases the company was directed to pursue, and the word was that everything came from Crowder. Haney was allegedly going to speak to regulators, but he'd been killed in a car crash. He'd blasted through an intersection one night and hit a tour bus. The Orange County Sheriff didn't dig too deeply into the accident, though the investigating officer noted that it was strange that Haney would be traveling at over a hundred miles an hour and made no attempt to avoid the bus.

Audrey Farre's information on Evelyn Hawthorne and her using NOVA as a carrot to get a massive influx of government money work into her nonprofit was certainly concerning. Nate McKellar had made some quiet inquiries on my behalf with people that overlapped with her in the White House. They'd all said Hawthorne was ruthless and had a reputation for ending the careers of people that stood in her way.

This didn't mean that Graves, Verala, or Singh were below suspicion, but I couldn't focus on six people. The three I'd prioritized all had strong motives, capability, and, in the case of Crowder, a curious implication of violent problem-solving.

After I'd built profiles on the five engineer names, I went into the NOVA office.

Julian, Graham, Amara, and the rest of the leadership team were huddled in Julian's office, doubtless discussing the fallout of his statement to the media.

"I'd love to see how you're going to steer them out of this," Brody Nash said from a lurking position behind me. I waited until the coffee machine that looked like it required a mechanical engineering degree to operate finished spurting caffeine into my cup before turning to face him. Nash was in his typical attire, a too-tight polo and an athleisure company's take on business pants.

Nash's tone, his posture, radiated arrogance and challenge. It would take a word, and he'd throw down with me right here next to the condiments.

"I was in the audience during Julian's demo," I said, acting as if I were too obtuse to pick it up.

The break room was empty but for us.

"I watched some of Julian's interviews today. Was NOVA really hacked?"

"That any of your business?"

"Maybe," I said. "Maybe not." I studied Nash's expression, his body language. He was guarded, and slightly aggressive. Protective, though not evasive. In backgrounding him I'd learned that he got into unnecessary fights online, typically about military subjects, but he also spent a significant amount of time and money on charities supporting the Naval Special Warfare community. On balance, he seemed like a decent human being, just an obnoxious one. Maybe I could bring him into the fold. "I told you that Julian hired me to manage conflict with the board of directors. That's mostly true. The full truth is that he's worried about a take-over."

"So, what are you, some kind of corporate super spy?" he said, making no effort to mask his derision. This mapped to the implications of my assailants.

"Yes," I deadpanned. When he didn't respond, I allowed a smile and a forced laugh. "My specialty is conflict intervention, and most of what I try to do is help leaders save their businesses. Julian has a revolutionary technology, and it seems someone is trying to take it from him. What I try to do is mediate the conflict and, in most cases, negotiate a soft exit for the aggrieved party."

"Aggrieved party? What kind of corporate bullshit double-talk is that? Someone needs to go to jail."

I patted the air with both hands, *Slow down*. "Maybe that happens. In my experience, it's usually best for the company to avoid that, unless this threat is fully external. Now, where you can help me, help Julian, is to tell me if you think this is coming from the inside."

"I don't follow," Nash said.

"Julian said someone hacked into NOVA during his demo. That's not supposed to be possible. Do you think there's anyone on staff, or maybe an early engineer that left with a grudge? How about someone that doesn't think they're getting recognition for their work?"

Give him credit, Nash actually thought his answer out. His face contorted into something like concentration.

"Thing about Julian is, people are pretty loyal to him. We don't have a lot of terminations here. Occasionally, you get someone that's not a culture fit, but the screening process is designed to weed out the ones who can't make it."

"How so," I said.

"Julian expects people to work hard and fast. That's what you sign up for when you come here. You've got to buy into the vision or you're not going to last. People understand there are sometimes going to be twelve-, fifteen-hour days. He has final say on any technical people they bring in."

"And no one ever took exception to that?" Like, maybe Wexler, I wondered.

"What are you driving at, Paul?"

"Someone hacked Julian's demo. Julian tells me only ten people have ever had that kind of access."

I could see the internal debate play out on his face. There was more he wanted to say, but wasn't sure if he could trust me with it.

"He told you that?"

I nodded. Finally, Nash said, "We had two people exit the company in the last year. Both of them were OGs."

"OGs?" I asked, using a supreme force of will to anchor my eyes in place to keep them from rolling.

"The initial group of developers that built the alpha version. I didn't know the two who'd been let go, and I personally screen people for potential compromise, you see, but I only came on in the last year. The story went that one of them, Travis Rourke, Julian asked him to leave because his code was sloppy. Cut too many corners. The other was Grant Matthews. Now, him, I actually met because he tried to confront Julian once. That's part of why I got hired. Matthews was a big dude and trained in a BJJ gym, so he thought that made him a hard case." The weight Nash put on Matthews's "training" suggested his Brazilian jiu-jitsu hobby wasn't quite up to the SEAL's standards.

"What happened?"

"He tried to get physical with Julian, so I put him into a wall."

"Why'd he get fired?"

"I don't know exactly, but I know it had something to do with an argument he and Graham Wexler had. I'm not the guy to explain this, mind you." Nash shook a negative and held his hands up with a slight smile. "It had to do with NOVA's neural interface. He said the kinds of things you can't take back. Graham and Julian huddled about it and recommended he resign. Now, both of these guys stand to make a lot of money if and when NOVA ever sells or goes public. Julian doesn't like animosity, so he gave them both generous exits. Dudes will both be millionaires if they aren't stupid."

"Thanks, Brody," I said.

Time to hit the bricks.

I'd start with Matthews. A few minutes with EchoTrace showed me that he'd moved with the company from Mountain View and now had a luxury townhouse in Costa Mesa. His physically confronting Julian suggested much unresolved anger over his termination, and there was a logical extension of that in proving his ideas were correct. Matthews hadn't joined a new company since leaving NOVA; rather, he'd founded his own company, called DarkStar. Which one could take to mean the natural evolution of a nova. That probably counted as clever where he came from. Matthews was the company's only employee, though the website suggested it was larger.

I followed him for two days, and I didn't make a secret of asking around about him. I called his condo manager. I spoke with his gym and some of the businesses he had relationships with. I may have implied, though never directly stated, that I was a state investigator. Little of what I learned was any use. In the two days I spent following Matthews, the fallout from the hack only amplified, as did the criticisms of NOVA itself.

Julian demanded progress, and I urged caution.

General Graves demanded the same, and I fabricated a report.

Neither were pleased or mollified.

Deciding to push it up a notch, I braced Matthews when he was coming out of his gym. It was in an industrial park that was a mixture of fitness businesses and low-grade manufacturing. I made my move when he got to his car, a blacked-out Ford Bronco with enough stickers that I could socially profile him just from his windows.

"Grant Matthews?" I said.

He turned to look at me, sizing me up. The look in his eyes suggested he wasn't threatened. Matthews was roughly my height, bulky but without purpose. He had black hair, which he kept short and unkempt.

"What," he said.

"My name is Matt Gage. I'm a licensed private investigator retained by Julian Kessler, and I'd like to talk to you."

"Fuck you, and fuck Kessler," he said.

"Well, you can talk to me, or you can talk to the police. Do you have an attorney, Mr. Matthews?"

That got his attention.

"I don't have anything to say to you," he said, which is what you say when your options are fight or flight. Matthews turned back to the Bronco.

"That's fine, Grant. Though, you should know they figured out you opened the back door into NOVA. You probably also know that two of NOVA's board members—people who have a significant financial and reputational stake in this—have deep connections in Washington. Alexander Graves, whom you may recognize as the former head of the National Security Agency, has the most advanced digital forensics tools ever invented at his disposal. He also tells me the FBI is involved."

Matthews's Adam's apple did some pull-ups as he swallowed hard. "I don't know what you're talking about," he said, stalling for time for his brain to catch up with a way out.

"You've got about a day. If you come forward now, Julian doesn't need to bring in Graves's...help. That will look better for you. Probably, it's the only way to avoid federal prison."

I took a step back.

"I still don't know what the hell you're talking about," he said, with a plaintive quality to his voice that didn't match his frame. "I have to go, I'm late for something."

"If you're smart, that something is a flight to a non-extradition country. In about twelve hours, you're officially a fugitive."

"You're full of shit," Matthews said without conviction.

I didn't respond. There's a great interrogation technique based on people doing anything to avoid an uncomfortable silence. Sometimes, all you need to do is stare an agitated person down and let them run. Their mouth will go to work before better judgment catches up. You'd be surprised how much a guilty person will admit to in trying to convince you of their innocence.

I waited him out.

Tendons tensed in his neck and his eyes darted, searching for a way out.

You're not finding it here, pal.

Matthews looked like he was about to puke.

"The back door was always there, and they'd never patched it. All I did was give someone access. I didn't *do* anything."

"How much did they pay you?"

"Fifty K," he said.

"That's a lot of money. Who was it?"

"I don't know. That's the truth. I never met them. Communication was anonymous, always. I tried to find out who they were, back tracing, stuff like that. As soon as I did, I got a message on my phone from a number I didn't recognize telling me to stop."

"So, this mystery person contacts you and just asks you to open NOVA up to them?" I asked.

"No. They said they knew that I'd been forced out and did I want to do something about it. Said Kessler's vision for the system was all wrong, dangerously wrong. He was going to hurt people because he wasn't careful. Said all they needed was a way in. I told them about the back door."

"They'd have to know it existed first. Otherwise how would they know to reach you? Who else did you tell?"

"No one."

"This is important, Grant," I said.

"I told you, no one. I probably talked about it on a Discord channel, but that's a closed group with just people I know."

Inasmuch as you *know* anyone online. Even a real-life acquaintance can be easily spoofed. Frankly, with the right technology—which was now publicly available—a bad actor could even deepfake a video. It's not perfect, but in a small window, when you're not paying attention because you already trust the person, you might not notice.

"How'd you get paid?"

"They set it up as a consulting engagement. It's all legit. I paid taxes on the money," he said with a self-satisfied air, as though it absolved him of any guilt. Matthews gave me the name of the company, which would certainly be a shell and probably already dissolved.

"Go home and stay there. I'm going to talk to Julian and square this. Don't speak to anyone, you understand?"

Matthews nodded.

I watched him drive out of the parking lot and walked over to my Defender. I called Julian.

"I've got something big. I just figured out who let in the hacker."

"I was just about to call you, Matt—we have bigger problems," Julian said. He hadn't even heard me.

"No, we don't. Didn't you hear what I said?"

"The board knows about you, and they are losing their minds. Hawthorne demanded I step down. It's all over the news."

Julian forwarded me an email that just went to him and each member of the board of directors, citing a *Los Angeles Times* article detailing that he'd recently hired Matt Gage, a Los Angeles–based private detective for unspecified "security consulting." The email went on to describe me as a "disgraced former CIA operations officer who'd been investigated by the FBI for espionage."

Okay, in a certain context, both of those things were *technically* true, but...

"Julian, this isn't what it looks like."

11

———

The mood in the board room was overtly hostile, and this is coming from someone who's been shot at more than once. The sharks hung in their seats when I entered, some practically vibrating with violent energy. Others practiced a more casual disdain. They'd been arguing loudly and with some malice, it seemed, before I arrived.

Julian joined me up front, spoiling for a fight. And he got one. Before his opening remarks left his lips, Hawthorne was shouting.

"Julian, you've gone too far! This is so extraordinarily beyond the pale, it shows how clearly unfit for this job you are."

Graves sent glances down each side of the table, leaned slightly forward, and said, "I've spoken to colleagues at CIA. The reporting in the *Times* was correct. Mr. Gage, here, was fired for cause."

"First of all, you don't have *colleagues* at the Agency, *General*. You're not an operator, and you've never seen the field. You have people you know from meetings," I said. Watching the self-satisfied, smarmy mien drain off Graves's face only to be replaced by a bright red flare of directionless fury was worth whatever this would eventually cost me. Verala snickered. There were a few other repressed smirks around the table.

Hawthorne took the opening to jerk the initiative out of my hand.

"Whatever he is, is irrelevant. The fact remains that Julian hired a private investigator to act under false pretenses. If you had concerns, you were obligated to bring them to us."

"What would you have done with that information?" I said. Hawthorne, unused to ever being questioned, let alone challenged, stammered. "If Julian had come to you, what would you have done?"

Crowder, surprisingly, came to her aid. "I have security people. Professionals. We could have looked into it."

"Oh, I'm familiar with your security people," I said. Let the others draw their own conclusions, though I still thought those were Nash's SEAL buddies.

"What exactly are you implying?"

Julian barked out a "hey," commanding everyone's attention. "I stand by my decision to hire Matt. And I stand by the decision to present him as a consultant. We knew you'd be suspicious of a private investigator."

"What do we have to be suspicious of?" Crowder asked. Verala and Hawthorne both nodded. Graves hadn't spoken and was still a shade I'd call "furious sunset."

"I hired Matt after some personal information about me was released to the public. Most of which you are already aware of. I believe this was done for the purpose of undermining my position as CEO. All of this information was taken out of context, and some of it was blatantly mischaracterized, if not overtly fabricated."

"That seems a little paranoid. It also seems like you're trying to shift accountability for some past indiscretions."

"Julian is prepared to address those allegations," I said. "Though it is obvious that someone is digging up and pushing dirt on him to force exactly this kind of conversation. Ms. Hawthorne has twice called for his removal. Someone is trying to take over this company by forcing him out."

"And is that your professional assessment? Not sure a private detective has the background—"

I cut Crowder off. "No, it's my professional assessment as a CIA case officer who used to do this sort of thing to the bad guys. This operation follows all the classic patterns of disinformation campaign. Frankly, it's straight out of the Russian playbook." Not exactly, but no one in here would know the difference, and I just needed a little breathing room. "Someone sent some people to try and scare me off. They got a little physical with me in a parking lot."

"Preposterous," Crowder said.

"No, felony assault. And it is now in Costa Mesa PD's hands," I said, as smugly as I possibly could. The police weren't doing anything about the assault, though no one around the table needed to know that. My conversational sleight of hand had the desired effect. The implication was like watching a shock wave fly out from a blast site. None of them gave anything away, other than shock. "Then there is hacking NOVA during Julian's demo."

"Again, we were never consulted on this," Graves said, finally reentering the fray.

"I have a former NOVA employee who will attest to being paid fifty thousand dollars to open a back door into the NOVA codebase. Another individual then used that access to take control of Julian's demo. Taken with the disclosures about his personal life, it's impossible to conclude anything else."

My eyes stayed on Crowder for a moment, then to Hawthorne, and finally to Wexler. Reactions were a mixture of righteous indignation, barely contained anger, and, in the case of Wexler, what appeared to be genuine surprise. I didn't know if it was because I'd proven they'd been hacked or because he feared being uncovered.

"I stand by my decision to hire Matt. It's time to fight back."

"Julian, an ex-spy fired for cause? That's all people are going to see. Those are terrible optics. Even you have to see that," Hawthorne said. She'd recovered her executive presence and dialed it up. "You have the company's reputation and our investors to think about. This isn't just you."

"My reputation *is* the company's reputation. And you heard what he said. This is right out of the Russian playbook for a disinformation campaign. Someone is digging up lies and spreading bullshit about me. I want to fight back."

Undeterred, Hawthorne turned her glower downrange to the end of the table with a look that would have frozen Medusa. If I hadn't been the piece of meat they were fighting over, this would've been fun to watch. "What does Graham think about this?"

When he didn't immediately answer, Hawthorne kicked him with a "Well?"

"I'm just learning about this," Wexler said, but his voice was distant, like he was speaking on autopilot. I caught him looking to Julian for some kind of confirmation, but his friend was too busy defending the castle walls to notice.

"If someone is attacking Julian, don't we think that's worth looking into?" Verala said. "It seems that we have a pattern here of, first, these disclosures. Some of them are embarrassing, some more...troubling. As a board member and an investor, I want to know if there is any truth to these allegations. Then, we have this demo. Now, Julian, we discussed this and decided that it wasn't the time." Verala opened her hands, palms up. The part about Julian going ahead with the demo over the board's objections was news to me. "Nevertheless, you went ahead with it anyway. Inadvisable as it may have been, knowing that a disgruntled former employee helped someone hack the system raises serious concerns."

"We don't know that he was disgruntled, that's speculation," Graves said.

"It's not speculation," I said. "Julian gave me the names of the only people who had that level of access, and I investigated them. I confronted the individual, and he admitted to it."

"What's his name?" Graves demanded.

"You don't need to know that. Not right now."

"I do if you expect me to believe you."

"I don't care what you believe. You aren't my client."

"Matt, I think it's important we come forward with this," Julian said.

What are you doing? In that moment I wished he had those glasses that I saw in the demo. The ones that told you the right thing to say when thinking on your feet.

I gave it a long beat. Revealing what we knew was a bad idea, because we didn't know who to trust with the information. But I wouldn't buck my client. Not in this moment. "Grant Matthews. He was one of the original NOVA engineers. He and Graham had a disagreement over technical direction, Julian sided with Graham, and they fired him. Not long after, Matthews threatened Julian."

"Are we involving the *legitimate* authorities?" Hawthorne asked.

"In time," Julian said, and the conversation quickly backslid out of control. This time, it was Hawthorne demanding we involve the federal government and Crowder countering that he wanted his people to handle it.

Verala dove back in. "The point is, we have these disclosures and now the system is hacked, I think there's something to it."

"I think it suggests insufficient oversight," Crowder said.

"Oh, this ought to be good," Hawthorne said acidly.

Crowder's face wrenched into an ugly mask, though he recovered it quickly. The various undercurrents moving here were obvious, and I wondered if this is really what Julian wanted me to see.

"These disclosures are too targeted and too tightly coordinated for it to be anything but a professional operation," I said. "That kind of help does not come cheap. I don't know that anyone in this room is behind it, but everyone in here potentially has something to gain by removing Julian and taking over."

In retrospect, raising suspicion that each of them was a suspect might not have been the wisest approach, as it certainly galvanized and vectored the anger against me. Gave them something to unify behind. That wouldn't last, and I felt I was long overdue for a counterpunch. Sometimes, it's useful for the opposition to know you know. I could expect a reprisal, and that might help me uncover who it was.

Unsurprisingly, I was invited to leave the room shortly after so they could bicker amongst themselves in private. I found Brody Nash in the break room.

"I saw the email about you. PI, huh?"

I nodded.

"A fellow sheepdog," he said knowingly. "So, how do you want to tackle this?"

"Tackle what?"

"Protecting Julian. I've got some thoughts."

Because, of course you do.

Hawthorne closed the distance between us with some serious executive purpose. Without breaking step, she looked at me and said, "It's just posturing. Don't take it personally."

Diabolical.

Of them, I'd expected something explosively public and decidedly threatening from Crowder. In every way, that would've been better. People normally make a show of something when that's all they've got. Crowder's eyes swept past me, and he left.

Julian emerged from the meeting harried. Graham Wexler and Amara Singh hovered behind him equally agitated. Wexler reminded me of old dynamite. He might just remain inert. He might also explode when you least needed it. Julian walked up to me. "Crowder called for a vote to remove me as CEO over this."

"It's pretty telling that when confronted with the knowledge that someone paid Grant Matthews fifty grand to open a back door into NOVA, the thing Crowder finds unacceptable is you hiring a private detective to prove there's a threat to your company."

Julian's expression was unreadable, and I knew his thoughts were elsewhere.

"Probably a good idea to get a report on everything you've found so far. I have a feeling my attorney will want it, at a minimum. I appreciate what you did, Matt. I know it wasn't easy in there." His eyes went to the floor. "What's it like, you know, having your cover blown?"

That's a weird thing to ask at a time like this. "Happens to everyone eventually."

Julian nodded, then turned and joined Wexler and Singh, and the three of them went to his office. Singh looked over her shoulder at me as she walked, her expression haunted. The door closed behind her.

I left.

Diana Verala was waiting for me outside the mirrored front doors. She was in an emerald blouse and black pants, working something on her phone. Without looking up, she said, "You probably heard about Crowder's power play."

"I did."

Verala's eyes tracked up and hit me with full wattage. She smiled, it was warm with a vaguely predatory quality, as if reminding me where I existed on the food chain. Her eyes went to the phone in her hand. "I'm interested in this insider threat. Why don't you tell me about it over drinks? What's your phone number?"

Every spook gets burned at least once in their career. The odds just aren't in favor of maintaining cover forever, no matter how good you are.

Back at my hotel, I messaged Verala and agreed on a time. I found a place in Costa Mesa, a trendy speakeasy that didn't advertise much. They were going for an "if you know, you know" vibe, and they didn't publicize the daily code word you needed to get in, obviously, but I'd have been a shitty spy and shittier detective if I couldn't figure that out.

Diana Verala and I met in the parking lot of the Oceanside, a new restaurant in Costa Mesa's northwest. The building was a blocky, post-industrial design, concrete, iron, and glass, which they hid behind a wall of vegetation, mostly ivy that crawled over the structure like it was the land-lord's kid.

I was there early and watched Dr. Verala's ride drop her off. She was again in green, a dark cocktail number that showed off her darkly tanned shoulders, which I could see even from a distance were nicely defined. I wore a navy polo over off-white pants and assumed this place didn't have a dress code. Though, I kept a blazer in a garment bag in my Land Rover, just in case. I'd learned the hard way that sometimes when tailing a subject, you needed to be dressed for the kinds of places they went.

"It's nice to see you, Matt. Thank you for meeting me," she said. Either the smile was genuine or she was very good.

"Thank you for the offer," I said. "Shall we?"

I escorted her inside, bypassing the hostess station and making our way to the back. There, I found a broad-backed man standing next to an alcove tucked into the corner of two massive age-of-sail paintings on rough seas. "Tsetse fly," I said, and gave him a cocky nod.

"I'm sorry?"

"You guarding the door or just holding up the wall?" His expression darkened. "I just gave you the word of the day."

"Do you have a reservation, sir?"

"If I gave you my name, wouldn't that defeat the purpose of a speakeasy? How I know you're not gonna give it to the first Prohibition agent that walks in the door?"

Crumbling before my irrefutable logic, he stepped into the alcove and opened the door there. "Enjoy your evening," he said grudgingly. He said "sir," but I know he didn't mean it.

I invited Diana to enter and followed her through. They called this place The Tides because they wanted you to believe it operated on some inscrutable schedule that one needed complicated charts to puzzle out. Normally, this sort of thing was far more pretentious than I was willing to stomach. The fact was that my cover had been rolled up by *someone*, and while all signs pointed to Graves, it was dangerous to assume he was the only threat. A place like this would limit who could come in, my name wasn't on any reservation system, and it was a little more secure than a walk-in bar. The booths were high-backed leather couches that wrapped around small tables, practically sealing you in. Between the house music and the outsized furniture, you couldn't hear the table next to you. We found an open booth, ordered drinks, and the server vanished.

We made a little small talk while the bartender worked on our order. I learned that Diana was renting a condo in Laguna, deciding to make a working vacation out of the board meeting. She asked if it was true that I'd been arrested for espionage, and I told her it was, but only because the FBI poorly managed their grudges. She thought that was funny. Diana told me something of her background, her mother was an American expat and her father Portuguese. She was raised in Lisbon, went to Cambridge for university and two elite graduate schools in Europe. As an adult, she alternated between the US and Portugal, moving where the jobs took her, eventually carving out a niche as a consultant and adviser to American technology businesses trying to navigate the increasingly complex landscape of European regulation. Her EU contacts got her noticed by the United Nations, where she occasionally advised today.

"What do you make of Crowder's threat to fire Julian?" I asked, over an unnecessarily complex iteration of an old-fashioned.

"Oh, he won't do it. This is a shot across the bow to remind Julian what Crowder believes is the pecking order. Crowder wants you fired, and he's angry that Julian hired you in the first place."

"Why is that?"

"The fact that Julian didn't go to him when he first thought someone was trying to destroy his reputation and ask for Crowder's not insignificant security apparatus was telling. He's losing face and embarrassed."

"He admitted all this?"

"Crowder admits quite a lot when he's yelling," she said, laughing musically. "It's no secret that he wants to buy NOVA. He's crafted a strategy for his portfolio of companies that relies on the technology. With Julian bringing you in, Crowder feels like it's Julian asserting his independence. Threatening to fire him was just Crowder trying to yank the leash. Most of this is reading between the lines. But we have had in-depth conversations about what he believes the future to be."

"And what do you think the future is? What do you get out of this?" I lifted my drink, to give her a beat to consider my question. "The others, I understand. Crowder wants world domination." That got a laugh, though maybe a nervous one. "Hawthorne, I know is making a play in Washington. It would be hard for Graves to telegraph his intentions any more."

Verala nodded, smiling. "That's quite true. My intentions are easy. I'm in it for the money."

She said it with such a casual, deadpan delivery, I almost spit my drink out. She devoured that reaction with a sly, self-satisfied smile.

"I know, I know, the global altruist. It's true, though. Yes, I pitched Julian on my ability to help him clear the EU's regulatory hurdles, which he will need. But it was mostly about the financial upside. Julian will be a billionaire by the time he's forty. I stand to make quite a bit, and with that money I want to set up an innovation ecosystem. Yes, I think that NOVA could offer some amazing advancements in the developing world, but those are mostly at the national scale—medicine, clean water solutions, resource utilization. Where it could really be a growth engine is helping countries across Europe, like mine, who have tech talent but not the national economies to develop something like NOVA. And this is as true in Europe as it is in South America or Africa. Perhaps you don't appreciate how much. Only deploying it to G7 countries creates a tech inequality that the rest of the world could never recover from."

"Don't we say that about every innovation, though?"

"Think of it this way, there is a time before America landed on the moon and a time after it. And only one country could be first."

"Right, but how many countries have space programs?"

Diana's lips parted in a soft, knowing smile. "That's exactly my point."

I was about to ask another question, but she beat me to it, saying, "And that brings us to you." She lifted a skewer of fruit garnish from her drink and pulled one of them off it in a gesture that was either flirtatious or threatening. "Tell me, what is the former spy, the man of mystery, wrapped up in this affair for?"

"Julian needed some help. After spending a little time with you people, I can see why. Someone is trying to take this company away from him. That's not right." Throwing Diana in with the rest of them was a calculated risk to see how she'd respond.

"Oh, now that is interesting. Julian hired you to save a company that was never his to begin with."

If you've ever driven a car on ice, you know there's a split second when you realize you are no longer controlling the car.

"I understand Julian had to give up a majority stake in order to secure the funding he felt that he needed, but together with Wexler and Singh, they still control it."

Diana tittered. "My dear, it would appear you're several steps behind. You cover it well."

I said nothing, refusing to concede her point. As a detective, you usually never have all the facts until the end. That's the bitter irony of the job. You should, however, have as much information as the person who hired you.

When I still refused to speak, she said, "This isn't public knowledge, but NOVA wasn't Julian's idea. It's Graham's brainchild. Wexler's problem is that he doesn't know anything about business. He founded NOVA under a different name, something ponderous and incomprehensible. They had a prototype, but no one would listen to them. So, he reaches out to his old college roommate for help. Julian agreed to come on as CEO to make it an actual product and an actual company."

"That's not right," I said. "They came up with NOVA in their college dorm. Julian tells the story all the time."

"A little bit of Cecil B. DeMille, I'm afraid. Oh, it's true enough that they theorized about this as undergrads, but he's stretching it to the Lagrange point of truth when he says they talked concepts there. Musing mostly. Graham created NOVA on his own and founded the company. Yes, Julian helped Graham make it a product, something non–computer scientists could interact with. I don't want to minimize that. Wexler never believed in 'AI for the masses,' and Julian convinced him that if they didn't have a broad acceptance, no one would invest. Julian's real value was making the technology into something they could sell. I would not be shocked to learn that he does not control much, if any, of the core IP." I watched her eyes play across my face, the corner of her mouth twisted into a coquettish half smile. I know when someone is trying to read me. Instead of giving away nothing, I lied and projected confidence. Let her figure *that* out.

My client lied to me. At the very least, he'd obfuscated the full truth and played a game of misdirection, which I'd bought. Considering that I'd just come off a case where the client intentionally misled me to garner sympathy, this pissed me off. Mostly because I should've been on guard for it.

"Julian hiring you isn't a good look, Matt. He should have come to the board. He should've trusted us. Bringing you in under false pretenses makes it so much worse. Is someone on the board trying to take the company from him? I can't speak to that. I worry that now that NOVA is up and running, Graham doesn't think he needs his old roomie anymore. That isn't true, but, you know, dollar signs. Crowder has always wanted to buy the company. Graves..." She shook her head in a weary gesture. "He thinks he can 'save the company from itself,' and would probably engineer a coup to do it. He still thinks he's a spy."

"He's a computer geek. He was never like me," I said, in one of those rare moments when my mouth's velocity exceeds my brain's better judgment. It happens so rarely, it caught me off guard. So I added a droll, "No offense."

Diana toyed with the cocktail stirrer in her glass. "There's one other possibility," she said, eyes fixated on the glass rather than me. "That this entire thing is Julian's play to make it seem as though there is a crisis that demands he take greater control. It's not fanciful thinking on my part, and I'm not the only one who's floated the notion. His name *does* bear an ironic similarity to Caesar's."

She leaned forward in her seat and considered me with a soft expression.

"If I could be so bold as to offer you some advice, Matt. You seem like a good person who is trying to do the right thing." She paused, and the humor, the vibrancy I'd watched throughout the evening, vanished as though it'd never been. "The most valuable lesson in business is knowing when to get out. This might just be a place where there is no right thing to be done, and only consequences if you try."

———

I waited with her in the parking lot for the black car to arrive, but I kept my distance in case she decided to go in for the hug. There'd been a brush with surveillance already. I'd also had a case a few years before where someone took photos of me with one of a case's potential antagonists, doctored them, and used it to sow doubt with my client. I'd play it carefully with Dr. Verala.

I decided to drive home rather than back to the hotel. Maybe I just needed to be out of the OC for the night, I don't know. I got home late and crashed hard. The next morning, I got my kayak out and hit the surf to work a lot of aggression out of my system. Afterward, I met some of the Dawn Patrollers for breakfast. Cosmic Ray's opened up a window and you could get breakfast burritos and coffee.

Somewhat refreshed and certainly cold, I went back home to clean up and get to work. I had quiet until about noon, when the phone rang.

"Matt Gage," I said.

"Mr. Gage, this is Detective Erik Ortega with the Orange County Sheriff's Department. I need to speak to you about a Mr. Grant Matthews."

"Okay, how can I help?"

"Mr. Matthews is dead."

12

We agreed to meet in person. Call me skeptical of my fellow man, but I wanted to visually verify this cop's badge before I said anything. He said he understood. I took his badge number down and entered it into EchoTrace, which confirmed there was a Detective Sergeant Erik Ortega in the Orange County Sheriff's Department. The system confirmed he was with the Homicide Detail. It took about ninety minutes for me to get to headquarters in Santa Ana.

Ortega met me out front. He was a bulky, bullnecked former street cop who wore his suit with contempt. It returned the favor.

We found a bench on the OCSD grounds and sat.

Ortega thanked me for coming down and started with some rudimentary questions, address and occupation. I said I was a state-licensed private investigator, shared the license number, and said that the context in which I'd met Matthews was related to a case.

"Can you tell me what happened?" I said.

"Matthews died last night in a car accident. Single car, appears to have lost control of the vehicle, swerved and went off the road at a high rate of speed."

"If Homicide is investigating it, rather than Traffic, that must mean you think someone was chasing him," I said. Ortega didn't acknowledge my point. Instead, he pulled the ubiquitous little notebook prized by cops the world over from a pocket and flipped to a page.

"How'd you know Mr. Matthews?" he asked.

"I didn't, really. We only spoke the one time. Two days ago, I think it was."

"What'd you talk about?"

"I'm a private investigator. Matthews used to work at my client's company. He'd been fired for cause, had physically threatened my client at one point."

"You were asking around about Matthews, though. Is that right?"

"Yes, I was."

"Who is your client?" Ortega asked.

"Julian Kessler. He's CEO of NOVA AI."

"Yeah, I heard of it. Saw him melt down on YouTube. That why he hired you?"

"Because Matthews threatened him?" I asked.

"Yeah."

"No, but I suspect it's related," I said. Normally, I keep any information about my clients locked down. There isn't any legal protection to back that up, but if a law enforcement entity wants that detail and the client doesn't want it shared—for whatever reason—I'll make the state produce a warrant. This time, I decided to cooperate. Maybe the time on the waves gave me a dose of zen and I wasn't feeling combative, or maybe I could feel the tremors and could guess what was coming. Either way, my spider sense was tingling. I'd unfortunately seen enough homicide investigations from the front row that I knew there was no way they'd have gotten my name within twelve hours of Matthews's death unless someone gave it to them.

Ortega was about to ask a follow-up question, but I headed him off. "You said you saw Kessler melting down on stage. Clip was all over social media. Well, the application he was demoing was hacked. Someone that wanted Kessler to fail got in and was driving during that performance. We don't know who that was, but we know Matthews got them access."

"How do you know this?"

"Matthews told me," I said. "He admitted to receiving a fifty-thousand-dollar payment in exchange for giving someone access to what software developers call a 'back door.' It lets—"

"I know what a back door is, bro," Ortega huffed. "How'd you know Matthews gave this person a back door to the app?"

"NOVA's engineers determined that someone outside the system hacked the demo. Julian gave me a list of names of the people who would have had that access. I whittled the list down and landed on Matthews."

"I'd like those names."

"If my client allows me to release it," I said.

"See that he does. So, you were saying about whittling down the list?"

"I eliminated some names and landed on two as the likely candidates. Indicators pointed toward Matthews, so I started with him." I immediately regretted my choice of words.

"How'd you *eliminate* these other names?"

I stared at him for a long, hard second and said, "Detective work." I have learned that police lack senses of humor in these moments, so I described how I backgrounded each of the people on the list, settling on Matthews. I explained how I surveilled Matthews, knowing that, too, could be problematic, as it could be used by a prosecutor to say I was setting up the target. Then I described confronting him outside of his gym, Matthews initially playing tough and then me revealing that we could prove he was one of a select few with that level of access.

"You knew all this, why didn't you bring it to the police?" Ortega asked. Reasonable question.

"You investigate cybercrime, detective?" I asked sarcastically.

"Matter of fact, we do. We were one of the first sheriff's departments in the country to set up a squad for it. Have to with all the tech companies around here."

Huh. Shows what I know.

"We'll come back to that question. Walk me through where you were yesterday," he said.

I explained that I'd spent the entire day at the NOVA AI headquarters, which could be verified by security camera footage, entry logs, and by a dozen people. I exercised and had dinner at my hotel, then met Diana Verala at the speakeasy at eight for a drink.

"You make a reservation at this bar?"

"No, that's kind of the point." That moment when you realize you're too clever by half.

"After you left the bar, what happened?" Ortega asked.

"I drove home. I think we were at the place for about an hour. I got home around eleven."

"Would you be willing to let me look at your phone's location data? Or the GPS in your car? I'd like to verify your story."

This was where my privacy obsession was going to come back and bite me. It's a perfectly reasonable position when you understand the threat and how easy it is to track someone, even one who takes precautions. But to a cop investigating a potential murder, all he sees it as is someone intentionally hiding their movements. Cop logic is always "why hide if you have nothing to hide."

"Detective, I know about a dozen ways that someone could take control of one of my devices and use it to spy on me. In my role as a PI, I am also frequently undercover. Location services are disabled on every device I have. My SUV is thirty years old and not equipped with GPS. I have every setting that could possibly geotag me disabled on my phone."

"You don't have anyone that can verify when you got home? Roommate, girlfriend or someone?"

"Nope," I said. Then, "Wait." I opened my phone and tapped my home security system's app. My landlord had it installed a year ago after a break-in. The break-in happened to be a black bag job by the Russian foreign intelligence service, so the security system wouldn't have been anything but a speed bump for them, but installing it made him feel better. And he barely increased my rent to cover it. I showed the detective the screen. "This is the activity log for my security system. It shows when I deactivated it to open the door, and there's video."

"Mind if I see that?" he asked, and held his hand out.

"You can see it just fine where you are," I said, because I wasn't giving anyone control of my device. Even, or more to the point, especially not a cop. As soon as you hand your phone over to a law enforcement officer, the privacy protections are no longer in your favor. Ortega's face clouded, though he kept any further commentary to himself. He made his notes. He asked me more questions. Ortega didn't admit this, of course, but the realization was dawning that there was no way I could have gone on a homicidal car chase and then made it back to Santa Monica given the timestamp on my security app.

That only absolved me from direct guilt; it did not absolve me of involvement. That much was clear from the frosty thanks Ortega gave when he said I was free to go. He walked me to the parking lot, which I figured out was to see the make and model of my ride. I would not be shocked to learn that Matthews was run off the road by a black SUV.

When Ortega spied my Defender, he said, "This isn't exactly what I had in mind when you said you had a thirty-year-old car." His tone was admiring.

"I'd driven ones like this in a bunch of weird places and kind of fell in love with them. So, I bought one and had it restored."

Ortega folded up his notebook.

"You said Matthews's crash was a single-car accident. Can I ask why you're investigating it as a homicide?"

"Brake patterns on the street suggest he swerved to avoid something. Could've been an oncoming car, or someone trying to overtake and not giving him any room. Maybe it was just really bad driving." Ortega sized me up one last time. "Or maybe it was really good driving."

Like the kind of vehicle control you learn in a combat driving course. I'd withheld that part of my résumé, but pieces of this were falling into place. He walked around my Defender, pretending to check out the restoration work, though he spent a lot of time on the front bumper.

"One last question. When I was looking you up, I came across a story in the *LA Times*. You used to be a spy. CIA, that kind of thing?"

"That's right," I said.

Ortega nodded. He didn't write it down. "Okay. You've been a help, Mr. Gage. Thanks for your time. I'll be in touch." He handed me his card. "You think of anything else, you let me know."

I left, and quickly.

Ortega had summoned me but hadn't brought me into an interview room because he knew who and what I was. Making this formal would've immediately put me in interrogation resistance mode, and that would just make it harder for him to do his job. This confirmed for me that he was acting on a tip. It was the only way they closed the loop that fast.

I drove back to the hotel, only this time I used some of the surveillance detection techniques from my spook days. Drove a circuitous pattern, doubling back at random intervals to check for tails. Once I got there, I took the portable electronic signal detector I kept in my kit and ran it over the Defender. If someone planted a GPS tracking device on my ride, this would pick it up.

Considering what I'd learned from Verala last night, did this put Wexler in a new light? Brody Nash, for all his vet bro affectations, business rucks, and machine gun coffee, could be an able guy Friday.

Matthews died hours after I revealed his name to the board. Taken alone, that wasn't conclusive. Could be someone was trying to scare him off and there was chain reaction. Could be Matthews was preoccupied by the situation and made a bad decision.

Or my revealing his name got him killed.

There was something about the method of Matthews's death that I couldn't shake. A coincidence.

Crowder.

One of Crowder's former employees caused a big dustup over the direction of the company after Crowder acquired it, made a big show of leaving. He was scheduled to speak with state and federal regulators about it, but he died in a car crash before he had a chance to. I had EchoTrace pull up a summary on the crash report and any related details on the victim. OC Sheriff closed it as a traffic fatality and, according to what I had here, they never assigned a homicide detective to it.

Contrary to what Hollywood would have you believe, there aren't secret enclaves of jaded ex-government assassins available for hire. That's not to say there aren't people that know how to engineer a murder.

Crowder made a show of bragging about his security team. Maybe Graves shared my information with him to garner favor in the fallout, or Crowder's people did their own digging.

Julian needed to know about Matthews, and it was news I'd rather deliver in person. A man was dead now, someone Julian knew well and worked side by side with. I couldn't say for sure that Matthews had been murdered, died accidentally, or somewhere in between. This case was escalating now, and we needed a new strategy.

I hadn't cleared Nash yet of organizing the assault in the parking lot, though I liked him for it less. And I'd need to figure him out quickly because Julian would need protection.

After a clean reading from the electronic signal detector, I got into the Defender and drove to NOVA. I didn't tell Julian I was coming, because I wanted to catch Brody Nash's reaction when I told him about the cop.

I arrived at NOVA and headed in, swiping my badge at the door. It made an atonal sound, different from the times before.

I swiped it again. The bar next to the reader flashed red.

A third time, the same result.

I was locked out of the building.

13

______

I called Julian.

"Hey, Matt, I can't really talk right now. I'm in a meeting. Can I call you back?"

Julian's tone was distracted, ambivalent. He didn't know about Matthews yet.

"When were you going to tell me that you'd revoked my access to the building?"

Julian was quiet as he thought about how best to answer that.

I realized that one of the people I was looking at for this was also responsible for the badging system. Brody Nash's stock on the asshole index started climbing. Could Crowder have co-opted him? That was definitely possible. Money was a powerful motivator, and Crowder could promise a lot.

When Julian still hadn't responded, I said, "Do you want me to keep working on this case or not? Someone is absolutely trying to take this company away from you. Now someone is hurt. You're mixed up with dangerous people, and I don't think you realize the trouble you're in."

"Hurt? What are you talking about? No one is hurt, Matt. You're not talking about the people that attacked you, are you?"

"No. Julian, I'm going to go to the Newport Beach parking lot now. I strongly suggest that you join me so I can fill you in on some information that you really need to know. If you choose to meet me, drive yourself and don't tell anyone where you're going or why."

"It's the middle of the workday," he hissed. "I have a *job*, running this company. I can't just up and leave."

"How much longer are you going to have it if you don't? Someone is coming for you, Julian. Newport Beach municipal parking lot," I repeated. "If you don't, I will assume you aren't interested in pursuing this case anymore. In that event, I will send you an interim report on my findings and a bill."

A beach parking lot is a solid choice for a meeting location. The skyline is typically unobstructed, so you can easily check for eyes in the sky, an unfortunate consideration these days. There is ample natural background noise from the wind and the water that makes it hard to listen in on a conversation with anything but the most sophisticated surveillance equipment.

To my surprise, Julian showed up, and he was pissed.

Someone driving angry in an electric vehicle just doesn't have the same effect. The scene called for the angry Rottweiler chugging of a traditional Mercedes G-Wagon; instead I got the electric whisper as he raced into his parking spot. It was like getting yelled at by a mime.

He also wasn't alone.

Brody Nash was with him.

Julian practically leaped out of the car, fury and righteous indignation at the interruption of his day. I took it for what it was. He needed a place to vent his anger, his frustration, his legitimately grounded existential fear, and the only place he could do that, in his mind, was on the one person he knew wasn't out to get him.

Twisted logic, that.

Nash had exited the car with authority, eyes sweeping the parking lot. Well, that's what I assumed from the head motion. His tacti-cool, wraparound Oakleys hid them.

When Julian was done fuming, I said, "Grant Matthews is dead." I kept speaking through his shocked, *What? Oh my God*, and the follow-up questions.

Nash, decisive and clinical, "How do you know this?"

Addressing only Julian, I said, "An Orange County sheriff's deputy called me this morning. Matthews died in a car accident, and they're trying to find out if it might have been forced."

"Why are they talking to you?"

"That's a great question, Julian," I said flatly. "Whoever is trying to get your company is now feeling threatened. According to Detective Ortega, he learned about me from my asking around about Matthews. He knew enough to look up that *LA Times* article, though. Maybe it's a legitimate traffic accident. Matthews would certainly have been nervous and distracted after I exposed him. But the fact that Ortega knew to call me to ask where I was the night before just twelve hours after the accident tells me he was doing this on a tip. I've been framed enough times that I know what it looks like."

"Really?" Julian said, but with a genuine curiosity.

"It's practically a trope," I said. "It's a solid strategy when dealing with a private investigator. Most of the time when someone like me gets jammed up with the police, they'll just walk away. Especially now."

"But you won't," he said, almost hopeful.

"This needs to be worth my while, Julian. We're in this, or we aren't. That means absolute honesty from you from here on out."

"I don't follow."

Knowing his guard was up, I pivoted. "Grant Matthews admitted to taking a fifty-thousand-dollar payment in exchange for opening a back door for some other hacker, someone he didn't know, to tank your demo," I said, and Julian nodded. "I told that to the board, which in retrospect I probably shouldn't have. I did it because I was trying to justify my presence, but I realize that I likely tipped them off. Matthews died that night. This proves that the person behind this was in that room." The latter I said for Nash's benefit. Build trust, see what he might kick loose.

Julian held his chin with one hand and looked down while he thought.

In the distance, waves crashed, and a strong offshore wind smashed both of our hair into impossible dimensions.

"And now, I'm locked out of your building, and you couldn't even call to tell me," I said, and that time I did look at Nash. He folded his arms across his chest, presumably so that I could measure his biceps with my eyes.

"I didn't have a choice, Matt," Julian said defensively.

"For someone who owns a company, you seem to have very few options, Julian." This was a dangerous tactic to take with a client, but so far no one was playing straight with me, and that frayed my last bit of good judgment. "Or is it that you *don't* own the company."

Julian looked away, and I knew what Diana Verala told me was true.

"You want to watch yourself," Nash said.

"It's fine, Brody," Julian said.

"So, it's true, then. You don't own NOVA?"

"I have a controlling interest in the company."

"Which you share with Graham and Amara. Which means you have a third of a controlling interest, providing the other two go along with you."

"I told you that. Mostly."

"You also told me it was *your* company, meaning *your* intellectual property," I said.

"I never used those actual words." Julian's expression was a mixture of sullenness and masked aggression. "Graham and I did come up with the idea in undergrad, but the technology didn't exist at the time. Most of it was fun riffing, something to take our mind off our coursework. We tried to build a language model that captured what we were thinking, but couldn't make it work. I didn't realize Graham kept working on it until he asked me to join the company. Initially, he just wanted me to invest because I'd just had the exit from my previous company. I convinced him he needed my help to make the idea into something he could sell. Before I joined, we talked with an IP lawyer, who said that my early contributions counted for about twenty percent. Amara, who joined before I did, gets another twenty percent. Graham has the rest."

I turned to Nash. "What's your relationship with Graham, Brody?"

He shrugged. "I provide equal security for the executive leadership team. It's just that with the threats against Julian, that's where most of my focus is."

Or you're keeping tabs on him.

"I didn't lie to you, Matt," Julian said.

Technically true, but enough sins of omission can still get you into hell.

"Why did you restrict my access to the building? And why didn't you tell me?"

Nash stepped forward, physically shouldering his way into the conversation. "That was a compromise we had to make with the board. They were going to force Julian to fire you."

"Which they can't legally do," I said flatly.

"Whatever. They voted and it happened," Nash said, as though it explained everything. I took it for what it was, the opposition putting up another wall between me and Julian, me and potential suspects. "You're also to have no contact with any NOVA employees."

Well, at least I wouldn't have to deal with Brody anymore.

"That's not enforceable," I said.

"Matt, please don't make this more difficult than it already is."

"Julian, do you want me to solve this case for you or not?"

Nash, again: "I don't know exactly what you think you do here."

Time to play a hunch. The opposition had to have employed an operative who'd get their hands dirty on their employer's behalf. Someone with street time and tradecraft. One of the most valuable pieces of insight in an operation like this was always having eyes on your target.

"Give me a minute," I said and stalked back to the Defender. I went to the back, opened the lift gate and then one of the concealed floor panels where I hid my kit. Inside, I had a clean laptop, clean phone, a small drone with a camera, long-range microphone, a disguise kit, and my electronics detection gear. There were other concealed compartments in the Defender where I stashed other kit—change of clothes, more disguise items, first aid and survival gear, but this was the main load. Oh, I also had a Beretta A300 tactical shotgun that I wanted to introduce Brody to, but now wasn't the time.

I removed the electromagnetic detector and closed everything up.

Then, activating it, I walked over to Julian's Mercedes and proceeded to scan the vehicle's undercarriage.

This was a nontrivial risk.

I'd made a big show of it and could easily humiliate myself by being wrong.

I wasn't.

The device hit as I ran it beneath the driver's-side running board. Reaching under, I searched with my fingers until I found it, a thumb-sized box magnetically clipped to the running board. Thirty seconds later, I found a second one attached to the passenger-side rear bumper.

I walked over to Julian and Brody, pushing the trackers into the ex-SEAL's chest.

"You asked what I'm doing here? Apparently, your fucking job, Sheepdog." I turned back to my client and his astonished face. "Julian, these are GPS receivers. Whoever planted them has been following your movements. An up-leveled hacker—which we know they have—can use these to bridge into your car, either through the vehicle's GPS antenna or, more likely, Bluetooth. You should assume your car is compromised."

"My...car?"

"It's a computer on wheels. And car manufacturers don't prioritize security as much as they do cool-looking features," I said. *Any security chief should be able to tell you that.* "This isn't something you take lightly. I had a case about two years ago where someone hacked into a Tesla Model 3 and remotely activated the car's autopilot. They accelerated the car into a curve and turned off the brakes. The victim went off the road doing about eighty. By the time the car stopped at the bottom of the hill, you could only conceptually tell that mess had been a vehicle." My eyes went from Julian to Brody as I let that seep in. Nash had a mixture of disbelief and scorn, he wasn't buying it because he didn't understand the technology, but I could see the awareness breaking on Julian's face. "I know someone that can check the vehicle, but I wouldn't trust it ever again. We should also sweep your house."

Julian handed Nash his car keys. "Take it wherever Matt says."

"No," Nash said, words practically punching the air. "You need overwatch. That's my job. He wants to get your car checked out, he can do it."

Julian wheeled on him, the explosion of words was as rapid as it was violent. "Securing my fucking company is *your job*. Stopping someone from trying to blackmail me is fucking *your job*."

The SEAL wilted in front of his boss, looked like a blow-up doll with a tear.

"I'm calling an Uber," Julian snapped, and he left.

I made a quick phone call. Then I texted Nash an address. "Drop the car off at this location in exactly ninety minutes. Lock it, leave the keys in it. Don't stay."

"This is downtown LA!"

I shrugged. *Enjoy the ride, asshole.*

After he'd gone, I'd climbed into the Defender and spotted Julian standing on the sidewalk, his back to the parking lot, staring out at the six lanes of Pacific Coast Highway in front of him.

I got out and walked over to him.

"Julian, you okay?"

"I didn't call a car," he said. His voice sounded far off. "Feel like I can't even trust my phone."

That's because you probably can't. I debated telling him. Maybe now wasn't the best time.

"You'd be surprised how many clients have had to buy me new phones. Come on, I'll give you a lift."

Julian followed me to the Defender, and I asked him where he wanted to go. He told me the office.

"Brody is a good guy. Means well. I think you threaten him," Julian said, staring out the window.

Not yet I hadn't.

"He's making the same mistake I did when I first started being a PI. I assumed that because I was good at one hard thing, I could do them all. Being able to kick in doors doesn't translate to corporate security, at all. You want someone that understands physical security, yes, and probably you need a body man. At least for now. But what that job really requires is someone with industrial espionage, cybersecurity, and countersurveillance experience."

"You mean someone like you," he deadpanned.

"Maybe. *Like* me, not *me*. Let's be clear I'm not trying to take the man's job. And I don't have deep experience with industrial espionage. You want, I can recommend some people."

"Who do you think it is?"

"I've interviewed everyone, though I haven't spent much time with Graham and Amara. Almost everyone has a clear motive and strong incentive." I stopped there. Telling Julian what I knew at this point could backfire. It could easily make him paranoid, looking for enemies in every shadow. And, at this point, I had theories, and indicators, yes, but no proof. Revealing the raw data would almost certainly damage his reputation with the board members that *weren't* out to get him.

"And?"

"I think it's best that I do not share anything else right now. I don't have enough information to be conclusive, and I don't want you distrusting the wrong people."

"Okay," he said, skeptical and nearly dismissive.

I wanted to ask him about Wexler and dig into their relationship, but this wasn't the time. My finding the tracking devices on his car clearly rattled him. The vote was out on Brody still. Special operators were frequently used to gather intelligence and conduct surveillance in the field, so he had some tradecraft. And there was still the question of who ran Matthews off the road.

Julian didn't speak the rest of the way. Whatever occupied his mind, he kept it to himself.

I dropped Julian at his office and made sure he had a ride home. He asked me when I could sweep his house, and I said at his convenience.

"The strategy here is to make you doubt everyone, to make you jump at shadows. Make you doubt yourself. They want you rattled and making mistakes. The point is to give the board enough evidence to vote you out."

"Thanks for the reassurance," he said.

"My job is to let you know what you're up against. I've seen this sort of thing before, Julian, and I know what to do."

He looked at me, holding the expression of a tourist realizing they only know a few words of the native tongue. Then he nodded and went inside.

After he was gone, I went out for some tacos and beer, collected my thoughts. Eventually, I made my way back to the hotel.

When I opened the door, I found a large envelope had been slid under the door.

I undid the clasp on the back and opened it. Inside were six photographs. Five of them were of Julian, Brody, and me talking in the parking lot earlier today. The sixth one was of Diana Verala and me outside the speakeasy.

14

High-quality telephoto lens, taken by someone with training.

The one of Verala and me was particularly troubling because that had been done at night, and across a couple lanes of traffic.

I packed and was checked out of the hotel within ten minutes.

My last words to Julian echoed in my thoughts: *...make you jump at shadows. They want you rattled and making mistakes.*

Between living in Southern California for a few years and my time on this case, I knew Orange County well enough that I could improvise a surveillance detection route. I found a new hotel just outside John Wayne Airport, a small chain that was on a main road and blocks from the 405. I didn't plan to be here long. I just needed an uninterrupted night's sleep so I could plan my next move.

I didn't bother unpacking, so I left my duffel on the floor and stretched out on the bed. The photographer did me one solid, which was to confirm that Brody Nash wasn't in on it. He couldn't be taking pictures of me if he was also standing in the parking lot.

Unless, perhaps, that was the point.

Show us together to throw me off his trail. If you wanted to turn a potential suspect into a confidant, this was the way to do it.

Again, my unfortunately prophetic words to Julian—*make you doubt everyone, doubt yourself.*

I just didn't think that'd apply to me.

My phone rang, breaking into my thoughts like an unskilled burglar. This was the regular ringtone, not the one I used for Signal. I didn't recognize the number.

"Mr. Gage?" It was a female voice, and I didn't know it. It didn't have Verala's continental accent, Hawthorne's contempt for everything, or Amara Singh's earnest lilt.

"How'd you get this number?"

"Let's just agree this is something I know how to do."

"Not good enough. I'm hanging up now."

"Wait," she said, almost pleading.

"What do you want?"

"To help."

"Why?"

"Kyle Haney was a friend of mine. We were...close."

Kyle Haney. It took a moment to place the name, but it flashed into my mind. That was the engineer who'd worked for Crowder, the one who'd tried to express some concerns to the government and had died in a car accident before he could.

"How well did you know Mr. Haney?"

"We were...together. It was quiet, because we both worked for Crowder. He, ah, frowns on that sort of thing. Plus, I knew how Kyle felt. About the company, the acquisition. Why he wanted to speak out."

"What do you do?" I asked.

"I can't tell you. If this ever got back to Crowder, I'd be finished."

I'd met Crowder's head of security, who was a woman. I'd also communicated with his chief of staff. Neither conversation was long enough that I could immediately place the voice, and considering their boss, both seemed equal candidates for being able to track someone down.

"You need to show me some proof, and tell me how you got my number." I maintained two phone numbers, one for my PI business and my personal one, both going to my iPhone. The business line was handled via an app on the phone. This call came in on the personal one.

Ignoring my question, she said, "I've seen the police report about his death. It's not what you were told. They didn't think it was an accident, but didn't have enough to prove it."

"That seems like a stretch," I said.

"I know because they told me," she snapped.

"Are you going to tell me who you are?"

"No."

The word was barely out before I hung up.

The photos shook me, got inside my head, I'll admit. And now, I wondered if this wasn't the same person basically doing a crank call just to screw with me. Give me another spinning plate to manage. This had been a long day, and I'd had enough of it. I went down to the hotel bar and decided to check out the scotch selection.

The bar had a retro quality, the sort of dated design you expect in an older hotel. Dark wood, tall booths, and a lot of brass, vaguely reminiscent of a neo–Gold Rush or Old West styling. They didn't have my usual, so I ordered a twenty-five-dollar Macallan. The place was quiet and the bartender wanted to chat. I did not.

After I'd finished the scotch, I debated having another because it'd been that kind of day. Instead, I went back up to my room and tried to look for sleep.

———

Nerves woke me early, so I drove down to the beach and went for a cold run. When I was finished, I swept the Defender for trackers and, finding none, coordinated with Julian to check his house.

Having someone be in your personal space when you're not there leaves you with a skin-crawling feeling that's hard to shake. A stranger peeling through your things, looking for secrets and maybe leaving a few behind. I'd need to wash everything I'd had with me, because there were things you could plant on a person's clothes. Though it had as much to do with another person's fingerprints on my things as anything else.

Julian lived in a gated community in Newport Beach. That was a good sign, because it restricted access. My relief was short-lived because as I followed the road to the end, I saw that Julian's home was the last on the street, facing the water. There was a privacy fence walling off the neighbor-hood from the beach, though most of the house still had unobstructed views of the water.

The home was spectacular. Two-story, four bedrooms, and a three-car garage. It boasted bright, exterior lighting with little for cover, meaning an intruder would have a long, exposed walk to an ingress point that would be bathed in light. Julian met me at the door, looking haggard. He invited me in and walked me back to the kitchen. "I made coffee," he said, and offered a cup, which I accepted.

I told him about the pictures, but not the phone call. I told him the logic of why I'd met Verala at that place.

"Does that mean you're being followed too?"

"I don't think so," I said, shaking a negative. I composed my thoughts around the mug in my hand. The coffee was quite good. "I'm confident in my countersurveillance techniques. We know they were following you by virtue of the trackers and likely followed Verala to get to me."

It was a good theory that I desperately hoped was true.

"Brody said my car is going to be tied up all day. I've got a rental," Julian said.

"That's a good idea."

"Well, I'll let you get to it."

I broke my gear out and set to work. After completing each room, I annotated that it was clear in my notebook. Julian stayed with me through the first floor, and then departed for work, asking me to lock up when I left. I told him I would.

It took me until lunchtime to finish sweeping. I used an electromagnetic detector to look for signals going out, but relied on a combination of other tools and visual inspection to fully clear a room. I didn't find anything.

I was packing up to leave when the phone rang.

It was the same woman who'd called me last night.

"Mr. Gage, please don't hang up," she said with an urgent quickness.

Now I was wondering if this was a coincidence, or had I missed a camera in Julian's house? I hadn't checked the property, nor had I looked at the neighbor's. These houses were built close together to maximize the available land, and someone could easily mount a concealed exterior camera. I didn't know what that would get them if they were also tracking Julian's car. Unless the point was to give me things to chase.

"I told you last night, unless you tell me your name, I'm not interested. I'm hanging up now."

"All right, all right. I'll tell you, but this *cannot* get back to Crowder. It won't just mean my job." She said that latter part with a dark certainty, and I found myself believing her. There was a strange quality to her voice, but I was having a hard time putting a word to it. It sounded…different, perhaps, than what I'd expected. I assumed she was the woman, the athletic blond in the sharp suit that guided me away from Crowder's august presence that day outside his office. She'd said but two words in that encounter, and I'd been so focused on what Crowder told me that I hadn't paid her much mind.

I waited for her to speak, and when she didn't, I took that to mean she expected some kind of assurance from me. "Maybe we should do this in person," I said.

"Are you out of your mind?"

"I'm getting tired of this. You have my word, I'll do everything in my power to protect your identity." I threw in some big words to make it official. It's funny, I was throwing back a line various cops had used on *me*. "As a licensed private investigator, I have no constitutional or statutory protection in this matter, but I will do my best to protect you. That good enough?"

"Thank you." A pause, which annoyed me. Then, "My name is Vanessa Holt, and I'm the chief of corporate security for Crowder Dynamics. In that role, I oversee the security practices for each of the companies in the CD umbrella, as well as coordinating personal security for Mr. Crowder."

Well, I could understand the secrecy, at least.

"You said last night that you were close with Kyle Haney. Were you romantically involved?"

"Yes," she said. It came out clipped. "I met him during the due diligence leading up to the acquisition. We hit it off, and…"

She sounded troubled, and I let her off the hook. I still wasn't sure where this was going and also not sure I wanted to be on the line for it. "It's okay, you don't need to tell me. What is it that you called last night to say? What does my case have to do with Mr. Haney's death?"

"Kyle wanted to talk to the state about Crowder. NexraTech is about using machine learning to optimize workflows for advanced applications like global logistics, but the system can also write its own code. They quietly released several apps into the marketplace designed by the Nexra-Tech platform without human involvement. Kyle thought that was questionable. He also worried that Crowder wanted to replace human workers at a pretty significant scale, and also that there was no regulation of AI-generated software. He thought Crowder could corner the global software market before the government got off their ass to figure out how to police it."

"So, Haney disagrees with Crowder, and he threatens to go to the authorities over it. Not long after, he's killed in a car accident." I recognized that these memories must be painful for Ms. Holt, though I still chafed at the whole premise of this conversation.

"The police contacted me shortly after he died."

"Which police?"

Haney had been driving on Newport Coast Road and lost control of the car. Conditions were wet, and he screamed through the intersection with PCH doing about a hundred, spun through the intersection, and collided with a tour bus. The bus driver was hurt pretty bad and some of the passengers had minor injuries. I'd learned this from various newspaper accounts.

"Orange County Sheriff," she said.

"You remember what he was driving?"

"You're fact-checking me?"

"Ms. Holt, as far as I'm concerned, you're still an anonymous caller."

"It was a white 2020 Porsche 911 Cabriolet. Satisfied?"

That car wouldn't need much running room to get up to a hundred. "I am. I hope you can appreciate this from my perspective. What did the police tell you?"

"That there were marks on the rear bumper consistent with a low-speed traffic accident, their words. The cop asked if he'd reported any. I said no, and then asked why. Then they went into whether I thought anyone would want to harm Kyle."

"What did you tell them?"

"Nothing." The words came out choked, like she had to force them out of her throat. "They said the car could've had a minor collision, or maybe it was pushed."

"There weren't any eyewitness accounts, at least that I read, that said another vehicle was involved."

"He was coming out of the Hills. I think...based on what the cop said... that someone tried to run him off the road. Kyle decided to outrun him and..."

And he got into a one-sided argument with a bus.

"You didn't tell the police any of your concerns, or about Kyle's?"

Her response came out as a harsh, hissing laugh. It was a clipped, scoffing sound. "You don't know Nathaniel Crowder. You think some state traffic cops are going to protect me from him?"

"You're so afraid of him, why do you stay?"

"I'll spare you the adages about devils you know and one's proximity to enemies and friends."

This was a weird conversation to be having in my client's kitchen, admittedly.

"So, why did you call me last night?"

"When I heard that Grant Matthews opened the back door into NOVA and then died in a car accident, it seemed like too much of a coincidence. I mean...Kyle. And then...I couldn't stay silent. I couldn't forgive myself."

I had to admit her point about the coincidences between Matthews's and Haney's deaths tracked with my own thinking. It felt like something was snapping into place. Finally, I was getting some momentum in the right direction. Two deaths connected to Nathaniel Crowder, even tangentially, was hard to deny. The links got a little clearer when contextualized. And the proximity between my telling the board about Matthews, the payment for enabling the hacker, and his death was undeniable.

The question was really, what to do with it now?

"Thank you, Ms. Holt, for sharing this with me. I can appreciate how painful that was for you."

"Thank you for listening. It should go without saying this conversation never happened. I don't know you and we never spoke. And if I ever meet you in person, I'll deny it."

"You did meet me in person," I said. "You threw me out of the Vanguard campus a week ago."

There was a short silence. "You'd be surprised how many people I do that to. You must not have made an impression."

She hung up.

That was a strange way to end an already bizarre conversation. I can only imagine Holt thought her rudeness would somehow convince me to never speak to her again and pretend this didn't happen. A one-night stand of transactional information sharing.

Here's to being used.

The question of what to do next about Nathaniel Crowder presented itself when I called Dr. Verala to inquire about her plans for the evening. It felt like she needed to know someone photographed us together.

"He's hosting us at his club," she said.

"The board?"

"Indeed."

"I thought you all couldn't stand him," I said.

"Oh, only too right, darling. But it's quite the club, apparently. I'm going just to run up his tab. I suspect that's what the others are in it for."

"Is this social or business?"

"One masking as the other. Have to go to figure out which is which, I suppose," she said.

"Just curious, what's the name of this place?"

"Oh, it's the Coastal."

"The Coastal Club?"

"No, dear. Just 'the Coastal.' It's the sort of place that doesn't need to say what it is." She tittered. Verala sounded different tonight as well. Perhaps she'd been drinking a little already, God knows I'd need a little insulation if I was going to spend a social evening with Nathaniel Crowder. Or it might just have been an outgassing of pressure from the last week.

"Unfortunately, I have to run. We're meeting there shortly. I'd love to meet you for dinner any other time," she said, and hung up.

I looked up the Coastal and saw their website was essentially a gilded splash page. You needed a special invitation even to view their web presence.

Perfect.

Earlier Crowder had called for Julian to be fired. Now he was summoning the board to his exclusive club for a meeting. The only reason I could imagine was that he was trying to whip support for his plan. And he was having it at a place where he felt secure, a SCIF for the elite.

A place he didn't think I could get to.

We'll see about that.

15

The Coastal, aptly named, lorded over the western edge of the San Joaquin Hills, a sentry against the lower classes. The club was tucked into a bend on Newport Coast Road, curiously, or suspiciously, along the stretch where Kyle Haney lost control of his Porsche and crashed into the bus on PCH. You could see the intersection from the club's front door. Though it was already on a hill, they'd raised the land slightly to give the structure more of an overlook to the coast. An overhead map showed me a huge driving range cut into the back lot, with several putting greens and a large outdoor pavilion.

The club itself was California mission architecture, flanked by an honor guard of palms. One accessed the club from Pelican Hill Road and by following an S-shaped curve that afforded the driver a stunningly unobstructed view of the Pacific before turning back toward the building. Luckily, my restored and updated 1993 Defender looked like the kind of eccentric ride a member here might own. All told, this car cost enough that it constituted a trade-off between four wheels and a down payment on a house, so I felt comfortable using it to sell the legend.

Before driving over, I'd gotten the disguise kit out of the back and transformed myself in my hotel bathroom. The Agency employs makeup artists that would put most Hollywood people to shame. Their real value, though, is their ability to teach. While we sometimes deploy them to the field, often a case officer has to put a disguise on in the back of a car or even on the fly. You'd be surprised how much you can alter your appearance in just a few seconds. For this, I chose a wiry brown-going-silver wig, cheek appliances, and some deft makeup brushing that would trick the eyes into thinking I was ten pounds heavier than I was. I added similar padding to my nose. A pair of thick-framed glasses intended to distract from the shape of my face completed the disguise. I didn't think it would matter, but the lenses were coated with a material that would hide my eyes on a video camera.

I kept a jacket in a garment bag and a few pairs of shoes hidden under the back bench. I rotated the jacket among the few that I own, depending on what I thought I'd need and what cover I had ready. My gun club check tweed blazer, gabardine pants, and loafers would sell this perfectly. When I pulled up to the entrance and a valet walked up, he didn't even look twice.

"Are you a guest, sir?" He knew by sight that I wasn't a member. I'd learned the hard way once that clubs like this had their staff memorize the members' faces. Ostensibly, it was to ensure they greeted them personally each time they arrived, but it was also a sound security practice.

"I am," I said. He tore off a tab from the check card as I handed him my keys. I grabbed a small leather notebook as I left. No doubt he confirmed my status into an earpiece as he drove off, because someone at the door intercepted me before I could make my way through the small groups of people waiting out front for their cars.

"Good evening, sir. Whom are you visiting tonight?"

When I spoke, I added a little gravel to my voice to go with the made-up years, miles, and pounds I'd put on my face. "I'm not a guest...yet," I added with a rakish tilt. "Carlton Trent," I said, offering him my hand. "I run a concierge service for, shall we say, a *bespoke* clientele," I said, adding emphasis and pretension onto the words. "I'm here to explore the Coastal's services on behalf of my members."

"I see," he said, with an equal mixture of genuine curiosity and not-my-problem. Cars were queuing up, and his body language said he clearly wanted to get back to his job as valet captain. "They can help you right inside, sir."

"Thank you, Rick," I said, spying his name tag.

Someone held the door for me, and I suspected that was the last time I'd touch a handle tonight. This was the kind of place that even ejected you with decorum. The entry foyer was a long, brightly lit corridor of warm wood, tan Italian marble floors, and an arched ceiling. There were arched accents along the walls at intervals, with a slight inset alcove beneath each one that held some large painting. Closed doors, set a little back from the entry and coatroom, showed a bar on one side and dining room on another, presumably in the front so both had views of the ocean. There were small clusters of members, some holding drinks, some not, greeting each other and chatting in the entryway. Staff members loitered like elegant flies waiting to guide them to the proper location.

I spotted at least two people I recognized—one of the regulars from *Shark Tank* was chatting with a former LA Laker.

Avoiding the maître d' would've been pointless because he was on me as if magnetized.

"Good evening, sir."

"Ah, good evening," I said, as though I were looking for him. "Carlton Trent, I'm with the Quintessential," speaking as if he should know and being embarrassed for him when he didn't. I watched the expression change, darken and flush.

"Yes, of course," he said, pretending to understand.

I leaned in and lowered my voice, letting him in on it. "We're an executive lifestyle concierge service." As I said this, I turned my head to Shark Tank and winked conspiratorially. "I'm here to explore the Coastal's services for our members. I spoke with Mr. Aguilar last week to make arrangements." Despite the exclusivity the club presented, they were quite open about trumpeting their board of governors, no doubt considering it a selling point to prospective members. It included several high-profile public and private figures. I'd spent a few hours that afternoon figuring out who each of them were and whether I could use them to support my cover. There wasn't enough time to cultivate a target, but I'd learned that Albert Aguilar, a one-time US ambassador to Colombia and now head of an international development firm, was out of the country on business.

The maître d' consulted his schedule and was visibly shaken that someone would gain access to the club without his knowing it, but the look behind his eyes suggested he wasn't going to push fate and test this newcomer's relationship with Mr. Aguilar. He said, "How may I help you, sir?"

Now to figure out where my target was.

"You have private event rooms, yes?"

"We do indeed."

"Are any of them occupied tonight? I thought I might have a look around."

"We're setting one of them up for a private dining experience now. I can arrange to have another shown," he said.

"Excellent. Perhaps I'll start in the bar."

"Very good, sir."

I was shown its location, and as I departed, the maître d' informed me, "I'll let our executive director, Mr. Parkhouse, know you're here."

Hopefully I'd be out of here before that happened. The bronze plaque next to the door leading into the bar read "The Library," because of course it did. The interior didn't disappoint. Stylish and inset bookshelves, backlit, lined the walls interspersed with paintings, also accent lit. A wide and long bar dominated the far wall. There were no tables in the center of the room, only along the walls, the presumption being if you were seated anywhere but a barstool, you were entitled to a private conversation.

Despite that, I spotted Crowder immediately.

Most of the board was with him, and they had a crescent-shaped booth in front of the window overlooking the ocean.

He was in a dark red jacket that had a faint sheen to it, patterned navy shirt, and a volcanic eruption of silk coming from the chest pocket. There was a whiskey tumbler in front of him. Graves sat to his right, his back was to me, and the half of his face I could see was furrowed in concentration or concern. Hawthorne was on the other side of the table in a suit, using a wineglass as a shield. Her ambivalent expression looked like it took effort to maintain. Finally, Diana Verala was next to Hawthorne and deepest in the booth. She was tastefully dressed for cocktail hour, but still managed to make it look elegant and stunning. In the thirty seconds I'd been here, I saw at least one ambush predator at the bar trying to figure out how he'd separate her from the pack.

The bar wasn't particularly busy that night, only half of the tables were occupied, with a few small clusters of members quietly talking in the center. By design, the booths were far enough apart that eavesdropping was difficult. However, the table next to them was unoccupied, and that gave me line of sight on Crowder. I was in that seat no more than ten seconds when a server came over and asked me for a drink order. I opted for a club soda with a lime. From a distance that looked like a gin and tonic, and I wouldn't need to wait for a bill in case I needed to make a hasty exit.

Crowder, unsurprisingly, was angry and speaking louder than he probably should. His voice carried and even at this distance, I could make out some of what he was saying. I opened my notebook, pretending to document my observations about the club. I positioned myself in the booth so that I was facing the bar, as if studying it, and this meant an ear was turned to their conversation. It was worth noting that the board members present were the ones who were external to the company. At the point of the conversation where I picked up, Crowder was first arguing that they needed a board injunction to prevent Julian from conducting another technology demonstration. Hawthorne seemed to argue every point Crowder made. Graves jumped in periodically, mostly seeming to side with Crowder, and Verala, for her part, seemed to just light conversational fires. It was hard to tell, as she was a little softer spoken than the others. Crowder was building toward his apex, though I couldn't tell exactly what that was. I was missing about every third or fourth word each of them said, and tone and pitch varied.

A shadow appeared at my table, and I looked up to see a silver-streaked man in a suit I'd never afford standing at a respectable distance. As soon as I looked up, he said, "Mr. Trent, it is so good of you to call on us this evening. I am Walt Parkhouse, the executive director of the Coastal."

"This is a fine establishment," I said, with an aloof disdain that I think went well with my jacket. I returned my attention to my notes, as though describing the amenities, and tilted the notebook slightly so he couldn't see that I was transcribing the conversation at the table next to me. Speaking of which, paying attention to two simultaneous conversations requires more processing power than my brain is capable of, and I was starting to lose the thread. Parkhouse continued, assailing me with facts about their exemplary services and why Julian Kessler was clearly now unfit to continue leading NOVA AI...damn it.

See what I mean?

With a hint of irritation, I set my pen down and closed the notebook, lifting my gaze to my earnest spectator. He very much wanted to take me on a tour of the facilities. "Mr. Parkhouse, I don't want to take up any more of your valuable time. In these early evaluations, I like to get my initial impressions and then schedule deeper dives with the leadership team. Would that be okay?"

He may have heard my objection, but it clearly didn't register with him.

Parkhouse enthusiastically probed into the concierge business that I'd made up earlier that afternoon. I hadn't made my mind up yet on whether he was trying to see if I was actually full of shit, or was he just very interested in closing whatever deal he'd arranged in his head.

Tactfully ditching a threat to your cover is one of a case officer's most valuable field skills. It's best done preemptively and, in retrospect, I should've intercepted Parkhouse as he entered the bar. He was, at heart, a salesman, and he viewed my obstruction as the thing standing between him and a win. By now, I'd completely lost what was going on at the board's table, and Parkhouse insisted I come with him on a brief tour.

I asked if I could schedule some of his time tomorrow, so that I was free now to compile first impressions.

Obviously, that simply would not *do*.

At the risk of having my cover blown entirely, I stood and joined him at the elbow.

As I was leaving with him, Amara Singh walked into the bar.

We burned twenty-five minutes touring the club, and I made no effort to hide my irritation. This was the one thing I wasn't improvising.

Parkhouse left me at the maître d' station with the presumption, I think, that I'd be leaving. I told him I intended to inspect the wine list and asked if I could return to the bar. Naturally, he escorted me there and stood with me at the bar while the bartender produced a large list. Parkhouse asked the bartender to get the sommelier.

Meanwhile, the board table had reached a hot simmer on its way to a rolling boil, with Crowder speaking loudly enough that Singh was visibly embarrassed and Hawthorne offended. I positioned myself so that I could at least observe it while Parkhouse talked about the "bespoke beverage program." If you were a member, they crafted a specific cocktail for you that you could request any time. For the love of God.

Crowder looked down at his phone while he blustered.

I focused on Singh.

She clearly looked uncomfortable and wanted to be out of there. Her eyes flitted to the door, and she held her arms tightly across her chest, moving in her seat.

Crowder said something explosive, and the tide broke.

I read on Singh's lips, "I have to go," and she slid out of the booth. Crowder stood, imposing his presence over the rest of them.

Crowder was drawing enough attention now that Parkhouse excused himself from me, walked over to him, and whatever he said was like water on a grease fire.

Crowder stormed out of the bar, and I followed.

While I never expected to return, it's best never to burn a cover if you don't have to. Seeing that Parkhouse was engaged mollifying Crowder's guests and trying to decide how best to deal with that now that their host stormed out, I gently grabbed him by the arm. In passing, I thanked him for his hospitality and would be in touch.

Crowder was out front, waiting for the valet to bring his car around.

I handed someone my claim card, and he disappeared.

Crowder's temperament had entirely transformed. The change was so sudden, it was like watching a window break. Crowder knew all the valets by name and was small-talking them as if they were his friends' kids. He was smiles and loud laughs, holding court in a high-end carport.

Everything inside was just a show to get him out of that room.

There was an unmistakable roar of a performance engine, and a vehicle that took obvious design cues from Christopher Nolan's Batmobile raced around the carport. Crowder stepped off the curb before the vehicle even stopped. He palmed a bill into the valet's hand, and climbed into his Lamborghini Urus.

The Urus was Lambo's answer to the SUV market, squat and aggressively angled. A fair extension of the driver, as I thought on it. Crowder revved once, to the delight of the valets, and roared off.

My Defender appeared a moment later.

I exchanged a weathered twenty for my keys and hoped the kid wouldn't be offended by the small change. Then I set about trying to catch a Lamborghini with a thirty-year-old Land Rover.

16

I watched the distinctive taillights race downhill toward PCH.

Crowder tried to convene a Last Supper, and it blew up in his face. He stormed off and was now putting his Lamborghini through its paces. Now, Crowder was enough of an asshole that this could just be the way he drove. My hunch was that it wasn't. His plan backfired, and I was betting he was moving to a backup. He'd made his play for the company, failed, and was now on the clock to save his goal of taking it over.

A proper tail involves a team of cars and coordinated with electronic comms. We'd seen that on this case for sure. Of course, you can do it solo, though it's best done in the city where you can blend in with other vehicles. The sun had already dunked itself into the Pacific, covering the sky with a bruised ochre turning to spilled ink. PCH was congested enough that Crowder had to slow down once he was on it, which gave me space to catch up to him. The Lambo wasn't hard to keep in view, allowing me to maintain a comfortable distance.

I followed Crowder a couple miles into Newport Beach. He turned off PCH after crossing Lower Newport Bay, heading north into a residential area on Dover Drive. Here, I had to back off a little. Crowder might not possess any tradecraft, but the human mind is wired for pattern recognition, and he may subconsciously notice the same set of headlights making all of his turns.

Crowder's route took us farther north, staying on Dover. We drove a long, roughly arced path until he made a right on Irvine. This was a two-lane road, and now I really risked getting spotted or losing him. If he wasn't in such a distinctive vehicle, I'd have to have considered ditching entirely. Instead, I dropped back, letting one pissed-off driver whip around me and one or two more in at a light. Irvine Avenue cut a roughly northeasterly path, angling back toward Upper Newport Bay and, after a few miles, the brackish bay and its wetlands appeared as a dark stain on the skyline to my right. The road opened up here, adding an additional lane in each direction, and Crowder picked up speed, then turned off onto a frontage road.

There was no way I could follow him directly and still maintain cover. Instead, I tried to stay parallel with him. The fork he'd taken looked like it went into a nature preserve or park that roughly followed the road's contour. Admittedly, this was guesswork. There was thick foliage between Irvine Avenue and the frontage road, which meant I was following Crowder through the gap in the trees.

Crowder maintained course for another quarter mile. Thankfully, the foliage thinned gradually, and I could more easily follow. He braked abruptly and turned about onto a dirt road. I could only tell because of the dust that the maneuver kicked up. He stopped.

There was a break in the median here on my left. I could make the turn and thread the needle of the oncoming traffic. The maneuver was sure to draw attention. Guessing this was Crowder's destination, instead I merged left, followed the road up another block, and made a U-turn. Backtracking, I turned right onto a side street perpendicular with Crowder and stopped.

There was enough ambient street light that I could see a blocky, black SUV pulled up on the frontage road. Both vehicles were far enough off the main road that they'd be outside the field of a car's low beams, and drivers averaged forty-five on that stretch. Chances were, it wouldn't rate a second glance, but it was still poor practice because it looked out of place enough. And there was the matter of Crowder showing up in a Lamborghini. These sorts of meetings were better handled in a place they'd fit in, like the parking lot of an upscale restaurant.

People who exercised bad tradecraft out of ignorance thinking they were clever was the fastest way to singe my nerves. It did make them easier to spot.

Now to see what they were doing.

The one downside to my vehicle's storage was that the only thing I could really access from the driver's seat was the Glock 34 hidden in the door panel. Everything else required me to get out and open things up. Thankfully, Miguel, the automotive wizard who'd rebuilt the Land Rover, included a kill switch for the interior lights so I could access gear without tipping off my presence. I climbed into the back seat, put the seat down, and crawled to the storage compartment. Popping the hidden latches, I accessed the concealed panel in the floor. I drew out a thin, carbon fiber briefcase, opened it, and pointed it in the direction of Crowder's Lambo. It took a few seconds to power up. I didn't bother connecting it to the truck's power supply, assuming this would be a short meeting.

Well, at least one good thing had come from working for Gloria Denmont, which was it allowed me to upgrade my surveillance package with a phased array microphone that, to a casual observer, looked like a laptop. I had the microphone set up and calibrated within a few seconds. Then, donning the headphones, I trained it on Crowder. It took a few seconds of fine-tuning to filter out the street noise, but overall, this was a nearly ideal environment, low ambient noise and a direct line of sight.

"...this is what I goddamned pay you for," Crowder barked, through a little static.

Yes, I am familiar with California's strict privacy laws regarding surveillance and how it's illegal to record someone without their permission. However, who among us wouldn't break the speed limit in an emergency?

"Sir, you pay me to protect your organization," the other person said.

"I don't draw a distinction."

"I understand that, but you have to acknowledge we're pushing the boundaries of what I'm comfortable with."

"You need to concern yourself with what *I'm* comfortable with."

If this other man was going to show some spine, now would be the time.

Crowder cooled himself a touch and asked, "Do you have it?"

"Yes. It's—"

Crowder held up his hands. "I don't want to know."

I'd have given a lot to know what started this conversation, and what Crowder had asked this guy to do. Based on the conversation, I gathered the other person was one of Crowder's security team, so why was he meeting with him and not Holt?

Unless he was something else.

While they talked, I searched in the dark for my camera case. I'd practiced assembling it without looking, and the camera came together quickly with the night vision lens on. I was less concerned about getting pictures of them together as I was seeing if I recognized the person Crowder was with.

"Now, is this Gage going to be a problem? Because you obviously didn't scare him off," Crowder said.

Well, that answered the question of who tried tuning me up in the hotel parking lot. Even money if I searched this guy's SUV I'd find a camera or, at least, an SD card with photos of me and Julian at the beach.

"Yes," the guy said definitively. "I've talked to some contacts. He's a legit operator. I can't find anything out about him, other than he's ex-CIA. The FBI investigated him once and he was arrested two years ago, but not charged."

"That's nothing we can use," Crowder said, declining his head in thought. I snapped a picture of the two of them for posterity. "Kessler is unfit to run NOVA, and the board understands this. I have the votes, but Kessler has Gage. He will be a problem if he uncovers something that proves Julian's case. We need to amp it up on him. You know what you have to do."

"Yes, sir," the other man said. That was it, he was dismissed. The guy turned to head back to his car, and I snapped one of his face.

The Lambo was already moving.

Julian needed to hear this.

I crawled out of the back and returned to the driver's seat, watching the murky outline of the other SUV in my rearview. I needed to find out who this person was so I could plan out my countermoves.

After a few minutes of contemplation, my new adversary got into his

SUV and drove off. He didn't even bother taking the frontage road, he just rolled over the bushes on the median and onto the street.

I hit the ignition, turned about, and blasted onto Irvine. This was still a Land Rover, but Miguel had tuned the engine enough that I had as much straight-line speed as the shitty aerodynamics would allow. I caught the other SUV, a Lexus GX with California plates, within a couple minutes.

I didn't need to follow him long. The Defender had a forward-mounted camera, which was just a higher-resolution version of a trail cam that many off-road vehicles now carried. I toggled the camera, and the Lexus appeared on my center screen.

The Lexus turned right at the next light, and I continued straight. Following him would be tough, assuming he was an operator with solid street craft. He might have military or intelligence training and could've certainly honed it in private security. So, I had to let him get a little bit of a lead so that I could cut over and pick him up on a cross street. If I turned and followed now, he'd pick me up for sure.

Once I was clear of the intersection, I floored the accelerator and raced up Irvine, making my first left. It was across traffic, and I damn near made a new friend the hard way. My luck being what it is, I found out this was a cul-de-sac. That actually worked out, because I could whip the Defender around and get back onto Irvine without having to go up a full block. I pulled out into traffic, made the right on University, and raced to pick up my target.

A 90s Land Rover chasing a Lexus SUV was like watching a pair of sumo wrestlers stalk each other into a ring. We weren't winning any drag races. I clocked the target when he was three car lengths ahead. He didn't make my job difficult, and I followed him into the industrial part of Costa Mesa. We crossed the aqueduct on MacArthur Boulevard, and he made a right on Hyland Avenue into an industrial park. Here, I had to let the line out a little more because it was well past business hours and if I turned, it'd look suspicious. Instead, I jetted up half a block and made the first right I could find. This took me in a long loop around a large building where I lost line of sight.

Finally, I'd caught a break.

Cutting the headlights, I cleared the building and picked up the Lexus. He'd driven down another block and turned back, heading in this direction on a road that dead-ended in a roundabout with a single two-story building at the end. The Lexus pulled into a garage.

I parked with a decent sight line to the other building. There was a strip of lawn with some landscaping separating my lot from the other one. The aqueduct was on the far side.

There wasn't much time to put kit together, but I assumed I'd be on camera. I had the camera-masking glasses from earlier and a ball cap behind the seat, within easy reach. I grabbed both of those and got out. The cap, which I may or may not have forgotten to turn back into the CIA's logistics division, had material in the brim and the cap that baffled electromagnetic signals. Basically, it made my entire head look like a cotton ball made out of static.

Mindful that I was still dressed for a country club, I ditched the sport coat and got out of the Defender. Though I couldn't remain out of sight entirely, I did what I could to minimize my profile. The air was crisp and cold, and I immediately regretted not having something heavier.

As I crept closer, I watched the garage door crack open and a BMW sedan emerge. He pulled out of the structure and accelerated down the street until it disappeared from view.

I decided not to press my luck with breaking and entering. If my instinct about this place was correct, I'd be on camera the entire time. Even if my appearance was obfuscated, there would be little question it was me. Instead, I decided to first figure out who owned that building.

Crowder was a powerful enemy. His allies included former Secretaries of Defense and military branch chiefs, current and former congressmen, and the governor. That was before we got to his legal team, which was what would do real damage to me. I wouldn't move against him unless and until I was absolutely certain.

Once I was back in my room, I entered the SUV's license plate into

EchoTrace. Even though I was licensed to use it, I had to justify access to some of the more advanced surveillance tools. For what I had in mind with Crowder's man, I needed to show proof that I was on contract for a client and that this was related to that case. The system's AI would review my entry and determine whether I would be granted access. What I was looking for was to run the plates and the vehicle through the various law enforcement databases, but also CCTV feeds. The automated license plate recognition feature would show me any time in the last month that vehicle popped on a traffic camera or on cameras belonging to any of the private businesses that participated in the program. That doorbell camera that everyone uses? That's in there too—read your terms of service, people. Anyway, what I'd hoped for was to get a traffic camera shot of the driver, and then feed that into the DMV and background check program to see who this guy was.

As that was running in the background, I removed the makeup and appliances, returning them to the kit. Then I went back to my laptop to check the results.

The system notified me that my request was approved. I set up live tracking and geo-fencing alerts. Whenever that Lexus popped up on a CCTV feed, I'd get an alert. I set up a second query for the system to look backward in time several days to see if it appeared anywhere within the search parameters I set.

The Lexus was registered to what looked like a shell company. You see enough of them, you know what to look for, but EchoTrace also had tools that interrogated businesses—checking websites, DUNS numbers, tax registries, and place of incorporation. It also looked to see if another business owned it, how many employees they had, and cross-checked the identities of any disclosed employees to confirm they were real. One of the really useful features the company added in the last year was integration with some anti–money laundering protocols used by the Treasury Department and some major banks. This helped expose things like shell corporations where people tried to hide funds.

Why was this important?

The man told Crowder, "You pay me to protect your organization." That meant he was an employee or a contractor. I suspected the latter. More and more this had the hallmarks of a deniable operation.

My hunch was that Crowder maintained a clandestine private security company. This sort of thing wasn't widely talked about, but they did exist. As industrial espionage became more prominent in a world where a company's value exceeded that of small nations, leaders like Crowder went to serious lengths to protect their empires.

While EchoTrace was working on that task, I set about to solve the very real problem of how to outmaneuver Crowder. With what I'd learned tonight, I knew that he was the one leaking secrets on Julian's past and doctoring them to undermine his position with the board of directors. Seeing that Crowder had his own dirty-tricks squad cemented that. The purpose of the meeting at his club was to get people on his side. And, apparently, that included Amara Singh.

The next pressing question was what to do with these revelations?

Proving to Julian that Crowder had a private security company nested in a shell corporation *and* that he'd directed them to dig up dirt on Julian was one thing. Proving it in court was something else. With Crowder's considerable resources and allies, we'd almost certainly never see a trial. The best Julian could hope for was negotiating a bigger exit package; the outcome would be the same.

The only way I could save my client's reputation, let alone his job, was to outmaneuver Crowder on the board.

For that, I'd need allies.

I called Verala.

...And stopped myself just before I dialed. She was the one who told me about the meeting at Crowder's club. If I called her now, it would surely tip off the fact that I knew the meeting was over.

I was staring at my phone when a text arrived, and it was from her.

The logical part of my mind knew this was completely a coincidence, but it still gave me that "you're being watched" sensation crawling down my spine.

Diana Verala: **Much ado about nothing. Crowder started a big fight & stormed out before dinner.**

Unsure how to play this, I replied with the obvious question, **What did you do?**

Diana Verala: **Had a four-figure dinner at his expense.**

That got a snort of laughter from me.

The rolling ellipses on my screen said she was composing another message.

Diana Verala: **Care to meet for a nightcap?**

17

____

EchoTrace dinged with an alert informing me that some task had just completed. I went back to the laptop and checked. First, I'd entered the SUV's plate, make, model, and color into the system and asked it to link it to any traffic or security data in the last five days. The day before my assault, a security camera in the neighboring property clocked that vehicle in the parking lot. They were staking me out. Now I could connect Crowder's clandestine operative with my ass-kicking.

I fought the impulse to fire off a missive to Julian. If I was going to make my appointment with Diana Verala, I needed to leave now. That seemed to be the theme on this case—frying pan to fire to boiling pot of water. Always some new crisis to manage and never enough time to unpack the problem I'd been trying to solve.

Thirty minutes after Diana's text, I was walking into a stylish, Mediterranean-themed steakhouse called Mozambique in Laguna Beach. After dining hours, this place turned into a three-level nightlife hot spot with a club on the second floor and a more subtle rooftop bar with a view of the ocean. Verala was already there at a table by the edge, flanked by a glass of wine. She'd changed from the cocktail dress I'd seen her in earlier, wearing a jacket and jeans. It was a cool night, but there were standing heaters near each of the tables.

I'd also changed from my earlier outfit. It wouldn't do to have her place me at the club based on my attire.

Verala flashed a warm and genuine smile when I approached and stood, moving in for a fast embrace like old friends. She held it for just a moment and let go.

"Thank you for coming out, this was a...it was a weird night," she said.

A server appeared and I ordered a beer. The music was 80s pop, a contrast to the thumping in the floor from the club below us. You could almost hear the waves coming onshore, though if it were light out, we were certainly close enough to see them.

"So, what happened, exactly?" Inasmuch as I was trying to see if Verala was a potential ally, I was also assessing whether I could trust her. Was her account of the night going to match my own?

"Oh, Crowder invites us to this place because he's trying to impress us. It's elite and exclusive." She rolled her free hand in a dismissive gesture to pair with a biting, mocking tone. "Trying to buy off a bunch of people who want for nothing is childish." She shook her head and took a sip of her wine. "He said it was to get us to talk about what we're going to do about Julian. I think Crowder was trying to see who'd side with him if he put it to a vote. Crowder started broaching the subject over cocktails, and Evelyn Hawthorne just laid into him. Those two started barking at each other, and it rather spoiled his surprise."

Then Amara Singh showed up.

"What was the fight about?"

"Oh, he talked Amara Singh into being there. Apparently, she's now got some concerns of her own."

That was news, and I bet it would be to Julian as well. He was counting on her support. In fact, she was the one person in all this I thought was squarely on his side.

The server set my beer down, asked if we'd like anything else, and left.

"So, Hawthorne doesn't agree with him that Julian should be removed? I assume that's why he called everyone there," I said.

"She hasn't said it, though I think she'd actually agree with him on that point, which is why they're fighting so much over it. The two of them just need to go to bed and get it over with."

"Hawthorne wants Julian out?"

"She hasn't *said* it, but, let's be honest, the allegations are disturbing. There are ethical questions about how the data is handled and how the system interacts with humans. Then there was the breach and that farce of a demo. Why bring it out in front of people if you aren't absolutely certain it's secure? Then the person who engineered it dies in a car accident immediately after? You're a detective, Matt. You have to admit that's suspect."

"I am a detective," I said, lifting my beer. "And I find it interesting that not twenty-four hours after I told the board that Grant Matthews sold a back door into NOVA, he died. I also find it interesting that the sheriff's detective investigating the crash knew to call me first." The look on Verala's face told me she was hearing this for the first time, or she was a damned good actress. That was valuable. I didn't relay what Vanessa Holt told me about Kyle Haney. First, I'd given my word, and second, you never know what someone does with information. Once something is out in the wild, its natural inclination is to metastasize. "Someone is trying to set Julian up so they can get him out of the company."

"I could've told you that." She looked up, a devious glint in her eye. "But you neglected to interrogate me." A wry smile lit her face.

"Everything I've seen tells me it's Crowder."

The smile drained off her face, and I felt guilty that I caused it. Verala turned solemn, and she drank in silence for several moments. The debate played out on her face, shadowed by the dim ambient light and a flicker from the heater beside us. Telling her my theory placed her in a precarious spot. By my saying that I suspected Crowder, it essentially put her in the role of agreeing or not. If the former, that put her on Julian's side; if the latter, it tipped her hand and made her potentially complicit in Crowder's coup. However, this was a time of choosing, and my strategy relied on whipping votes since I didn't think I could beat Crowder in court.

Hawthorne would certainly side against him.

Graves, I was fifty-fifty on.

Wexler wasn't at the cocktail party to kick off the Night of the Long Knives, so presumably he wasn't working with Crowder. Especially given that Singh was there. I still wasn't sold on Wexler, and it was always possible he was Crowder's hole card. I assumed, for now, he'd vote to keep Julian if Crowder was exposed.

I had three that I was sure of, counting Julian. Diana didn't make it a lock, we'd need Wexler for that, but we also couldn't do it without her if Crowder had Singh.

"You haven't mentioned Graham. Was he there as well?"

"No. I think that would be too suspicious. And anyway, they're a package deal. It's almost like the two of them aren't fully formed humans without the other. This company doesn't work without Julian. NOVA, as an algorithm, might have been Graham's brainchild, but it doesn't work without Julian. He was the one who came up with the idea for the noninvasive neural interface, or whatever they call it. He's truly a visionary. At least in that regard."

"Then why is he at risk?"

"In this business, you're indispensable until you aren't. You and I are both adults, so let's not pretend anything I say to you doesn't make it back to him. He's your client, and I understand how this works. Julian has a vision for NOVA and is guiding development in a way that Graham Wexler never could. Graham doesn't *interact* with people. He writes code. He just doesn't get that a non-engineer would find value in the way it collaborates. But Julian, for as awkward as he can be around people, he understands the interaction of humans and tech better than anyone I've ever met. *That* is the unique alchemy of this place. That is why NOVA could change the world. Julian's personal life has put him on a timer. If it continues to get worse, we'll have to decide that NOVA is good enough now."

I'm rarely speechless. That was a powerful admission, even if it was intended to be a message to my client.

She set her glass down, reached both hands across the table, and set them atop mine.

I'd be lying if I didn't admit it sent a warm shiver up both arms.

"I'm not sure that I trust Julian right now, Matt, but I do trust you. I don't think you'd be part of something you knew was wrong."

"You're a quick study," I said, not entirely offhand.

"I'm a woman in international business and tech. I have to be. You think America is sexist, you should try Europe. That's not the point. The point is that if you're telling me that everything I'm hearing about Julian is bullshit, I'm inclined to believe you. So, is it?"

"I think the truth is being manipulated for effect. I've looked into his sister, she's blatantly lying and doesn't have a great track record of holding steady work. Julian did have an affair with that woman. He—" I caught myself before I said what I was thinking. I didn't know Diana and couldn't trust what she would do with the information. Julian had grown up awkward and learned confidence through technology; he was very naive around people. I couldn't say for fact that his judgment was clouded because a pretty girl showed interest in him. I couldn't disprove it either.

"He what?" she said, not letting me off the hook.

"He didn't terminate her because of the affair. Julian doesn't think that way. He hyper-compartmentalizes everything. And anyway, he said they've turned their entire BD team over several times. He wouldn't go through that kind of churn just to cover up an affair. You and I have already talked about the money. The thing with his sister, the thing with the classmate, those are designed to undermine his character. The affair and the alleged embezzlement are intended to paint him as a corrupt leader. The demo was character assassination in real time. Unfortunately for him, I don't think this is the last we'll see, either. But I don't think he's amoral, and he's certainly not what this phantom adversary is painting him as."

"Then that's good enough for me." Her eyes returned to the distant water, and she lifted her glass back up for another drink.

"What do you get out of all this?"

Her eyes returned to me. "I told you before, I want to create an innovation ecosystem, I want to democratize technology. Few countries have the kind of tech incubation environment that America does. I truly believe NOVA can help with that, and in exchange, I help Julian navigate the European regulatory environment. This is just the first step, though. NOVA has the potential for so much more. Imagine a virtual schoolhouse where every student had a tailored learning plan based on their individual needs and unique circumstances. One that could contextualize for the student, rather than standardize based on historical norms. Now, imagine that in the poorest, most impoverished parts of Africa." She shook her head slowly.

"With that, you could change the world in a generation. We can't do that if we sell it to the US military or the Intelligence Community."

"The board had a very negative reaction when they found out I was a private detective. It seems natural to me that Julian would want to investigate this. Are you comfortable sharing why they reacted like that?"

She laughed, sharply and caustically. It still sounded like music.

"Because you have Julian's ear and we don't. He fawns all over you when you're not around."

"So it's about control, then? You have to know I'm not influencing his decisions about the company."

"I think Julian might be a little drunk on the idea that someone is trying to take him out."

Her hand crept back across the table and rested atop mine.

"Matt, you need to be careful. Julian has a right to protect himself. As much as I hate to admit it, though, Crowder did have a point in that this could have been handled in house. They're going to come after you."

"What the hell for?" I said.

"Crowder is convinced you're an operative and all this is your fault," she said, an almost comedic flourish in her voice. Was this a joke, or did she just think the entire situation was absurdly funny? "Now, it's been quite a long day, and I think I've had enough of business. I'm renting a house down the beach. Why don't you walk me home?"

I would, but I was getting answers about Crowder on the way.

I signed for our drinks, and my phone rang. While I was on a case, I had a different ringtone for my client. Julian had just messaged me in Signal, asking if I was still awake.

"Everything okay?"

I didn't answer immediately, as I was asking that same question of Julian.

Julian.Kessler: **We have a big problem. Need to talk to you now.**

My eyes tracked up from the phone to meet Diana's expectant gaze. "I am afraid I'll need to postpone our walk."

I dropped Diana off at her condo. She leaned across the center console and kissed me gently on the cheek, a hint of what I'd probably missed out on.

There are certain decisions we make when the sun is gone that don't look as good when it returns. Julian's missive undoubtedly saved me from one of those.

The drive to Julian's was thirty minutes straight up PCH, and when I arrived at a few minutes from eleven, I found him erratic and stalking.

"What took you so long?"

"I was having a late dinner," I said, deflecting. Technically true enough. There was something about Julian's demeanor that suggested telling him I was out with Diana Verala—even if it was to get information—wouldn't go over well.

Julian turned and walked back inside, leaving me in the doorway. I stepped in, closed the door behind me, and followed him into the kitchen where he had two laptops and a tablet open. One of the laptops was opened to a terminal window and looked to be compiling code, the second was on some internal NOVA interface, and the tablet had a cluster of news sites and blogs.

"What's going on?" I asked

Julian was in yoga pants and a light blue sweatshirt, his face drawn and gaunt, haunted.

By way of response, Julian waved a hand at one of the screens, though it wasn't clear which one. "When Amara started with the company, she set up an anonymous system for submitting feedback and concerns. It's an encrypted passkey system that leadership couldn't get into even if we tried. We actually tried to hack it once, in a town hall, to prove we couldn't do it. So, she got a message on that today, a whistleblower saying they 'know' we're using the neural interface to test the interactions with people without disclosing it to them that we're testing. Which is preposterous."

"And illegal," I said.

"We're not doing it, Matt. The complaint also says it's so we can test whether any of the wearables introduce adverse side effects that people wouldn't otherwise disclose."

"Julian, I need you to put that in context for me." This was curious. The last anonymous "whistleblower" message came from an external encrypted email. This was through an internal system.

Irritated, he said, "The complaint says we're testing the interface technology, the wearables, without telling people what they are, or under false pretenses, to collect 'unbiased data.' Basically, that we gave people these and told them to wear them all the time because it was like a health monitor, not because it was a neural interface. Collecting biometric data without consent is patently illegal."

He said that in the way that suggested it was an original idea and not one I'd literally just voiced.

"They sent logs from NOVA showing where all of this happened, but I can't find any record of it anywhere. And I don't understand why they'd use the whistleblower system. Like, why not just blackmail me and be done with it? That's what this is, right?"

Julian's speech was fast and oddly syncopated. Once I got close enough to truly see his face, I saw that his pupils were dilated. Hopefully, this was just stress chased with Adderall.

"Blackmail would involve a threat. That would give us sufficient cause to bring in the police. Sending this through your closed loop system reminds us that they are still inside and can control information. That's a threat in and of itself. Then, we assume that this is also somehow leaked to a board member, likely two to make it harder to figure out who's behind it. That's how I'd do it." I gave Julian a second to process it, really wishing he had a clear head. "Could that data be faked? The logs?"

"I don't see how. Not unless they had root-level access and went in and covered their tracks. And NOVA would need to be in on it, because we have security protocols trained into the system to prevent exactly this." His mouth turned down at the corners, a combination between a frown and a pout. "Guess anything is possible at this point."

"When did you learn about this?"

"Like, an hour ago," he said quickly.

So, after Amara was at the Last Supper and with enough time to sit at home, stewing over her options. I couldn't know if this was decided in the few minutes that I was being forcibly escorted around the club by the executive director, or if Crowder set this up outside of it. The fact that I could place her at that meeting, and then this happened not hours later, told me she was in on it.

"I want to know what's goddamn going *on*, Matt. You're supposed to be out there doing some Jason Bourne shit."

"Have you spoken with Graham yet?"

"Yeah, she told us at the same time. I asked him to look at the logs, which is what I'm doing. I can't find any...any trace of *anything*. It's like it's not fucking *there*." Then, in a hollow and chilled voice, Julian said, "Assuming he's telling me the truth."

It took me about a half hour to get Julian back into a low earth orbit.

I couldn't be sure if he'd taken anything, or if the erratic behavior was just what was after the equals sign of several weeks of some ugly psychological math.

All credit to the man, his bar was well stocked. I poured us each a couple fingers of bourbon, and that seemed to ease him off the ledge he'd been on.

Once I saw him get on solid ground, I told Julian what I'd found out about Crowder. I wanted to give him something to anchor himself on, some measure of hope that we had a way through this. And despite whatever assurances I may have made, I think he needed to hear all of it.

"Julian, I'm convinced that Crowder is setting you up. I think what you're seeing is a protracted campaign to undermine you with the board of directors. The intent is for one of them to introduce a no-confidence vote and move for you to be removed. This won't come from Crowder, but from an ally. Then he swoops in during the aftermath and arranges to acquire the company. That was the plan, at least."

"I don't follow."

"I tailed Crowder to his club. He invited the entire board, minus you and Graham."

"How do you know?"

"I used a disguise and an alias and talked my way in. I watched the whole thing from the other side of the bar."

"Sick," he said. There was a flare of interest and excitement. It died just as fast.

Learning someone is trying to take your life's work isn't easy news. I've seen men in his position rant and fury, I've seen them break down. One guy pulled a gun. But he was a Russian oligarch turned private army chief and something of a dick. That was probably a one-off.

Julian handled it well, especially considering the state I'd found him in.

"That's a serious allegation, Matt." He held up his hands in a placating gesture, one of which was still wrapped around his whiskey tumbler. "It's what I hired you to do, I'm not accusing, and I know I'm the one who suggested it was a board member in the first place. I guess I just hoped that you'd prove it was an outsider threat." The latter, he said seemingly to himself.

"Let me walk you through it," I said, and I built the case.

I started with what he knew, but put the timeline into context. The disclosures and the media leaks. Then the situation with the demo, the back door and Matthews's curious and untimely death, my conversation with Detective Ortega. "Now, this next part, we need to be careful of. This is coming from a confidential source, and there can be repercussions for them, which should become clear when I tell you what they said. So I'm not going to reveal their identity."

"I understand," he said.

"This person was...involved...with a man named Kyle Haney. Haney was an engineering director with Crowder's company NexraTech. He was going to speak with some government officials about ethical concerns he had with how Crowder ran that company, what they were doing with the tech. He died in a car accident before he could testify."

I watched that news break on Julian's face like the dawn when you know a storm is coming. He only said, "Continue."

"That person felt compelled to tell me about the similarities between Haney and Matthews. It isn't proof, and it's nothing I can take to the police—"

"Why not?"

"Like I said, it's not proof. Second, it would be nearly impossible *to* prove without having Crowder under oath. Crowder wouldn't have done this himself. I'll get to that." I paused to take a drink and let Julian process what I'd told him so far. "So, back to the meeting at Crowder's club. Apparently, this was supposed to have been some kind of summit in a private dining room, but they didn't make it that far. The meeting imploded during the cocktail hour, the group getting into an argument loud enough the manager had to step in. Amara was there as well. I found this strange because she was the one who first told me about the financial disclosures."

"Do you know why she was there?"

"I have a thought. I'll get to it. She walked in late. I've seen things like that staged for effect, and that's what it looked like to me. Judging by the looks around the table, the others weren't expecting it. Then Crowder got a phone call and he left. I followed him. He met with a private security operative. I'm not sure the connection yet, whether that person is an indie like me, or whether Crowder actually has his own corporate black ops team."

"That sounds like him," Julian muttered. I nodded my agreement.

"They met in a nature preserve. I recorded their conversation." I got my phone out, accessed the secure drop box, and played the file, setting the phone down on an end table between us. Julian's expression went from bewilderment to naked anger as the sound played back. When it was over, I said, "We can't use this in court. Or even in a board meeting. I debated sharing it with you."

"Why?"

"This kind of surveillance is illegal in California without a warrant, and Crowder has the kind of lawyers that could make it a big problem for me. I decided that I wanted you to hear it, because he admits they tried to scare me off and that he's trying to oust you from the company. We also have Crowder directing him to 'amp it up.'"

"But we don't know what it is."

"That's correct. I suspect he's being intentionally vague so there's no way to trace anything back to him. Then, an hour or so after the meeting at Crowder's club, Amara gets this 'anonymous' email in your whistleblower system."

"That can't be faked, though," he said, shaking his head. "We have a public/private passkey system. It's not hackable."

"Julian, the former head of the National Security Agency is potentially conspiring against you. *Everything* is hackable."

Julian leaned forward in his chair, resting his elbows on his knees and cradling his tumbler between both hands. I wasn't sure if he was going to launch, puke his guts up, or just sit there and stew. Maybe all three. Either way, he practically vibrated with a nervous, frenetic energy, which renewed my concerns that he'd taken something earlier. Reading his expression, his body language, I could surmise that this was the first time Julian truly considered the implications of having Alexander Graves so close to his business. "Listen, I want to believe Graves wouldn't do that. It'd be an incredible violation of the law, and I'm not sure someone in his position is going to do that. However, I've also seen men like him justify some pretty terrible things in what they define as the greater good. I need you to be aware it's plausible, if not possible."

Julian nodded, eyes still downcast and his position unchanged. "I understand. What do we do now?"

"I think the best way to defeat Crowder, the cleanest way, is to get him off the board. That keeps us out of court."

"I agree. But how do we accomplish *that*?" he asked with the kind of skepticism one might give a magician suggesting they could disappear the Statue of Liberty.

"Hawthorne is against him, and I think Verala is too. If Graham sides with you, that should be enough." I didn't know that to be true. The math between Wexler, Singh, and Julian wasn't totally clear to me, but Julian didn't object to my logic.

"I can't believe Amara would do this."

"For what it's worth, Julian, my read on her is that she takes her role as an ethicist seriously. Put yourself in her position and look at the information that has come out since this started."

"But none of it is *true*," he protested.

Well, it *was*, or rather a flavor of it. That's not what the client needed to hear right now. "That's the point, though. It's to give any normal person reasonable doubt in your ability to run this company. Think about any scandal you've seen in the last decade. Man, it's never one thing. Once that first allegation is out, more just leaks out of the woodwork. People come forward. That's how this had been engineered. Nathaniel Crowder couldn't do this on his own, he's got someone working behind the scenes, probably someone like me that knows how to manipulate opinion. I don't blame Amara for believing it. The question is whether we can get her back onside."

And whether Graham was in on it.

We'd ground out a hard hour past midnight, and we both needed sleep. I set my drink down on the table and pushed myself to my feet. "This is going to be a hard question, and one I want you to give some thought to. Can you trust Graham?" I left the thought on its own merits, not needing to spell out for him that *someone* with talent hacked the NOVA demo.

Diana's words from earlier in the evening came back to me then. Maybe that was the first time someone put all of this into the proper context for me. There was a dynamic between Julian and Graham that I hadn't appreciated.

Julian was still considering my question. "I'll think on it," Julian assured me. I nodded, told him to get some rest, and I left.

I woke early and got in some cold reps in the hotel pool.

Over a room service breakfast, I reviewed the data runs I'd scheduled in EchoTrace to see if any new patterns emerged. So far, nothing else on the shell corporation.

My phone rang midmorning, a number I didn't recognize. The caller ID read "US Government."

That's usually good news.

I answered.

"Mr. Gage, my name is Mark Blackwell, I'm with the Bureau of Industry and Security. I was hoping I could get a few minutes of your time."

"I'm afraid I'm working and am going to be tied up for some time. Perhaps we could schedule something in a few weeks."

"Mr. Gage, I'm going to have to insist on now."

18

I wasn't immediately familiar with the Bureau of Industry and Security and had to look it up after the call. The bureau was part of the Department of Commerce, primarily focused on export controls, treaty compliance, and protecting the US defense industrial base. Blackwell explained the bureau's LA field office was right here in Irvine and that it would be a good idea for us to speak immediately. He gave me the address, and I agreed.

While I was looking up the bureau, I tried to figure out what they did at this LA office and found it was staffed with special agents charged with export enforcement. They were credentialed federal law enforcement officers. So, I had that going for me.

I reasoned that I could get cleaned up for a trade cop, so I threw on the blazer I'd worn last night over an oxford and jeans and drove to the address he gave me. As it turned out, the office was only about ten blocks from my new hotel. I orbited the block several times until I found a spot to park. Call it a best practice, but I tend not to use government garages when my truck has a pistol, a shotgun, a disguise kit, and multiple pieces of surveillance technology.

It was a bright November morning and warm. The BIS office didn't appear to be in a government building after all but an upscale office park. The building itself, rather two of them, were cylindrical in shape and styled to look like one building separated in the middle, with a courtyard in between. The location made sense. Orange County was to defense what Silicon Valley was to tech at large. Industry types can be wary of taking meetings in government buildings the farther away you are from DC. The two buildings faced each other with a courtyard beneath a canopy of palms.

A man rose from a bench in the courtyard and moved to intercept me.

"Mr. Gage?" he said, extending a hand when he was about three steps out.

"That's right," I said.

"Good guess, then. Mark Blackwell," he replied with a manufactured smile. I shook the offered hand. He was average height, and I put him in his late forties or early fifties. Brown hair, fit but not obsessive about it. He wore a charcoal suit with a subtle stripe, white shirt, and a black tie. Blackwell wore sunglasses of a conservative, classic style. They looked like Clubmasters. "It's a nice morning, and I thought we could do this outside."

"Sure. What exactly *is* this?" I asked.

Blackwell indicated to a spot in the courtyard some distance away. I took his lead and followed. "The Bureau of Industry and Security has the responsibility for protecting our country's defense industrial base. We ensure sensitive technologies don't fall into the wrong hands. In the past, that was things like weapons systems, but in this day and age, I'm sure you can appreciate our mandate has expanded quite a bit. You'd be shocked if I told you the things that could be weaponized nowadays."

Not really, but I let him have the point.

"Cyber technologies have been in our portfolio for some time, but now we're forced to contend with artificial intelligence. These latter technologies introduce some interesting complications in export controls. Which brings us," he said, "to NOVA AI." He stopped and turned to face me.

"What makes you think I know anything about that?"

I hate speaking to people wearing shades because the eyes are among the body's best tells. However, the way Blackwell cocked his head and the dry smile that cracked his thin lips brooked no question about what he meant. He explained it to me in a weary voice, as though repeating it to a dull child.

"It was in the *LA Times*," he deadpanned.

And they say nobody reads the paper anymore.

I shrugged nonchalantly.

"Wait. Why are you even talking to me? If you have a concern with my client, you should be speaking to him, or his legal team. What you're asking is completely outside the scope of what he hired me to do."

"Mr. Gage, I think you're in a position to help your client before he makes a serious mistake. Our office has made some effort to reach out and clear this up. Mr. Kessler has ignored us. This is quite a serious matter, I assure you."

"And I assure you that the tree you need to be barking up is that way." I motioned vaguely southwest.

"We have some intelligence," Blackwell looked back the way we'd come, a gesture I took to be purely for effect, "that suggests a foreign power is attempting to acquire the NOVA platform."

Something hit me then. Evelyn Hawthorne had been an Undersecretary for Commerce. I needed to dig into this, but BIS may have been part of the department that she ran. Even if it wasn't, she'd have maintained ties with the lingering bureaucracy that didn't turn over with presidential administrations. If this whole exercise was just another board member flexing to further their agenda, I was going to start pushing back.

"While I am not at liberty to discuss my client's interests, I can assure you Mr. Kessler has no intention of selling the NOVA platform to a foreign government. Again, though, my capacity is in working for Julian Kessler, and I am not involved with the technology in any way. I think you're wasting your time talking to me."

"The NOVA platform is an unprecedented expansion in AI capability, and one that would level the playing field, if not outright tip the scales in favor of any nation that might acquire it. AI requires a massive amount of energy and processing power to work at scale. There are states in Asia and in the Gulf that are very interested in this technology, ones that would build whole data centers just to support something like NOVA. The Saudis, the Emirates, they've got some deep pockets. Their security services are also not shy about operating here."

Buddy, you have no idea.

"Mr. Blackwell, I appreciate your concern, but again, Julian isn't trying to sell his technology. And he sure isn't going to hand it to the Saudis because they can write a check. Every tech giant in this country and most of the investment firms are practically shooting money out of cannons for this." Before this torpedo campaign, that is. Blackwell was obviously ignoring the part where I told him talking to me was a waste of time, and that just made it seem more to me that this was Hawthorne's doing. The question was, is her strategy to manipulate me into acting out her aims or to scare me off?

"We already know that Nathaniel Crowder intends to acquire NOVA AI. Because of his own foreign military sales and technologies on the control list, he had to file paperwork with the department to express his intent."

"And that's what started all this?"

"No. As I said, we had some intelligence that suggested foreign influence may already have permeated Mr. Kessler's inner circle, if not himself."

Crowder filing an intent to acquire NOVA AI was something. For one, it meant his plans were more advanced than I'd assumed. I wondered if we could use that somehow. If there was a paper trail, did that give us something more actionable than just ejecting him from the board of directors?

"You'll have to forgive me, Mr. Blackwell. As a private detective, I'm not as up on my foreign influence of commerce as perhaps I should be. Don't other countries invest in US tech all the time?"

"It must be disclosed and controlled, Mr. Gage. That's the point. I reached out to you because, according to what I read in the paper, he hired you as a security consultant. If it's true that a foreign government might be trying to financially incentivize or direct development of this technology, that's something we have a duty to be concerned about. It also gives you an avenue to approach your client about."

"Again, that's not what I'm here to do, and you even asking me about it seems inappropriate."

"Perhaps there is a board member or another company officer you might be able to approach," Blackwell said.

"What good would that do? Also, that's not the sort of thing you'd need me to facilitate for you. I'd imagine your credentials could get you in to see any of them. Especially Crowder."

Blackwell sighed, as though my obtuseness was embarrassing the both of us. "For example, what if you were to speak to Mr. Wexler about the matter. He would certainly know if Kessler was taking investments."

"Stop." I held up both hands. "Blackwell, I gave you my time in coming out here. You have wasted that time with a bunch of unfounded accusations and vague hints. You keep using the word 'intelligence,' though I don't think it means what you think it does."

Blackwell's face soured. "Do you know the name Sheikh Omar Al-Fahim?"

"No," I said, though that was a lie. I knew exactly who he was.

Al-Fahim was a minor noble in one of the UAE's seven ruling families, and had achieved some prominence in their intelligence service. He was a businessman now. Though, I suppose Al-Fahim was a "businessman" the same way that Jeff Bezos ran a bookstore. Al-Fahim was now one of the richest men in the region, but maintained his ties to government and the security service.

While the UAE was technically an ally, what most people failed to recognize about the Near East—forgive the Agency parlance—was how transactional those relationships were. American officials tended to think all alliances played out like they did in Europe, meaning they were long-term relationships you could count on. In my experience, that was rarely, if ever, the case. The Gulf states in particular had an ends-justifying calculus that would make Niccolo Machiavelli wonder if they took it too far.

"It's unfortunate that you don't, Mr. Gage, and doesn't speak highly of your acumen. If you were truly looking out for your client's interests, that's a name you should have come across by now."

In truth, I could take this guy to school about Al-Fahim. I knew him personally, if distantly. Our paths had crossed at least once. This was an area that I actually had an advantage. When Nate McKellar retired from the Agency, he was running an IC-funded venture capital business that invested in technologies of interest to CIA. He also used that to run counterintelligence operations against foreign security services trying to penetrate American tech companies. If the Sheik was playing in our sandbox, Nate would know or would know who would. Even though he was recently out, those connections were still fresh.

"We understand that Dr. Verala has significant contacts in the European

Union, but also with the United Nations. Her intent to, how shall I say, 'internationalize' NOVA AI is quite clear. It is possible that Al-Fahim worked through her. Something to consider." Blackwell looked at his watch, an Oris. Clearly they paid him enough to live in LA. "I asked about Wexler because they're partners. If you don't think this topic is safe to talk to Kessler about, perhaps you trust Wexler enough for that. If not him, do you know anyone on the board of directors well enough, someone that Kessler might see as a confidant or an adviser?"

"To what end?"

"We don't want to see NOVA shut down, Gage. I don't want that. If it works, it advances the state of the art by a decade and gives our nation vital tech. I don't want to see this company get broken up, or parceled out in a fire sale. We are, I assure you, trying to help your client from making a serious mistake."

"In all honesty, I don't know anything about this. Again, it's way outside the scope of what Julian hired me for. But I'll think on what you said."

"I hope you do," Blackwell said. He reached into his jacket and handed me a business card. I looked it over, noting the raised Bureau of Industry and Security seal on the right side. Good weight, expensive. It went with the suit and the watch. Blackwell wanted to be taken seriously by high-profile industry types and was trying to look the part. I flipped the card over and noted a QR code on the back. Seeing my curiosity, he said, "It links to an anonymous tip line." His tone was frigid. "If we find that your client is selling sensitive information to foreign governments, or setting up a potential acquisition outside technology transfer protocols, he could be facing serious federal penalties. And if we find that you, in any way, attempted to obfuscate that, so could you. Good day, Mr. Gage."

I reasoned that if we were getting to the point on this case where a federal law enforcement officer should threaten me with jail time, at least that was on schedule.

So, when a local cop called to threaten me with something, it didn't have the gravity that it probably should've.

It was Detective Ortega.

Sometimes, knowing a punch is coming doesn't make it any easier to dodge.

19

"This is Gage," I said, picking up the call. I started power walking back to the Defender.

"Gage, this is Erik Ortega with the Orange County Sheriff's Department."

"How can I help you, detective?"

"Where are you right now?"

"I'm in Irvine. About fifteen minutes from you."

"Then I'll expect you by noon. Headquarters. You already know where that is."

"Great. What's this about—"

But he'd already hung up.

This was not what I needed right now, another fire to put out, another thing to take my focus away from this case. I also needed time to process that bizarre conversation I'd just had with Mark Blackwell. There was a lot to unpack, and it introduced several complications—running down Al-Fahim and whether Diana had been involved in that. Had to admit, there was a dark logic to it. The Wexler angle was also something, because it made me wonder if he wasn't really on Julian's side?

Or if this whole thing was to cover up the fact one of them got caught taking foreign money.

While I drove, I called Nate, shared what I'd just heard about Al-Fahim, and asked if I could draw on the favor bank. Nate laughed and said he wondered why it took me so long this time.

At least he wasn't hiding me from a Russian hit squad like the last one.

Ortega and I talked in an interview room. I liked that experience less.

He wasn't waiting for me outside; rather, I walked in and talked to a desk sergeant behind glass. He paged Ortega, and after a pat down, he escorted me back to the interview room. There was no casual conversation along the way.

The room was cramped, with a single table, four chairs, and gray walls. Antiseptic light shone down from buzzing halogens overhead.

Ortega set his phone on the table, opened a transcription app, and set it to record. He identified himself, the date and time, and why we were there.

"I need you to describe your movements yesterday," Ortega said.

"And I need to know why."

"You are *not* in an asking questions kind of position, Gage."

"I am if you want to have this conversation with just me, or do you want me to involve a team of lawyers?"

"That's not what you want to do here," Ortega said.

"Man, spare me that tired-ass line about only guilty people call for lawyers. We both know I didn't kill Grant Matthews. If I need to bring a shark into this to clear this shit up so that I can get back to figuring out who is trying to steal my client's business, that is money well spent."

"You done?"

Let's face it, I probably wasn't.

Ortega repeated, "What were your movements yesterday?"

Now that's where things get complicated. First, I was infiltrating Nathaniel Crowder's private club under false pretenses. And admitting to a cop that I was a master of disguise while he was investigating a potential murder seemed like what Agency brass called a "career-limiting move." Then there was the probably illegal surveillance of the same. After which, I had drinks with Diana Verala, who had still not been cleared as a suspect in the—whatever the hell was going on with my client's business. I don't know why that was sensitive, it just was. I didn't want Julian finding out about it, I guess because of the appearance, even though I was just trying to get information.

I wanted to start with the phone call from Crowder's chief of security, Vanessa Holt.

Seemed like telling Ortega that another person in Crowder's orbit died the same way after crossing him would be information he could use. Of course, I couldn't tell him how I knew that Crowder also had his own private security team, because if this got to court, I'd be forced to testify how I knew that. There wasn't a way I could hide the fact of how I got it. Yes, it's probably only a misdemeanor, the point is that his legal team would use the fact that I'd broken the law to get information and it would undermine our entire case.

"I'm waiting, Gage," Ortega said.

"Turn that off first."

Ortega's already prominent frown found a way to deepen and, for a moment, I wondered whether I was getting arrested on the spot.

"That ain't how this works."

"I'll talk, but it's got to be off the record. If not, I'll lawyer up and you can see how much a filtered conversation is worth to you."

I'd pushed my luck about as far as it would go, and if I'm being honest, about an inch beyond. When I'd spoken to Ortega before, he'd been convinced that I wasn't involved in Matthews's death. Something changed, or I wouldn't be here now.

Crowder's instructions to his operative came back in a haunting echo: … *Kessler has Gage. He will be a problem. We need to amp it up on him. You know what you have to do.*

Want to bet that was why I was here?

Again, not that I could use it.

Ortega and I continued staring each other down, seeing who'd break.

He stabbed his phone with a finger that could drive a nail, and I was half shocked he didn't crack the screen. "If you're wasting my time, I swear to Christ I'll Mirandize you right now."

The challenge "for what" bounced off the back of my teeth before it got into the air. Thank the patron saint of private detectives for throwing me a solid.

"Fine. We trade. I give you info on Matthews, and you tell me why I'm here."

Ortega grunted a breath and leaned back in his chair, folding his arms across his chest, just to let me know how irritated he was. The sand was running out of that hourglass like it was on fire.

"What do you know about Kyle Haney?" I said.

"Nothing."

"He worked for a firm called NexraTech. Nathaniel Crowder purchased the company and pushed them in a direction Haney thought was questionable. Haney quit and tried to go to some state officials to drop the dime on Crowder. Only, he never got the chance to. Day before the appointment, he's speeding down Newport Coast Drive and crashes into a tour bus on PCH."

Ortega's shoulders lifted in an annoyed, *So what?*

"Sheriff's department handled the call. The investigating officer had at least one eye wit who said Haney was chased. His intuition was that the accident was forced. He couldn't prove it, so it got written up as reckless driving."

"How do you know all this?"

"The deputy called Haney's girlfriend and asked if anyone had been threatening him, or if he had problems with anyone. I don't know the deputy's name, but you should be able to look up the crash investigation. The girlfriend is in a position to know about both Haney and Matthews. Once she heard that Matthews died in a car crash, she called me."

I've been called full of shit too many times to count in my life, but there is nothing quite like a cop's face when they aren't buying it. "And you think Nathaniel Crowder drove this guy off the road? That's your big theory?"

"Of course not. He's not getting his hands dirty. But I've got reason to believe he's got his own private security company."

"This is some bullshit," he said, reaching for his phone. I went for mine, opened the folder where I kept my case files, and showed him the Lexus's license plate.

"Run that plate," I told him. "You're going to find it's registered to a shell company. You can roll them up. Go up far enough, you're going to see that Crowder is funding this outfit somehow, and is doing a great job hiding it." The latter part was hypothesis, but the only reasonable one. And I was counting on the fact that Ortega wouldn't spend the hours trying to disprove it.

"How'd you get this?"

"A couple days ago, I spotted two cars tailing me. One was a Lexus SUV, and the other was an Audi sedan. At one point, I'd maneuvered behind the SUV and snapped this pic from my dash cam. I lost them, but they showed up outside my hotel and got a little rough with me. Wanted to scare me off the case. After that, I used EchoTrace to search security camera footage and caught the Lexus."

Everything I'd told Ortega was true, I'd just altered the order a little.

If my telling him that someone jumped me made any kind of difference, he didn't show it.

"Where were you before that?"

"I spent the morning at Julian Kessler's house sweeping it for surveillance equipment. The afternoon I spent at my hotel. I met with one of NOVA AI's board members to interview her. Kessler called me at about ten thirty, asking to meet because someone sent a message in the company's whistleblower system alleging unethical activity. Only, it's all fabricated." I gave Ortega a moment to absorb what I'd just told him, but not enough for a counterattack. "Kessler hired me because he thinks someone is trying to force him out of his company. They've dug up a bunch of information about his past, recolored it enough that it seems sketchy, and sent anonymous messages to the board, the *LA Times*, and some tech papers. Crowder is the one behind it, I'm sure of it."

"You got something more than just speculation?"

This was another sharp reminder of the vast differences between this world and the one I was used to working in. Intelligence is gray, educated guesses, fragments of truth buried in lies. I was used to swimming in charcoal-colored waters, brackish swamps of fact and fiction. Cops looked for certainty.

"When you called me, I'd just finished meeting with someone from the Department of Commerce's industry security bureau. He admitted in that meeting that Crowder filed paperwork to buy NOVA AI. I guess he had to because Crowder's company exports sensitive technology. When I add that to what seemed like private security contractors threatening me off the case, seems hard not to make a connection."

Ortega dropped his arms to the tabletop and let out a long, tired breath. This was way more than he'd signed up for.

"Someone broke into Matthews's apartment last night. Security cameras caught it, but the guy was in and out in about two minutes. Knew what he was looking for, got it, and got out."

"What did they take?"

Ortega shook his head. "Nope. You haven't earned that yet. Who was the girlfriend, the one that tipped you off about this Kyle Haney?"

"Her name is Vanessa Holt. She's chief of security at Crowder Dynamics. You should know, after Haney and Matthews, she's scared shitless about a retaliation. Could be her job, could be something else. She made me promise not to reveal her name to anyone, even you. I'm doing it because I need you to believe me. And I'm really hoping you can help."

Ortega nodded, understanding the position I was in. An informant wanting to preserve their secrecy was probably the one part of this that did make sense to him.

"Here's what I can do. I'm going to pull the investigation report on Haney's death, see what shakes loose. Talk to the patrol officers involved. If that report is anything different than what you told me, or the investigating officer doesn't know this girlfriend, you and me have words and those words end with, 'Do you understand your rights as I have explained them to you?' We clear?"

"Yes," I said.

"Lemme see that plate number again."

This was a gamble.

If Vanessa Holt was lying to me, or even pulling on the truth just a little, Ortega would know. Hell, even if the officer that investigated Haney's death half-assed his notes and didn't bother including the conversation with Holt because it didn't go anywhere, it could tank my story's credibility.

That blowback would be immediate and bad.

I had several missed calls, but no voicemails, so I ignored them. The phone rang again before I got to the Defender. I answered.

"Mr. Gage, this is Evelyn Hawthorne, and we need to speak immediately."

Because, of course we do.

"Ms. Hawthorne, this isn't the best time. Give me a good time to call you back."

"It must be now."

I sighed and made sure she heard it.

"Okay, shoot."

"Not over the phone."

"Yes, over the phone. If you need to speak to me that badly, that's how it's done."

A curt, cynical laugh. "You misunderstand the dynamic here, Mr. Gage. I have time in an hour. You can meet me at my foundation. Pacific and Main, in Santa Monica."

Now it was my turn to laugh.

"I'm at the ass end of Orange County. You're at least an hour away, and that's if there's a loving God. You've given me zero reason to fight my way up to you and, it's worth mentioning, you aren't paying for my time. It's also worth mentioning the last time we agreed to meet, you didn't show and it felt awfully intentional."

Hawthorne simmered in that for a few silent seconds. These people were all used to jerking the chain and having all manner of underlings snap to. They were all equally guilty, but Hawthorne and Graves, by virtue of their positions in government, had the least experience with people telling them no.

"Your job is to prevent someone from taking NOVA AI out from under Julian, is it not?"

If I weren't on a crowded street, I'd probably vent my frustration at the sky in the loudest bellow I could muster. People like her asked rhetorical questions as a matter of conversational course when we both knew the answer to them. I didn't give her the satisfaction of a response and wished I could've watched her annoyance deepen when I didn't.

"Very well, then. I know who is behind it, and if you'd like to save your client's job, if not his company, I suggest you find a way to make it here for us to discuss it. If you don't, I shall assume you aren't interested, and I will act accordingly." She paused a beat for effect, giving me a dose of my own. "And in concert with my own interests."

Hawthorne hung up.

I climbed into the Defender and prepared to do battle.

20

It took me ninety minutes, and for my sins, Hawthorne made me wait another forty-five.

I called Kessler twice on the way and didn't get him.

I also called Benjamin Blake. That, too, went straight to voicemail, but he texted immediately and said he'd call as soon as he was able.

Hawthorne's foundation, Catalyst for Humanity, was a think tank that existed to bridge the public-private technology divide. According to their website, C4H worked with governments, grassroots organizations, tech companies, and academic institutions to align "advanced technological resources and harness the transformative power of AI." I'm giving the direct quote here because I couldn't bring myself to say it. They claimed to have created innovation hubs in traditionally underserved communities and regions, what they called "tech deserts." Hawthorne managed this in conjunction with a socially focused venture fund called the Horizon Impact Fund.

I had time to look this up because she kept me waiting for so long.

C4H had the fifth floor in a building just blocks from the beach. Naturally, Hawthorne's office faced the water. The waiting area was white, brightly lit with tan furniture. Digital displays highlighted the foundation's good works. I could almost see my house from the window, and I did make out Cosmic Ray's.

Wouldn't shock me if that was my next stop.

Something told me after this conversation, I was going to need a drink.

Eventually, a polished young woman appeared and told me that Ms. Hawthorne would see me now. She clutched a tablet like it was a talisman to ward off anything that would jack up Ms. Hawthorne's schedule

She guided me into the office, which had an expansive and nearly flawless view of the ocean. Hawthorne was at her desk, typing behind a large screen, and did not acknowledge my presence. The pair of them discussed something in low tones for at least three minutes before the acolyte dutifully made annotations on her tablet and then said, "Mr. Gage is here."

It was nearly three thirty.

"The schedule is rearranged, I see," Hawthorne said in a hushed yet piqued intonation that was entirely for my consumption. "We'll make do, I suppose."

The acolyte disappeared, and the door closed.

"Mr. Gage, would you have a seat?"

I took the chair in front of her desk and waited a few more moments before Hawthorne finished on her screen. She hit a key with a decisive, final stroke and turned to face me. "Thank you for coming."

We both knew she kept me waiting because she could. I decided not to point it out, but any grace I'd offer was in a chalk outline in the lobby alongside my patience.

"So, you're interested in keeping Julian at NOVA AI," I said, not stating it as a question.

"For the record, I never wanted him out. It was a matter of whether he was viable to remain. And, I might add, if the things we were hearing about him proved untrue." Her eyebrow lifted. "Is it true you are a disgraced ex-spy?"

"It's true that I was a spy," I said. We already covered this when the news broke.

"Indeed."

"I've engineered disinformation campaigns before, so I know what they look like. I'm convinced someone wants to undermine Julian's position and get the board to vote him out. Each of you seems to have a vested interest in Julian's ouster."

Hawthorne scoffed at that. *Hope you don't wring your neck clutching those pearls.*

Hawthorne's expression softened. "How is Julian holding up?"

"He's tired, understandably jumpy," I said. He was shaken, exhausted, jumping at shadows, and probably abusing stimulants. "I took a GPS tracker off his car. So, not only is someone coming after him, they were also following him. Our antagonist has help."

I didn't discount the possibility that any of these people were teamed up with each other. Hawthorne and Crowder openly going at it every chance they got while maintaining an alliance behind the scenes would be effective cover. If she was in on it, I wasn't telling her anything she didn't already know. If she wasn't, then revealing this might get me an ally.

Or it would just convince her to go to the authorities.

"What do you make of the engineer?"

"You mean Grant Matthews?" She nodded. "The police aren't sure if he was murdered," I said, and watched for a reaction. Admittedly, Hawthorne was hard to read. She was a seasoned Washington operator and didn't give anything away for free. I added, "I haven't finalized my own opinion, but I think it's curious that Matthews died within twelve hours of me revealing his name."

"And you're completely convinced it's one of us?"

"I'm not going to share confidential information, or conclusions, with anyone but my client. I've already told you each of you has a motive. No one has cleared themselves in my eyes. If one of you would work with me, it'd go a long way to convincing me you aren't in on it."

The eyebrow lifted again, and the faintest hint of a smile crept onto her lips. Just as quickly, it was gone. "I suspect one of us *is* working with you," she said, toying with the words.

"And you've got something to back that up?"

"Crowder showed us all photos of you and Dr. Verala leaving a speakeasy. Looked rather cozy. Claims that they were sent to him anonymously, though none of us bought it."

Well, at least now I knew who was having me followed.

"You don't always get to pick and choose where you meet sources. Sometimes it's a cocktail bar, sometimes it's a ninety-minute slog across the Southland."

"Commendable. Well, as it happens, we agree that someone is trying to take NOVA from Julian, and I am reasonably sure I know who that is." Hawthorne pushed back from her chair and stood. She wore a black sleeveless blouse over a cream-colored skirt. The matching jacket was on the back of her chair. Hawthorne was tall, and in her mid-fifties. She was naturally tan, but the darkness and tone on her arms suggested golf or tennis. Hawthorne's eyes were dark and intense. She paced over to a section of the window—which ran floor to ceiling—and looked out. "Last night, Nathaniel had us to his club for a summit." She said this with unmasked derision. "He tried to call for a vote to oust Julian."

"Who was there?"

"The externals. Myself, Verala, and Graves."

Interestingly, she didn't mention Singh.

"Wouldn't Crowder need either Singh or Wexler to force Julian out?"

"He would. Claims to have Amara Singh in tow, though I doubt that. He wants to buy NOVA outright, offered us all a deal on the spot."

"Let me guess, did this include offering Graves the CEO role?"

Hawthorne smiled. It made me uncomfortable. "You've done your homework. But no. He offered Graves a carve-out—and I found this out later and only because Graves is a braggart. It's a nothing role that Graves would think is important. My guess, Crowder will fund it for six months until the ink is dry on the acquisition and then shutter the thing, putting Graves on the street."

"What did he offer you, if I might ask?"

"We're running a pilot now, placing generative AI systems in impoverished communities. We're using it to teach young people to code, we're also using it as expert systems to help places that don't have sufficient health care to service more patients. Help educate them on living healthier lifestyles so they need to seek care less. Crowder promised to deploy NOVA AI to that effort."

"That's exactly what you've been trying to convince Julian to do," I said.

"As I said, you're well informed. Crowder offered me exactly what I want, which is how I knew he was lying."

I stood as well. I've got this weird thing about talking to standing people when I'm sitting down. Reminds me too much of being interrogated.

"What happened after Crowder made the offer? And did he say something to each of you individually or just go around the table like it was Christmas?"

"He called me this morning to smooth things out. The meeting got a little heated. I have to admit to baiting him into an argument, for little other reason than I despise the man and wanted to press his buttons. He threw a temper tantrum and left. Pretended that he got a phone call."

I'd seen Crowder outside waiting for his car, and it was like nothing had ever happened. I thought at the time he was faking, though I couldn't figure out why he'd pretend to blow a gasket if he was trying to convince people to join his little coup d'etat. Apart from omitting Amara Singh's presence at the Last Supper, everything Hawthorne said appeared true. She also hadn't told me anything I didn't already know, though from her perspective she wouldn't know that.

"So Crowder leaves you at his club and storms off. What happened then?"

"Well, the party broke up, I suppose. The manager, or whoever, came over and said the drinks would be on Nathaniel's tab. He was a bit embarrassed, but it was clear he wanted us to leave, so we did."

"All of you?"

"Yes, why?"

"Just curious." Because Diana told me they'd had a four-figure dinner at Crowder's expense, an FU for leaving them hanging.

"Ms. Hawthorne, you didn't call me all the way up here to tell me about a spoiled dinner. Now, I already suspected Crowder was the one trying to oust Julian. I appreciate that you want to head that off, but what was it that you wanted to tell me? Crowder saying he wants to buy NOVA outright doesn't necessarily square with him running a disinformation campaign to undermine my client."

"Are you convinced that Crowder was the one digging up all the dirt on Julian? Can you prove it?"

"I never said that I thought he was. You were the one bringing that up," I said.

"It'd go a long way to convincing the others that he needs to be voted off the board. He's got enough of a stake in this company that hearsay won't do it."

She was fishing for a deal. These people traded in secrets. Power was a game to them, and outmaneuvering their rivals was more addictive than any drug. Hawthorne wanted something she could bank to use against Crowder when it would hurt him most. She was more interested in outmaneuvering a rival than she was saving my client.

At some point, this case turned into solving a murder before the shot was fired.

"Ms. Hawthorne, Julian Kessler is my client. Unless and until he tells me that I can release information to you, whatever I may or may not have discovered on this case stays between him and me."

"Matt, there is some damaging information on your client out there. Allegations that he's used the system for unethical research and data collection. Allegations that he stole the IP from someone. Now there's a whistleblower complaint that he is using the system to hack employees' personal accounts to prove they aren't leaking proprietary information. One of his former employees died suspiciously after you learned he'd taken a bribe." Hawthorne folded her arms across her chest and leaned against the window.

"How do you know about the whistleblower complaint?" I asked. This was a new revelation. And one that I did not appreciate hearing first from Hawthorne.

"Amara Singh shared it with the board. It's protocol to show that they take those situations seriously," she said archly. "Now, I'm hearing questions about where NOVA's initial investments came from, and that concerns me."

"Have you been talking to some of your old pals at Commerce?"

"I would be foolish not to. No one on the board except Nathaniel Crowder wants NOVA AI to end up in Crowder Dynamics. Crowder is dangerous and not just because he has no moral compass. If you expect me to side with Julian Kessler and keep him in play, you need to convince me that he's worthy of it. Because there are two options on the table here, Matt. One of them is voting Crowder out. The other is doing the same to Julian and choosing a new leader. As the saying goes, both things can be true."

"Why would you go to the effort of ejecting Crowder and then doing the same thing to Julian?"

"NOVA is a moon shot, but if it plays out, it could be one of the most impactful technologies ever developed. Today, it can predict what a user might do because of a dialogue-based interface. That's the first stage. You've seen the neural interface. That will change humanity's relationship with technology in ways we don't appreciate yet. Would we, as a society, entrust that to someone who wasn't absolutely worthy?" Hawthorne leveled a smoldering gaze on me. Had to admit, her eyes had that "abyss staring back at you" quality that I rarely found outside third-world interrogators. "Said another way, we eliminate Nathaniel Crowder as a threat now. I have the votes. Cooperating would be the best way to show us that Julian is sincere about his responsibilities."

21

This case had squeezed and twisted itself into some unexpected shapes. When I started in this racket, a friend of mine in the FBI cautioned me not to view everything through the lens of being an ex-spook. This case had gone far afield of what Julian Kessler hired me to do. I told myself that I didn't have the ability to prove Nathaniel Crowder was trying to oust Julian in court, and that was probably true. What I had on him was inadmissible surveillance.

Well, perhaps that wasn't all.

I did have a Commerce agent tell me that Crowder filed paperwork to buy NOVA AI. Then, almost immediately after, Evelyn Hawthorne summons me for a meeting. Speaking of covert influence operations. An inelegant one, perhaps, but I knew one when I saw it.

So, camped out at my usual table at Cosmic Ray's beneath the Christmas lights and the tribal masks and the surfboards, I typed my findings in an interim report for my client. I omitted sources and methods, particularly the ones that might land me in questionable legal waters. However, I did include that Crowder employed security personnel seemingly outside the corporate hierarchy of his family of companies and that those operatives had, at least once, attempted to scare me off this case with force. I noted Grant Matthews, the former NOVA engineer who activated a back door in the code for someone to hack during Julian's live demo. And I noted that I had been the target of a technical surveillance operation using drones. Taken together with the events that precipitated Julian hiring me, this was a clear and concerted effort to first damage my client's reputation by uncovering and then manipulating information about past associations and businesses. Then, illegally accessing both his technology and his corporate assets to further that goal.

Julian should have everything he needed to force a decision and get Crowder out of his company. I'd also gotten two members of his board to go along with it. Amara Singh and Graham Wexler were still variables to me, though I wondered what Singh would do when presented with this information. She seemed smart enough to recognize manipulation for what it was.

Yet, this didn't seem like everything.

Verala's statements about Graham Wexler.

Hawthorne's offer to remove Crowder and end this.

I hadn't identified who hacked NOVA during Julian's demo, only that Grant Matthews had been paid to make it happen. Maybe that wasn't strictly necessary. If Crowder was employing a dirty-tricks squad that rolled up to a shell corporation, it wasn't a big logical leap to suggest they had a hacker on staff. Especially if they were the ones who helped Grant Matthews into the next life.

Taking Hawthorne's deal without answering those other questions felt like leaving Julian at the mercy of the board and giving them a loaded gun.

I called General Graves.

"I'm a little disappointed about your updates, or lack thereof. I was about to have a conversation with the state licensing board about your methods," Graves said.

"Call them, General. I'm sure my contacts at certain watchdog organizations, not to mention my attorney, might be interested to hear how you're using your position to coerce me." I held it a beat. "Sorry, former position. Look, Graves, we can do this like a knife fight, or I can trade. What is it? I'm sick of you threatening me, so if you want to go that route, I'd rather know now so I can send people after you and focus on my real job."

Graves brooded in silence, which seemed like it was as much for effect as it was for him to figure out how to recapture the advantage.

"What do you have for me?"

"Crowder's offer is bullshit. He just wants you to side with him. He was never going to make you the CEO of NOVA. Once he bought it, he was going to carve out a company for you to run for six months and then decide it wasn't paying off. He gets your vote, gets NOVA, and removes you as a potential threat until it's too late for you to do anything about it."

Graves thundered for a lot longer than I'd have thought possible. Eventually, he lost steam. I knew he was running out of gas when he started repeating threats. Against Crowder, against me, against Julian. Graves finally understood that none of the status he enjoyed in Washington translated here, there was no force of will, no charismatic gravity he could exert on anyone to create his own physics. If he hadn't been such an asshole, I'd have felt for him.

I said as genuinely as I could, "I wanted to save you the embarrassment."

"Thank you. I appreciate that."

"Now, here's what I need in return. You're always telling me about your resources. Let's put them to good use. I need to know everything you can dig up about a Bureau of Industry and Security investigation into NOVA. The lead agent's name is Mark Blackwell. Hawthorne may have set it in motion, so don't involve her. Do you know Sheikh Omar Al-Fahim?"

"I've met him," Graves said.

"According to Blackwell, Al-Fahim was an early investor in NOVA. If it's true, it'll be through intermediaries. There isn't anything stopping Julian from taking foreign money, necessarily, but it'd close him out to a government contract if he did and didn't disclose it. It feels off to me."

"I'll see what I can find out," Graves said.

Nate would tell me if the Al-Fahim thing was true, I didn't need Graves for that. Pitting him against Hawthorne could buy me some breathing room, and giving him a nugget of intel would convince him I was playing nice.

If this thing had any more sides, it'd be an Escher painting.

My phone rang then. It was Blake.

"Matt, how goes it?" Blake's voice was boisterous and amiable. He was a consummate wheeler-dealer, and I'd experienced him flashing that klieg light smile at me when he was trying to shine me on. Of course, I'd seen the darker side to that personality, and I knew Blake could be ruthless when the situation called for it. In another life, that ability to switch between the two would've made for one hell of a case officer.

"Thanks for calling me back, Benjamin. I, ah, could use your advice."

"Wasn't expecting to hear that," he said, tone still jovial, but I could sense the wariness at the edges. "You're not looking to invest in your client's business, are you?"

"No, nothing like that."

"I'm glad you called. I wanted to ask you how it was going. Was a little hesitant to do so, not wanting to get involved in your work or anything. But after that demo, frankly I'm a little worried."

"That's a great starting point," I said, wrestling control of the conversation back. I told Blake about Matthews and the money, then his death. I left the peripheral details on the wayside, but I told him about Crowder's instructions to his operative to take care of me. When Blake asked how I found that out, I told him it was best not to ask. He thought that was funny.

"So," I said, "I can't conclude anything but Crowder being behind it. I know you're a little biased there."

"He's a goddamn snake, Matt. I trust your instincts, if not your tradecraft. I wouldn't say this, mind you, if you hadn't brought it up first."

"Right. That's where I could use your opinion. I don't have any experience in this kind of thing. Company politics. People that can hire entire law firms to come after me. Shit like that. The evidence that I've got on Crowder is solid in my world..."

"Just not in this one," Blake said, finishing for me.

"Exactly."

"I guess my question to you is, what do I do with it?"

"Well, Julian hired you to prove someone was trying to trash his reputation, right? And I'd say you've done that. From what you've told me, you've done it in a way that would lead any reasonable person to conclude the intent is to force a sale, taking advantage of your client's uniquely unfortunate position with regard to ownership of his company. What Julian does with that information is up to him. I think you owe it to him to educate him on what he can and can't do with that information, like, don't go threatening a lawsuit with that as the basis. And I think your instinct on not wanting to go toe-to-toe with Crowder is right. As much as I'd love to see you get under his fingernails as only you can, that might not be the best investment in your future."

Funny that Blake reinforced much of the same conclusions I'd arrived at earlier.

Part of me was ready to be rid of this entire lot.

"Thank you for this. I really appreciate it." I paused, a question dangling on my tongue. I didn't want to ask it because I had a sense the answer would either confirm my suspicion, or it'd be the truth Blake thought I needed to hear. I asked it anyway. "When I started this, I'd asked you what you thought of Julian. You told me you wouldn't have given him the money if you didn't trust him."

"That's right."

"You trust him to deliver on your investment," I said, voicing aloud what had been creeping around my subconscious. Therein was the distinction that I hadn't appreciated at the time, and not until I put words to it. "What is your opinion of him as a person?"

"Does it matter?"

"Let's say it does," I said.

"I won't do business with someone that I think is patently amoral. To be clear, I've invested in businesses run by some real assholes. Some of them delivered and some of them didn't. None of them were criminals." Blake paused and then added, "At least not at the time. That's a story for not now. The question you're asking is whether Julian is someone you should be working *for*. I can't answer that for you, Matt. Truly. You're in a different position than me. If my judgment proves wrong, all I lose is money."

There it was.

"Thank you, Benjamin."

"Think nothing of it. Listen, I might be down your way soon. There are some companies I'm prospecting. If it works out, I'd love to buy you dinner."

"I'd like that," I said.

I hung up.

Blake mentioning dinner reminded me I needed to eat some myself. Ray did a serviceable burger, so I ordered one and ate in silence. I paid my tab and went home. Once there, I packaged up my report for Julian, loaded it to our secure portal, and sent him a note that it was ready for his review. My hand was on the bottle of Lagavulin when the phone rang.

It was Graham Wexler.

Now, I'd suspected Crowder had help on the inside and hadn't cleared Wexler yet of not being that person. Of anyone, he also had the cleanest motive for betraying his business partner.

"This is Gage," I said.

"Matt, this is Graham. I just got a ping on our network from a previously registered device. It's Grant Matthews's phone."

"What?"

"Grant Matthews's phone is attempting to log into NOVA's code repository right now."

I was on my feet and out the door to my Defender. It took a second for the phone to complete its handoff to the car's speakers. "Matt, are you still there?"

"Yes, can you tell me where I'm going? I'm up in Santa Monica."

"I only caught it a couple minutes ago."

"That's not what I asked, Graham. Where is the phone?"

"Right," he said, and I heard furious typing in the background. "Sorry, it's taking a second to triangulate the IP."

There's no fast way to get to Orange County from my house at any time of day, but I opted for the 10 to the 405, hoping to loop around LAX. If I was lucky, I could do it in less than an hour.

This town.

"Okay, I've got it. The phone is logging on from Irvine."

"Graham, listen, I'm most likely an hour away. Can you text me updates?"

"Yes, of course."

Time to drive like I stole the car.

Wexler called me back about twenty minutes later.

"I'm getting location pings all over," he said.

"Talk to me like I don't have any idea what you're talking about. And how are you following him? You didn't use NOVA to break into Matthews's cell company, did you?" I wouldn't have felt the need to ask if my day hadn't been going distinctly in that direction.

"No...no, nothing like that. We let employees bring their own devices, so we load a security program that monitors traffic for suspicious activity. We can shut down access remotely if we think the device is compromised, or if it's stolen." Stealing from a dead man seemed especially ghoulish. "Once you told us about Matthews, I was worried something like this might happen...so I flagged his device."

"Catch them in the act, rather than shutting office access preemptively. That was smart, Graham."

"Thank you," he said, sheepish.

"Where is the phone now?"

"Like I said, I was getting location hits all over the place. Costa Mesa, Irvine, Huntington. Now it's in Fountain Valley."

"And as long as the phone is on, you can track its location?"

"As long as it's trying to access our network, I can follow the IP addresses," he said.

If I didn't know better, that would look suspiciously like a surveillance detection route. Or a blanket of false flags to hit as many cell towers as possible in a short period of time to hide their location.

Likely, it was a bit of both.

When Wexler told me where it stopped, I got that ugly feeling of finality. The kind of thing that ranks somewhere up with "I told you so." The phone was at Crowder's off-the-books security shop.

The phone wasn't moving.

"Call Julian and tell him what's happening," I said.

"*I* don't know what's happening, Matt."

"I know who took the phone and probably why. Crowder has a private security firm that he funds through a series of shell corporations. I bet if you dug into his corporate ledger, you'd see a bunch of innocuous line items like 'special projects' and things with generic code names." That's how we did it at the Agency. I said, "Look, I need to go. Just tell Julian to have a lawyer ready."

At least I knew Wexler was on our side.

I took MacArthur over the dead canal and into the industrial park, yellow lights over white buildings and the shadows between them. The facilities in the industrial park were separated by alleys, thin streets abutting narrow parking lots coiled around their structures like snakes. I took the second alley and parked behind a large warehouse with no line of sight to my objective.

I got out, taking the Glock 34 from the hidden space in the door. Holstering the pistol, I hugged the side of the building and made use of the cover. Turning the corner, I had line of sight to the security outfit's entrance. I spotted a single vehicle out front, an SUV of some type, though I couldn't make out what from here. The lines told me it leaned more toward the "sport" end of the spectrum, rather than "utility."

I didn't see anyone. There weren't lights over those parking spaces and nothing on the building's exterior. Maybe they'd already gone inside, I didn't know. But I could wait just behind that SUV and get the drop when he came out. It was pushing ten now, and I doubted this guy was staying overnight.

I crossed from this lot to the next in fast strides and made the building's shadow. Then I worked my way around to the front, staying inside that perimeter darkness. Now I was just a few feet from the garage door where I'd first spotted the Lexus GX pulling in. I was close enough to see the SUV in the parking lot was a Porsche Cayenne. I took a few steps toward it, and a voice cracked the silence.

"Okay, Gage, we're going to do this calm and easy." It was a female voice, with an unmistakable hard edge. And, naturally, was right behind me. My first question was, *Do what?* "Hands," she said.

I recognized the voice, but couldn't place it.

No one tells you to put your hands out if they aren't covering you with a weapon. Or, they want you to think they are. Since she hadn't identified herself as police, I decided to take the chance that she wasn't prepared to shoot me.

I turned.

Vanessa Holt stepped into the yellow field of street light, about fifteen feet from me.

She wasn't openly carrying. Holt had a casual light jacket on, so I assumed that covered a pistol. Ever since she called me, I'd wondered about the correlation between her and Crowder's dirty-tricks squad. As the head of security, I found it hard to believe she didn't know. Which begged the question, what in the hell was she doing here?

"Holt, what in the hell are you doing here?"

It was too dark to read her reaction, though I could make a good guess. Holt had said *we're going to do this calm and easy*, which told me she'd been expecting me.

"No bullshit and none of your games, Gage. You want to hand it over and we can get this done?"

"Hand *what* over? And, seeing you here, I have to assume we're being covered by your buddies inside."

"Are you playing dumb for a recording? Is this some bullshit stunt to play back in court?"

Well, if Vanessa Holt and I had anything in common, it was that we were both equally confused. Playing dumb for a recording?

"I'll make you a deal, Holt. You can give the phone to me or to the police."

"What phone? What the hell are you talking about?"

"Shut up, both of you," a third voice commanded from behind me. "Don't turn around, Gage, I'll shoot if you do." A voice sounds different when there's a gun backing it up. I did as instructed. Then, the unmistakable pressure of a gun pressing into my spine confirmed that I had the biggest game of catch-up to play.

22

The principles of investigation told me that the man with the gun was Crowder's man. I'd only heard him over a mic before, so I couldn't peg the voice.

"Gage, are you armed?"

"No."

"If I frisk you and find one, it's going to go poorly."

"Okay, tough guy. I'm armed. If you want, we can match your rent-a-cop academy skills against mine and see who wins. Holster is on my hip. Make a play," I said.

"You talk too goddamn much."

I get that a lot.

He said, "Left hand behind your head. Remove the pistol with your right hand, first two fingers only." I felt a subtle shift in the pressure of the gun against my back. Then I saw why. His attention shifted to Holt, who was going for her own weapon. "Don't touch it," he added.

"You can't shoot him and me," Holt told him.

Whose side was she on?

And I meant that genuinely.

"I'd rather he didn't try," I said.

"Shut up, Gage," they both said. I think Holt added a word. I'll let you guess which.

Without moving my hands, I said, "I came here because I tracked Grant Matthews's phone to this location. When I saw Holt, I thought she had it." Risking a shot, I turned my head slightly to the side. "But asshole-with-the-gun-in-my-back, it makes a lot more sense that you'd have it. Holt, I take it you don't know what your boss does here."

There was a sharp jolt in my back, and I guess he didn't like me sharing.

Holt's gun was out, but her math was still correct on who'd get shot first. Guess I'd have to save myself. As usual.

I spun on my heel and, in the same motion, struck his wrist with the heel of my right hand, knocking the gun away. He fired on reflex, and it went wide.

Things went off the rails quickly after that.

Holt shouted for us to stop and, seriously, when has that *ever* worked? I grabbed the guy's wrist so he couldn't bring the gun back on me. Then I knuckle-punched him once in the throat to back him off. Sputtering, he staggered backward, and I let him go.

A shot cracked the relative quiet.

Holt cried out and fell to the ground. At first, I thought the shot had been hers, but after she dropped, I turned back to Crowder's man. He stared hate daggers at me. "You brought backup?"

"What? No," I said, but he was already raising his gun again. The guy pivoted, looking for whoever had the drop on him. He must have spotted something in the darkness, because he loosed three downrange.

I still had my pistol because we got distracted arguing with each other before I could disarm myself as instructed. I drew.

There was another shot, and the security man's head snapped back. His body dropped to the ground like it'd been unplugged.

The ruin of his forehead told me I didn't need to check for a pulse.

I dropped to a knee, pistol up. It was the only cover I was going to get.

Simultaneous cries of pain and pleas for help from Holt told me she was still alive.

Eyes went to the dark distance, looking for the shooter. I knew from reconning this place before that there was a parking lot between this building and the one across from it, trees on the far side that backed up to the aqueduct. There was a metal security fence, maybe eight feet tall, with anti-climb spikes. If the shooter was on the other side of that, I'd never get to him.

Time to find out.

There weren't any other shots incoming, so I dashed hard at a ninety-degree angle to the left, aiming for the far side of the parking lot. It was darker there. Then I sprinted for the corner of the parking lot.

Sirens exploded all over, and I saw about a hundred lights, red and blue, spots.

Shit.

The thunderous crash of helicopter rotors drowned out everything else.

There was a car parked in the lot next to the fence. I hit that at full speed, jumped onto the hood and vaulted over the metal fence. I tried to plant a foot onto one of the flat metal spikes, but mistimed it and got the gap between them. It threw off my balance, and I careened into the pine on the far side. I bounced off that and then to the ground, landing hard. A shock wave of pain blasted through my right side.

I rolled over, fought for air, and when I found some, grabbed my gun. Then I started running. The shooter would be going south. The MacArthur Boulevard bridge was in the opposite direction.

It looked like my initial orientation was off. This wasn't the aqueduct; rather, it was a strip of land between the industrial park and the concrete riverbed that was being excavated for something. There were dirt mounds and construction equipment everywhere.

No sign of movement. I poured on some speed to pursue. The right side of my body disagreed with that. If I got to the top of the mound, I'd have enough of a vantage to see where he was going.

I hit the dirt mound, surged up it, and was painted by a spotlight.

"Freeze immediately! Drop your weapon!" the helicopter pilot commanded with his voice-of-God speaker.

There was a power line directly overhead, so he wasn't getting any closer. I needed to catch the shooter, or this was all coming down on me.

Which, I suspected, was the point.

I crested the dirt mound and dropped to the other side.

No one.

I broke out of the spotlight, but was momentarily blinded and couldn't see anything.

Except, maybe, for how much shit I was in.

On the other side of the mound, I found a kicked hornet's nest of pissed-off sheriff's deputies. And they were closing fast. My brain tried to process the competing commands of putting my hands in the air, my face in the dirt, and dropping my gun.

The flying body tackle and mouthful of gravel sorted that out, though.

One thing I've learned about cops is that they do not like it when you run, and that tends to lead to some flexible interpretations of what constitutes "police brutality." For a group of people that spent half the day in the gym, they sure got mad when you made them use it.

The Orange County Sheriff's SWAT team covered that industrial park like flies in August, though I only saw that as they were frog-marching me back from the construction site. The rest of the time I spent facedown on asphalt. Eventually, someone yanked me to a seated position, and some deputies in tac gear swarmed me, yelling questions and suggesting the horrible things that were going to happen to me in jail.

Whatever.

EMTs rolled in not long after the sheriff's department secured the scene. They put a sheet over Crowder's security guy, affirming what I'd already seen. Holt was alive. I heard the cops say the bullet was a through-and-through, clean exit from the shoulder. She'd be fine, but was on the way to the hospital now.

The officer-in-charge pushed his people aside and laid into me. He was also in tactical gear, and lobbing accusations. To listen to him, I was half convinced I needed to change my first name to Lee Harvey.

Once he was done shouting at me, I asked, "You know Detective Sergeant Erik Ortega in Homicide?"

"No," he said, biting off the word.

"Well, maybe you could call him," I said in the kind of helpful tone that usually got me punched in the face.

The cop stayed angry and attempted to intimidate me, which I found funny but got tired of quickly. I informed him of this to save us both time and to preserve LA's already flagging air quality. That landed about as well as you'd expect.

We went at each other like a couple that just couldn't wait for the divorce attorneys to get there. In my defense, I was wrongfully accused of a murder and an attempted one. And someone tricked me to get me here. That made me angrier than anything else.

"Listen, guy, we can go at it all night, but this is how it's going to end. You're either going to call Detective Ortega and get him to come down here and sort this out, because he's the guy who's even tangentially aware of what's happening. Or you can haul me into your station and I say nothing until my lawyer gets there. Then he explains to you that there was a fourth person here, who did the shooting, which you will learn once you confirm that my weapon had no bullets fired from it. And if you think to search that dirt over there and find a gun, you'll see that it has either someone else's prints or none at all. My guess is the latter. Since you didn't find any gloves on me, or in the immediate area, and there was no possible way that I could've cleaned a weapon *and* thrown it in the time it took you guys to spot me and knock me down, my guess is you're going to look pretty stupid for letting a shooter get away. Am I going too fast, or should I slow down so you can take notes?"

"Anyone ever tell you that you run your mouth too much?"

"Yes," I said.

For all his bulk, the lieutenant didn't have a chin and his head looked like a singular extension of his neck. It reminded me of the eraser on the end of a pencil. Once that image was burned into my thinking, I couldn't take him seriously, and that certainly didn't help my situation.

"I don't know any Detective Ortega. If he is working on your case, he'll get an email in the morning telling him you're booked on suspicion of murder. We've got one person dead and another shot, and you were caught fleeing the scene."

"I wasn't fleeing, I was chasing the shooter!"

"We didn't see anything."

"You also didn't *look*."

The lieutenant found that unhelpful.

23

They booked me on "reasonable suspicion" of murder and processed me into county jail.

Then they played shell games with my Fourth Amendment rights. Repeated requests for an attorney or my phone call went ignored.

At least they gave me my own cell.

There were no clocks. Jails were more like casinos than you might think. Eyes and volatility everywhere, and the odds were never in your favor.

I counted time by the shift changes.

I assumed people got fed around here, it just wasn't me. At some point, I slept, because I woke up to the sound of my cell door opening and a deputy grunting at me to get up. The deputies they put in jails are a bigger breed than the ones they let out on the street. This guy was six and a half feet of unmasked menace and raw power. His face practically demanded you try something and showed equally that he wanted you to. He frog-marched me through a labyrinthine connection of corridors and finally to an interview room where he shoved me down into a chair. The deputy handcuffed me to the table and left.

Detective Ortega came in a few minutes later. He wore jeans and a sheriff's department polo and looked like he'd been at it awhile. There was a bag that smelled like food with him. He opened it and put a foil-wrapped package on the table and then removed a couple coffees. "Figured you hadn't eaten," he said. He pushed the burrito across the table, then leaned over and unlocked the cuffs.

"Thanks," I said.

"You made quite the impression on Lieutenant Hennessy last night," he said.

"Oh, the fascist meathead has a name?" The look on Ortega's face said that was probably too far. "I want to talk to my lawyer. Now."

"Man, you are not in the demands-making business."

I could only imagine the number of times someone on this side of the table promised an attorney would open the gates of legal hell if they didn't get what they wanted.

"Goddamn it, Ortega. I have rights. Those don't go away because I pissed off some cop."

"Ease up, Gage. I'm on your side," Ortega snapped. The unstated "for now" hung in the air between us.

"What time is it?" I asked.

Slightly confused, Ortega looked down at his watch. Then he realized my question was genuine. "It's a little before noon."

I unwrapped the burrito and started eating. It, along with the coffee, was now lukewarm, and I was damn grateful for it.

"What is going on here? They can't seriously still think I shot anyone. They arrested me with my own gun, and it hadn't been fired. By now they'll have confirmed my gun is registered and I have a license to carry it. Your forensics people will surely have figured out now that I couldn't shoot a man that was behind me. I'm a good shot, but not that good." Ortega's face again reminded me that I was dancing over the line. I filed that along with most of the good advice I tended to ignore. "The shots, I assume, came from behind the fence. Holt got hit first, then Crowder's man. Before he was shot, he said something like 'you brought backup.' Man, no one there knew what was going on." I stopped. Through the fog of fatigue, it finally hit me that I was doing all the talking. Ortega brought me food and a coffee and said very little, other than cautioning me against trashing his colleague. "After what happened last night, you'll forgive me if I'm a little uncomfortable saying anything else without my attorney present."

I watched the drama of calculation play out behind Ortega's eyes. If I lawyered up now, this interview was over. It would push his case out by days, if not more, and Ortega would lose any valuable information he might get. He'd also never explained to me why I was talking to him and not someone else.

He picked up his own coffee, took a sip, and downcast his eyes to the notepad he'd brought with him.

"The deceased's name is Lucious Kett. Employment records list him with a company called Aperture Systems, Limited, which sounds like a bullshit company. The weapon we recovered from his person was not registered."

"Did Holt make it?"

Ortega nodded. "She's stable. It was a through-and-through. Stayed in the hospital for observation. I interviewed her this morning."

"So this is your case now?"

"This is where it gets complicated. Whenever there's a shots fired call, a homicide detective gets dispatched. Last night wasn't my night, so one of my colleagues took it. We have a system that flags an investigating officer any time someone connected with one of their cases has an interaction with us. You dropped my name to Hennessy last night. He thought we might be friends or something, so he delayed putting you in the system until he absolutely had to do it. Because of your connection to my other case and the fact that Ms. Holt works for Nathaniel Crowder, they pushed this one over to me. After you told me about Kyle Haney, I had Crowder listed as a person of interest in the Matthews investigation. So, you're just the gift that keeps on giving." Ortega leaned back in his seat. "The responding detective last night interviewed Holt at the hospital. I followed up with her again this morning. She says you called her with damaging information on Crowder, that you wanted to make a trade."

"What?"

Ortega nodded grimly and offered nothing else.

"That's bullshit. Or it's a lie. Check my phone records. I was at that spot because Graham Wexler, NOVA AI's number two, called *me* and said Grant Matthews's phone was trying to access the company network."

One of Ortega's thick eyebrows stood up. The expression was otherwise tough to read.

"Gage, I don't think you shot either of them. The angles don't work. There were no shell casings, and there was no gun. Holt doesn't think you shot anyone either. The question is whether you had help."

Neither of us spoke, two marble statues in a staring contest. His intent was clear. He'd given me all the free information he'd planned to. Meanwhile, I was trying to understand why Vanessa Holt would say I called her.

When I'd gotten into trouble with the police before, it'd usually been by circumstance, and the situation eventually worked itself out. Or I'd engaged my attorney and he played hell with them until I solved the case and the situation eventually worked itself out. This felt different. Gripping my coffee cup, though not hard enough that we had a Vesuvius of caffeine spurting into the air, I told Detective Ortega what I knew.

Mostly.

Starting with the Commerce agent, I worked my way through the afternoon, who I met with and what we talked about. I gave him the details about my conversation with Wexler, how he called me to say that he found Matthews's phone accessing their network and how I followed that to the site.

"Remember when we spoke after Matthews's death? I told you that someone jumped me? Then I used EchoTrace to show that black Lexus was outside my hotel the day before? Well, that's Lucious Kett's car. It's registered to a shell company, but you open that building up and you'll find it in the garage. I think Kett works for Nathaniel Crowder, he's some kind of corporate troubleshooter. I told you about this before. Didn't you follow up on it?"

Ortega cocked his head.

"Industrial espionage, man," I said. "The Commerce agent I met with yesterday, Blackwell, said Crowder was trying to acquire NOVA AI, he'd filed paperwork to do it."

"They have to do that? File paperwork?"

"I don't buy a lot of companies. I took him at his word. Then, I've got all these targeted disclosures about my client's past, all designed to make him seem untrustworthy with his board of directors. Force him out of the company, then Crowder sweeps in and buys it."

"And you think that's what this Lucious Kett was doing?"

"I didn't call Holt."

"Not from your phone, no." Before the thunder was even out of my mouth, Ortega held up his hands like a conversational traffic cop, advising me once again that I was exceeding the speed limit. "I think you got ghosted, man."

"What?"

"The number you gave me for Wexler? It's bogus. We traced it to an IP address, so it was probably just an app call. We were able to get in touch with Julian Kessler, who gave us Wexler's real number. He says he didn't call you."

"Can he prove it?"

If Crowder was going to maneuver Julian out of the company, he'd need one of the officers to do it. Maybe he used an app to make the call, but I spoke to Graham Wexler last night. Frankly, for as dangerous a man as Nathaniel Crowder was, I didn't think he was *that* kind of dangerous. Murder was big medicine, even for someone like him.

It didn't seem to fit, yet here we were.

On the other side of the scale were the lingering specters of Grant Matthews and Kyle Haney. Two men who had been in Crowder's orbit, and certainly one of whom, Crowder had good cause to silence.

I also couldn't ignore my intuition about how Crowder gave orders. I'd watched him with Kett that night. All he'd said was to handle the problem; he let his underling figure out how it should be done.

Everything about this felt wrong.

"Wexler and Kessler were together most of the night working. They'll both swear to it," Ortega said.

"We got call logs from the telco for Holt, Wexler, and Kessler, as well as yours. There's no record of Wexler calling you or you calling Holt. At least, not from your cell phones."

"What about Wexler? He's the one who told me someone had

Matthews's phone in the first place." Ortega shook his head. "It was him," I insisted. "I know his voice."

"We think you might've been deepfaked."

"How the hell do you know?" I said, and I'll admit I sounded like an asshole.

"Gage, OCSD has one of the best cybercrime squads in the country. All the tech companies around here, think about it. We're starting to see a lot of deepfaking, mostly on fraud cases, so I admit this one is new." Ortega took a swig of coffee and opened his notebook. He pulled a computer printout from his folder and slid it across the table. "We got a 911 call last night claiming multiple shots fired at that office park. But look at the timing. That call came in well before everything went down because the units were already rolling when the shooting started. That's why they arrived on scene so fast."

"Swatting," I said.

Ortega's big head bobbed twice. "Looks like it. This is a pretty sophisticated roll, Gage. Deepfaking Wexler and then calling in the heavies. Now, I've met you, so it's not hard to believe you could piss somebody off that much, but this is serious. Whoever did this knows what they're doing. I believe you didn't call that Holt woman and offer dirt on her boss. Just doesn't sound like you, and frankly, it just doesn't make sense. Nathaniel Crowder's lawyers would destroy you, you tried shit like that. But it would be enough to get her out to some office park in the middle of the night. And yes, I know what industrial espionage is. People like Holt do a lot more for their companies than process badges."

I nodded, taking it in and saying nothing. Ortega tapping his pen on the notepad suggested it was my turn.

"Did you ask her about Lucious Kett?"

"Said she'd never seen him before. And you don't know Kett worked for Crowder, that's speculation."

"Right," I said, practically pulling the word apart at the seams. "The building you guys found us in front of, that was a private security company —for lack of a better term—that Nathaniel Crowder funded through a series of shell corporations. I can't prove it beyond showing the building is leased to a fake company, and there are a few vehicles in the garage registered to a different one. I suspect if there was some forensic accounting done of his companies, you'd find the line items that will ultimately trace to that. I think I may have told you about this before."

"Yeah. You mentioned it. You also told me you caught some conversation between them, but were a little light on the details. Leaving that aside for now."

"At the time, I thought the shots came from the other side of the fence, near the aqueduct. Did they find shell casings, or a gun, or anything?"

"Nope. The helicopter is equipped with a forward-looking infrared camera, but it wasn't working. Plus, they were so close to that power line when they dusted you, the pilot backed off super quick. We found some footprints in the dirt, but not much else. No way to prove those didn't belong to a construction worker. If there was a shooter, they slipped away in the chaos."

That basically confirmed for me that it was a setup.

"What about Grant Matthews's phone?"

Ortega laughed, it was a cynical, glass-cracking sound. "That's been in evidence since we found his body."

Someone pretended to be Wexler, and someone pretended to be me, to maneuver the three of us into a place to get shot. Then called in an emergency sufficient to get a SWAT team rolling in hard. I couldn't tell who the intended target was, or even if it mattered.

Ortega was right about one thing. This was a professional job, and they were good.

And scary.

Ortega pushed back in his chair, exhaling a huge breath while he did. Looked like it took him some effort. It also looked like he was weighing his words carefully. When he did finally speak, his words were slow and measured, almost practiced. Like something he might say on a witness stand.

"The department is dropping charges related to the shooting, and you'll be processed out."

"So that 'suspicion of murder' stuff, that's gone?"

Ortega nodded and started packing his things up. "You're going to want some sleep. After that, we need to talk. Our digital forensics people want to look at your phone, if you're willing. See if you've been hacked."

I nodded, though it was more acknowledging the request than acceding to it.

"What's going on with Grant Matthews's case?"

"There is some pressure to close it as a traffic accident. Between you and me, I think someone bumped him and he lost control of the car. There's a mark on the rear passenger-side fender indicating a light collision."

I knew that maneuver, but with all the speculation on me, this did not seem like the time to point that out.

"Can't prove it with what I have. Even if I can prove that the nick on Matthews's bumper came from that night, it's currently speculation to say it was intentional," Ortega said. "The link with the Haney death is…something." Ortega paused before he opened the interview room door. "One more thing. SWAT is an additional duty. Hennessy's day job is he's the second-shift OIC for patrol. If it were me, I'd walk between those hours. He's really got it out for you."

"Thanks."

"Listen, I know you haven't told me everything. I get that you're trying to protect your client and all. Whatever your reasons are. Someone did try to kill you last night. No reason not to think they won't try again. You hear something, you see something, you call me. Don't do anything on your own."

"I understand. And thank you."

I processed out of jail, and they gave me my things back, except for my Glock, which they kept because it was "part of an ongoing investigation." My phone was dead, but there were always plenty of cabs loitering outside of a jail. I got one, and he took me to my Land Rover.

I drove back to my hotel room and showered the jail out. By the time I'd finished, my phone was charged, and I almost wish I hadn't checked it.

Among the dozen or so voicemails and close to thirty texts, Julian called seven times between last night and this morning. I didn't bother tallying the texts. They were all a variation on "where are you," "need to talk to you immediately." Hell, even Diana messaged early and asked if I knew what "this" was about. I think she was worried about the photos of us together and it implying she was taking a side.

Curiously, there was one from Benjamin Blake telling me he was flying down from San Francisco today.

I had no idea what any of them were talking about, and no one wanted to mention it in clear text.

Something was going down at NOVA, so I got in the Defender and hauled over.

Of course, I no longer had building access. No one was answering phones, and that told me they were all together and behind closed doors. I tried Brody Nash, who met me out front.

"Not sure I'm supposed to let you in, bro."

"What is happening? Julian called me about a hundred times. I was... unavailable."

"Yeah, he's pissed about that," Nash said.

"I spent the night in a cell at county. Someone set me up, after they tried to kill me."

Nash whitened. Honestly, it was kind of funny to see.

"If Julian is behind closed doors, I can only imagine that person wanted me away from whatever is going on here."

Nash said, "I think they're kicking Crowder off the board." Nash's phone buzzed. He looked down at it and then said, "Sorry, I gotta go. Need me inside."

"Brody, we need to talk. You, me, and Julian. Wexler and Singh, too. They need to know what happened last night. Whatever it is, I don't think this is over."

"Is Julian safe?"

"I can't promise that he is until I know what's happening."

Nash nodded for me to follow, and he badged us in.

Whatever they'd done to Crowder had the brutal efficiency of a Texas execution. It was a solemn group that filtered out of the board room, probably because they'd all realized their own corporate mortality. Julian locked eyes with me. There was something in there, and it wasn't welcoming.

Julian nodded stiffly to Nash, who was off like a shot. I was close enough to hear his gruff instructions.

"Mr. Crowder has resigned from the board and will no longer require building access."

Crowder gave me a look that would spoil milk behind three feet of glass.

"I suppose you're proud of yourself," he said, loud enough for everyone in the foyer to hear.

"You took your shot and missed." We locked eyes, and I added, "So to speak."

Nash made quick steps to Crowder, putting a hand on his elbow. "This way, Mr. Crowder." He shook Nash's grip off with a broken wing shake.

"You're being played, Gage. This is exactly the outcome they wanted, and you just served it up."

24

"I can appreciate that this isn't a good time for you, but I really need to brief you on some things. Graham and Amara should hear them as well."

"Is this about the police interviews?"

"It is."

Julian's mood was hard to read. He'd just been through what had doubtless counted for a broken-bottle street fight in his world. Ejecting someone that had been a mentor to him couldn't have been easy.

He called the other two in, and they looked as ashen-faced as he had. It was a good reminder that most people don't deal with serious conflict in their lives.

I started by chronologically telling the story from when I met with Evelyn Hawthorne the day before, transmitting my report to Julian, and the deepfaked phone call from Graham. Nash appeared at the door then. Julian looked at me, I nodded, and Julian waved him in.

"Sorry, Crowder gave me an earful in the parking lot."

"Matt was just catching us up on the situation," Julian said, still hard to read. "By the way, flipping Verala like that. Sick. Crowder showed us pictures, said it was evidence of collusion. She's, what do you call it, an asset?"

"Agent," Nash offered confidently.

"They mean the same thing," I said, suddenly very uncomfortable. "Shall I continue?"

I picked the thread up, describing how the deepfaked Graham led me to the office park where I met Vanessa Holt, Lucious Kett, and then the shooting. Then the SWAT team. I also told them how I'd connected Kett to my assault earlier.

"Kett appears to have run a covert private security company. We'd need some forensic accounting to do it, but I suspect that you'd find some highly obfuscated payments from Crowder to some dummy corps that ultimately track back to Kett. Crowder paid him to make problems go away. Problems like me. On surveillance one night, I'd caught Crowder telling him to get rid of me."

"Well, it's a good thing we kicked him out," Wexler said.

"I don't understand why he'd want to kill his own person, though," Amara said.

"Matt, you said that you and this Holt woman both got deepfaked phone calls telling you to be there. Is that right?" Julian said.

Before I could respond, Nash jumped in. "I know her. Vanessa Holt. I've worked with her on some security agreements between us and Crowder Dynamics." The perplexed looks from the others in the room at how that was relevant were unmistakable. I think Nash just wanted to participate.

"Someone shot Holt and then Kett. Holt's was not fatal, Kett's was. I could not identify the gunman. The SWAT team rolled in immediately after. My police contact said the 911 call that triggered the SWAT team came in before we got there."

"How could..." Amara said, thinking aloud.

"Swatting," Nash said, and I decided to let him have that one.

"I get everything you're saying, Matt, I just don't understand why Crowder would try to kill his own people. And who would do it?" Amara said.

There was no question that Crowder used Lucious Kett to scare me off the case, and had I not caught them that night, he would've moved on me before I knew it. Despite all of that, murder didn't fit Crowder's profile, a thought I'd repeatedly circled around. Kett appeared to have the skills and disposition to dig up seemingly unfavorable information on Julian and manipulate it. Not a far cry to believe someone like him would have the kinds of connections in the Intelligence Community that he'd need to uncover my background either. Doubtful that Kett was also the hacker, but he'd know where and how to find one.

Still, no matter how hard I tried, I could not figure the logic in that shooting.

Lost in my own thoughts, I hadn't realized everyone in the room was looking at me. They were all waiting on the answer to Amara's question.

"I believe I was the intended target," I said. "They just shot the wrong person." It was a convenient lie, or at least a half truth, and it seemed to mollify them.

Crowder's admonition that I'd played into "their" hands stayed with me. Whoever "they" were.

Had I eliminated a threat or just removed a rival?

"I'm sharing this with you all because I don't think the threat to Julian is over." I exchanged a pointed look with Nash, letting him know I wanted his help. Saddle up, Sheepdog. "Graham and Amara, I wanted you both to be aware of potential attempts to coerce you or otherwise get you to align against Julian in the future. I don't think this is over."

"What? Of course it is," Graham snapped. "We just fired Crowder. What else is there?"

"Assume he goes down swinging," I said. Feeling the pulse in the room, this wasn't the time to share my concern that Crowder might not be Julian's only threat.

The meeting broke, and Graham exited quickly. Amara made an awkward orbit before departing. Nash stayed, waiting for instructions. Julian asked for the room. Nash nodded and left, closing the door behind him.

"I'm glad you're okay, Matt," Julian said, still brusque. He sat at his desk.

"It's the job."

Julian tented his fingers, resting his elbows on the desktop.

"I hope you can appreciate how exposed I am now," he said.

"I don't understand."

"The kind of lawsuit that Crowder can, and inevitably will, bring on me now. He's going to allege that I hired you to dig up dirt on him to get him off the board because I was threatened. Basically, the reverse of what he tried to do to me."

"What bright-eyed genius gave you that idea?"

"You haven't met Adrian Beckett yet. He's our corporate counsel. Adrian stayed in Mountain View because we moved during the school year, and he's got kids. He told me not to hire you, for basically this reason. You ever have a lawyer say, 'I told you so'?"

Buddy, more times than you got fingers to count.

Julian stood from his desk and walked around to the front of it, just a step or two away from me.

Julian continued, "Anyway, he was dialed into the board meeting just now. We were texting while the meeting was happening. He said I need to sever this relationship immediately." Before the words of caution were out of my mouth, he held his hands up. "He doesn't know about what happened last night, so I'm going to ignore it for now. Crowder is pissed, and he moves fast. I suspect he's meeting with his legal team already. I'm not sure they picked up on it, but I could read what you weren't saying. You think there's someone else involved."

"Let's call it a theory. The shooting is the thing I can't figure out. Holt said *I* called *her* to trade dirt that I supposedly had on her boss. Only, I didn't. Someone must have deepfaked my voice and called her and gave her that spot to meet. Which just happened to be Lucious Kett's off-the-books security outfit. Feels an awful lot like a setup to me. But, to do what?"

"I'm going to give you a week to prove that there is someone else involved. After that, Adrian says I've got to turn everything over to the police."

"I understand," I said. Julian walked me to his office door. I stopped before we reached it. "Yesterday, I got a phone call from someone in the Department of Commerce's Bureau of Industry and Security. He said Crowder filed paperwork with them to acquire NOVA AI. Does that sound right to you?"

Julian thought it through. "Possibly. He'd need to clear it with the Federal Trade Commission and Department of Justice first. Get a CFIUS review. There's SEC filings as well. I don't know much about BIS to know when they'd get involved, though if they are, it's downstream in the process."

I nodded and left, assuring him I'd be in touch.

I grabbed a red-eye, a coffee with a shot of espresso in it, and headed back to my hotel. What I needed was about two days of shut-eye. However, considering that I was now on the clock, sleep would have to wait. I couldn't even afford to grab a couple hours, because I needed the afternoon to work.

First, I called my own attorney and learned that Thomas Coogan was out of the country. His firm's focus was international law, with Thomas running the civil liberties practice. He also did a lot of work with refugees and conflict mediation. How did he end up representing me? The firm, Case Ritter, did pro bono work for a collective of investigative journalists called the Orpheus Foundation, who I used to do contract security work for. Thomas bailed me out of trouble enough times it was something of a running joke between us, and we'd become good friends. Unfortunately for my current situation, his assistant told me he was at Guantanamo Bay, arguing with the government about deportations.

So, I was without a safety net.

Next, I started reframing my investigation. In a real sense, this was a new Day One. I didn't bother with the usual questions of "Who benefits?" Because they all did. Everyone except General Graves had wanted Crowder gone. And as for the good general, his goals could still be accomplished with or without Crowder, so he wasn't off the hook. Telling him Crowder never intended to make good on his offer likely swung Graves in our favor. That also didn't absolve him of culpability and, if I was looking at people who could have hacked this demo, he was the leading candidate.

I powered up my laptop and set EchoTrace onto seeing what I could learn about Lucious Kett and his phantom security operation. There was value in knowing how much of this was Crowder's doing and how much was this other person. I also assumed Crowder was going to retaliate— against Julian in the courts and perhaps a little more viscerally with me. If Kett wasn't his only flying monkey, I needed to know about it.

While the system was running on Kett, I opened another search dialogue. I asked EchoTrace to do a government records search to see if Crowder Dynamics, or any other entity, had filed paperwork to acquire NOVA AI. I quickly bounced off that one. The Justice Department and Federal Trade Commission antitrust reviews were only disclosed after an acquisition. The system also checked if a new corporation was charted to facilitate the transaction. Often, these were formed in Delaware, because that state traditionally had low barriers to entry for incorporation. Again, nothing. The reason I was burning time on this question was that someone laid an elaborate trap and I'd waltzed right into it. I had to understand how deep that went.

Then, I hit on that Bureau of Industry and Security agent, Mark Blackwell. I didn't know whether he was an "agent" or not. BIS did have export enforcers who were federal law enforcement officers, but I hadn't actually seen his badge or credentials. Just his business card. I found that and scanned it. There was only one number on it. This was common, as companies were shedding traditional phones in favor of employees just using their personal mobile devices. However, this was a federal government office, and in a sensitive role like that, they'd need something more secure than a cell phone.

I looked up the BIS office in Orange County online and called. It took a while to get to a human, and when I did, I told them I was with the Office of Personnel Management doing a periodic background check on one of their people, Mark Blackwell. The person on the phone said there was no one there by that name. She bounced me to a couple different offices, but it was the same thing. No one there had ever heard of Mark Blackwell.

Checking the time, I called Mickey—Mikhail Iliescu—my Romanian hacker on Signal. Blackwell had a QR code on his business card that was supposed to automatically store his information in a phone's contacts. At the time, I thought Blackwell was just trying to look cool in front of the SoCal tech companies he allegedly did business with. I took a photo of the card, front and back, and sent that to Mickey. He called me back a few minutes later.

"I opened this on a clean laptop," he said. "There's a tracking pixel embedded in the QR code. When you scan that, it basically has a line of executable code that the camera can read, but the human eye can't. It's a common trick with spam, too. Anyway, if you'd have scanned this, he'd have owned whatever device that was on."

"Shit. I don't know if I scanned it or not."

Best to assume my phone was compromised until I knew it wasn't.

This "Blackwell" could have been tracking my every move the last two days. That could explain a lot.

Mickey opened a VPN and connected to my phone and scanned it for spyware. Which he found, and removed, after not an insignificant amount of telling me that I knew better than that. He said whether I trusted the phone after this point was up to me—he wouldn't. It was possible Blackwell snuck something else in there. I thanked Mickey and hung up.

So, I had something, at least. Which was that I knew for certain now the other side had an operative.

Several things were possible.

One: Blackwell worked for Lucious Kett, in which case Crowder would certainly unleash him on me. Probably Julian, too. When this started, I'd assumed Crowder would stop if we got him out of the company. That was a dangerously bad assumption.

Two: Blackwell worked for someone else, and the threat from the other board members remained.

Three: Julian was wrong, and it was never coming from the board of directors, that it was someone else entirely. I believed his assessment, his logic, and never really pressure tested it. Because it fit. Seeing how elaborate this frame was, again, a dangerously bad assumption.

I had no way of getting to Blackwell, but maybe I could figure out who the hacker was.

The police had Grant Matthews's phone and his laptop. They'd have taken anything of evidentiary value from his condo. Matthews would know enough about cybersecurity and digital forensics that he wouldn't use either of those things to break into NOVA. Which meant there could be a clean phone and a laptop somewhere. Ortega didn't say they'd found multiples of either.

I got in the Defender and raced over to Matthews's place in Costa Mesa.

He'd owned a luxury townhouse at a complex near city center. The exterior was blond wood, brushed steel, green glass, and seagrass. The manager was a woman in her mid-forties, California tan and dressing on the business side of athleisure.

She identified herself as Lora and extended a hand like it was a damp towel. Judging by the length of her nails, I hoped her job didn't require a lot of typing.

"My name is Matt Gage. I'm a private detective, and I'm assisting the Orange County Sheriff's Department with the Grant Matthews murder investigation." I flashed her Ortega's business card. "They've spoken to you, yes?"

Astonished hands went to her face, and she flashed a look just this side of playacting.

"I didn't know Mr. Matthews well, but I try to build a relationship with each of the residents. I'd see him at one of our events from time to time, but he mostly kept to himself. I told all this to the police," she said. Her defenses and suspicion raised immediately, resentful that she had to answer the same questions again. And to someone who wasn't even a real cop.

"I'm sure you did, ma'am. I am just here to check the residence, if that's okay. I think the forensics team has already been through. I'm supposed to just do a quick inventory before they turn everything over to next of kin." That seemed plausible enough, and I didn't think they'd give his possessions over to the family until the case was closed.

"Oh, okay," she said. "That makes sense, I guess. I've been trying the people he left as his emergency contacts, but they weren't his parents, and I can't seem to find them." Lora leveled her eyes at me, like this was her personal moment of truth. I'd invoked the police, and she was deciding if she believed that or not. "They didn't say anything to me about anyone coming back."

"I'm not surprised, there's like four different divisions involved right now. I work for the lead investigator, but now that it's a crime scene, we have to send our requests over to the forensics people. The DA is in this now, it's a whole thing."

"They really use private detectives for stuff like this?" she asked, still doubtful. I nodded earnestly.

"Yeah, budget cuts. It's cheaper to contract someone like me for routine stuff like this than to dispatch an officer." I shrugged for effect. "Money isn't bad. Fills in the gaps, means I have to spend less time taking pictures of dirtbags cheating on their wives."

As I said this, she disappeared into the back office, where I could see her in profile opening a small safe. She returned with a pair of keys. "They took that yellow tape up everywhere and told us not to go in it."

I pulled a pair of latex gloves from my pocket and held them up. I had a backpack over one shoulder so I could sneak the laptop out, if I found it.

"Same kind as they got," I said. I kept a box in the Defender. Lora asked me to follow her and led me through the well-maintained property.

"Here we are," she said when we'd arrived. There wasn't any caution tape on the door. Lora explained she'd negotiated with the sheriff to remove that so as not to upset the residents. She opened the door, and we stepped inside.

"You've probably got more important things to do than watch me inventory. If you want to leave me a key, I can just lock up and bring it to you when I'm done."

"I should probably stay." She stretched the words out, as if saying them required too much effort. "Just in case the police have questions. You know?"

I put the gloves on, pulled a notebook and pen out of my backpack, and set to work. "Work" was writing down random things that a regular person might think were important to a murder investigation. I made up a numbering system on the fly, in case she happened to look over my shoulder. I made it look as boring as it was.

Lora made it a whole ninety seconds before her phone was out, demanding her full attention.

It was forty-five seconds longer than I thought it would take.

The townhouse's interior reflected the design aesthetic throughout the complex: wood, brushed steel, and marble. Lots of light, natural and LED, the latter ultramodern bordering on sci-fi. I hovered in front of his massive TV and home theater setup, documenting the numerous media and gaming consoles. I kept it up for another few minutes and then tested her attention by stepping into the hallway.

Lora said nothing.

There was one bedroom on the main floor, which Matthews converted to his home office. I could tell he spent a lot of time on video calls, because the area directly behind it was created to look like a corporate office rather than a home one. Listening for movement, and not detecting any, I started searching. The police would have picked up anything obvious. What I was looking for was hiding spots.

The desk was too easy, though I cleared it anyway. No hidden bottoms. Next, I inspected the floorboards for false panels and then moved on to the room's closet. Same. I didn't think Matthews was savvy enough to engineer a covert cubby into his place, like I had in mine. Nor did I think he'd have the time. It still paid to be thorough. While I was in here, I copied the MAC and IP address from Matthews's router, which the police oddly hadn't confiscated.

The credibility of my story was running a footrace with Lora the Manager's patience for leaning against the kitchen counter and scrolling Instagram. I needed to keep selling the tedious fiction to make it believable, just being careful not to draw it out so far she decided it wasn't worth the trouble. Or, worse, called Ortega to double-check my story.

Finding nothing, I stepped out into the hall and flashed a look at Lora. She had one elbow on the counter, the other arm cradled the phone with her thumb doing all the work. I turned around the corner and started up the stairs.

The step creaked as soon as I put weight on it.

"How's it going?" she said, and I froze.

"Fine. I've got a list of things I'm supposed to look at," I said. It sounded good in the moment, something I could riff off of if I had to. "Should only be a couple of minutes."

There was a long pause, and I heard all the pins drop.

"'Kay," she said in a bored voice. There were about ten grains left in this hourglass.

Moving upstairs quickly, I found Matthews's bedroom. Wall-to-wall carpet, and a fast feel showed it was still connected to the floor beneath.

Nothing behind the dresser. Then I lifted the bottom drawer out, nothing in the space beneath.

Closet was also clean.

An investigator's breeze through the en-suite bathroom confirmed the same.

I tried to put myself in Matthews's head. *I've got a burner phone and disposable laptop. I want to keep them near me, but also out of sight because I'm doing some crazy illegal shit with them. Where to hide them?*

Would he?

There are a dozen clandestine communication methods I could name right now. None of them as anonymous as a burner you bought with cash, though.

These people wouldn't let him off the hook. This job wasn't a one and done. So there had to be a phone. He owned the house. Where would he keep it?

I checked the ventilation grate, and it was securely attached. A multitool is an invaluable addition to your kit, and I've carried one ever since I was a first-tour case officer. I pulled my Leatherman out, flipped the screwdriver head, and removed the grate. I felt around, and there was nothing.

I replaced the grate and screwed it back into place.

The bedroom was clear.

Human psychology says that people tend to hide things in the places where they feel safest. For most people, that's the room where they close their eyes. Grant Matthews had a hiding spot, though, and it wasn't here.

I stepped out into the hallway.

Choice time. I could pull off one more search before I had to call it, or blow my story entirely.

Matthews had another bedroom across the hall. When I stepped out into the hallway, I saw there were stairs leading up, which meant there must be a roof deck, because there wasn't a third floor.

Worth a shot.

I padded down the carpet and up the stairs, and opened the door when I reached the top. It opened to a wide, open space with a long, sectional outdoor couch wrapped around a coffee table. Son of a bitch had a wet bar up here with a beer fridge. Pays to get fired. Good work if you can get it. Beneath the pergola, there was a grill, and judging by the label on the cover, it was worth more than I'd made on some cases.

If I'm hiding something, where is the last place someone is going to check? Something with fire.

I walked over to the grill, removed the cover, and lifted the lid. It smelled like grill. There wasn't time to take this damn thing apart, so I lowered the cover and put the nylon top back on. There were a pair of doors beneath the grill, so I bent down and opened those, pulling the trays out.

And there it was.

In the back of the bottom pull-out tray, something you wouldn't have seen if you hadn't looked right at it, was a phone.

"Mr. Gage? What are you doing up here?"

25

I palmed the phone, sliding it underneath my notebook.

Pressing both against my hip, I turned. Lora stood in the doorway, hip cocked to the side and a pissed-off expression painted on her face.

Flashing my best sheepish smile, I said, "Just being thorough. They asked me to inventory everything. Even the grill shit."

"I think it's time you left," she said. Picking up on the contextual clues that I'd overstayed my welcome, I decided it was time to leave. Lifting up my backpack, I dropped the notebook and phone into it, then zipped it closed. If she saw me pull it out of the cabinet, she didn't let on. I didn't think Matthews would've had time to ditch the computer he used for the hack before he died, and I obviously wasn't getting a second chance at his condo, so the phone would have to do.

Lora watched me, a hawk eyeing a field mouse and calculating the descent physics. I shouldered my backpack, and she said nothing as I passed.

Once we were downstairs and she was locking up, Lora asked me if I found what I needed.

"Just doing an inventory so the real cops don't have to. Thanks for your time." I flashed her a dull smirk.

Lora followed me all the way down, made a show of locking the door, and gave an icy escort back to the Defender. She was wordless the entire time.

I raced back to the hotel. First, I powered up the phone and entered its details into EchoTrace—the phone number, MAC address, and any IPs it used. Then I entered the numbers from the call log, which Matthews hadn't bothered to erase. I ran an open source intelligence search against those numbers, and then did the same for the dark web.

While the reports compiled, I checked the calls and texts I'd missed while I was in the townhouse. Diana Verala had called, asking if I was free for dinner.

Graves had called as well, said that he had an update on my "query" and that I should return his call immediately.

The longer I considered him, the more Graves rose on my list of suspects. I was trying hard not to let personal bias affect my professional judgment. So far, many signs pointed in his direction.

Ignoring Graves for now, I called Diana back, told her I'd love to meet her for dinner but that I'd be tied up with casework. The truth was I needed sleep. We made plans for tomorrow night, and I suggested she pick the place. She asked me if I'd ever had Portuguese food, I told her I hadn't, and she said she'd love to cook. That sounded fine to me. I'd bring the wine. Getting her perspective on the other board members and, specifically, what went down in their meeting today could be important.

At least, that's what I told myself at the time.

Shifting my attention back to my laptop, I saw that the reports finished.

Matthews covered his tracks well, but he wasn't a true hacker and he still left crumbs. A human might not pick up on the trail, but EchoTrace could kick over an unlimited number of digital rocks. Matthews used an onion router, which was a web protocol designed to obfuscate a user's IP address. Matthews appeared to use it every time he communicated with his "employer," except the one time he didn't. That gave me metadata on the dark web chat room he used and, most importantly, his handle. Using his handle as my search parameter, and I could piece together several conversations in the black chat rooms that existed in this corner of the internet.

There in black and white was the text record of a conversation between Grant Matthews and *someone* grooming him, getting him to brag about how he'd left a back door in NOVA AI. That person left a phone number, which matched one of the numbers I had from Matthews's phone.

Switching to the returns on the burner, it showed him calling two numbers. EchoTrace automatically ran scans on any numbers it found. It confirmed that both were registered to SIM cards purchased in cash from two different locations in West Hollywood, and on the same day. I had the system try to target the location using the date-time-groups of the transactions. This sort of data exists in the digital ether. It just requires a machine to find and compile it.

EchoTrace's developers just launched a new feature in the app, which allowed a user to clone a cell tower for the purposes of triangulating cell phones. This pissed off the civil liberties people because it was a functionality only law enforcement agencies were supposed to have, and they'd launched multiple lawsuits in-state. Amazingly, the State of California hadn't shut the capability down. According to the call log, Matthews called one of the numbers immediately before the demo.

I directed the system to run the call trace. Sometimes this worked, sometimes it didn't. Phone companies shouldn't provide this information without a warrant, but groups representing state and local law enforcement —and duly appointed private investigators who often worked for them— lobbied to allow it.

It worked.

The call showed a ping in a downtown LA cell tower. I had the system bring up the property records for every building and residence within the radius. This would take time to sort through given the population density and the number of mixed-use structures. The phone call lasted twenty-two seconds. I created a geofence around that block for that time and had the system retrieve any CCTV footage if the phone pinged again.

While that compiled, I pulled up the previous camera request, and a cold shock ran through me.

There was a grainy photo of a man at an electronics store on Wilshire buying one of the burners.

It was Blackwell, the Commerce agent.

He wore glasses and used the same trick I did with the coated lenses. I recognized the shape of his face anyway.

I clicked on his face, and the image recognition dialogue appeared on screen asking me if I wished to search for him. I did, even though I knew the results. With the disappointment that can only be delivered at machine speed, EchoTrace told me it didn't have enough detail to search.

I didn't have any better luck with the cameras during the time that Matthews called before the hack. Probably, that meant the phone was inside at the time. However, I had something else. EchoTrace connected Matthews to a hacker in some dark web forums who went by "Ghost." A summary appeared next to the Ghost alias, describing him as a hacker wanted by the FBI and several other law enforcement agencies across the country. I saved the alias as a "person of interest" in my case file and checked his activity in California.

This Ghost had to be the hacker that took control of NOVA during Julian's demo.

Zooming in on Ghost's suspected activities in Los Angeles, I saw that the name appeared in a client report for a cybersecurity firm based in downtown LA called BlackICE Defense. The report would normally have been labeled "client confidential" or "proprietary" or something, but because it'd been included in a court deposition, it was not a public record and therefore accessible to EchoTrace. The report stated that the client, an investment bank called GBS Financial, contacted BlackICE after a hacker identifying themselves as Ghost conducted a ransomware attack on the firm. GBS Financial hired BlackICE to conduct a "post-intrusion remediation." BlackICE's CEO, Asher Nolan, stated that he'd identified the "human and technical attack surface" and provided technical support and training following the event. Nolan wasn't interviewed directly, they'd just referenced his final report to the client.

I bet Nolan didn't even know the client used his report in their deposition.

An icon of a glowing yellow-orange exclamation point inside a triangle appeared next to BlackICE with the tag "Possible Case Connection" beneath it. I clicked it, and EchoTrace informed me that BlackICE's office was on the same downtown block that the phone tracker pegged the burner that Matthews called the night of the NOVA hack.

I ran Asher Nolan's name through the system and got a generic return. It did give me his driver's license picture and home address, though. Setting the image recognition to run as a background process, I got into the Defender and headed north.

So, now we had Grant Matthews communicating with a known hacker called Ghost. Ghost was named in a deposition where a cybersecurity firm was called in to undo some of his damage. BlackICE Defense's HQ was on the same block as where Matthews called Ghost just before Julian's demo. What were the odds that Ghost and Asher Nolan were the same person?

I couldn't tell yet how Nolan could plausibly connect BlackICE's "legitimate" business to repair the damage he'd done as Ghost, so I'd leave that to the police. It wouldn't be the majority of BlackICE's business, that would be too easy for the police to detect. My best guess was that he would hack a high-value client as Ghost. Then, Nolan would pitch his services as BlackICE Defense to clean up the damage. So, on top of being a hacker, he was also a solid con man. Good to know, though, to frame how I'd handle him.

It was late afternoon. I could probably make downtown LA in ninety minutes if I pressed it.

————————

"BlackICE" was a nod to the seminal cyberpunk novel *Neuromancer*, by William Gibson. In the book, the term "ICE" stood for "Intrusion Countermeasures Electronics," or the computer programs that prevented hackers from accessing systems in that world. "White ICE" was like a firewall, while "Black ICE" was a program that could kill you.

For the first time in forever, I felt like I was making headway.

Bluffing my way into Matthews's condo had been a risky move, and I was sure there would be some blowback with Ortega. He'd been fair with me, and I didn't want to piss him off. Still, I hoped he could appreciate what I was trying to do. If he ever found out about this, his official response would be that this was something I should turn over to "the real police." How long would it have taken them to make the connection between

Matthews and Nolan? If I could prove that this Nolan really was Ghost and my hunch about his business was true, maybe that would smooth over any feathers with the police. It wasn't their jurisdiction, but a crime was a crime.

BlackICE was in a run-down, old industrial building on the corner of Broadway and Fourth. Nolan must have purchased the building just before it was condemned and renovated it himself. I knew the city was trying to entice businesses to come back downtown after many of them fled when those blocks were seemingly given up to a tide of homeless camps. So I could see how a small outfit like this could afford the two-story structure.

I parked the Defender, put on my ball cap and glasses to baffle any cameras that might catch me, and did a quick walk-by of BlackICE. Mostly, I just wanted to get the lay of the place. Staking it out wasn't a great use of my time. I learned that the building was owned by a real estate development trust that Asher Nolan ultimately owned, and he'd split it up among four tenants—BlackICE, a cocktail bar, a clothing shop, and a bodega. The latter three all appeared to be legitimate and not connected to him.

After an hour downtown, I'd reasoned I'd had enough detecting for the day and headed back to the office. I'd gotten eyeballs on Nolan's business and proved it was a real place. For today, that was enough. I'd left downtown just before the wave of traffic fully broke on the street, so it only took forty minutes to get to Santa Monica. I parked at Ray's, grabbed my laptop, and headed inside. Happy hour was just now getting underway, and since it wasn't tourist season, everyone inside were locals. Most of them were the surfers that called Cosmic Ray's home, or the people like me that didn't have their own tribe and glommed onto theirs. I, at least, was enough of a fixture here that I was welcomed by the locals.

In surfer argot, a "local" is someone who surfs the breaks in a given area, not necessarily a resident.

There were some head nods as I entered the tiki bar and sauntered back to my usual table. Carrie, one of the semi-pro surfers who rounded out her income by working tables here, clocked me as I sat down and glided over to see what I wanted. She wore a sun-faded sweatshirt that was a size too big and cutoff jean shorts showing tanned and athletic legs. I ordered a bottle of Pliny the Elder and tacos.

I called Vanessa Holt. She'd be out of the hospital now and convalescing at home. It went immediately to voicemail, a digital "FU." I left a message anyway, saying that I hoped she was recovering well and to call me. I had information that I thought she'd want to hear.

It wasn't a very compelling message, I know, but I've learned to be cagey with voicemails. Same rules as a Miranda warning, anything you say can be used against you.

I needed to speak to Holt, though. I wanted to find out what *she* knew, and it wouldn't have been appropriate to call before now. Still, someone had tried to kill us both, and I had a good idea who was behind it. Seemed like something Holt deserved to know. I also didn't think the sheriff's department was as forthcoming.

I messaged Julian in Signal and told him that I had a lead on the people who hired Grant Matthews. Given that NOVA's attorney was now pressuring him to shut this down, regular updates were critical. I took a screenshot of the link analysis that connected Matthews's phone to the geofence around Asher Nolan's building and sent that to a cloud storage account. I didn't have time to compile the full report and wanted something handy if Julian called me back.

My food arrived, and I folded up the laptop. Carrie asked if I wanted anything else, and I told her I'd just take the check. I wanted to get home and get back to work, maybe try Holt again. I gave Carrie my debit card and she walked back to the server station to run it.

My phone rang as Carrie sauntered away, it was Nate McKellar. I answered with my usual, "Hey, boss."

"I did some asking around about our old pal, Sheikh Omar."

"Yeah?"

"He's not anywhere near this thing. My contact couldn't go into details for reasons I won't discuss on the phone, but he made it pretty clear that investing in an American tech company, especially one like NOVA, would jeopardize some ongoing 'security cooperation.' Wouldn't get any deeper than that."

Carrie was walking back to me, her expression a little off.

"Thanks, Nate. I owe you a scotch. I'm sorry to cut this short, but I need to go."

"Godspeed, kid," Nate said, and disconnected.

Carrie walked up to the table and handed me my debit card. "Matt, there's a problem with your card."

I took that and did an embarrassed exchange for my credit card. While she ran the new card, I pulled up my bank's app on my phone.

My bank account was empty.

26

The machine-shortened language for "account transfer" appeared in angry red on the screen.

By the time Carrie returned with the bad news that my credit card was similarly declined, I'd already checked that bank's app and confirmed the same.

I stared at the phone screen in disbelief.

No matter how much of a regular you are at a bar, the line "I can't pay my bill because a hacker stole my money" isn't going to get you very far.

I don't carry a lot of cash. It's not like the old days, or at least what I understood the old days to be. Rarely had I had an occasion to pay someone for information. One time, the guy wanted me to Venmo it. But for the grace of the patron saint of itinerant private detectives, I had enough on me for dinner and the beer, but forced me to stiff Carrie on the tip. I showed her my bank balance so she'd know I wasn't being a cheapskate.

"You can get me later, Magnum," she said with an eye roll.

I was on the phone with my bank before I hit the parking lot.

This sort of thing was supposed to be difficult by design. Checks and balances.

By the time I got back to my house, I'd gotten some part of the puzzle solved.

Someone—I'm assuming this was Asher Nolan—called, pretending to be me. They'd properly authenticated themselves using my bank's procedures and informed them they were closing the account. These requests typically take up to three business days, and the person on the phone told me she couldn't tell from her screen when I'd asked to do that. She also seemed confused as to why I didn't know. Any attempt to stop or reverse the transfer was beyond her powers. I explained that I didn't authorize the transfer, and she really stuck to her guns about this being properly authenticated. Eventually she got accusatory, like I'd had some buyer's remorse or something. My repeated statements about being impersonated and suggestion her bank may have been hacked didn't have the effect I'd hoped they would.

"I understand that, sir, but the *system* says..."

I got about fourteen variations of that.

Because "the system" absolves the person looking at it from either critical thinking or empathy, apparently.

After some back and forth with this, she agreed to open a case with their security team and said that someone would get back to me within a few days. I erupted with the kind of urgency that only a person who'd just been cleaned out like a hurricane hitting a blackjack table could muster, but it didn't do any good.

There was a similar story with my credit card company.

I called the Santa Monica police and navigated the menu, slamming my finger into whatever phone key represented my choice. Eventually, I got a duty sergeant. I explained the situation, said I hadn't thought I should call 911 because of this but that it was definitely a crime and definitely urgent. He took my information down and dutifully informed me "someone would get back to me."

I stopped, forced myself to calm. At the Farm they teach you how to maintain your composure in the most extreme situations, like a secret police official that just isn't buying your story. There are calming exercises you can do that slow the heart, slow the mind, ease yourself enough to think objectively. I leaned on that training *hard*.

Okay—break it down.

I knew Mark Blackwell was an operative and not a Commerce agent. I could assume he'd been on my phone for two days. Mickey couldn't tell if he'd done more than just plant tracking software, so it was possible he'd moved upstream and gotten access to apps. Or, Nolan just hacked my bank. He wouldn't necessarily need an exploit to do it. He might have gotten in through social engineering or impersonating a bank representative, or some combination of tricks.

I sent a message to Mickey, but it would be the early hours in Romania, so he was likely sleeping. Told him it was urgent and to call me back immediately.

Next, I called Ortega, but he didn't pick up.

Then, Wexler. I explained what happened as quickly and succinctly as I could.

"You should assume that this Asher Nolan is still inside your systems," I said.

"We checked everything," Wexler protested.

"I get that, but if he really is this 'Ghost,' then he's a top-tier hacker and wanted by the FBI. You need to check *everything*."

"Okay, I'll get with Nash, and we'll start in the morning."

"Goddamn it, Graham, you need to start *now*. These people already tried to take me out with a fake SWAT call, and now they're giving me another fire to put out. Whatever they're planning, it's happening soon."

"All right, all right. We can do a full physical security audit, replace access cards, force password changes, and lock virtual access. I'll get the engineering team on it."

"You need to look at NOVA again, too."

"Don't tell me how to do my job," Graham snapped.

"Do you know where Julian is? I've been trying to reach him," I said.

"Yeah," Graham said, and it wasn't a happy sound. "He was meeting with some potential partners. We need a new data center, NOVA takes a lot of computing power to run, and we'd hoped to do a joint venture with these guys. They just pulled out. Julian is trying to talk them into sticking with us."

Isolate me to keep me from helping Julian. Isolate Julian's business to keep him from getting help from anyone else. Then, an offer appears when he's got nowhere else to turn.

Or something worse. Though I tried not to think about that.

"If you talk to him, tell him I need to speak with him right away," I said. Graham said he would.

The most important thing I could do right now was to figure out who this Blackwell really was. Then I could work on who'd hired him. I'd long suspected there was an operative orchestrating this. This Asher Nolan was certainly a hot shit on his turf, but that rarely, if ever, translated to the real world. When I'd worked in a covert action unit, we'd had a cyber operator in our squad who was a fully trained case officer who had additional qualification in dark keyboard stuff. Those guys were a rare breed, and I doubted very much Nolan was one of them.

I tried Detective Ortega again and got nothing.

Then I messaged a friend in the FBI. Maybe I should've called Katrina Danzig long before now, though to be fair to her, I'd overdrawn that favor bank lately—running trend, it seemed. When I'd first met her, during the Johnnie Zhou investigation, she'd worked on a counterespionage squad in Silicon Valley. Likely, she'd be familiar with NOVA AI, but that's not why I wanted to talk to her. I wanted to get Ghost into the penalty box, and fast. We chatted briefly, I told her that in the course of an investigation I'd come across evidence linking a local cybersecurity firm with a hacker on a Bureau wanted list. Danzig said she didn't have a lot of active contacts in their cybercrimes division, but would ask around. Give her a day or so. I thanked her and said I'd forward what I had. It was late in DC, and I didn't want to keep her.

Next up was the Los Angeles Police Department.

Unfortunately, I didn't have deep contacts there. They had a computer crimes division, but I didn't know anyone who worked in it. I put some calls into the detectives I did know, however distantly, hoping someone would have a buddy. I also did a cold call to their central tip line. I identified myself as a private detective, provided my license number, and left a version of the truth that would hopefully get someone to call me back. I did the same with the LA District Attorney's cybercrimes unit.

Now what?

The need to move, to do *something* was almost overwhelming. It was like an itch beneath my skin. There's a panic, a mania, that sets in when you know you're truly powerless.

The thing that I could do was start following Asher Nolan.

One option was to force him to act, to get him scared enough that he'd call whoever this Blackwell was. Assuming they were still using the burners, I could pinpoint his boss's location. Better yet, I'd scare Nolan enough that Blackwell would want to meet in person. Of course, that introduced the additional complication of my being comically broke. This time of night, I could burn a lot of gas just sitting in traffic. LA had a light-rail system, and there was a line that could get me from Santa Monica to downtown in about forty-five minutes, but that wouldn't be much help if Nolan decided to bolt and he had a car. I pulled up the Metro map on my phone. The blue line would take me to within three blocks of BlackICE.

Good enough.

I made one last attempt at Ortega.

This time, he answered.

"Hey—I've been trying to get you for hours. I know—"

"Gage. Stop talking. You're in deep shit, man. There is a warrant out for your arrest."

"What the f—"

"They got you on camera at Matthews's house. We thought the killer might go back and clean up, so we put some hidden cameras in. We got you sneaking around, looking through his shit. The complex manager called us as soon as you left with that bullshit story. The department is convinced you offed him, or you at least are covering up for whoever did. They're coming to arrest you now." He let that sink in. After some dead seconds, Ortega said, "I don't think that's true, which is the only reason I'm telling you this much. Someone is coming for you."

We agreed on that much at least. Ortega also admitted they thought Matthews was murdered. Previously, he'd only said it was a possibility.

"Okay, I admit I went into Matthews's house."

"You don't have to admit it. We got you on camera."

"Whatever. I bluffed my way in there, and I found a burner phone."

"Which is tampering with evidence in a crime scene. Congratulations, you just fucked the case. You putting a hand on that thing means we can't touch it. That's bad enough, now if you actually *took* the goddamn thing, which I know you're not dumb enough to do, then that would be a felony, and you'd lose your PI license."

There wasn't a lot of time. I needed to get mobile if these guys were indeed coming for me. If this was true, the only reason I wasn't in custody now was that I lived outside OCSD's jurisdiction and they needed to coordinate with Santa Monica PD or LA Sheriff's Department first.

"I traced the phone—"

"Do not say another word to me about anything you did or didn't do with that phone."

"Then consider this an anonymous tip. I can connect Grant Matthews with a hacker who goes by the alias Ghost. Matthews covered his tracks well, but not perfectly. I've got communication fragments of the two of them on some dark web chat rooms. Ghost's real name is Asher Nolan. He runs a cybersecurity company in LA called BlackICE Defense. He's got a side hustle of hacking big clients as Ghost and then getting his firm hired to fix the problems he caused. I can connect him with that guy I told you about who's pretending to be a Department of Commerce agent." Someone reading off the lawyer words at the end of a drug commercial hadn't spoken as fast as I did just now. I hoped Ortega caught it all. "You can run with this."

"No, Matt, I can't."

"What? Why not? Nolan will prove they paid Matthews, and he'll lead you at least to Blackwell."

"It's not my case. They moved me off."

"What? Why?"

"They didn't like my theory that there might be a connection between Kyle Haney and Grant Matthews," he said dully.

Oh. And I'd given him that lead, and I was now tainted.

I started to speak, and Ortega cut me off. "Shut up and let me think a minute." While he was thinking, I walked over to my window and peeked through the blinds just to make sure there wasn't a caravan of cops rolling in on me. "Gage, this is what I'm willing to do. The detective they reassigned the Matthews case to, he's a friend. We're meeting tomorrow for handoff. Send me what you've got, and I'll figure out how to give it to him. He's also been told to wrap this up quick."

I opened my laptop and pulled up EchoTrace. An angry red banner flared to life on my screen informing me in thirty-point font that my access was suspended.

Because there was a warrant out for my arrest.

Remember all that talk about how AI can do the work of dozens of investigators and lets you move way faster than you could alone? Turns out that can work against you.

"You still there?" Ortega said, barking at my silence.

I just stared at that blazing banner.

"Yeah," I said, trying not to sound as defeated as I felt. "I use an investigative tool called EchoTrace."

"I know it. Department won't spring for it, but I know what it is."

"That's got all of my information on Asher Nolan, and now I'm locked out. Because of the warrant."

"Man, someone really has it out for your ass," Ortega said. This guy was a street cop to his bones, and despite my mood, there was something about his growling bluntness that I appreciated. "It can't be a coincidence that I got pushed onto some bullshit detail and my case reassigned, then this happens to you. I gotta talk to my captain and figure some things out. You need to stay low. Don't be home, got me?" I could hear him banging away at a keyboard. "Oh shit."

It's rarely good news when anyone says that.

It's usually the worst news when a cop says it.

"What?"

"Remember that SWAT lieutenant, Hennessy, that hauled you in the night of the shooting? He picked up the warrant service."

Fuck.

"Look, man, I've met contract hitters. I know that's not you. Hennessy, though, he's looking for a reason. He flexed on me in the hall yesterday, asked why I let you off."

"What the hell is his problem?"

"He's a good cop, just a hard-on. Lot of the SWAT dudes are cowboys. With him, though, he's got a bug up his ass over you. He thought you tried to kill that Holt woman and doesn't want to listen to shit else that'll convince him you didn't. He's a touch righteous."

"Thanks for the warning," I said, and I meant it.

"Do yourself a favor and stay mobile. And I did not say that. This conversation never happened. If it comes to subpoenaing phone records, I will say this call was to get you to turn yourself in. You got a lawyer?"

"Sort of."

"Call him. Don't assume you'll hear from me again. And for Christ's sake, don't call me."

"Thank you, Erik. I appreciate this."

"Just be careful. Someone wants your ass."

Ortega hung up.

I hadn't even told him about my bank account.

Asher Nolan and I were about to have an uncomfortable conversation. Before I did that, I had to sanitize my Defender. If OCSD thought I was a killer, finding a bunch of surveillance and disguise equipment on me would go a long way to convincing them they were right.

I brought everything into the house. I had a wall safe, though it wasn't big enough to hold the disguise kit or the long-range microphone that I'd used on Crowder. I hid those things in the garage. There was a concealed safe beneath the bed, which my landlord did not know about. That contained my emergency kit: five grand in cash—in both dollars and euros —a clean, untraceable pistol, and a few passports that I may have reported as "turned in" after an operation in my Agency days. It was a small space, designed to accommodate the two ballistic nylon pouches, but I managed to cram a few items from the truck into it.

The combat shotgun I kept in the Defender was also a problem. There was nowhere to hide it. It was legally purchased and licensed, so I placed it in the rack I'd built into my bedroom closet, next to the wall safe where I kept the Glock when it wasn't in the Defender. I secured the trigger lock. It'd have to do.

It took about thirty minutes to get everything stored in the house. I kept my ball cap, though. The one with the materials sewed into the lining to fuzz electronic surveillance. I put that on.

Before leaving, I grabbed five hundred dollars out of my emergency funds. Gas, food, and a hotel. I hated breaking into the reserve; that was supposed to be used if I needed to bug out. I made a mental note to replace it.

I got into the Defender, filled up at a Shell station, and pulled onto the 10, heading east.

Commuter physics are never in your favor in Los Angeles regardless of the direction you're going, and I was racing against several clocks.

Maybe countdown timers were more accurate.

There were several working against me.

The first was how long it would take the Orange County Sheriff to serve the warrant. I assumed there was an APB on me and that measured my time in hours. I needed to ditch the Defender. The problem was, in favor of what? Without a credit card, I couldn't easily rent a car. There were places that would rent one without—perfectly legitimate enterprises that catered to, shall we say, "privacy enthusiasts." The trade-off was it cost you twice what a typical rental would and you had to pay in cash.

Next was the clock of finding Nolan and his boss before they did something to Julian that couldn't be undone. Removing Crowder now appeared to be part of the plan. He was the one obstacle preventing one of the other three from taking over—assuming it was one of them. I wasn't sure now. Hawthorne and Graves were both ruthless in their own right, but they wouldn't countenance a murder. My train of thought froze. If Kessler and Wexler fully realized their vision, this would fundamentally change how humans interacted with technology. You couldn't measure that impact in mere dollars. Would someone kill for that?

Probably, they would.

Back to that calculus of justifying terrible things for the "greater good." That kind of thinking was exactly how evil got the edges rounded off.

If it wasn't one of them, finding the real mastermind was going to be a problem.

While I was driving, I called Benjamin Blake.

"There he is," Blake said. The background noise told me he was at dinner.

"Ben, I'm sorry to bother you, it sounds like you're out."

"I can take a minute. What's up?" The tone in his voice changed.

"Have you spoken with Julian yet?"

"Do you mean about Crowder? If that's what you mean, then yes. Who do you think replaced Crowder on the board?"

"The person that's trying to take NOVA AI tried to kill me the other night."

"What?"

"I don't have time to get into it now, but they've hired some heavy people to make this happen," I said.

Crowder out, Benjamin Blake in. What did that tell me?

I continued. "You probably knew they had a top-tier hacker in the group. He's the one who took over NOVA during Julian's media demo last week. They've just turned their sights on me, hacked into my bank account and my credit card. Cleaned me out."

"Jesus Christ, are you serious?" Blake said. It was quieter around him now, he'd moved somewhere he could talk. It's hard to gauge sentiment over the phone, someone can fake concern easier than they can hide a subconscious tell. Still, he sounded genuine.

"That's what I know about. It's possible that there's more," I said.

"How can I help, Matt?" Blake asked.

In a manner of speaking, I'd gotten Blake his board seat back. That meant he was either in on it, or the person behind it didn't think he was a threat. There was a third option, I supposed, which was that they hadn't intended for the seat to be filled, and this was a surprise move. In which case Blake was also now at risk. As were some combination of the others.

"It gets worse. Remember after Julian's demo, I told you a disgruntled ex-employee sold a back door to whoever hacked it?"

"He was killed in a car accident," Blake said.

"Right. Orange County Sheriff isn't so sure it was an accident. Thing is, there was a similar situation with a guy that worked for Nathaniel Crowder about a year ago. Similar enough that I told the detective about it, and I think Crowder may have been questioned."

"Is he threatening you or something?" Blake asked, sounding genuinely confused.

"Not directly. But there's a warrant for my arrest, and the detective who had the case had just been reassigned. The sheriff is an elected position. I don't know that Crowder called in a favor. I also don't know that he didn't." This murder frame came together quickly, and it seemed like a stretch that Crowder could pull this off, even with his influence. Still, I reasoned that Blake was looking for some payback, and this might just be the thing to motivate him to do what I needed. And if he balked, that'd push him into the top position of suspects.

"My attorney is out of the country. His firm gave me the number of someone to call, but I'm not so sure. I was wondering if you still had that lawyer you sicced on me."

Blake gave a dry chuckle. "Arty McWhorter. Yes, he's still my attorney. He's not a criminal defense lawyer, but he'll have people. And I'm happy to help."

"Thank you," I said.

"No problem. Let me make some phone calls. And Matt?"

"Yeah."

"Be safe."

The sun had nose-dived into the horizon about an hour and a half ago, leaving only the darkening afterglow in the skies. That red to purple filled my rearview as I neared downtown. My next call went to Vanessa Holt and, again, she didn't pick up.

"Someone tried to kill us both. They voice-cloned me to get you there and did the same with your voice to draw me out. I have information for you. Please call me."

Hopefully, she read the voicemail transcription.

I spotted an LAPD ride as I was nearing the city, so I took the first exit, which was the Santa Monica and Harbor Freeway interchange. This dropped me in the southwest corner of LA proper and about fifteen blocks from where I needed to be.

The opposition had put a large team in the field against us, and they appeared to be A-players. I wasn't going to last long without some help of my own. Once I'd found a spot to park down the street from BlackICE Defense, where I could observe, I called Nash.

"Brody, it's Matt."

"Hey, man," he said, tone noncommittal.

"I could use your help with something. You want to do something to protect your boss?"

A pause, then, "Depends on what it is."

"When you were with the teams, you did surveillance, right? Sometimes sniper spotting, stuff like that?"

"Yes, but if you think—"

"We're not shooting anyone," I said. *Yet.*

"Is this the part where you tell me Julian is in danger?" There was more than a hint of sarcasm in Nash's voice, since I'd already pulled that particular lever.

"I found one of the people that called the SWAT team in on me. They tried to come at me again today, so this thing isn't over. Will you help?"

"Guess I will."

"Then I'll fill you in as soon as you get here."

"Just tell me where and when."

"Downtown LA, and as soon as you can."

27

Nolan's building was on the corner of Fourth Street and Broadway. It was early and the streets were full. We weren't far from the arena, or the Disney Music Hall. Crowds also meant there were a lot of cops. Which, admittedly, I didn't love. As the homelessness epidemic got worse, crime increased at a commensurate rate, and the police responded. Downtown was their turf. I was only a few blocks from the LAPD headquarters, too. When police roamed in their vehicles, they used an automated license plate scanner to check if any cars they encountered were associated with a want or a warrant, or if the vehicle was stolen. Now that there was a warrant for my arrest, my license plate would flare out on their computer screen like an oil rig on fire.

So there's that.

I didn't want to wait on Brody, but part of his being here was backup in case Nolan decided to rabbit. I parked around the corner at a metered spot on Grand and posted outside a barbeque restaurant on the opposite corner from Nolan's place. The ground floor was a bodega and a cocktail bar, the second floor was registered to BlackICE, but Nolan also used that as his home address.

There was a steady flow of traffic into the cocktail bar, well-off people who wanted to seem edgy by drinking in a transitioning neighborhood.

The bar was called Revelation. The bodega stayed open until nine, and I'd watched the owner go through his closing routine. No sign of Nolan, but there were lights on in his windows. The building occupied the corner lot and was painted gray, with a dark accent line between the first and second floors that followed the windows and doors. The corner rounded, giving it an almost art deco appearance. The skyline of the reimagined, rebuilt downtown loomed directly above, a sharp contrast of brightly lit modern architecture just a few blocks in the background as if to say, "We're coming." I couldn't immediately see where the entry to Nolan's part of the building was, but the address for his business read Fourth Street. It was probably tucked into an alcove.

Since I had time before Nash arrived, I did a loop around the block so that I could identify all the exits. I spotted the sign for BlackICE on Fourth, a small dark plaque that I had to lean in to read. On the building's far side, which it shared with a parking lot–sized EV charging station, I found several vehicles parked in spaces that threatened towing. They all looked like the kind of cars that you'd leave in downtown LA at night, so probably not Nolan's. I did not bother with the narrow, unlit alley between the buildings.

Nash arrived at nine fifteen. We met on the far corner of Broadway and Fourth. I said a silent prayer of gratitude that he'd shown up in street clothes and not the tactical wardrobe I assumed occupied half of his closet.

"What do you need me to do?"

"I'm going in to question him." I pointed out where the recessed doorway was. "This guy is a hacker and con artist. I don't expect things to get physical. What I'm going to need you for is keeping an eye on him for a few days. But be visible about it. I want him to know I'm not working alone and that we've figured out who and what he is. I want him rattled enough that he contacts his boss for help."

Nash's expression changed immediately. "I don't know, man. I got work."

"I'll tell Julian you're helping me."

"I got out of the Navy so I didn't have to crouch in shitty neighborhoods watching for assholes in run-down buildings anymore," he said. I laughed. Nash would do all right.

"Let's hope it doesn't come to that. I want the threat of it to be enough. Be on the corner where I can see you."

"Roger that."

I clapped Nash on the shoulder and walked over to BlackICE's door. The alcove was well lit, and I spotted the black bulb of a surveillance camera. I pressed the intercom button, keeping my head low and the ball cap's brim shielding my face from the camera. It should scramble the image, but I didn't want to take any chances.

"We're closed," a tinny voice said through the intercom. "You can make an appointment through the website."

"This is Dean, I'm the manager at Revelation. I need to speak to a Mr. Nolan. Owner sent me."

"What?"

"Something about the fire code. Said you knew."

"I don't know anything about it," the voice snapped. So, confirmed that Nolan was home. "Tell him I'll talk to him in the morning."

"Can't dude, sorry. City fire inspector is, like, here. We gotta talk now."

"Hold on."

There were a lot of things that a landlord could put off until tomorrow. Meeting with a city fire inspector wasn't one of them.

About a minute later, the door opened. Nolan's eyes flared with recognition when he saw me.

"Surprise, dickhead," I said. To my amazement, I didn't break his nose.

Nolan didn't fill the air with stupid questions like *What was I doing there* or *How did I find him?* He waited for me to speak. He was about my height and put in some heavy hours in the gym. I could tell from the way he moved that he didn't know how to handle himself. These were vanity muscles, prizing size and definition over function. All the muscles in the world won't do you any good in a fight if you don't know how to throw a punch.

"You're in a lot of trouble, Asher. You can help yourself by helping me."

He folded his arms across his chest and flexed for show, a move he'd likely practiced enough to appear nonchalant. I put Nolan in his late thirties. He was early bald, head stubble and the two days' growth on his face were about the same level, creating this kind of elliptical orbit of lazy grooming around his face. Bug eyes sized me up, and his skin was the archetypal sallow, spoiled-milk color of one who spent too many hours in front of a computer screen.

When he still didn't say anything, I wondered if maybe the guy was deaf.

"Okay," I said. "Does that camera also have audio?" I gave a slight nod toward it, without looking up and exposing my face. "Because I'm going to say a few things you probably don't want recorded. Things that have to do with some of your extracurricular activities. Things that might connect you with—"

Nolan pulled the door closed behind him and shouldered past me onto the sidewalk. I let him pass.

He'd stepped out of view of the camera. Music from the bar poured out onto the street, it was this electric jazz, but with a hip-hop backbeat. There's a name for it but I don't care to know it.

"Talk," Nolan said. He turned to face me. I was looking up the block now and clocked Brody Nash on the far corner.

"I know you hacked Julian Kessler's demo and that you used a back door a software engineer named Grant Matthews gave you access to. I know you communicated with Matthews on a Nokia 105 cell phone. And I know that you, or your boss, paid Matthews fifty thousand for the job."

"That's a funny story. What a wild imagination you must have," Nolan said.

I went for my phone and he jolted.

"Relax," I said. I accessed the screenshot I'd taken of the link analysis and held it up so he could see. "That's the phone tracing Matthews to you. I mean, I suppose someone at the bar here could've done it." I offered a comical shrug for effect. "I can connect at least one of Ghost's ransomware attacks with your business." He stared at me, unblinking, unspeaking. If it weren't for the slight lift in his shoulders to show he was breathing, I'd think he'd gone catatonic. "Your client, GBS Financial, sued their insurance company for not covering the ransomware attack. The report you gave them stated an 'attack signature of a known cybercriminal using the alias Ghost.'" I spelled it for him. Again, outside of his eyes flaring slightly, there wasn't much of a reaction.

Nolan was the type who got careless because he was arrogant. He didn't think anyone was good enough to catch him. Over time, caution eroded to complacency. He probably used his alias in the attacks he perpetrated against prospective clients in order to raise his cred in hacker circles, or to make Ghost more of a threat. Which meant BlackICE Defense could charge more cleaning up his messes. It wouldn't be a card Nolan could play often, but when he did, I'd bet it landed him a sizable paycheck.

"What are you hoping to get out of this conversation?" Nolan said with minimal inflection. Now he was fishing.

"You owe me a lot of money. I came here to tell you that draining my bank account isn't going to scare me off. My client has deep pockets. So does the State of California."

A cocky, self-satisfied smile painted his face, and it all but assured me of his guilt. And his feeling of invincibility. Time to pop that bubble.

"People are going to get hurt before this is over, Nolan. Maybe you don't care about that, but one man is already dead, and that will have consequences. You're looking at serious time for hacking NOVA and even more for my bank, because money is involved. That's on top of what the feds will hit Ghost up for." Those bug eyes bulged at the mention of his handle. Watching an asshole like this fully grasp the riptide just yanked them out to sea was fun. "Grant Matthews died right after he told me you lot paid him off. You're not going to beat an accessory to murder rap. And if the police find out you were the one who swatted me, there's a whole other shitstorm of trouble that puts you in."

"You can't prove anything."

"I already have. The question you need to be asking yourself is, who have I told?" I gave Nolan a second to let this sink in. "Let me tell you how this is going to play out, Asher. You're going to give me a name and a phone number. If you do that, I will leave and you'll never hear from me again." I motioned casually to the end of the block and nodded. "I have an associate there. Take a look." Nolan did. "My man is going to stay here for a while. Once I've decided he can go, he'll leave. Until then, he will follow you wherever you go."

"Do you have any idea what I could do to you? I can end your life by the time you get to your car, asshole."

"You may want to rethink that. You've certainly heard the phrase 'the most dangerous man is the one who doesn't have anything to lose'? Your best hope at staying on two feet, Asher, is to make sure I still have something to lose." I gave him a beat, then set the hook. "Your only real option is this. Tell me what I want to know, or I give that link analysis I showed you to my contacts at LAPD, the DA's cybercrime unit, and the FBI. From there, it'll be a fun game to see who nails you to the wall first. If you try to run, my friend there will follow you. And if you try any more shit with me, or anyone connected to me, *he* comes down on you like the asteroid that wiped out the dinosaurs. He's an ex-SEAL, so you decide how far you want to play this one out. And I mean it about leaving me alone. I'm assuming you're going to put the money back in my bank account and unfuck my credit card, along with anything else you've done. Because, and I swear this to almighty God, Asher, if you try *anything*, I will come for you. I made a career in the CIA of taking down people that would make you piss your sheets. And my pal over there? He's the type that we'd just drop into a terror cell and order to just do maximum violence." I stared Asher Nolan down.

I doubted this guy had ever been confronted in person. At least, not since he'd taken up this life. Nolan was an apex predator in his environment, and was just figuring out that he was in a totally different zoo now.

To my great surprise and disappointment, Asher Nolan told me to go to hell.

"Well, that's certainly a choice," I said. "I'll give you the night to think it over. You already know how to get ahold of me." I stepped forward, closing the distance between us, and pushed Nolan out of my way with a hard shoulder. I stopped, half turned, and said, "This is coming. I've already filed a police report about the bank theft, so that ball is in motion. They'll ask me if I know anyone who'd want to do me harm and, being the good citizen that I am, I'll have to share what I know. This kind of crime goes federal almost immediately. The smartest thing you can do for yourself is to help me now. It's your best chance to stay out of prison, pretty much forever. The worst thing you can do is come at me."

I turned and walked up the street.

I could feel Nolan's eyes on my back as I walked to meet Nash. I did not look back.

Everything rested on Nolan coming to his senses and calling me to make a deal. That had to happen before the Orange County Sheriff's Department caught up with me.

One more clock to manage.

"He's still watching," Nash said when I reached him. "How long we going to stand here?"

"Long enough to make it awkward for him," I said. "You know, the entire time I talked to him, I'm not sure he blinked even once. He's weird."

"How long you want me here, I mean, like tonight?"

"If he's going to run, he's going to do it within the next hour."

Nash nodded. "Is this, you know, legal?"

"Anyone asks, you're conducting lawful surveillance of a suspected criminal. You are subcontracted to a licensed private investigator."

Nash nodded again. "So, this is the guy who hacked Julian's demo, huh?"

"He is," I said.

"Caused a lot of problems, that." A dark look passed over Nash's face.

"Brody, don't do anything. Just watch him. This is important."

"I know," he said.

It occurred to me that in his role, Brody Nash probably had enough shares in NOVA AI that he'd never have to work again. Nolan had threatened that, put it at risk.

I hoped I hadn't made a mistake bringing him in on this.

"Give it an hour."

"I'll stay."

"He moves, you call me. Only communicate on Signal, never in the clear."

"Roger that," Nash said in an operator's monotone.

28

I drove south.

Bracing Nolan hadn't gotten me what I'd wanted, and now I needed to regroup. Given what I'd learned about him, I thought I could coerce him into rolling on his boss. He didn't. That told me he wasn't afraid of the police, or was more afraid of his employer than he was of the law. Neither of those were good. Or maybe he knew what I knew, which was that in taking the burner from Matthews's townhouse, I'd tainted the evidence. It couldn't be used in court now. Even the bank would be hard to connect back to him.

I needed to stay moving, find a safe place to crash for the night.

My house was out, and so was the hotel in Costa Mesa.

Heading back to Orange County was risky, almost stupidly so. But that was where the information was and, I suspected, the man who hired Asher Nolan.

First, I needed to sleep.

I'd stuck to residential streets leaving downtown and then picked up the 405 south, exiting in Seal Beach. I took that to PCH and drove along the coast, looking for a dive motel. The kind of place that catered to tourists and would take cash. It hit me motels like that hadn't been on this stretch of road in close to thirty years, and if I'd really wanted to stay in a pit like that, a Motel 6 with bars on the windows along I-10 eastbound would be my best bet. That was also the wrong direction.

I found a place that looked promising and the lights were on. I parked and checked them out. The Surfside Inn was on PCH, just over the line to Huntington Beach. According to their website, people came from all over the world to surf here, and the Surfside Inn existed to serve them. You could tell from the site that they'd take in tourists if they had room, but made it clear who their preferred clientele was. Given that, I reasoned that this place likely had taken all kinds of payments, brah.

The guy behind the desk was about thirty, and this was the only time of day he spent inside, other than sleeping. I gave him a story about my credit card being stolen, which he bought, and asked for a room and could I pay cash. When he looked at my driver's license, he said, "Santa Monica. Why don't you just go home, dude?"

"Renovations," I said, though that might have been in another language.

"There's a great hang up there. It's called Cosmic Ray's. Dude who owns it is a legend." He said the latter like it was two words.

"I'll have to check it out," I said.

The dude handed me a key card and told me how to find the room. All of them faced the beach.

I keep a go bag in the Defender because cases often have me away from home or might require spur-of-the-moment travel. Or, prevent me from using my home base because of an arrest warrant for a murder I didn't commit. It was one of the few things I didn't clean out. It was just a few days' change of clothes, toiletries, and backup batteries to charge devices, nothing that a cop would find out of the ordinary.

Anyway, I grabbed that and headed up to my room on the weather-beaten wooden stairs. It was a clear, cloudless night, and a thick moon cast an unworldly glow over everything.

I dropped my bag on a chair, stripped, and crawled into bed. I had one text from Nash saying that Asher Nolan hadn't moved. I assumed that meant he hadn't left his apartment, not that he was still standing on the street staring at Nash. Though after today, I supposed anything was possible.

Exhausted as I was, sleep did not come easy, or fast.

Eventually it found me, because when I opened my eyes, the room was bathed in gray light. I checked my watch, it was barely six. I'd gotten maybe four hours. It would have to do. I had the room until ten, so I had that long to plan.

A quick check on my phone showed a coffee shop a couple blocks up PCH. I showered, dressed, and walked there. The morning cold slapped me awake. I grabbed a coffee and a walking breakfast and went back to the motel. Early morning traffic rolled by, and waves crashed beyond the highway.

I considered my situation and my ever-withering set of options. I didn't like what I saw.

Back in my room, I powered up my laptop and opened a mind-mapping app. I'd have to re-create my suspect board from memory since I couldn't even log into EchoTrace right now.

I started with a circle in the middle and wrote "MARK BLACKWELL." I drew a link beneath it and added "ASHER NOLAN." I drew a second link under Blackwell and added "SWAT shooter???" Blackwell wouldn't do that himself, and there was no way Nolan knew his way around a gun. The sheriff's department helicopter's infrared camera wasn't working that night, so they'd relied on the spotlight, but couldn't get directly overhead because of the power lines. By the time the SWAT team got to me, the shooter was already gone. I drew another line from Blackwell, this one going up, to another circle where I wrote "BOARD MBR?"

The mind map was an exercise to get my subconscious thinking about pattern matching. The kind of thing EchoTrace used to do for me automatically.

My phone buzzed and I looked down. It was Mickey asking if I was awake.

I called him on Signal. I explained the situation, the connection between Ghost and Asher Nolan, and what Nolan did.

"What do you want me to do?" Mickey asked.

"Burn him to bare metal," I said.

"Say no more."

I tried Vanessa Holt one last time. It was close to seven now. Straight to voicemail. "Listen, Holt, please call me back. After Matthews died, you called me to tell me that you thought Crowder might have been connected to your friend Kyle Haney's death. You obviously felt that was something I should know—" I stopped.

Holt never called me with that tip.

It was so perfectly, shatteringly clear now.

They'd gotten a sample of her voice, cloned it, and called me with that information. That's what set me on Crowder's trail. It was all a setup to get Crowder off the board and give me an incredibly dangerous new enemy.

I hung up.

I messaged Nash in Signal to see if he'd learned anything overnight. He wrote back saying he'd gotten a few hours of sleep at the Westin down the street, once the second-floor lights went off. Nash said he was back in front of Nolan's by 0500. Been there ever since. There was no movement. I said to use his best judgment, but he should get home soon and get some decent rack time. He rogered again.

My next call went to Bo Fochs, the retired PI that I knew from Cosmic Ray's. Bo was one of the Dawn Patrol, the veteran surfers that rode out just as the sun was breaking over the water, so I knew he'd be awake for the call. They'd surf until the waves died and usually paddled into Ray's for coffee and breakfast burritos. Luckily, for once, it seemed, I caught him before he locked up his phone and paddled out. I asked Bo if he could recommend a good criminal defense attorney, someone he trusted. He told me he did, said he'd worked with her for years and gave me her contact information.

Her name was Vivian Vaughn, and her practice was in West Hollywood.

I ticked away the hours until it was okay to call.

"This is Vivian," she said. She'd picked up almost immediately.

"Ms. Vaughn, my name is Matt Gage."

She chuckled knowingly into the phone. "You're Bo's friend. He just texted me to expect your call."

"What's so funny?"

"His exact words were, 'you're in deep shit and you need a snorkel.' Don't worry, I practically made a career of getting him out of trouble. Most of which he made for himself." I liked her already. "I have a full client load right now, but as a favor to Bo, I'll take you on. Can you come in today? I've got lunch free. I'm in Hollywood."

"Ahh, so here's the thing. I'm in the middle of a case. I can give you the details later, but my client is Julian Kessler. Someone is trying to force him out of his company, NOVA AI. They've got a fixer working for them who framed me for a murder, and there is now a warrant for my arrest in Orange County."

"Got it. So you're going to need something a little more than the standard pamper package."

Finally, someone I could work with.

"Where are you now?"

"I'm in Huntington Beach, crashed at a motel. Oh, and these same assholes hacked into my back account and tanked my credit card. Don't worry, I can pay you. Just that the idea is to drain my resources so I'll fold."

"That's just mean-spirited," she said flatly. Vivian paused while she thought.

I quickly ran through the situation with the Orange County Sheriff, the SWAT team, and this Lieutenant Hennessy who clearly had it out for me. I was in such a bad mood, I couldn't even laugh at the bad irony of how much "had it out for me" sounded like the cop's name.

"Here's what I'll do. We need a police report for the bank stuff."

"I called Santa Monica PD. They haven't gotten back to me yet."

"Ugh. Okay. I'll get someone on that. Next up, stay moving. Normally, I'd say your best bet is to turn yourself in, but even to me, this feels like a setup."

"There's one more thing."

"There always seems to be. You really are like Bo," she said.

"Right. So, one of the people trying to buy Kessler's company was Nathaniel Crowder. He's—"

"I know him, or of him. He's the Larry Ellison of lethal drones. And an asshole."

"You have no idea. Anyway, long story I'll fill you in on later, but I kind of got him kicked off the board of directors. I think this shit with the arrest warrant might be him leaning on the sheriff."

"I'll look into it," she said. "Stay mobile. You'll hear from me. If you get arrested, give them my phone number and don't say anything."

My phone rang, breaking me out of the flow. And by "flow" I meant nervous pacing across the motel room because I couldn't do anything else.

I picked up the phone.

"Hello, Mr. Gage." The voice was as smooth as a frozen lake and just as cold. It was Mark Blackwell.

"I'd say good morning, Mark, but that's not your name, is it."

"No."

"I don't like talking to an alias I know is bullshit. How about you tell me your name?"

"I don't think so."

It was worth a shot.

"I'm glad this is fun for you. You murdered Grant Matthews."

"I haven't killed anyone."

"I'm sure the police will see it that way."

"That's why I'm calling. I appreciate you getting to the point. I've heard you don't mince words."

"That right? What else have you heard about me? How about my atomically short fuse?"

"Oh, that's well documented," he said. "Associates of mine from the Agency have shared your reputation. It's a bit checkered. Nicaragua was interesting. Your work against the Russian intelligence service last year was inspired." His voice warmed up at that one, and if I didn't know better, I'd say the praise was genuine. "I hope they didn't do any permanent damage."

Jesus, this guy was connected. Nicaragua was a reference to my last job at CIA, the one that got me fired. This guy had serious traction. The Nicaragua story was highly classified, though it was well known within Agency circles. I was eventually exonerated, though too late to save my job, and there were still some people in ops that thought I'd been reckless—accurate—or incompetent—unfair. And not accurate.

"Okay, I'll give you a point for that." Denying it would just make me look naive. "Now, what do you want?"

"My client wants this situation to come to a swift and resolute conclusion. Julian Kessler is a dead man walking." He paused just long enough for the thought to plug into my brain. "So to speak. Defrauding investors, lying to the media, abusing family members, stealing intellectual property." He spoke like he was reciting a section of the newspaper rather than sharing his plot to destroy Julian.

"You know all of that is bullshit. At best it's manipulated, and at worst, entirely fabricated."

"The truth is highly subjective, Matt. You of all people should know that."

"Fine. Your client is trying to illegally take over this company. What do they want for it?"

"My client hasn't broken any laws. And neither have I," he said. The accent was strange, and I couldn't immediately place it. It was similar enough to the way he spoke as Mark Blackwell, Commerce agent, that I hadn't picked it up right away; still, the difference was there. Could be he was running it through a modulator, or some other tool to throw me off. I couldn't record the call without him knowing, so I didn't bother, though I really wanted to run this through EchoTrace when I got it back.

Then I remembered I couldn't.

"Right," I said. "What is your client offering? That's what this call is about, I take it. You're here to make an offer for this all to go away in exchange for Julian stepping down?"

"Stepping down *quietly*. He's going to go, it's just a matter of whether he wants to take the company down with him. He could still have a place in NOVA's legacy."

This was a bullshit offer.

"You won't tell me who your client is now, but I'll find out when this is over. And then Julian drops a massive lawsuit on them. So do I, for that matter. Then the authorities get involved, and they come for you. So do I."

That got a chuckle. It sounded brittle and forced, like it lacked practice.

"I suspect he won't. If you can convince Julian to announce his departure, today, I'm willing to reinstate your bank account, your credit, your identity, and the few other little land mines I'd laid."

"Giving me back what you stole from me is your idea of a carrot? And how is it you haven't broken any laws again?"

Julian would never agree to this. And he shouldn't. It was blatant extortion, not to mention the two men who were dead and the two others, me and Vanessa Holt, who could've been.

Why make the offer if it would never go anywhere?

Why call me at all?

To get me on the phone.

This guy was good. He possessed solid tradecraft and the same kinds of tools that I had. Perhaps even more questionable ones given Asher Nolan. If I could trace their phones, they could do it to me. They'd already sent a police raid to my location under false gun charges. No reason to believe they wouldn't try that move twice. They also had someone on their side that wasn't afraid to pull a trigger.

This Blackwell wouldn't do it himself. He'd operate through agents. His actions already suggested that, but everything about our interactions softly whispered the spiderlike manipulation of strands in a web. He was operating more like a consigliere, or an intelligence officer.

I took the phone off my ear and texted Detective Ortega.

How fast can you get to Huntington?

"Are you still there, Matt? I hope you aren't doing something foolish like...texting that friend in the police department. Because I'd know."

A bluff. Mickey cleaned my phone, and if he really knew, he'd have said "sheriff's department." It was the logical guess, but still unnerving.

As a rule, I didn't unpack when I stayed in a hotel because I often found myself in situations where I needed to leave quickly. I folded up my laptop, dropped it in the backpack, grabbed my bag, and made a fast look around the place to make sure it was clean. "Oh, I'm still here. So, you're offering to give back the money you stole and whatever else you did, if I convince Julian to abdicate the throne. That's what this is?" I raced out the door, making fast steps to the parking lot.

"Exactly," he said. I could already tell from his personality that he liked pulling the strings. Forcing me into a rat trap would be as much fun for him as delivering the outcome his client wanted. I didn't know how long I had. At a minimum, they'd have the closest cell tower.

"It's a generous offer," I said, as seriously as I could. "Tell you what, why don't we meet over a beer and talk it out?"

"Tell me, if everything is a joke to you, how are you going to react when you find out the punch line is a bullet?"

"Oh, that's a good line. Can I use that?"

Interesting, this was the first overt threat he'd made. It struck me, because until that moment, Blackwell—or whoever he was—claimed that he hadn't broken any laws, as if he was stating it for the record.

"Matt, you aren't taking me seriously. That is a mistake. I'll make sure that when Julian Kessler is looking at the ruin of his life, he'll know you thought it was a joke."

I made it to the Defender, got in, and started it up. Most modern smartphones canceled out background noise, though I wasn't sure if it could filter out something like a vehicle door closing or an up-tuned mid-1990s SUV engine growling to life. He didn't say anything in reaction to it, though. Could be he didn't want to tip me off that he'd heard.

I plugged my phone into the adapter—I don't connect anything via Bluetooth—and the call transferred to the Defender's speakers. I pulled out of the parking lot and headed north on Eighth Street.

My phone beeped, and I looked down to see Ortega was calling. No choice but to send it to voicemail.

"Blackwell, it's a bullshit offer, and we both know it. You won't reveal who your client is, which Julian would demand to know. And you aren't promising anything other than a 'soft landing,' which you also aren't detailing or guaranteeing. You've given me nothing to take back to him. And anyway, all this secrecy ends as soon as you get to endgame. Your client *has* to reveal themselves."

Except that they didn't. Now I got it. It was entirely possible that our phantom interlocutor was going to appoint a patsy, someone to run the dance to the steps they called. That subterfuge wouldn't last forever, but it'd last long enough.

I still believed this guy didn't want to kill me. Not unless I forced it. He wanted to discredit me, pay me off, or make me want to quit. I'd already made enough noise that if I turned up dead, heat would come in so hard and so fast there would be no way to hide that this had always been a take-over plot.

I'll give him this. He was a hell of a card player.

"I wonder how many lawsuits you'll survive when both your client and the state discover the evidence you'd collected was illegally obtained. You've committed a felony. How much longer do you think you'll be a PI? You might want to reconsider my offer. You *are* falling, Matt. The difference is will you have a parachute...or bounce off the concrete."

"Let's talk about the police, shall we? LAPD's computer crimes unit is super interested in how a hacker who goes by Ghost—that's *G-H-Zero-S-T* —could launch a ransomware attack on an investment bank downtown, and then it gets cleaned up by Asher Nolan's company. They're also interested to know why this Ghost was talking to Grant Matthews. That is, right up until Matthews was killed. After *someone* paid him fifty thousand to give Ghost—who, again, is Asher Nolan—a back door into NOVA AI. With me so far?"

That short-circuited him a beat.

I couldn't keep this going much longer. I kept him on the phone to see if I could figure out how they were tracking me. They hadn't bugged the Defender. I'd checked daily for that. Mickey assured me the phone was clean. My working theory was they'd hacked the cell towers. So, I cut a crisscross pattern with random double backs across as many coverage zones as I could. I also watched for tails. Hopefully, Ortega had gotten off his ass and was heading this way.

"Asher Nolan is more expendable than you," he said in dull monotone.

Christ. Don't sign me up for his team.

"This is your last chance, Matt. More to the point, it's Kessler's."

"If you've done *any* amount of backgrounding on me, you'd know there is precisely zero evidence I'd sell out my client. Jesus, do you know how many punches to the face I could've traded in? You—"

The line went dead.

His constant use of my first name implied a familiarity, a broken barrier of anonymity. It creeped me out.

I kept working my way north, cutting a stair-step pattern by driving two blocks west, then one north. At random intervals, I'd switch it to heading east and vary the two-block rule. It was a classic surveillance detection technique. I did not find anyone tailing me yet.

I called Ortega back, and turned right onto Talbert, looking for a place to park. I spotted a Walmart parking lot on the right, and pulled in. This was a good spot, lots of other cars and a lot of motion, easy for me to blend in. As soon as I was off with Ortega, I'd find an observation post, maybe near the store, and watch for a vehicle trolling.

"What the hell, man?" Ortega bellowed.

"They're following me. The ones who set me up."

"What? Who? How do you know that?"

"Because the guy just called me with some bullshit offer to make all this go away. Give back the money they drained out of my bank account. It was stalling. I think they were tracking me through cell phone towers. I'm driving around now, just making myself a target. If I stop somewhere, can you get here? Arrest them?"

"On what charge on this thing that isn't my case anymore?" Ortega was pissed at the question. He also wasn't wrong.

"Start with hacking into my bank account."

"Hacking your what?"

That's right. I hadn't told him. "Asher Nolan, the hacker I told you about, he drained my bank account and maxed out my credit card. You said you've got one of the best cybercrime squads in the country. Go after that. Or suspicion of murder for killing Grant Matthews."

"There's a warrant for that on you, asshole." Ortega caught himself. "Matt, I'm sorry. I know you didn't do it, but there is nothing I can do. It's not my case anymore." I tried to protest, he cut me off. "Look, I think you're a good dude, trying to do the right thing. But if I get caught trying to help you, it's my job. The best thing for you to do right now is lawyer up. I'm sorry. Don't call me again."

Ortega hung up.

29

Getting the cops on my side was a long shot. Hell, just getting a fair shake seemed Sisyphean.

Now that I wasn't going to have police backup, waiting around for a hired killer to roll into a Walmart parking lot seemed less of a good idea.

I've said before that if you're doing an escape and evasion run from the police in your own country, something has gone horribly wrong.

The phone rang. Maybe Ortega had a change of heart and decided to play good cop.

Whatever fleeting hope I might've had drained away as I saw Amara Singh's name on the caller ID. I was just saying to myself, what this day needed was a fresh complication. She also didn't have a habit of calling me without reason.

"Amara, is everything all right?"

"I don't know. I came across something, a name. I don't know if it means anything, but I wanted to give it to you in case it did."

"A name," I prompted.

"His name is Denis Kwan. He owns a private equity firm called oX Capital. Kwan is an investor in the company."

"All right. Why is this name important?" I don't like being spoon-fed information. It was a psychological reaction people had when they were deciding in real time whether to reveal something. It was a common pattern with new assets. If you pushed them too hard, got frustrated, often they'd turtle and you'd learn nothing.

After a few moments of hesitation, Amara said, "I can't tell you how I know. It'll be too easy for it to get back to me. I think Kwan *could* be involved somehow. So, I'm just going to give you the name, and you can consider it a hunch or whatever."

"Amara, I can't go bothering some random person without evidence." Especially not while possibly dodging hit men.

"I know him. At least a little."

"You need to give me something to go on. There's already too many balls in the air for me to go catching strays. If I take my focus off my leads right now, Julian could get hurt." *And I don't know what side you're on.*

"Look, I heard part of a conversation with him. It sounded like they were trying to set Julian up. That's all I'm comfortable saying. Please tell me you'll try."

"And you won't tell me who the conversation is with because you're afraid of it getting back to you."

"I'll bet Grant Matthews would say the same. Not that we could ask him."

I had to give her that one.

Against my better judgment, I said I would look into it.

My nerves were frayed from running improvised escape and evasion routes from the police that stretched well into the afternoon. I needed a safe place to crash, and to sleep.

Julian phoned around five, and he was coming in hot.

"A cop just called and said you're wanted for killing Grant. What the fuck, Matt?"

So much for subtlety.

"Julian, we need to talk and do it now, but not on the phone."

"What? Why not?"

"Because someone could be listening, that's why."

"I'm not talking to you if you're a fugitive."

"It's a setup, Julian. I'll explain when I see you. The people who are doing this, they're getting ready to close the noose."

"Fine. Where?"

I just told you someone might be listening.

"Remember that place we got drinks? They made a good martini," I said.

"What? We—" The gears clicked, and he remembered the code we'd worked out. "I, ah, need to stop by the grocery store first. Nothing in the house."

Once they'd hacked the demo, I knew we were dealing with a top-tier adversary, and tapping a phone would be right in their wheelhouse. I just hadn't figured on that phone being mine. So, I'd worked out a code with Julian in case we needed to meet somewhere and had to do it over a compromised line. He wouldn't get any marks for selling it, but he did well enough.

We hung up, and I drove to the Home Depot.

There was a restaurant in the parking lot's upper left corner. I parked behind that, shielding myself from the street and giving a view of who came in. Julian called me thirty-five minutes after we'd spoken. "I'm here."

"Look to your left. Far side of the lot." I hung up. Julian eventually figured it out. I got out of the Defender and met my client. He looked ragged. Heavy bags under his eyes that already had a haunted look to them.

"Matt, I'm sure this isn't what you want to hear right now, but I have to let you go. Our attorney says that with this situation, I've got to cut you loose. He said I should even void the contract, but I don't want to do that to you. If you can tell me what I owe you..."

"I didn't have anything to do with Grant's death. I think this is Crowder looking for some payback for getting him kicked off the board." Can't say I blamed him. "He leaned on the sheriff, probably calling in a favor from campaign contributions. It's the only reason that comes together so quickly. It's not like they have real evidence." I mean, except for me pretending to be helping the police to get access to Matthews's house, and camera footage of me removing evidence, but that's beside the point. "My lawyer is on it." I explained the situation with my bank, Asher Nolan, and how I connected him with Matthews. Leaving out the evidence tampering part.

"Jesus," Julian said, shaking his head.

"They want you out, and they aren't pulling any punches to do it. I'm the biggest thorn in their side, so they're focusing most of the effort on me. Whatever their coup de grâce is, you should expect it soon."

"Yeah, about that. So, our attorney, Adrian, thinks that whoever this is, they'll have to reveal themselves at some point. And when they do, even if I've been forced out, we can sue them and get my position back."

"With what evidence?"

"Well, whatever you've gotten so far."

I knew Julian was in the middle of this, that he was parroting whatever his lawyer was telling him to say. That didn't make it any less infuriating. I'd found that when he was outside of his turf, namely tech, he tended to reiterate whatever voice was whispering in his ear. I knew he was doing that with me to the board, and now with his lawyer. It was like his brain didn't want to allocate any processing power for the unnecessary, so it defaulted to whatever he'd heard from the closest "expert." That explained a lot of why the board was so threatened by me. Hawthorne and Crowder both believed they could control Julian, and by extension, NOVA.

That cast the threats to oust him in a diabolical new light.

Maybe firing him was never the plan, or at least not the primary one. You keep dangling that stick disguised as a carrot in front of Julian to keep him in line, deliver the product, and move him in the direction you wanted him to go.

These people.

"Julian, listen to me carefully. If you fire me now, you cannot come back and ask for my help later. I'll give you a report on everything I've uncovered for you up to now, but it will be incomplete. I can't say whether it'll hold up in civil court. So far, I've been arrested, almost gunned down, my bank account stolen, and framed for goddamn murder. I think I've earned the right to protect myself. If you, or your lawyer, or anyone else has a problem with that, I wish you good luck. I have a small measure of what your technology is capable of. Seeing that end up with people like this scares the shit out of me, but if you aren't willing to defend it yourself, I don't see why I should."

I turned and started walking back to the Defender.

"Matt, wait."

We took another pass at the conversation. Julian said he understood my position. I've learned over time that people tend to either ignore attorneys outright, or take their word as, for lack of a better term, the law. Rarely did there seem to be middle ground. Julian also said he understood that I wasn't threatening him, nor was I trying to extend my contract longer than necessary, that I was just trying to do the job.

"Do you think Crowder is still a threat to me?" he said.

"Honestly, yes. He's angry, vindictive, and now feels he has cause to justify whatever he does. I can't say that he is implicated in Kyle Haney's death. I can say that the circumstances are strange and are worth someone looking into. That's now a police question. I do think he'll try something else with your business. A lawsuit seems likely. I just can't discount the fact that he had this Lucious Kett and certainly others acting as operatives for him. That's on the one side. He's not the one who hired this Blackwell and Asher Nolan. Right now, I don't know how far they'll go, and that's why I don't think I should quit."

We agreed that I'd keep at it. Julian said it'd be a hard sell with Adrian Beckett, but that was Julian's problem and not mine. I said to put Beckett in touch with my attorney. Better that I not talk to the guy. I've learned the hard way that punching lawyers is only cathartic in the short term.

With my client momentarily satisfied, I had to refocus my energy. The opposition had done an effective job in giving me too many fires to fight at once that it prevented me from focusing on the main problem.

During the Cold War, the case officers working in the Soviet Union came up with a set of practices designed to keep them alive in the most dangerous city in the world. This doctrine, codified as "the Moscow Rules," has guided espionage operations ever since. We all memorized them, canonized them. Two came to mind immediately.

Assume nothing.

Everyone is potentially under opposition control.

I did not want to believe Benjamin Blake could be involved. He also wasn't cleared until I cleared him.

I didn't ask Julian about him, or how he came to replace Crowder's spot on the board. I was afraid that might tip my hand that I suspected him. I knew he and Julian were close, and as much as it pained me to say, I couldn't trust Julian's judgment in the moment.

For now, I needed to get off these streets. Ortega told me that Lieutenant Hennessy was the patrol shift commander for second watch. Most departments, that was late afternoon and evening. I was right in the middle of his shift now.

The last of the Moscow Rules came to mind: Keep your options open.

I had a place I could go for a few hours, and it'd be the last place Hennessy and his roving goon squads would look. Might even learn something.

Two birds, and all that.

I called Diana Verala.

Maybe I was a little lean on the details, but we *had* made plans for dinner tonight. She'd told me seven, which meant I had ninety minutes to kill. The question was now how to get there. Unless you've got a boat, there are only two ways to Laguna Beach, PCH, and Highway 73. The latter cut straight through sheriff's department patrolled areas, so the risk was much higher. Similarly, the community of Dana Point was also one of the municipalities they policed, so my idea of taking the San Diego Freeway south and coming back up was out. Instead, I carved an improvised surveillance detection route from Costa Mesa to Newport Beach, hiding out in parking garages and lots and creeping through cozy upscale neighborhoods. And burning a lot of gas in the process. My entire strategy was based on them having gone to my house, found me not there, and concluded that I'd run. I was hoping they didn't think I was crazy enough to still be in their territory. This was undoubtedly overkill, though the logic was sound.

At least what passes for logic in *my* life.

I'd gotten several confused, angry phone calls from my landlord. I didn't pick up, scanning only through voicemail. Guess the authorities reached out to him.

I watched the sun begin its final dive into the sea from the parking lot of a Pilates studio in Newport Beach.

Then I made the last run to Diana's place on PCH, and couldn't help but note when I'd driven past the spot where Crowder's whistleblower had died.

The sky was an incredible dark golden color when I arrived at Diana's condo complex. It's true that there are some scenes that can make you forget just about anything, and this was one. I could probably just stand here and stare until I got arrested—and that thought jolted me back into motion. True to California's ethos of building on every available scrap of land that faced water, this entire complex perched on the edge of a cliff hanging over the Pacific like a skydiver with second thoughts. The complex had a parking garage, so my Defender wouldn't be in view. Before going inside, I pulled a fresh shirt out of my go bag, a black polo, and threw my jacket over it.

Diana greeted me at the door with a quizzical look. The condo's entire wall behind her was windows opening out to the ocean, and it backlit her with that blazing golden light. "Won't you come in?" she said, in that accent that wasn't quite European and not fully American either. "You look like you could use a drink." Diana led me into the spacious condo, which might rival the house I rented for square footage. She pulled a bottle of white from a chiller on the counter and poured a glass. "After the little dustup about our date for drinks, I figured it was safer to meet at my place."

"Dustup?"

"Oh, Julian screamed his face off at me in the board room when Crowder brought it up."

"I'm sorry that I didn't have time to properly dress for dinner. It's been a day." I caught myself.

"Well, I didn't have time to prepare the dinner I'd promised, but there is a great Thai place down the street, so I ordered in."

"That sounds perfect," I said.

"Come," Diana said, grabbing my hand, and led me out to the balcony overlooking the water. She indicated a chair and we sat, enjoying the sunset for a few moments. I felt the tension begin to drain into the chair. Again, I checked myself and held a little of it back. I was working, after all.

I did not tell her about Crowder or the warrant. If Diana was the one, she'd already know. If the sheriff knew I was here and broke the door down in the middle of dinner, it wouldn't matter if she was in on the plot against Julian or wasn't. Might as well enjoy the drink.

"You're renting this place, is that right?"

"I am. They couldn't find a buyer. I negotiated a short-term lease until they do. Originally, I'd planned to stay for a few weeks, but I don't know, Laguna is growing on me." If I had this view every day, it'd grow on me too. "There's no pressing reason to go back, I can work from here, so I figured I'd stay a bit and decide from there." Diana took a sip of her wine and then said, "General Graves went back to DC today."

"Why is that?"

"Well, the board's business has concluded." She waved her hand in a vague, dismissive gesture. "At least, as much as it can under the circumstances. Personally, I think the general is just licking his wounds," she said, though in an ambivalent tone. There was none of the parting-shot venom I might've expected.

"Is that because he was hoping Crowder was going to buy out NOVA and let him run it?"

"He won't come out and say it, but Evelyn and I think that's what it is."

"You two close?"

Diana's shoulders lifted and then fell. "Not especially. I don't trust her. It's more solidarity of women in the boys' clubhouse."

"You say the board business had wrapped up. Seems like there's still a lot going on," I said.

"Oh, without question. How much of that can this group help Julian with, though? Now, I've got some experience with crisis management. And I've advised someone through a transition like this before."

"A transition?" I said.

"How to exit a crisis. There are genuine questions about Julian's fitness to lead this business and whether he has the ethical grounding to safely bring this technology to market. That is, if this situation were over today. I gather from how I found you in my doorway that it isn't."

"Touché," I said. Her comment reminded me of my conversation with… well, I guess I still called him "Blackwell." It was interesting how he'd said *he* hadn't broken any laws and neither had his client. Wasn't sure a court would see it that way, but the conviction in his voice had been unmistakable. Hard to tell on the phone if it was skill or belief. Blackwell's implication was that Julian had done those things he revealed, and Blackwell just bent the law to uncover it. He viewed himself like an opposition research expert in a political campaign, exposing the other side's dirt for others to decide on. If that dirt needed to be muddied a little more, well, that was immoral, just not illegal. It was like marketing.

Diana rose from her chair and went back into the condo. She returned with a light sweater and the wine. She bent low to refill my glass, and I caught her perfume. Diana set the bottle down, brushed the hair over her ear, and went to the railing. I joined her. She was looking at the explosion of color in the sky. I wanted to see her head-on, though, to evaluate her expression.

"Maybe it's not about economics, then," she said. "Maybe it's about safeguarding that capability for the betterment of humanity. We all have known Julian for years. Graves was the only one who hadn't had some kind of prior relationship with Julian before he became CEO. We knew his flaws, or thought we did. Recent events are forcing us to ask hard questions. Have you ever considered the fact that whoever is doing this might believe they're genuinely acting in our collective self-interest?"

"Preventing a technology they see as dangerous?"

"Or even just slowing it down."

I'd never considered that as a motive.

Was she sharing an insight, or telegraphing a move?

Diana smiled, part coy, part something else. "Worse men have come back from bigger problems. My job as Julian's adviser is to ask these kinds of questions. And *your* job, Mr. Private Detective," she said, pressing her index finger into my chest. Like the smile, it was a playful gesture. "Is to ask those kinds of questions *also*. From me, from Graves, from Benjamin Blake, and from Evelyn. Julian as well. And those around him."

"And here I've been just randomly calling people in the phone book for clues," I said.

She smiled again, this one a little more fiendish, and poked me harder with her finger.

"I'm hungry." Diana turned and went inside. I grabbed the wine and followed her.

"Speaking of Blake, what do you think about him?"

"Oh, I've known Benj for a long time," she said from the kitchen. *Benj?* "He was on the board when I joined. I voted to retain him, for what that's worth. My take, I think he'd rather just be an investor than the leader. He only took the seat back to spite Crowder."

Diana finished warming the takeout and slid the contents from the frying pans into serving bowls. She opened a new bottle of wine and brought the steaming bowls of food over to the table.

"You guys have insight into any partnerships that Julian is considering, right?"

"It depends. He doesn't need to get our permission to explore, but he would need authorization to move further than that. Why?"

"Oh, I'd heard that he was considering a joint venture with a small cybersecurity firm called BlackICE Defense."

Diana looked down at her plate, speared a piece of pad thai chicken. "I hadn't heard that," she said.

I watched her for a reaction.

"That seems like an odd move. Did he say what he'd get out of it?"

"No. Again, it was just something he'd said in passing."

"Cybersecurity would be more Graves's lane than mine," she said. "Maybe it's some old NSA buddies of his."

Pressing too hard would give away the fact that I was using this as an end around to see if Diana knew about Asher Nolan. The physical indicators suggested she didn't. That wasn't necessarily decisive. The operator may have kept that from his boss. More likely, the boss insisted on complete deniability.

I let that thread expire, and Diana didn't press further. It occurred to me that I hadn't thought once about my being a fugitive since I'd been here. Even a few hours free of fight-or-flight was an incredible psychological relief.

We finished dinner, and Diana would not let me help with the dishes. I took that time to check my phone. Interestingly, there were two missed calls from General Graves. *Ears burning?*

I had a missed call and follow-up text from Vivian Vaughn asking if I was okay, since she hadn't heard from me. She reassured me she was on it and would have answers soon. I texted her back to let her know I was okay and out of sight.

Brody Nash was looking for instructions.

I also had a message from Mickey telling me that he expected to have some updates by morning.

Diana appeared next to me, took the phone from my hand, and set it facedown on the table. She slid her other hand around the back of my neck and guided me in to kiss her. I didn't fight it.

Why would I? I didn't have anywhere else to go.

I was awake to see the violet dawn.

It was a stunning display of pastel color splashed across the sky that deepened and gradually faded to blue. I'd slipped out of Diana's bedroom and stood on the balcony, listening to the surf break and letting the cold shock me awake.

I stayed for a long time. When I went back inside to check my phone, I found a flurry of messages from Mickey. And one from Asher Nolan.

Asher Nolan: **You've made your point. Call off the dogs.**

30

I woke the son of a bitch up.

"All I want is out of this," Nolan said. His voice had that same lack of intonation.

What had Mickey done to him?

I decided to roll with it. My AirPods were in the Defender, and I couldn't talk to him and scroll Mickey's messages. "That depends on you, Asher. You know what I want to know."

He went silent, and I thought I'd lost him.

"His name is Silas Grey. At first, we only worked through aliases. Once I found out what he wanted me to do, I told him I wouldn't unless I met him in person."

I described Mark Blackwell to him as best I could from memory. Also remembering that Blackwell had worn sunglasses the entire time. "Five foot ten, brown hair, early to mid-fifties?"

"Yeah. That's him."

"And he hired you to hack NOVA AI?"

"Yes, but I won't tell that to the police. No matter what they offer."

"Did he tell you to drain my bank account, or did you come up with that on your own?"

"He said we needed to take you 'out of the game.' Those were his words."

"Why?"

"Why what?"

"Why am I a threat to him?"

"Don't be stupid."

"People lose teeth talking like that," I said. "Answer the question." *Careful*, I cautioned myself. I'd spooked him, but that would only play so far. I had to keep my temper in check. Take it a notch past the line and he could retaliate or bolt, or both.

"He needs you preoccupied so you can't stop him. Originally, I was just supposed to hack the demo. Then you turned out to be more of a problem than Grey expected. He turned me onto you."

Really, I was Grey's only threat, but I'd asked the question to see if Nolan kicked anything loose. If Grey wasn't overtly violating the law, he didn't have to worry about the police. He'd handled Crowder and his private Gestapo, so I was the only thing standing between him and unseating Julian.

"How do you communicate?" I already knew the answer to this, and wanted to check Nolan's response to see if he was being truthful.

"Always on Signal. He bought the phone and gave it to me."

"I take it you're reversing what you did to my bank account and credit card."

"Yes," Nolan snapped. I think it was the first time I'd heard emotion from him.

It occurred to me that perhaps this wasn't a conversation that Diana should walk in on, so I stepped back out onto her balcony. Still wearing only jeans and no shirt, it was cold.

"What about the Orange County Sheriff and my arrest warrant?"

"You can't fake that!"

"I know you can't. But you can doctor a case file in a database to make it look like I did something I didn't."

"I didn't touch that, Gage. All I did was get the cop moved off. Evidence files have digital signatures now. It's a lot harder to manipulate. I couldn't touch that without them knowing, not with the time I had. What I could do was manipulate the chain of custody so it looked like the detective was sloppy. Change logs, shit like that."

"All right, all right."

"So are we good?" he said.

"No, we are not. What does Silas Grey have planned next?"

"Hell if I know." Now there was a petulant, "not me" quality to his voice. We'd gone from no emotional displays to the full gamut, as if Nolan had no middle ground.

"Not good enough."

"He doesn't *tell* me anything, Gage. Even you should be able to figure that out."

"Fine," I said. "What did he have you working on next?"

Nolan didn't immediately respond, and my ability to threaten him was, at best, complicated. Without knowing what Mickey did, I didn't know what levers to pull on. I still wanted to see this asshole in a courtroom and testifying for what he did to Julian. Taking the phone off my ear, I chanced a look at Signal. Putting it on speaker would make him think I was setting it up for others to listen in. Mickey had sent a dozen messages, each with an increasing level of malicious glee. I skimmed through them as quickly as I could, putting my old speed-reading training to good use. In the field, you often had just a second to look at a mission-critical piece of information.

Mickey had impersonated the LAPD's computer crimes division and blasted Ghost's favorite dark web haunts with covert inquiries. Mickey pretended to be a cop that was trying to cover his digital tracks. He'd started poking around Ghost's environment, which would trigger Nolan to see who it was. Mickey laid a trail of cleverly hidden digital breadcrumbs back to a source. Mickey would make it look like he was obfuscating his moves, relying on Nolan's arrogance that no one could hide from him online. Nolan would conclude the police were investigating him but trying to make it look like something else. It was a digital false flag.

That didn't seem to be what did it, though.

Mickey had simply asked the question, in a roundabout way, on a dark web forum, whether Ghost was Asher Nolan.

The last thing I saw before Nolan started talking again was a message from Mickey saying Ghost was believed to have stolen millions in cryptocurrency from a Russian-backed criminal syndicate in Hungary, draining their spoils of a series of ransomware campaigns. By associating the two in a place where the gangsters could easily find it, Mickey put Nolan's life immediately at risk. The intent, I suspected, was to force him to seek witness protection.

Mickey, though, had been trained first by the Russians and then we got ahold of him, turned him, trained him better, and used him as a kind of digital black operative. Ghost was very good. Mickey had few peers that weren't actual intelligence agencies.

The phone went back to my ear when Nolan was midstream in some nonsensical invective. I hadn't missed much.

"Asher, stop," I said. He didn't, so I just talked over him, hoping words would get through. "It isn't too late for me to tell my friends in the police department that you've decided to cooperate. You might even be able to wrangle some kind of witness protection, especially if you think this Silas Grey is a threat."

"All right, all right, all right, okay, fine," he said in a verbal torrent that made it sound like just one word.

"Do you know anyone else Grey is working with? Who shot at me the night of the swatting?"

"I don't know," he said plaintively.

Pushing a deal with the police that I could not guarantee would backfire and probably spook him. Nolan was already on a knife's edge, and leaning on him too hard could have consequences.

I said, "Asher, do you still have the phone that Grey gave you?"

"Yes."

"Good. Do you know what a dead drop is?"

"Yes," he said.

"Good. I'll text you with instructions tonight."

"Why don't you just give them to me now?"

"Because I don't want you to dump it and run."

"Then come meet me. I'm not waiting around, Gage."

"You will if you don't want to have this conversation with the police."

I waited until Nolan gave me his word he'd wait for my instructions and then hung up.

I went back into the condo and its welcome warmth to find Diana standing in her living room wearing my shirt from last night and nothing else.

"Working?" she said.

"This job doesn't stop, sometimes it slows down enough for me to sleep." A slight smile on my face, I said, "I'm going to need that shirt back."

"Then come get it."

She made a compelling argument.

Unfortunately, I really had to be moving. Diana relented and gave me my shirt back, though my hasty exit from her place was stalled a bit by the fact that my overnight kit and change of clothes were still in the Defender. She found this funny and teased me when I had to leave and come back. Once I was showered and changed, Diana kissed me long enough to regret my decision to leave. Somehow, I mustered the personal fortitude to do it. I found a beachside cafe where I grabbed a quick breakfast and a coffee, scanning my missed texts and calls while I ate. It was just past seven now. I messaged Brody Nash, apologized for being out of touch, and suggested we meet up later.

There was also a message from Vanessa Holt. This one had come in not long ago, probably while I was talking to Nolan. I tossed my wrapper into a trash can, grabbed my coffee, and walked back to the Defender. Before returning her call, I made a fast check up the street in both directions. Everything looked clear.

I called Holt. She picked up immediately.

"Can you really prove someone deepfaked me?"

"Where are you right now?"

"I'm at home," she said.

"Send me your address. This is a conversation we need to have in person," I said. *So I can tell if you're lying.*

"I'm not telling you where I live."

"For f—" I paused and checked my temper. "I can look it up, Holt, I'm being polite. Fine. Meet me on Ocean Boulevard in Newport Beach in fifteen minutes. At Inspiration Point."

I could just make it.

"No," she said. "Not outside. There's a mall in Irvine. University Center.

Meet me at the Coastal Commons. You said fifteen minutes. I'm not waiting."

That was something. And insisting on meeting inside, too.

I raced up PCH and took Newport Coast Drive inland.

University Center was a multi-geometry cluster of upscale, modern shopping and dining in the middle of the UC Irvine campus. It had an orange-tiled, Mediterranean-style roof and abundant green space. Even at this early hour, between the two restaurants that served breakfast and the Peet's Coffee, there was a decent amount of foot traffic. Easy to blend in. Solid tradecraft on Holt's part.

Coastal Commons faced the parking lot with several tables outside on the large patio. I cut a path through these and went inside.

To my great surprise, Holt showed. She was in athletic gear and wearing sunglasses and a ball cap. Hollywood incognito. I tried not to sigh.

I also noticed Holt wasn't in a sling. She wore a bulky hoodie that concealed the bandage. She still looked pale.

"How are you feeling?"

"It was a clean wound. Didn't hit anything important. Nicked my collarbone."

Just like that, clinical and antiseptic.

We ordered a pair of coffees and Holt a pastry, then found a table. I followed her lead, and she found a spot well in the back.

"The deepfake," she said once we were seated. Holt took her sunglasses off, finally, and set them on the table.

"This thing got set in motion when I got a call, allegedly from you, saying Kyle Haney tried to inform on Nathaniel Crowder to state regulators. This was right after Grant Matthews died in a similar accident. I didn't put this together until after the swatting, when Detective Ortega told me you said I called you. Were you and Haney involved?"

"No," she said flatly. "I barely knew him." Her eyes darted to the side, and I knew she was lying.

"How about we try that again?"

"We weren't dating. It was more casual than that. We became friends during the vetting and due diligence, then hooked up a few times. I liked him. Crowder knew I was friendly with him, so once the whistleblower stuff started, he wanted me to leverage that. I told him I wouldn't do it, and he about lost his mind. Nathaniel Crowder doesn't get told no often and doesn't react well when he does."

"The sheriff's department investigator thinks that Haney was chased. He lost control of his car and crashed. They couldn't prove it, so the case didn't go anywhere."

"I think that's true," she said.

"Did Crowder task Lucious Kett to follow him?"

"I assume so. But, Gage, you have to understand, I didn't know *anything* about Kett or that whole operation until that night."

If Kett hadn't been killed then, I'd have assumed he was the one orchestrating all of this. Made me wonder if his death was intentional or not.

"You don't think Crowder would have tried to silence you, do you?"

"Not...then," she said. That was something I was going to have to follow up on.

"Here's what I'm trying to figure out. I get why someone wants me dead. My job is to cause problems for people. What I don't understand is who would want you there too. Originally, I thought Crowder figured out you tipped me off. Once I realized you calling me with that info was a deepfake, that made less sense. And what was Kett doing there if Crowder wasn't involved?"

Holt nervously toyed with a sugar packet while she thought it out. She said, "The best way to frame Nathaniel is to link him to Lucious Kett. A murder draws a pretty hard line." It's not technically a frame if they actually *did* it. This probably wasn't the best time to argue semantics. "Isn't that what this was about? Getting Crowder off the board?"

"That was step one. I know they called in an active shooter at that location, which is what got the sheriff to roll the SWAT team in. And the call went in before we even arrived. They timed it so SWAT would show up right after you were shot. I believe the plan was to make it look like I'd shot you so the responders would take me down."

"That seems complicated. Is that even realistic?"

"It's a stretch, though I've done worse," I said. "And we're dealing with a top-tier operator here." I lifted my coffee mug. "And overly elaborate seems like his style. He's incredibly arrogant. It makes sense, though, tactically."

Holt pursed her lips, thinking it through. "He's flooding the zone," she said, nodding. "Create as many shiny objects as possible for the authorities and his client's opponents to chase. Enough that no one can focus on any one thing." She shook her head. "Fucker."

My eyes lifted off the table to study Holt. She looked angry, confused, agitated. A bundle of nervous energy screaming for an outlet. To look at us, you'd think she was the one running from the cops. "You have friends in law enforcement? Or, better yet, the private security community?"

"Both. I was a badge before I went to work for Crowder. Why?"

"Can you reach out to some of your friends, see what they can find on the name Silas Grey?"

"That the guy?"

I nodded. Holt took her phone out, made a note, and put it away. "I'll see what I can do. So, who do you think hired him?"

"Well, it's got to be Graves, Hawthorne, or Verala. Unless it's coming from completely outside the company. On paper, Graves is tailor-made. He unraveled my cover at the start of this very quickly, so much so that I wondered if he used national assets to do it. He tried to get me to tell him what I knew, said he'd expose me to the board if I didn't. Kept it up for a while, but he didn't seem to have much useful information to share. He tried to run me like an agent, though the case accelerated faster than he anticipated, and that idea got away from him. He's pretty much backed off." I picked up my coffee and took a sip, just needing the space to organize my thoughts. "The plan was to make Kessler radioactive. Dig up and release dirt on him, manufacturing it when necessary, to force the board of directors to vote for his removal. They hit him on all sides—business stuff to make him look nefarious and personal stuff to undermine his character and activate the non-tech crowd online, people that otherwise wouldn't know who he is but are now engaged. The media is now talking more about that than they are the fact that someone hacked his demo in real time. Then whoever was behind this would swoop in and take over."

"That makes no sense. That would trigger, like, a million lawsuits."

"I said the same thing. Hell, I told Silas Grey that."

"Wait, you've spoken to him?"

"Oh yeah. He called me to gloat. Well, he called me to triangulate my location, but also to gloat. Anyway, they think that they'll release enough bad shit on Julian that it's impossible for him to remain in place. He negotiates an exit and this whole thing goes away quietly."

"It *still* doesn't make any sense. What's to stop you from telling everything you know?"

"Well, remember, I wasn't supposed to be alive. Or at least, not a free man. The swatting either gets me killed or jailed. Once I'm a felon, anything I say is tainted. Only, that didn't work out the way they wanted, so they hacked my bank account and bled me dry." Time to shift tactics slightly and see whose side Holt was on. "You should know, I'm also being investigated for Grant Matthews's murder."

"That's insane."

"Yeah, well, it was your boss that did that. I imagine he's a fairly big donor to the Orange County Sheriff's reelection campaign. Crowder must've told the sheriff that I was doing the things Silas Grey was and that I probably killed Matthews to hide my tracks. And it worked. Figure it's out of spite over getting him kicked off the board. There's a warrant for my arrest right now. I've got a lawyer on it. Crowder is a distraction, though a convenient one for the opposition. Grey's strategy is to tar my reputation enough that I'm not credible in court, or I decide it's not worth the harm and walk away."

"That's pretty ruthless," she said.

"Yeah. Well, as I have come to understand this technology, if NOVA AI is even moderately successful, it changes the way we interact with machines. Imagine the kind of wealth that comes along with that."

"It'd be like inventing a whole new currency," she said.

I shook a slow negative. "It'd be like inventing a new economy. With those as the stakes, even decent people could rationalize the decision to do terrible things to justify what they believed was a noble outcome. And none of these are decent people."

"So, what's your next move?"

"Stay a step ahead of the police until my attorney sorts this out. Then I'm going to brace Silas Grey. I'll use him to connect me to his boss. Evelyn Hawthorne is fast becoming my chief suspect. I know through some Washington contacts she's making moves there. I think I've eliminated everyone else. I'll still look at Graves, but like I said, I think he's out. Once I have this thing with the sheriff sorted, I can stop worrying about Crowder."

"Ha! You think Nathaniel Crowder is just going to up and quit because someone kicked him off a board. He's still one of the majority investors, and NOVA AI is bleeding cash. He's just going to wait whatever this shit is out, and pounce on whatever and whoever is left. And buddy," she laughed bitterly, "I would not want to be you. Or Benjamin Blake, for that matter."

"Without Lucious Kett, Crowder is just another rich asshole having a temper tantrum because he didn't get what he wanted."

"Lucious Kett wasn't the only one. He's got a team. I've done some digging since that night. It's well hidden, like you'd expect, but I know how to look and have privileged access. Gage, you have no idea what you're up against. Vanguard Defense Systems. Crowder bought the influence to get exemptions or waivers or whatever he needs from the local governments here so that he can fly Vanguard's unmanned aerial systems for 'testing.'" She actually made the air quotes. "Crowder can conduct surveillance on anyone he wants using company R&D assets."

"That's illegal."

"Is it? He used PACs to influence local policy regarding flight restrictions, and to donate to political campaigns, here and in Sacramento. He figured out what causes local politicians care about, same with our congressman, and makes donations in their name. When the time comes, he gets his way with the law. Who's going to stop him? And how would you prove it anyway?" Holt wrapped her fingers around the coffee mug, leeching off the warmth. The corners of her mouth pulled at the edges, a drawn, tight expression. "Vanguard has a contract with OCSD. They lease surveillance drones to the sheriff at a ridiculously low cost and provide the engineers to run them. On top of the opportunity for real-time testing in an urban environment, Vanguard gets copies of the data as long as any personal information is obfuscated out. For operation testing. Anyway, the company has a lot of contacts in the department. Once Crowder heard that SWAT lieutenant was out to get you, he offered to lend the department whatever they needed. Wouldn't surprise me if Vanguard has a drone on you now. I learned about them coming for you through a colleague in the department. The only reason I agreed to meet you here is I thought you needed to know."

"Going behind your boss?" I ventured.

"I'm on convalescence, but I'm not going back. Look, man, I don't know what Crowder is involved in. I don't know if he was part of this thing, or if he's just waiting to scoop up the pieces. All I know is that once I found out about Lucious Kett and his goon squad, I wanted out. I can guess what Crowder has them doing, just knowing him. He'd always talked about wanting problems to just 'go away,' how it'd be great if some rival had skeletons in their closet, or something he could use for leverage. I always thought it was just talk, you know. Didn't think he'd do it."

It no longer shocked me that people like Crowder paid people like Kett to "troubleshoot" for them. Most of what they did was legal, in the strictest sense, though questionably ethical for sure. And it would certainly raise questions coming from someone designing lethal combat and surveillance systems for the government. I also suspected Crowder wasn't the only one. I bet this was far more common than people wanted to believe. There was too much money at play to not create every advantage.

"Does Vanguard manufacture armed drones?"

"What do you think? You know what the Switchblade is, right?" I did. It was a low-cost suicide drone, hand-launched and highly effective. Kind of like a flying grenade. "Well, he's got one several generations advanced. And they're working on a sniper drone. Apparently, firing Hellfire missiles from twenty thousand feet is passe." I didn't want to tell her the Agency had these already. Some secrets are better left kept. The Israelis had been using sniper drones for about five years, though, and weren't shy about the public knowing. Early versions were basically quadcopters with assault rifles on a stabilizer platform. Vanguard's systems would be far beyond that. "Why do you ask?" she said.

"The night we were shot. Sheriff responded with a full SWAT team and a helicopter. They didn't find anyone. I made it over the fence, practically to the aqueduct before they swarmed me. I didn't see anyone."

"What, you think Crowder had something to do with it?" Holt's tone was scoffing, but there was real concern over the implication in her eyes.

"I don't know that it was him. These guys hacked into NOVA and took it over in real time. How hard would it be to redirect a supply system? Vanguard is a big company. How long would it take before someone noticed a drone was missing?"

"Like, immediately," she said, with conviction.

"But would they admit it? Would they tell Crowder? If they did, would Crowder tell the public?"

We let that topic rest. I think we both understood that whoever tried to kill us that night was ultimately irrelevant to the objective. Another shiny object to chase.

Holt's brow creased, and I watched her eyes go tight, clearly thinking something through. Eventually, she said, "This operator, Silas Grey?"

"What about him?"

"You could use some help, I'll bet."

"You offering?" I asked.

"Matt, I almost died so that some asshole could steal a computer program. Whatever help you need, I'm in."

31

I went out to the parking lot and retrieved my laptop and go bag from the Defender. I'd have to leave the vehicle here until it was safe for me to drive again. Once I had my things, I navigated through the mall to the other side, and emerged without my jacket and wearing the ball cap. Holt pulled up in her Porsche Cayenne, slowing just long enough for me to get in. I didn't know if they had aerial surveillance on me, again felt paranoid, but if they did, we'd taken what countermeasures we had time for.

We drove north.

Holt spent the first few minutes on the phone calling old law enforcement contacts. I'd learned she'd started her career as an officer in the Air Force's Office of Special Investigations. I knew about OSI because they were also a member of the Intelligence Community, part of the subset that Agency personnel referred to as "the kids' table." One of OSI's responsibilities, which I didn't know about until this conversation, was to police defense contractors. It was a mission that started because of the Air Force's deep ties to the aerospace industry. They investigated allegations of fraud, as well as potential foreign penetration. After her military service, Holt did a brief stint with the IRS's Criminal Investigation Division going after money launderers and terrorist financiers before Crowder recruited her.

"Once he found out about you, Crowder had me look at all the other board members," Holt said as we drove.

"Oh yeah?" I said, wondering where she was going with this.

"Kessler doesn't know. Crowder just wanted dirt on the others. That's not how he phrased it, of course. Said he wanted to know who was 'potentially compromised.' Like someone was manipulating them. Anyway, I put my team on it and also outsourced to some private security firms."

"Surprised he didn't have Kett doing that," I said. Though, I knew Kett was busy following me.

"I came to most of the same conclusions you did about Graves. Hawthorne, I don't know much about, she was one of the ones we outsourced. Verala, though. That one concerns me."

"Why?"

"She runs a PAC, not unlike Hawthorne's Horizon Impact Fund."

"I know about it," I said.

"Well, over the last year, that group made a lot of donations to nonprofits and an umbrella organization advocating for greater AI oversight. One of those groups even suggested NOVA AI should be a nonprofit, that the research be put into a kind of public trust. The PAC's second largest donor is PaxTech. They're—"

"I know who they are. A carve-out from three of the biggest US tech companies trying to solve the same problem as NOVA, and one of NOVA's biggest competitors."

"Verala also had a law firm draft a filing that would limit Julian's power as CEO."

"You find out why?"

Holt shrugged. "Isn't it obvious?"

"I mean, that isn't the kind of thing you do casually. She'd have to have a reason."

"We didn't get that far."

Maybe it was nothing.

And maybe I shouldn't have slept with her.

"Graves isn't off the hook," she said. "He just isn't the top of my list right now. You know what I don't get? Why doesn't Kessler just dissolve the board? If all these people are coming after him, just fire them."

"He can't. He never had that power. Kessler didn't found the company, and doesn't own the majority stake. Graham Wexler, the COO, founded NOVA AI. Julian convinced Wexler that he needed help, and that's when the company took off. Wexler didn't give Kessler total control, though."

"And you don't think Wexler is behind this?"

"I considered him at first, but he convinced me otherwise. I think I know the answer to this, but I'll ask anyway. Did Crowder have you look at Benjamin Blake?"

Those two hated each other with a vigor one didn't usually find outside the Middle East. Crowder had engineered Blake's ouster from the board, and then maneuvered his way into that seat. He'd be furious that Blake was the one who replaced *him*, though that wouldn't mean Crowder would suspect anything other than spite being behind it. I still didn't believe that Blake hired Silas Grey, or that he'd even know how to find someone like him. Blake was a ruthless businessman, just not like that. I'd also been wrong before, and that made it worth running down.

She laughed, harsh and shrill. "He did, once he heard that Blake hired you."

"Blake didn't hire me, Julian did. Blake just told Julian about me," I said.

"Crowder doesn't draw that kind of distinction."

"What did you find out?" I asked.

"I wasn't allowed to touch that. When I asked, he said 'I'll handle it.'"

"Kett," I ventured. She nodded.

"I'll tell you this for free," Holt said. "You already know Crowder is coming for you. Even without this thing with the sheriff, you need to watch your back. And I hope Blake has security."

"You don't think Crowder would try anything, do you? He'd go after his businesses, maybe. Same as with me. I think he has to know that this thing with the police isn't going to last long. There's zero evidence."

"Oh, I think he knows you don't go to jail. He wants to ruin you, though. And he'll spend a lot of money to do it. Crowder knows he's made an enemy, and he thinks you're just the kind of person to come after him when this is over. He figures Blake will pay you to do it. Crowder will try to take you out before that can happen."

"You implied, though, that Blake needed to watch his back. You just said he needed security. Do you think Crowder would try to kill him?"

"Matt, you have to understand that he would never say something like that to me. He's like a mob boss that way. I've worked for him for ten years, and closely. Trust me when I say he defines 'corporate security' very broadly. I've done opposition research on his rivals, exposed their secrets to the press or *their* boards. Looked for corner-cutting and painted it as malfeasance. Everything happening to Julian is exactly the kind of shit Crowder has done to other people." Holt's voice trailed off, and she concentrated on the road. I gave her the space of a few moments. "The reason I'm helping you now is I didn't fully grasp what I was a part of until I saw it happen to someone else."

There wasn't much to say after that.

I texted Ortega. **Anonymous tip for your cyber guys to check out. Evidence chain was altered remotely. Have it from the source.**

He did not write me back.

As she drove, Holt took sporadic returned calls from her law enforcement friends. And I got a phone call from my attorney. With nothing better to do and needing a few hours to kill until I could meet Nolan, I agreed. I gave Holt the address to Vivian Vaughn's Westwood office.

Holt dropped me off and said she was going to post at a nearby coffee shop where she could keep working her contacts. I thanked her again for the ride. I might not have made it out of Orange County without it. She didn't seem to want the gratitude, accepting it awkwardly, like it was a fruitcake at an office Christmas party.

Vaughn's practice was on the twelfth floor of the Westwood Place building on Wilshire with views of the mountains and the ocean. An associate in the season's current power color met me in the lobby, confirmed that I was already overly caffeinated, and led me back to Vaughn's office. She had an impressive view that stretched from one wall to the other. Vaughn had pictures on her walls in tight, thematic groupings, of her with select celebrities but also prominent LA power figures—to include, I noted, the current police chief and more than a few officers. Interesting art for a criminal defense attorney.

"Matt, it's so nice to meet you in person." Vaughn stood as I entered. She walked to me, extending a hand in greeting. It still took her a while to get there. She wore a navy suit and minimal jewelry, though what she had on could probably float my rent. Vaughn was tall, mid-fifties with sharp features only slightly rounded by time. Brown hair fell at her shoulder, and she had a slight, amused smile. The eyes, though, were like surveillance cameras—electric and watchful, missing nothing. Vaughn had a presence to her, a don't-fuck-with-me aura that simultaneously suggested she'd go to the ends of the earth for you. I could tell why Bo worked with her for so long. If half of his stories were true, I imagine he needed it.

"Bo tells me a lot about you," she said as we shook hands.

"We talk shop on occasion," I said.

"Please, sit." Vaughn motioned to a spot on the long leather couch. She sat, crossed her legs. "Is it okay if Laura stays? I'd like her to take notes."

"Fine by me," I said.

"Okay. Great. First, I have some good news. My husband was a prose-cutor for the Orange County DA for about fifteen years, and we have a lot of connections there. Their case against you is paper thin and, frankly, I'm amazed the judge granted the arrest warrant. It's going to be dismissed today."

"Really? That's amazing. You work fast."

"If it wasn't for my husband's connections there, this could've taken a week to sort out. But don't thank me yet."

It's usually not good when a lawyer tells you that.

Vaughn continued. "They have no real evidence that connects you to Grant Matthews's death. You probably know this already, he died in a single-car accident. They can't prove whether he was hit and lost control of the vehicle. However, there is the matter of you unlawfully entering Matthews's home, which was a crime scene. They have you on surveillance footage, and the manager will testify that you falsely represented your asso-ciation with the Orange County Sheriff's Department."

She didn't say anything about the phone.

"A hacker named Asher Nolan paid Matthews fifty thousand dollars for access to NOVA AI. Nolan accessed and manipulated the system while Julian Kessler was giving his demo."

"I've seen the clips," she said.

"Matthews died the day after I told the board about him."

"I know."

"I went to Matthews's house looking for a connection between him and the people who paid him. I could connect him to Nolan, who goes by the alias Ghost, through dark web posts. I can't prove yet that they gave the order, but Nolan admitted to taking the payment. I found a burner phone which led me to Nolan, and Nolan flipped on his boss, an operative named Silas Grey. This is who tricked me into going to that industrial park where they phoned in a bogus shots fired call, and almost got me killed."

"Matt, I appreciate your passion for this case," she said, her voice calm, almost soothing, but there was a hard line through it. "Without court authorization, your motives ultimately do not matter. Unlawfully violating a crime scene is a felony, and this will most likely cost you your license. I'm sorry. You need to prepare yourself for that."

Vaughn paused while the weight of it fell on me.

None of this was news to me, yet somehow it never truly registered. Not until Vaughn said it.

On one of my first cases, I'd done something similar. Broken into a crime scene looking for something the police missed. After that, I told myself if I was going to be a PI, I needed to play by new rules. For the most part, I'd followed them. I broke that promise to myself, and this time it would cost me.

Silas Grey seemingly being a step ahead of me at every single turn no doubt colored my judgment. I'm not used to being outmaneuvered. It made me act stupidly. I had to wonder if Grey profiled me and set this up for this exact outcome.

After getting ejected from the Agency and taking the fall for someone else's mistake, being a detective gave me new purpose. It was a way to use the things the government taught me to do to help people that needed it.

I'd just pissed that away over Julian Kessler's power struggle.

"There might be the possibility of an appeal as well. And it may be possible that we can get it reinstated in time. Though, I don't want you to get your hopes up."

"I understand," I said in a voice that sounded distant to my ears.

"OC's District Attorney has agreed to drop the charges against you. They are filing a motion with the state to have your license revoked for professional misconduct, and they are placing a restraining order on you that says you cannot enter Orange County for ninety days. If you do, you'll be arrested."

"What do I do now?"

Her face softened into a somber mask. "Lie low. I'd wrap up your work for Mr. Kessler. I can recommend a few investigators that I trust, if there is more work to do. Bo is retired, but his license is active. He's agreed to help. Given all the attention on you, that might be an unexpected move."

"I want a civil suit against Nathaniel Crowder, and another against the Orange County Sheriff. I'm also going to reach out to some friends in the FBI on the public corruption angle." I explained the situation with Crowder and what I'd learned from Vanessa on the drive up.

"You think this is credible?" Vaughn asked, not in an accusatory way, but rather one of true concern.

"Vanessa Holt has been eyewitness to this kind of thing for a decade. When I piece that together with what she's told me about him buying political influence in Orange County so that he can test his security systems with impunity—not just drones, but everything."

"He doesn't think the rules apply to him," Vaughn said, nodding.

"No. Nathaniel Crowder thinks he writes them now."

"We'll take a look at options," she said and stood. I did the same. "In the meantime, Matt, remember what I said about lying low. Do not engage. This is no longer your fight."

"Well, if I go back there, it's a race to see if they arrest me or if Crowder shoots me off the road," I said in a flatline tone. Then I added, "I'm mostly kidding."

Sometimes I needed to point that out for people.

Holt met me out front, and I asked her to drive me home.

"You check your phone?" she asked when I climbed into the Porsche. It was the universal preamble to "I found out bad news, but I don't want the responsibility of breaking it to you." I'd had the phone on "do not disturb" while I was in with Vaughn and hadn't thought to turn that off until she'd asked. The millisecond I changed the setting, the red eyes of a dozen different notifications blew up on my phone, staring up at me like pissed-off Cyclopses. Swearing, I navigated to a news app. I had it configured to immediately surface any breaking news about Julian, NOVA AI, or any of the board members. Maybe I'd gotten lucky and Crowder wrapped his Lambo around a tree.

I picked the story up after the headline, which in and of itself read like a car crash. "Leaked internal documents from NOVA AI appear to show embattled CEO Julian Kessler reporting a five-million-dollar R&D contract through the Defense Advanced Research Projects Agency (DARPA), though no record of any such contract exists. Officials at DARPA confirmed they have only had exploratory conversations with NOVA AI. The company's balance sheet shows four million dollars in internal research and development reclassified as an 'infrastructure investment' in recent shareholder communications. 'It raises significant questions on how our money is being spent,' W. Allan Buckley said in a phone interview with *WIRED*. Buckley is a minority shareholder in NOVA AI. Perhaps most concerning is a monthly recurring transaction of fifty thousand dollars to a firm called Aether Consulting. However, no such company exists, and filing information reveals it is little more than a shell." I put the phone down. I'd seen enough.

Embezzlement.

If there was a shred of truth to this, Julian was going to jail.

At a minimum, he'd lose this company.

This was Silas Grey's finisher, and he'd timed it perfectly. Stripped of my assets, my tools, and nearly anyone that would help me, and fighting fires on every conceivable front, I was in no position to investigate this, certainly not in the time I had.

Even if this *wasn't* true, the allegations were out in the world, and no amount of reputational laundry was going to change it.

There were calls, texts, and Signal messages all from Julian and all demanding to know what, with varying degrees of invective, was going on.

I called him.

"What the fuck, Matt? Have you seen *WIRED*? Jesus, have you seen *anything*. This shit is all over the news."

"I just saw it. You'll have to forgive me. I was meeting with my attorney discussing how I beat this murder charge Nathaniel Crowder engineered."

Julian sputtered a moment and stopped.

"Is it true?"

"No," Julian shouted into the phone. It was loud enough that Holt heard it, because I saw her eyes go up. "What are you doing about it?" he demanded, regaining some of his destructive energy.

"If it is completely untrue, then we have legs to stand on. Is it *completely untrue*, Julian?"

"Yes."

"Because if it isn't, I am going to walk away right now. I will not cover up crimes for you," I said in a tone as calm as my current state would allow.

"Goddamn it, Matt. This is all bullshit. I didn't *do* any of this."

"Okay. I will be in touch. I need to consider my next move. For right now, you need to get that PR firm I introduced you to on this. I also need you to have your corporate counsel contact me immediately."

"Adrian? Why?"

"Because I asked you to, that's why. When is the last time you spoke with Brody?"

"It's been a couple of days."

Shit.

"Never mind. What's Graham doing?"

"He's reviewing all of our internal records, trying to see where this came from."

I hung up with Julian and called Graham. "Graham, do you have a relationship with a cyber forensics team?"

"No. But I know people," he said.

"If you haven't done so already, call them. When this started, I gave Julian the name of a PR firm that specializes in damage control. He appears not to have called them. They also might know someone. You need to get on that right away. Assume that Grant Matthews helped Nolan get into more than just NOVA. I think they're messing with your corporate ledger."

"Right. Okay. I'm on it."

I hung up and exhaled a hot blast of frustration.

What good is good advice if the subject never takes it?

"Now I know how all my former bosses felt," I muttered under my breath.

"What?" Holt said.

"Nothing. How fast does this thing go?" I asked.

"Let's find out."

Even though the arrest warrant was rescinded, it would take a few days before that worked its way through the system and I got access to Echo-Trace again. The bureaucracy rarely moved swiftly in one's favor. There was a search warrant taped to the door. The police are required to leave one when they enter a residence and the owner isn't there.

As one might expect, they were not good houseguests.

My place was trashed.

Actually, it looked like a slash-and-burn job from a particularly corrupt banana republic.

My couch cushions were torn and the stuffing pulled out. You know, because that's where people typically hide the evidence of murder conspiracies. Everything was upended. I made a room-to-room assessment, and with each one, I found fresh reasons to believe they'd never read the Fourth Amendment. Everything in my kitchen was pulled out and left all over the place. What little food I had was out on the counter.

The assholes even confiscated my scotch. Including a special bottle of thirty-year-old Macallan that Nate McKellar gave me when they booted me out of the Agency. The bottle, which hit the low four figures, was James Bond's label in the Daniel Craig films and was something of a joke between us. It had been accompanied by a note, "The proper function of man is to live, not to exist. I shall not waste my days in trying to prolong them. I shall use my time." It's the toast M gives Bond after his death in the last film.

They took it because they could.

The odds of me coming out of this without shooting anyone were near zero.

I videoed everything, room by room, providing as calm a narrative as my temper would allow.

When I was done, I sent that to Vivian Vaughn.

Throughout the entire thing, Vanessa remained silent. I think she could tell that I needed some space.

When I came back downstairs, I found her in my tortured living room, looking like someone who'd just returned home to find a tornado hit while they were out.

"They took my shotgun," I said, not expecting her to understand what I was talking about.

Vaughn called me back and told me not to touch anything. She was sending one of her people over right now to document the situation. Whatever the hell that meant.

The police got a safecracker to break open my gun safe, though that didn't matter because the pistol that I kept there was already in their possession. Their search team did not find the safe hidden beneath the floorboards under my bed.

Amateurs.

I removed the pistol, two magazines, and a holster from that safe. I checked the action, holstered it, and clipped that to my belt. I grabbed a black Harrington jacket out of the closet. This was designed for people who did the kind of work that I did, or wanted to dress like they did the kind of work I did. It featured concealed internal pockets that could hide smaller items, like a passport or spare magazines. It wouldn't stand up to a dedicated frisk, though it would hide them from a casual search.

"What are we going to do now?" Holt asked when I returned to the living room.

"Get Silas Grey," I said.

"Right, but what are you going to do when we find him?"

Million dollar question, that.

32

Most of the gear I stashed in my garage had been confiscated. However, I'd hidden the surveillance microphone that I'd used to listen in on Crowder's conversation with Lucious Kett well enough that they hadn't found it. The device was designed to look like a regular laptop so it could be used covertly in a public setting, which meant that it had a small form factor and easily slipped between other things. I grabbed that and some other pieces of kit, and by the time Vaughn's people arrived, Holt and I had our plan together.

I gave them a spare key and said do what you need to do.

Laura, the power-suit-wearing assistant from earlier, incredulously asked why I wasn't staying.

I just said I needed to find a hotel for the night and wasn't in the mood to pick up.

We drove downtown.

I still hadn't heard from Brody Nash, and now I was concerned.

We knew Silas Grey had at least one shooter. He'd convinced me he wasn't a trigger puller himself. The point to putting Nash on Asher Nolan was to make him seen, so that Nolan—and Grey by extension—knew there was heat. Grey might've responded poorly to that. I had no doubts Nash could handle himself in a fight, but he didn't necessarily have the street craft to know the fight was coming.

I hoped I hadn't put him in harm's way.

Normally, I wouldn't stop. However, we had time to burn before the dead drop pickup, and both of us were running on fumes. It could turn into a long night, and we'd need the energy. There's a food hall on Spring Street, places for chefs to try out new restaurant concepts without having to go all in. Kind of like a food truck that doesn't move. I got a couple of tacos and a Gatorade, Holt got some kind of curry. We sat at a small round table and enjoyed the companionable anonymity of a crowd. I'd brought my laptop back with me. Holt wasn't happy about leaving her Porsche street parked downtown, and I wasn't giving a would-be thief any extra incentive.

"Most of my hits on Silas Grey came back empty," Holt said, picking at her curry with a plastic fork.

"Doesn't surprise me. Imagine it's an alias."

"I said *most*, not all," Holt said, sounding a little peevish. "That's his real name. There's no criminal record in any of the national databases. He's also never had a security clearance. I had some friends at the IRS run him down."

That didn't surprise me. You can run from just about anybody but the taxman. "What'd they find?" I asked.

"Just his SSN and a few addresses. Proves he's a real person, though. Thing I don't get is, why all this?"

"What do you mean?"

"If he wants to take you out, why not just have you killed? No offense."

"Murder is big medicine, and hard to cover up. Even for someone like him."

"Could you do it?"

I was not answering that. Instead, I said, "Grey works inside the law, mostly. When he does break it, my guess is that it's in ways he knows he can get away with and not face any serious consequences. I don't think Lucious Kett's death was intentional. It was dark, we were all close together, I think the shooter was trying for me and got him by accident. If your boss hadn't leaned so hard on the sheriff, they wouldn't have thought I was involved and maybe I could've gotten some help. Everything Grey has done against me has been to convince me to quit, not to take me out at the knees."

A flash of recognition lit her eyes, and she nodded along. "Because if you've got nothing to lose, you're going to respond like someone with nothing to lose."

"Exactly. That might be his mistake, though."

"Oh, I don't doubt that. You're much too much of an asshole to give up."

"Not that," I said, pulling my laptop out of my bag. "Jerk."

I opened my laptop, balancing it on my legs because there wasn't enough room on the small table. I reached into the bag and retrieved my mobile hotspot, activated it, and tethered it to the computer. Vaughn had filed a motion to quash the arrest warrant, but it could take up to forty-eight hours to process. This was unfortunately verified when I found I still didn't have access to EchoTrace.

Worth remembering that the Orange County Sheriff might not get word for a few days. Of course, going there would be against the advice of counsel, but if I'd made a habit of listening to good advice, I'd be in a different line of work. I floated a soft f-bomb and stowed the laptop back in the bag.

"What are you doing?" she asked.

"You know what EchoTrace is?"

"Yep."

"I'm still locked out of my account because of the warrant."

"Want to use mine?"

"Will you marry me?"

Holt gave me a look that would generally be categorized as "I'm too old for this shit," but she smirked a little too. Tried to hide it, but it was there. I handed her the computer and started clearing the food away so we could work. Because I'm paid to notice things like "clues," I spotted a coffee shop and made a line for it. Of course, this was "upscale urban food hall" coffee, so you couldn't just get a cup, you had to mentally page through a bunch of bullshit just to arrive at "Two drip coffees, please." And it still took them ten minutes to prepare it.

Anyway.

Time and a bunch of unnecessary ceremony later, I had two scalding paper cups of certified organic artisanal jet fuel and returned to the table. I slid one across the table and said, "Careful, that will melt steel."

"Here's what I got," Holt said. She rotated the screen so I could see. "We started using this system for background checks last year. Crowder is also borderline paranoid, so he's got me looking at everyone he does business with. Or," Holt leveled her eyes at me, "wants to take a closer look at."

"How'd you even get access? I wasn't aware they extended this to corporate security types."

"I'm a state licensed investigator, same as you."

That was a chilling thought, honestly. Nothing illegal or unethical about it, just an insight into the way Crowder conducted his business.

Pushing that to the side, I read the summary on Grey.

Genius-level IQ, polymath, speaks German, French, and Dutch fluently, and is conversational in Italian and Spanish.

His father was a diplomat, and he grew up primarily abroad. Grey's undergrad was at the University of Chicago, with a major in interdisciplinary studies focused on "solving big problems" and a minor in data science. Harvard Law. The profile flagged a few pieces he wrote for the *Harvard Law Review* where Grey argued the value of a law degree was as a tool for problem-solving, less for the strict operations of a legal framework or society. After graduation, he was hired by a global risk management firm, first in Boston and transferring to their London practice within a few years. There, he was scooped up by a private intelligence firm. Though they were becoming more common in the US, the Europeans and especially the British had a longer tradition of corporate intelligence. The entire MI6 was the size of a single division in CIA, so they outsourced a lot. Grey honed his tradecraft here, learned surveillance—physical and digital, was trained in advanced psychology, and he applied his problem-solving and data science acumen to great effect. Grey's profile showed an increasing aptitude for corporate intelligence, first in exposing and thwarting industrial espionage. The rest of it is, forgive the pun, a little gray, but reading between the lines it appears Silas moved into corporate and political sabotage. One interesting note, he even went undercover in one company—an English tech firm looking to be acquired by a rival of his client. Someone figured out he was feeding information, exposed him, and caused a bit of a scandal. Knightsbridge Security fired Grey immediately, accusing him of exceeding his mandate. Again, knowing how these things play out, Grey was clearly scapegoated.

He disappeared for a bit, reemerging as a freelance operative. His profile highlighted speculative connections to several corporate and political scandals, each with varying levels of confidence on the level to which he'd engineered them.

So many pieces fit together now.

And something else. The accent. That's why I couldn't place it. It was that same continental inflection Diana had, partway between American English and the King's.

"What now?" Holt said.

"Well, obviously we have to kill him."

"Your biggest problem is that I can't tell when you're joking."

"That doesn't seem like *my* problem."

Holt sighed loud enough that people at the next table heard it.

———

Her Porsche wasn't stolen, so the day was definitely trending up.

Nolan texted me again on Matthews's burner, making sure I'd be there to pick up the phone. I replied, asking where "there" was, and he said he'd tell me.

At 7:50, he texted back with a location and told me he'd drop at eight. If he saw me, he'd keep it and disappear. The Angels Flight trolley, only blocks away from his building, as if we could get more clichéd for a dead drop.

Christ, I hated dealing with amateurs. Maybe losing my license wouldn't be all that bad.

While Vanessa drove, I was still on my laptop, in her instance of Echo-Trace. Something about Grey's profile kept nagging at me, floating just outside of view like an afterimage.

His specialty seemed to be corporate sabotage, which sounded obvious in hindsight. But that's not the kind of person you just come across. You have to know where to not only look but even to start. You'd also have to know people like that existed in the world.

I tasked EchoTrace to research Silas Grey's businesses. He'd use a shell corporation, but it would still have to be incorporated. And he appeared to run a legal operation—more or less—just one that narrowly toed the line. Employers would pay him through an intermediary or holding company, something he could cut ties with if he had to. It'd be a hard thing for a human to unwind, especially with the time we had. I also had world-class AIs at my disposal.

I still had access to NOVA AI. When this started, I'd asked NOVA for briefings on the board members. This time, I cast a wider net and asked it to give me analyses on all the investors, not just the board. Then I set up a separate query in EchoTrace to identify any of the financial transactions going into any corporation registered to Silas Grey. This would take time to unravel, even for an AI. It still had to link trace both the multitude of incorporations at play and the transactions. I also opened the aperture up to include cryptocurrencies.

Even now, I started getting hits on the IRS and SEC databases with employer ID numbers linking to various consulting firms and LLCs that appeared to have only a few employees. Almost all of these were subsidiaries of companies chartered in various offshore locations—Vanuatu, Panama, Grand Cayman, and other places. Some were the traditional offshore banking haunts, others less so. The pattern was established, however. I had the system cross-reference EINs with payments received and where those came from.

The real breakthrough was an aerospace corporation in Texas that employed Grey and was also flagged in a separate DoJ investigation. That link provided an entirely new line of data to plumb, the same way that Asher Nolan being referenced in court had.

Within ten minutes, I had a list of corporate clients. My hunch on crypto was solid, almost all of those transactions were in cryptocurrency.

Like I said, you can outrun anyone but the taxman.

I set up a separate thread to identify any aliases Grey might use.

Next, I had EchoTrace scan for repeated metadata patterns in encrypted communication. I was looking for any IP activity between Grey and employers, or the shell companies one or either might use to communicate. I was going to use that to link to the list of investors exported from NOVA.

It felt like a floodgate had opened up and fresh data was just pouring out.

Asher Nolan's phone was still important, if not vital.

Then, I decided to play a hunch.

I'd never followed up on the name Amara gave me, Denis Kwan and oX Capital. There hadn't been time.

I wasn't beating Silas Grey by setting him up for the police. I was going to take him down by giving Julian's legal team enough that they could bury Grey and his employer in a civil suit. If the government wanted in on that, so much the better.

I had a photo of Silas Grey buying the burners and would soon have one of the two phones he purchased. I'd have the call records from Nolan's phone. The burden of proof in a civil case was lower than in a criminal one. This, with other data I was now collecting, should be enough.

"You're obviously onto something," Vanessa said. I looked up from the screen and found we'd parked.

I sent all of this to my own EchoTrace account, so that I didn't lose progress. With luck, I'd be back up tomorrow.

"I think we've been chasing the wrong person," I said. "What if it's not a board member, but an activist investor that wants to take NOVA down? Or, at least, someone that wants to radically change the company's direction. I was thinking that the reason they wanted to torpedo Julian was to take over the company. Maybe what they're looking to do is take over so they can shut it down. His tech is making a lot of people nervous." Diana had started me on this path, raising the idea that the threat could have come from entirely outside the company. This was also a chance to pressure test Holt and see what she really knew.

"How would that even work?" she asked, skeptically.

"You get enough private equity money you can reverse gravity. They could shut down the controversial part and sell the core AI to any tech company."

"Crowder would buy that in a flat second. That's what he wanted in the first place. How'd you hit on that?" she asked.

"Silas Grey. He specializes in corporate sabotage, undermining companies so that they can be picked apart. Sure, it might very well be Evelyn Hawthorne, but that feels off to me."

"Can that wait? If we're going to get this phone, we've got to move now."

"Let's go."

My phone rang. It was Nolan.

"Hey—this isn't the plan."

There was no voice, just a muffled sound that could've been a hard exhale. Then I heard the phone crash against something.

"Nolan!"

A second of static, and the line went dead.

"What is it?"

"Someone is moving on Nolan. We have to go, now." I opened the Porsche's door and put a foot on the street. "Take the car, cover the back entrance. They might try to run that way."

"Wait—I don't..."

I was already out the door and sprinting down the sidewalk.

Without waiting for traffic to stop, I blasted across Hill and cut through that EV charging station adjacent to Nolan's building.

I skidded to a stop just in time to make the alcove.

The door was a thick, industrial number with a heavy metal handle. It opened with a push. Immediately inside the doorway, stairs ascended to the second floor. I took them. Electronic music, loud and pulsing, emanated through the walls, though I couldn't tell if it was coming from Nolan's apartment or the bar downstairs.

BlackICE Defense was a lobby with four UHD monitors displaying the company logo bolted to the walls. A long, black leather couch ran along one wall, a table in the center, and two chairs. A door leading deeper into the building was open a crack, and the source of the music came from the room beyond. I pushed open the doorway and drew my pistol. There was a meeting room on the left side, presumably for letting clients in behind the firewall, but no offices to speak of. If BlackICE employed anyone but Nolan, they didn't work here. This looked like a front. Something he'd pass through on his way back into the real world, how he calibrated himself. Once he passed through these doors, he wasn't Ghost, he was Asher Nolan.

The door at the end of the hallway was open, music pulsing through, and the lights were on.

You do this long enough, you get a sense for a setup.

Nolan wouldn't have seen this coming.

I knew his type. He was an apex predator in his domain and convinced himself that applied to all the others. Pushing the door fully open with my knuckles, my suspicions were confirmed immediately.

I stepped into the room and saw him.

Nolan was lying facedown in a pool of blood.

He'd been shot in the back of the head at point-blank range, and he hadn't seen it coming.

I turned, just in time to see the punch.

33

Knuckles smashed into the side of my face and knocked the glasses flying.

My head snapped around with them, and it was like a million flash-bulbs went off in front of my eyes. The rest of my body followed the direction of my head. That was a hard hit and precisely delivered. A hand grabbed my pistol and wrenched it out of my grip. I heard it clatter against the ground as another strike hit the side of my head.

It was by luck alone that I was still conscious.

Not that I had much control of my body. I felt like somebody just pulled out my plug.

Two kicks in rapid succession immediately followed the punch. Totally disoriented, I had no idea where they'd come from and couldn't hope to block them. My body lurched in a direction I didn't intend, and I felt like someone who'd woken up and learned the hard way they were still drunk. Another punch, again from a direction I hadn't expected. Apparently, I was fighting an octopus.

I planted my back foot to steady myself and yanked my arms up in a hasty block. The world still looked like Salvador Dalí choreographing a boxing match.

Another punch rocketed toward my face, and this time, training took over. I snapped my wrist up, blocking the strike, and managed to grip my opponent's wrist. I threw a punch of my own, an imprecise knuckle jab aimed at his trachea. It connected, but was a glancing hit and landed on the meaty side of his neck.

My opponent was about my height with another twenty pounds of muscle, at least. He moved with the easy combative grace of someone used to fighting. And he wore a ski mask, because of course he did.

It didn't matter. I knew the build and I knew the eyes.

Damn. I honestly felt a flash of regret over that discovery. I'd come to appreciate Nash, if not almost like him. I'd certainly trusted him enough to have him be my backup.

He chopped hard on my forearm and my grip dissolved; shock waves of numb sensations raced up my arm and I couldn't even flex my fingers. He must have short-circuited a nerve.

Lurching forward, I closed the distance between us. It was a dangerous move, going inside his reach like that, but I needed a break from the frenetic assaults. I knuckle-punched his larynx. That was a strike intended to put someone down, and if I'd had my stance calibrated, I'd have ended this thing with a crushed windpipe. Nash stumbled backward, sputtering and coughing, and I shot the heel of my palm into his nose. Blood spurted out onto my hand.

Before I knew it, before I could react, his two hands grabbed my shoulders and held me in place while he delivered three knee kicks to my sternum. Nash let me go and I fell away from him, feeling about as in control as a spacewalker that just lost his tether. Nash side-kicked me and I flew backward.

Asher didn't invest much in decoration, but even as I hit and slid across the ground, I was looking for something I could use as a weapon. At least until I could find my own pistol.

Electronic music still pounded out its rhythmic thunder. It was nearly impossible to concentrate in here.

I dove for a floor lamp and snatched it up, yanking the cord free from the wall in the same motion.

Nash went for his gun. He must have holstered it after he shot Nolan.

I surged forward, holding that lamp like a trident, and jabbed it into his face. Say this for lamps, the thing had a hell of a reach. The force was enough that the halogen bulb cracked. The music was too loud for me to hear, but I saw the shards falling out. I'd have done serious damage if Nash hadn't been wearing a ski mask.

I kept jabbing Nash with lamp's broken end, just to keep him at bay while I looked for my gun. I got three good thrusts with the thing before Nash wrapped his free arm around it and yanked it out of my grasp.

I dove across the gap to my pistol, but Nash was on top of me instantly. God, this guy was *fast*.

A kick to the ribs and, because I was already hunched over, a heel to the side of my head that sent me to the ground.

Before I knew it, there was a serpentine arm wrapped around my neck with a bicep pushing my Adam's apple back to my spinal cord. Already the darkness closed in around my eyes.

I had about five seconds to come up with something absolutely brilliant, or I was done for.

So, I hit him in the balls.

I jabbed my elbow into his crotch with as much force as my crumpled form could generate. I'm not proud of this, mind you. I know turnabout is fair play and all, but there are rules even in combat.

He grunted, and the pressure on my neck released.

I backpedaled to give myself space.

"Amateurs wear ski masks, Brody," I said, huffing. "Professionals disable security cameras."

"Go to hell, Gage."

Nash leaped forward, though he was still bent over in pain, and I'll take that glee to my grave. He closed the distance between us in three strides.

But before he got there, I pulled my pistol and shot him.

It's never as dramatic as it looks on film. Plus, it was basically a wing shot, firing as I drew. My normal rig is a Glock G34, this was a compact G23 with a .40-caliber round. I hit Brody in the chest, and he dropped like a meteor.

Probably hurt like hell.

Then I did something stupid that I'd regret immediately.

Believing Nolan had cameras on the inside, I walked up to Brody and yanked off his ski mask. For a normal person, getting shot would leave them down for the count. This might not have been Nash's first time.

Just as I was saying, "Surprise, you're on Candid Camera—"

Nash's legs shot out, wrapped around mine, and down I went. My gun clattered across the floor and out of my grip.

Nash was sprinting for the door, leaking blood, before he was even fully on his feet.

Guess fear of being caught overrode whatever desire he had to kill me too.

Or maybe that wasn't the plan. Admittedly, we were pretty far off the map here.

I didn't try to stop Nash. All I could've done was shoot him. Self-defense is an easier case to make when a combat-honed special operator is bearing down on you. Harder to convince a jury if you shoot a man in the back while he's running away.

More important was to figure out what in the actual hell he was doing here.

Was Nash working for Silas Grey all this time…or had my client finally snapped?

To be honest, staring at Asher Nolan's body, I couldn't answer that question.

I called Holt.

"Nolan's dead, Vanessa. Brody Nash did it. He was here. He's probably got the phone, God knows what else. I'm on my way down. We need to call the police."

If she had eyes on the back alley, she wouldn't have seen Nash running out the front.

There was crushing silence on the line.

A strange thing when you're standing next to the dead body of someone you know.

Finally, she spoke.

"I'm sorry, Matt. I'm sure you understand. It's just a job." And Vanessa Holt hung up.

What—the hell—was going on?

Then I remembered all of this would be on camera and I absolutely should not stick around. I heard the distant wail of sirens bouncing off skyscrapers. LAPD's Central Division was just two or three blocks from Nolan's building.

There's no way she could've *known* the hacker would be facedown with his brains splattered across the floor. It wasn't a giant leap for someone with her background. When Nolan didn't show, Holt would have made the same conclusion I did. She just wouldn't know that it was Brody Nash who pulled the trigger. Holt guessed Nolan was dead and called it in.

Maybe I was making mental leaps when it should be baby steps. This wasn't the time for debate.

Time to move, Matt!

If the phone was here, Nash had it now.

That had to be what this was about.

I made fast steps to the stairwell and took them two at a time. Once I hit the street, I looked around and saw police cars in the distance. Where to go? The ground-floor bar was open; that was a risky play, though. It was a weeknight, and even through the windows I could see it wasn't crowded. Instead I cut across the street and headed southwest, away from the oncoming police cars. Figured I could make the end of the block by the time they rolled up and, if luck was with me, make the corner.

Three minutes later, I crossed Hill Street into Pershing Square.

As the adrenaline faded, I felt my limbs go heavy and I had to stop for a breath. The pain from the ass-kicking I'd just received was starting to take shape. That fight could easily have gone another way. I was lucky to have escaped it.

I couldn't make out my reflection in the dark, but I had to assume I looked like I felt.

I cut over four blocks and up three to the Westin Bonaventure. It meant backtracking a little, but it was a huge hotel, four blue-glass towers around a central structure. Even at this time of night, there'd be a cluster of taxis out front.

I still had about two hundred dollars on me, and that should cover cab fare to wherever I needed to go.

Holt was lying all along. She wanted to find out what I knew. The theory that made the most sense was Crowder wanted Silas Grey's identity and who hired him. Crowder wanted to take out the competition, make himself a hero to Julian.

Everything she'd told me—about Kett, about the drones, about how Crowder used her to take down rivals—all of that, plus the fact she'd taken a bullet likely meant for me, was intended to get me to trust her as fast as possible, and I fell right for it. Most of that stuff was very likely true. The part Holt lied about was how she felt about it.

And she had all of my gear.

My laptop.

Shit.

I'd logged into EchoTrace using her account, so she had all the research. And now she knew Brody Nash killed Nolan.

She showed up today to pump me for information, found she was playing with house money, and decided to see how long she could ride the cards. Holt wouldn't have known I'd used EchoTrace until I'd pulled my computer out and showed it to her. Her having an account of her own was just a shitty coincidence.

I'll give her this, Vanessa Holt was a hell of an opportunist.

Unless she wasn't.

I'd known that Grey compromised my phone. It wasn't a hard leap to believe a hacker of Nolan's caliber could access my computer. Was Holt working with them?

Or, had she used some of Crowder's tech? It also wouldn't be a stretch to believe his companies had some offensive cyber capabilities. Christ, even General Graves...

I stopped myself. When it's under stress, the mind has a way of jumping at shadows because of the monsters it's convinced are there.

Focus on what you know.

Nash was hard for me to square. Initially, I'd suspected him, but I judged him completely loyal to Julian. Truly I didn't think Brody Nash was capable of murder. That, I hadn't seen coming.

What was Nash's next move? Who was he a threat to?

Asher Nolan was a ghost, no pun intended. He barely existed in the real world. No relations that I could find.

If he was even remotely tethered to reality, Nash wasn't murdering Julian. Didn't mean he wasn't a threat to Julian, though. Nash was still in play, even with a gunshot wound. He had battlefield experience, knew how to fight hurt, and given the number of ex-SEALs per capital in Southern California, he had someone that he could call in an emergency.

I caught a cab outside the hotel. At first, the guy didn't want to take the fare. He took one look at me and decided that I was too much trouble. I convinced him that I'd been mugged. As soon as the words left my mouth, I amended it to "attempted." He wanted to see the money in advance.

Forty-five minutes and a hundred and twenty-two dollars later, I was across the street from the University Center Mall. It was eleven thirty, and the mall was dead. I'd had the cab driver drop me a block from the mall. I couldn't know whether Holt would go for some scorched earth and call the location of my Defender into the sheriff's department, though that really seemed like her kind of move.

I worked my way around the parking lot's perimeter. Everything was closed, and there were no bars or local hangs nearby, so I was it. I spotted a patrol car on the far side, maybe a hundred yards from the Defender. His main lights were off, but I could see the two yellow ones beneath them letting me know the engine was running.

Now I had a choice to make.

If that cop was watching my car, I'd had it. I had an unregistered firearm in my possession, which I wasn't getting rid of because there was now a psychopath ex–Navy SEAL on the loose, and I was the thing between him and a murder rap. Might as well go all in. I cut back, breaking line of sight with the cop, who I was sure never saw me anyway at this distance. With the mall between us, I jogged across the parking lot to the sidewalk and walked around the mall's west wing. The police car was much farther back, with a view of the mall's entire southern face, while the Defender was parked on the far west side. Because of the building's geometry, the cop could see my ride but he couldn't currently see me.

I walked quickly to the Defender. One of the advantages of a thirty-year-old car was that it didn't have a remote unlock that simultaneously flashed its lights. I got in, turned it on, and didn't turn the headlights on until I was out of the cop's sight. I drove the opposite direction, exiting to a frontage road.

Next stop, Julian's.

It seemed to be a truism of the tech community that its members were night owls, and my client was no different.

The lights were on when I pulled up to his house. Of course, I'd had to tell him I was coming to get past the gate guard.

I couldn't call him from the cab and warn him about Nash, so a detailed explanation would have to wait until I got there. I had texted him from the cab, saying that I had updates and wanted to know if he'd be awake. He said he would be.

For all the good it would do, I called Sergeant Ortega. Knowing there was a murderer on the loose and he might go to ground here seemed like a good citizen thing to do.

It went straight to voicemail.

Speaking of cops, I still needed to deal with LAPD on Nolan's murder. There would be more questions if I didn't. The longer I waited, the more complicated the answer became.

What would I say? How would I explain my fleeing the scene?

If I told them I was concerned about Julian's safety—which I was— they'd just say I should've contacted the police.

You know, maybe this wasn't a "Matt Problem." Maybe it was a "Matt's Lawyer's Problem."

Julian was not happy when I arrived and, from his perspective, I could understand why.

His pupils were dilated, he was sweating slightly, and within a second of seeing him, I knew he was wired for sound. I'd suspected he'd been taking Adderall for some time, and all the classic signs of amphetamine use were on panoramic display.

He waited until his front door closed behind me before he started yelling, because I guess he had to yell at someone and I was the person he paid. I saw

Wexler in the kitchen. He looked like a contestant for *The Running Man*, his face a cocktail of indignation and nerves. There was something else, regret, maybe? Wexler had given his life's work, this world-changing idea, over to Julian and was now watching as his college roommate burned it to the ground. Or someone did that on Julian's behalf. In the end, was it any different?

Julian followed me, still shouting. Wexler couldn't decide if he was an inmate or a guard.

All that time hanging out at Cosmic Ray's with those veteran surfers, I'd picked up a few things. They all believed that the ocean had its own energy, and surfing was about tapping into that energy to ride the wave. You couldn't just go whenever, though. You had to wait for your set. Sometimes that meant waiting your turn until the surfers who got there first went, sometimes it meant waiting for the sea to tell you.

When Julian shouted, "They can't fucking *do* this!" I knew it was my set.

"Yes, they can," I said calmly. Julian had not expected that and sputtered, an outboard motor that wouldn't catch. "If half of what you tell me about NOVA is true, you're getting off easy. Julian, you've said this technology could change the world, right? Now, let's say you didn't invent that but are very close to it. How hard would it be to convince yourself that a little invented scandal, a small bad thing in the grand scheme, was morally justified? If you can't get there, pal, it's a failure of imagination."

"Matt, do you have *any* idea who's behind this yet?" Wexler asked, both desperate to know and angry it had taken this long.

"We'll get there. First, there's some things I need to make you both current on."

"We don't have—"

"Julian, you're my client, and that gives you a lot of latitude, but for right now, shut up. Please sit down."

I followed them into the front room where Julian and I had drinks what felt like an eternity ago.

When they were seated, I pointed at the bar. "May I?"

Julian shook his head but said, "Be my guest."

This was a little bit of theater, admittedly, space to get him to calm down. I found a bottle of Yamazaki twelve-year, no slouch but not the most expensive thing in his bar. It'd be bad form to reach for his best spirits under the circumstances. After setting the bottle and three glasses down on the table in the center, I poured myself one and walked over to the window to peer out through the curtains. Again, a little bit of theater.

"Asher Nolan, the hacker who co-opted your demo, is dead. I was supposed to meet him this evening. I'd convinced him to help me. When he didn't show, I went to his home. The door was open and I found him. He was shot in the head. Brody Nash killed him." I gave them both the time it took me to take a sip of the Japanese whiskey to spit protest words into the air before continuing. "I saw Nash there, so there's no point arguing that it wasn't him. Or that it was a frame. I caught him, he tried to take me out. No, I didn't kill Brody."

Though not for a lack of trying.

Julian's chemically amplified state cycled him through the emotional journey at lightning speed. He landed on grief quickly, head in his hands. I walked over to the table and poured him a drink.

Wexler looked confused, if not baffled.

"Have either of you heard from Brody recently?"

I stared them both down, studying their faces.

"I haven't talked to him in days," Julian said.

"Why would he do it?" Wexler asked, now reaching for the bottle himself.

"My guess is money. The operative behind this is a man named Silas Grey." I watched their reactions as I revealed the name. Julian expectedly erratic, Graham was looking around the room. I continued. "Grey is a kind of corporate hit man. Made a career of doing stuff like this, curating scandals to facilitate corporate take-overs, tank political campaigns." I studied them both as I delivered the news. Neither of their eyes were on me. Julian was in his own world. Graham's hand shook while he poured, and he was intently focused on the glass. "I think Grey recruited Brody to be his man on the inside. It seems like Grey is tying up loose ends. Asher Nolan was a recluse hacker and a criminal. No one would miss him. Maybe that's how Grey justifies these things. Or, maybe he just told Brody, 'Wouldn't it be easier if.' I don't know."

That would mean Grey planned to kill Nash, too. He couldn't risk Brody being arrested and flipping on him.

"Have you spoken to the police?" Graham said, finally looking up.

"Not yet. There wasn't a great way to explain what I was doing there without blowing a lid on this entire thing. And I'd be tied up with them for hours. That would give Nash and Grey all the time they'd need to end this."

"Are we in danger?" Julian asked, seeming to have gotten hold of himself now. That was another thing I'd noticed, at least with him. His reactions swung wildly when he was using, at least with amphetamines. He'd go from wildly erratic to manically focused.

"It doesn't make sense that they would try to kill you. If the goal is to take over the company, they wouldn't execute this elaborate smear campaign just to shoot you in the head at the end."

Julian's expression paled, and I regretted my choice of words.

"What if that was the point?" Wexler asked. What was that, anger?

"I think you're about to find out how involved a murder investigation is," I said. Graham's face whitewashed, and he said nothing else.

"No," Julian said, and he sounded mostly convinced. "Do you know who did it? Who hired this Silas Grey?"

"I do. If I tell you now, I need your word you aren't going to do anything, Julian."

"What I'm going to do is bury the bastard."

"I need to know that you're not going to fly off the rails and try to expose them before we're ready. First thing in the morning, we three need to meet with your corporate counsel and decide what the next move is. Can we agree?"

Julian practically vibrated, impotent rage bouncing off him in waves. The desire to do *something*, to lash out, to find any vector for his anger nearly overwhelmed him.

He stood and stalked across the room, then back. Julian paused near the table, with Wexler and I trading confused looks. He mumbled, "Fine," and grabbed his glass. It took him a moment to recognize that it was empty.

"Graham?"

"Yes," he said, almost a stammer.

"Okay, then. It's Evelyn Hawthorne."

I watched them process it. Julian's face purpled with a fury he didn't have a vector for. Graham looked...relieved? He sank back in his chair, hiding his mouth behind the tumbler before he drained his glass. It didn't quite hide the smirk.

"I'll give a more complete accounting in the morning, but I'm sure. Silas Grey impersonated a Commerce agent using credentials he only could've gotten from the inside. I also learned from some Washington contacts that she was making deals with the Senate Appropriations Committee for NOVA trials in DoD. So, it fits that she'd try to throw Crowder under the bus, seeing as Defense is his playground."

Julian sputtered, a broken sprinkler of invective.

"Graham, why don't you go home and get some rest. Tomorrow is going to be a long day. I'll stand watch here."

Graham rose, saying, "That's a good idea."

He walked to the door, opened it without another word, and we watched him go.

Once he was gone, I said, "Do you have your laptop here? Can you fire up NOVA?"

"Of course," Julian said. "Why? What's going on?"

"Graham is the one who did it, and now we're going to nail him to the wall."

34

Julian didn't move, didn't speak.

He sat, filled his glass, and stared at the table.

Honestly, I was expecting a fusillade of invective and threats to fire me. The fact that he didn't was telling.

Julian looked like he needed time to process this, so I gave him that space, saying nothing until he looked up from his glass with eyes so weary they were barely up to the task.

"Let's hear it," he said.

"I have an AI investigative assistant and case manager called EchoTrace."

"You've told me about it before," Julian said in a clipped voice, glass halfway to his mouth.

"Right. Well, I ran extensive link tracing on all your investors. There's a group called Velocity Foundry, do you know them?"

Julian looked confused and shrugged. "No."

"You don't, because it's a bullshit company. They're owned by another fund called Blueprint Alpha, which is also bullshit. It's a series of shell corporations that ultimately rolls up to a private equity company, oX Capital. This group is a little cagey about revealing who they are, they just can't hide everything from the IRS. EchoTrace, because it's only available to law enforcement agencies and licensed PIs, can also tap into the IRS's anti-money laundering systems. oX Capital is owned by a man named Denis Kwan. Denis and Graham are old friends. They came up at Google together, Kwan cashed out and used that money to become a PE fund manager." I held a moment, to make sure he was following. "Let's fast-forward to the good stuff. Three years ago, Kwan tried to engineer a buyout of an East Coast machine-learning firm called AIgnition. Their CEO didn't want to accept the offer, until it was discovered that he had some skeletons in his closet. He quickly retired to 'focus on his family,' and sold his shares. Want to guess how Kwan got his leverage?"

"Silas Grey," Julian said.

I nodded.

Knowing that I wouldn't have EchoTrace access for some time, I'd forwarded a soft copy of the report I'd produced with Vanessa's account to my own email.

"What was all that about Hawthorne?" Julian asked.

"I wanted Graham to think I fell for it. Grey did pose as a Commerce agent, probably to implicate her."

"What do you need NOVA for?" Julian said.

"Right now, we've got a smoking gun, but I still want the fingerprints from the grip."

Julian got his laptop from the kitchen island and brought it over. "Hi, NOVA."

"Good evening, Julian. How can I help?" NOVA said. Had to admit, the speech was very good.

"NOVA, do you remember my associate, Matt Gage?"

"Of course. Hello, Mr. Gage."

"Hello, NOVA. Do you recognize my voice?" I said, responding the way Julian coached me what felt like months ago.

"I do," the computer said.

"NOVA, grant Matt CEO-level access." Julian recited a passphrase. NOVA asked him to confirm it and asked how long I should retain access. Julian told him two hours. He then used the fingerprint scanner and camera for two levels of biometric validation. Once the security procedures were completed, I asked NOVA to identify any financial transactions executed over the last six months, eliminating any that were recurring. It took a few minutes of back-and-forth refining but eventually homed in on several that were deleted. Upon inquiring further about those, we found the security access logs had been redacted. I asked to see that information, NOVA informed me that I was not authorized and not even Julian could override it. I instructed NOVA to reconstruct the erased timestamps if possible. Instead of financial transactions, which were a long shot, what we found was that two days ago, Wexler restructured the executive access protocols. Effectively creating a wall around certain datasets that only he could access.

We kept at it, bouncing off his executive-level privileges for the next twenty minutes or so.

More than that, we learned that Wexler didn't just delete data, he scrubbed it, removing the digital breadcrumbs that would lead us to him.

But the neat thing about artificial intelligence was that it could learn.

"Matt, may I ask what you're looking for?" NOVA asked.

I shot Julian a glance, who nodded his assent.

"NOVA, we believe Graham Wexler is conspiring with Brody Nash to take over the company illegally. We are looking for proof."

"I understand." NOVA paused for a few seconds, a near eternity in machine time. "I have something you may find useful. I have identified encrypted internal messages with similar syntactical patterns between Mr. Wexler and Mr. Nash. These logs were deleted."

"Is it possible to re-create them?" I asked.

"It is possible to re-create them by accessing an older version of a server backup."

Okay, then why not just do that?

"NOVA?" Julian prompted.

"Our corporate security policy prevents me from this type of investigative analysis unless duly authorized by two corporate officers."

"What policy is that?"

"Mr. Wexler enacted this recently and was co-authorized by Mr. Nash," NOVA said. Watching a coup in real time is an experience few people get. I don't recommend it.

Julian attempted to bypass those new security parameters, but NOVA stalled him each time, bouncing off the protocols Wexler set. Then, I got an idea.

"NOVA, can you infer anything from data fragments of deleted messages, or their server backups?"

"Yes, I can infer coordination between Mr. Wexler and Mr. Nash. Specifically, Mr. Wexler's desire to keep these conversations secret."

A partially rebuilt message appeared on the screen:

Brody.Nash: ...status?

Graham.Wexler: Don't update me here.

Brody.Nash: We need to move soon.

Graham.Wexler: I said not on company servers.

NOVA continued, "Following this exchange, all associated messages were purged. However, I have recovered additional financial data showing that Mr. Wexler has diverted special project funds to an external account."

"NOVA, any financial transactions above five thousand dollars require CEO and CFO approval. Do you see a record of that?" Julian said.

"Julian, it appears Mr. Wexler entered your authorization. According to session logs, your passphrase and username were used to authenticate the transaction."

"I authorized no such thing," Julian said. "NOVA, Graham used my credentials without my permission. This violates our security policy and potentially the law. I need you to override the new protocols."

Another pause, then NOVA said, "I understand, Julian."

"NOVA, where did the special projects money go?"

"To a consulting firm called Blackroot, Inc. It is chartered in Delaware. Corporate records indicate five employees. However, I cannot correlate these names with any digital patterns, electronic behaviors, or online communication."

"Meaning they aren't real," I said.

"That is a valid assumption. Blackroot, Inc., is a subsidiary of—"

"NOVA, stop. Can you roll up the companies that Blackroot is owned by? A common tactic with shell corporations is that they are nested within other shell corporations."

NOVA displayed the results on screen. I sent a copy of my EchoTrace report to Julian's corporate email address, and he instructed NOVA to ingest and analyze it.

"NOVA, can you find any connections between the shell corporations in this document and the ones that Mr. Wexler sent payments to using special projects funds?"

"Yes, Matt. I can also determine from corporate filings that Blackroot was dissolved the day after the transaction processed."

That was everything.

"NOVA, can you create a chronological summary of Wexler's activities. Include timestamps and command inputs for proper attribution when appropriate."

"Of course, Matt."

"Thank you. Once that's done, I would like you to send that summary to every member of the board of directors. Include the EchoTrace analysis file that I gave you."

"I will get right on it," NOVA said.

I looked at Julian. His face was ashen, but steeled.

Julian said, "NOVA, I want you to conduct a predictive analysis on Graham Wexler's likely actions. Use your interactions with him since inception as the basis for the analysis. Be sure to factor these most recent steps, including his new security protocols."

"Mr. Wexler is attempting to physically and virtually lock you out of the company and our information environment. I have detected a security system configuration change, which is scheduled to take effect within the next hour. This was logged in the last ten minutes. Security verification protocols prohibit this from being executed immediately. This will terminate physical building access and cut off your digital access to all corporate systems, including me."

"NOVA, rescind that immediately."

"I am unable to, Julian. The code was entered directly into the servers at headquarters, with instructions that I am not permitted to override. It leverages the new protocols Mr. Wexler just implemented."

"Julian, can you undo that if we're in the building?"

"Probably." He'd gotten distant and distracted. The full realization of

Graham's betrayal was only now starting to cut through the chemical fog. Graham knew Julian on a level and with an intimacy that I doubted anyone else in his life ever had. Graham understood Julian, knew what drove him on a fundamental, essential level. And Graham used that knowledge to undermine Julian, to usurp him. He offered that up to Silas Grey, and the operative conducted Wexler like a dark maestro.

I grabbed the laptop and handed it to Julian, who stood there, dumbfounded. Then I grabbed his arm and pulled. "We need to go. Tether that computer to your phone."

We were almost to the door when the lights went out.

"NOVA, is there a power outage?" Julian asked.

"Southern California Edison has not reported one," NOVA said from his computer speaker.

"Julian, do you have a panic room?"

"No, why would I?" He asked it like I was a consummate fool to suggest the idea.

"Then get down."

"What?"

I grabbed his shoulder and pushed him to the floor. I joined Julian in a crouch and drew my Glock. "Is NOVA wired into your home security system the way it is at the office?" That seemed a very Julian thing to do.

"I don't have a security system yet. There wasn't time to put one in."

He'd been here for six months, but this wasn't the time for debating the point.

Okay, ingress points for an intruder. There was a door in the back of the garage, and there were three sets of doors leading out to the patio. The first, double glass doors, off the kitchen; the second set of double doors was in the living room; and a third door was in a study. The patio faced the beach with an eight-foot privacy fence surrounding the property. The patio was well lit, though there was a deck off the second-floor master suite that wrapped around half the house, and those lights weren't on now. Julian's house was nearly four thousand square feet. It was a lot of area to cover.

If Julian had his faculties together, I'd have him sneak out to the garage and blast out of here in his G-Wagon while I caused a diversion. That vehicle would be plenty fast. In his current state, I wasn't sure he could operate a car at all, let alone potentially handle evasive maneuvers. The Defender was parked in the driveway. I didn't want to break for that without knowing what we faced.

Graham left twenty minutes ago, and it'd been at least two hours since my confrontation with Nash. Grey wasn't a trigger puller, and he also didn't have combat experience. He'd never get into a straight fight with me. He would send a proxy. Nash was hurt but still combat effective. Nash would be alone. One of his SEAL buddies might patch him up, one of them might even help him tag-team me if Nash could invent a good enough story—though I didn't think he was crafty enough for that. None of them would join him in assaulting Julian Kessler's home.

"W-w-what do we do?" Julian asked.

A rock through a pane of glass has a way of galvanizing action.

"I want you to get upstairs. Get into your bedroom and lock the door. Call 911 and tell them there is a home invasion in progress. Tell them I'm here, that I'm licensed and armed and defending the property. Do you got that?"

"Yes."

"If someone tries coming through the door, you can get out from the deck."

"What? There are no stairs!"

"Climb over the railing and drop. You hit the grass, you'll be fine. Go!"

I watched Julian disappear into the darkness.

The glass breaking came from the back of the house, one of the windows that I didn't have eyes on. Then I remembered the front door wasn't locked.

Using a wall as cover, I crept out of the kitchen and got line of sight on the front door as it slid open. Without hesitating, I put two rounds through it.

Breaking cover, I stalked forward into the foyer, pistol level.

The door burst open. I heard the muffled shots of a suppressed pistol and dove for the ground. Looks like I'd missed.

I hit the ground, rolled, and got to a crouch in the shadows just in time to see the murky form racing across the foyer and deeper into the house.

Goddamn it, Nash.

I pivoted and silently retraced my steps to the kitchen. Nash wouldn't know Julian ran upstairs and would clear the first floor before checking anywhere else. He wasn't here for Julian, though. I was the only link to Nolan's murder. I assumed Nolan had video cameras inside his house, it fit the profile, but I didn't *know*.

With my back to the wall, I crept deeper into the house.

Nash's path would've taken him into the living room, through a stubby hall between the wide staircase and wall. There was a chance he'd taken the stairs, though those were wood and I'd likely hear the creak. He'd clear the ground floor anyway.

I slipped back into the kitchen, listening for any sounds of Nash's movement—shoes on the floorboards or labored breathing. Maybe a gasp of pain as he tweaked the gunshot wound I'd just given him. Then I remembered who I was dealing with. He'd be trained not to give anything away. The house was silent, though there was a lot of wall between Nash and me.

There was a little more ambient light in the kitchen. Its back wall faced the ocean, and Julian kept the blinds up for the natural light. Moonlight spilled through, and I could make out the lines of glowing surf through the window.

I paused.

Still nothing.

Back to that central wall, I rotated around, leading with my pistol and clearing the corners. The kitchen flowed into the living room. I advanced into it slowly, creeping like a thief. Unless the bastard vanished, he'd have to be in here.

With an aching slowness, I holstered my pistol.

A blind gunfight is tactically stupid and viscerally dangerous. I also wanted Nash alive. The police would be on their way now—if not from Julian's call, certainly from my first two shots. Those had been a reaction. I needed to subdue Nash for the authorities. He could link Wexler to Grey and everything else.

An inky shadow detached itself from the wall, and I surged forward. Nash pivoted, but I closed the gap between us too quickly for him. I was there in three strides, planted my foot, and delivered a side kick with all the force I could generate.

My foot landed square in Nash's center of mass, and he went flying with a surprised grunt. Something wasn't right. I'd fought Nash recently and knew how big he was. Punching that asshole felt like boxing with a wall. This was not that. This was *half* that.

Two suppressed rounds broke the wall next to my head, and I dove for the ground.

"Time's up, Gage."

That was Vanessa Holt.

35

Holt, I guessed, was crouched behind a couch. This made no sense. She had all my files. She could just serve that up to her boss and he could use that for his endgame. There was no logic in coming here.

This was also not the time for questions.

Breaking cover, I sprinted across the room. I saw her murky form rise out of the gloom. Couldn't tell in the dark whether she was right- or left-handed, didn't know exactly where the gun was, but aimed for the right. A split-second realization that I didn't remember where she'd been shot. I struck out with my hand, grabbed what I thought was her wrist, and yanked it forward to take her off-balance. In the same motion, I brought my knee up to her forearm to smash her grip on the gun.

Holt grabbed my wrist with her other hand, and we battled for control of the pistol. The Air Force trained her how to prevent a larger male opponent from disarming her. The CIA taught me to fight dirty.

Forcing the barrel down with my right hand, I pushed further into her reach and snapped a punch with my left at her neck. The strike landed. Holt coughed and jerked back in a violent, uncontrolled reflex. I jerked the pistol out of her hands, but the action cost me. If the lights had been on, I could've seen the counterattack. Holt kneed my rib cage, recalibrated with incredible quickness, and kicked me in the balls.

Karmically, I probably had that coming.

Seizing the advantage from my, um, discomfort, Holt tried wrenching the pistol back out of my grasp, but doubled over as I was, I'd just appear as an amorphous blob of shadow in the dark room. All she managed was to grab my elbow, which I promptly sent into her jaw.

I tossed her pistol away from me. The weapon clattered down the hall and landed somewhere in the foyer. Once I backed her up a few feet, I'd draw my own weapon and end this thing.

"Vanessa, what the hell are you doing?" I said, watching her shadowy form to see if she'd press the attack or make a dash to find her gun.

"You're on the wrong side of this, Gage. You always were." She surged forward. My eyes had adjusted enough that I saw a jab coming from her left hand and blocked it.

That was a feint.

A sharp pain exploded in my head, filling my vision with a billion glittering stars of hurt, the formation of an entirely new and terrible galaxy. My head snapped around, and I was dangerously off-balance. Too dark to see what she'd hit me with, but I knew it was metal and about as wide as my thumb. I staggered to the side and Holt was on top of me, panther-quick. She landed another strike in my rib cage and I felt something give way. Holt tried kneeing me in the face but mistimed it in the dark, and I moved out of the way just in time to feel her knee brush past.

Recovering my footing, I had both arms up in a defensive posture. I could mostly make out her form and pushed forward. Holt saw that, too, and punched as I moved. The hit landed awkwardly and probably not where she intended, but the metal drove into my right shoulder with an excruciating lance of pain. My arm went numb.

I jabbed with my left hand and connected. Felt like just below the eye. I put some knuckle on it, and she'd be seeing stars now too. Holt chopped, and that metal bar hit me just below the chin. I fell backward, unable to breathe. Panic flooded as I couldn't find my breath and I feared she'd crushed my windpipe. Holt was on top of me instantly, kicking and driving me backward.

A reflexive lungful of air rushed in, and the panic subsided.

Holt loomed over, and I caught her silhouette framed against a window.

I saw the punch just as she tried to send it, brought both arms up to block, and caught her hand just before it connected with my face. I clamped down on her wrist and realized what the weapon was. An impact kerambit was a blunt-force version of the curved blade of the same name, a J-shaped length of metal with an end extending forward beneath the wielder's pinky finger and a metal loop around the index.

Holding onto her wrist with both hands, I used as much force as I could generate to torque her body off-balance. I planted a side kick, mostly to push her further off her feet, and stood. I drew my pistol and fired a warning shot.

The muzzle flash lit the room for a fraction of a second, blinding us both.

"Stop!" I shouted.

Holt lunged to the left, through the hall toward the front of the house. She was going for her gun.

I guess we were doing this.

Stupid.

I ran back the way I'd come, looping through the kitchen. Running was hard. She'd shaken my equilibrium like it'd been a snow globe. I crashed into the kitchen island on my way, knocking something off. It shattered on the floor.

Bracing myself against a wall, I said, "Vanessa, stop. You don't need to do this."

When she didn't respond, I pushed forward into the dining room, taking up a position behind Julian's massive and never-used formal table. The table was ebony, and the room itself was pitch black. I'd be a ghost in here. I had line of sight to the foyer and saw Holt, framed against the windows, questing for the gun. The dark plays tricks with your eyes, which was why I'd not wanted to have a shootout here. I thought I saw her, but I wasn't *sure*, certainly not enough to send lead into Julian's front room. I broke cover, moved around the table, and edged in on the foyer so I could see her. The front door was still open.

"Holt, I have you covered. It's over. Place your hands on top of your head," I said, hoping the bluff would hold.

I heard her rack the slide, chambering a round.

The lights came on, and a gun fired.

36

Brody Nash stood framed by the front door, a pistol in his hand and confusion on his face.

He'd come in just as the lights came on, saw Holt, and made a split-second decision to fire. Thankfully, he missed.

Holt recovered her pistol and, now that she could see me, had a bead on me. I had her covered, though it was just a couple-degree pivot to Nash. Still, if someone's trigger slipped, none of us were walking away.

Holt and Nash had both come here to kill me. That was apparent. Nash's logic, I could back into. I could identify him as Nolan's killer. I still couldn't fathom what Holt was trying to do. If she was still working for Crowder, fine, murdering me would coffin nail any plans he had for NOVA.

"Someone want to explain what the actual fuck is going on here?" I said. Then added, "And maybe explain without shooting."

No one offered an answer, and we all stood there longer than was comfortable. *The Good, the Bad, and the Ugly* in a beachfront mansion.

"You patched yourself up quick, Brody." Maybe reminding him that I'd already shot him once today would shake something loose. Or clue Holt to the fact he was injured.

"Is there ever a time when you *don't* talk?" Holt said.

"What are you even doing here, Vanessa? You have my laptop. You have all the evidence that proves *his* boss was behind it." I jerked my chin at Nash. "What do you even need?"

"Right. That's all fake, Gage. This entire thing was a setup."

"I've been trying to convince you all of that for about three weeks."

"No, idiot. Julian. The whole thing is staged. He faked all of this to hire you, find someone he could finger, and use that to justify terminating his board of directors. *That's* how Julian takes control of the company."

"What bright-eyed son of a bitch put that idea in your head?"

"Silas Grey," she said, without a second's hesitation.

"Silas Grey told you that? When?"

"Doesn't matter. He said this entire thing was a ploy by Wexler and Kessler, they hired him to do it. Crowder knew this all along, it's why he put people on you."

That explained so much. That was why so many of them believed I was an actual threat to them. They were attributing Grey's moves to me.

"Why would Grey admit that to you?" I was too many steps behind right now. "Hold on, I'm not following. Grey tells you that Julian and Wexler are in cahoots, that they conspired to eliminate the board. He also told you that Julian hired me as some kind of smoke screen? How does that even work?"

"Julian hired you to follow the breadcrumbs that Grey left, push all the right pressure points. You were here to sell it," Holt said.

"Okay, but then he sent you here to kill me. That doesn't make any sense."

"Yeah, I'm not following that either, to be honest," Nash said.

"Grey told me you killed Nolan, Gage," Holt said. "Nolan was scared for his life after you threatened him, and Grey had a camera feed up in the apartment to watch him. He said you figured it all out, that you were a plant, and after you killed Nolan, you came here to confront Kessler. Grey told me that if I could stop you, I'd be a hero. Said I was the only one in a position to do it."

"That's not true," Nash said. His voice had a dreamlike quality, like he was just waking up. "*I* shot Nolan. I was afraid he was going to skip town, and I didn't want him to escape. He pulled a gun on me. It got out of hand. I got the drop on him and shot him."

It sure as hell looked like an ambush to me, and I didn't see a weapon anywhere. Though, I also didn't look.

"Guys, I'm lowering my weapon now. Maybe you can do that too. I think we've all been played here." Holding one hand out to stay them, and praying I wasn't making a fatal miscalculation, I dropped my gun off level and holstered it.

To my amazement, no one shot me.

Grey was a master manipulator. He knew exactly the right lever to pull with Vanessa Holt and at exactly the right moment. I didn't know how he figured out we were together, unless he'd been watching me. Anything was possible with him.

Brody looked to me, then to Holt, and lowered his weapon. Confusion and anguish played a rapid chess match across Holt's face. She might have had this the worst of all. She'd been manipulated very nearly into taking an innocent life. That's a hard fall for an ex-cop.

A flood of decisions played out in rapid succession in my mind. Having both of them here, in custody, would mean whatever Graham Wexler tried tonight would get stopped dead. Holt wouldn't know where Grey was, he was too good for that. She could at least confirm he existed. All that was on one side of the balance.

I made a different call.

"The police are going to be here any minute. Maybe you two shouldn't be," I said. "Brody, Nolan was a career criminal and an asshole. He won't be missed by anyone but the homicide squad. They will nail you to the wall for him. If they find you, that is. You should disappear. You can be in Mexico in a couple hours and from there, just fade away. No one is going to come looking, not over Asher Nolan."

Holt interjected, "I'm not going anywhere. I need to explain what happened to the police. They need to know about Grey."

I shrugged. For all the good it would do.

I walked over to Nash, who was still standing in the doorway. "Brody, I have a...friend...in Panama City. If you make your way down there, tell him I sent you. He can get you set up with a new identity."

"Why would you do that?"

That was a great question.

"This one of those times your mouth is getting in front of your brain?" Holt asked, with a mixture of equal parts curiosity and sarcasm. I flashed her the flick of a side-eye, otherwise I ignored the jab.

"Because we both got duped, Sheepdog," I told him honestly. Brody laughed at the moniker, snapping the tension. "I'm tired of being a pawn. Letting you two go is going to make it harder on me. Still, we all nearly killed each other over this thing. That's not right either." Nash nodded and faded out the door.

Halfway out, Brody stopped and turned back to me. "Thank you, Matt."

"*Vaya con Dios,*" I said with a dull wave, and he was gone.

I got it. Julian, Graham, and the rest of them got all these people drunk on changing the world. They would have fortunes to ride shotgun with their history-defining power. They were all swept up in it, a passionate and furious tsunami. And they were all equally blind to the destruction it wrought.

When Brody left, I said, "You should reconsider leaving."

"No," Holt said.

"Right now, Julian doesn't know you're involved. If he finds out you came here to kill him, it's going to end badly for you."

"I already told you. I wasn't here for him."

"He won't see it that way." I walked closer to her and lowered my voice to just about a whisper. "His ego is not going to let him see it any other way."

The dawning of a starkly different future formed in her eyes. After the briefest contemplation, Holt nodded and moved to the door. We could hear sirens getting closer. Holt wouldn't have been able to park in the neighborhood because security wouldn't let her in at this hour without clearing it with a resident first.

"What do I tell the police?"

"The truth. Everything you told me tonight. You just got away in the confusion."

"Okay." She took a step and turned back to me. "Back in the car, when you were talking about who you suspected, you told me you thought it was Hawthorne. You knew by then, didn't you, that it was really Wexler." I nodded. "You did that on purpose."

"I did," I said.

Holt gave me a strange look, as if surprised that I'd deceived her. Then she nodded and quickly moved away.

Holt disappeared, hopefully avoiding the now growing number of curious neighbors. One of the exterior doors from the back of the house opened and closed. I whipped about, pistol out.

Julian stepped out of the kitchen. I holstered the weapon.

"You got the lights on?"

"I'm an engineer," he said, incredulous. He'd climbed over the side of the deck and dropped down in the dark. I wouldn't have thought he had it in him. Julian surveyed the damage. "Who was it?"

I held my response for a few seconds while I considered him, and what Holt told me about him. I didn't believe her, exactly. It was Silas Grey's manipulation. Still.

"It was Vanessa Holt, Crowder's head of security."

"What was she doing here?"

"Silas Grey somehow got ahold of her, convinced her that I'd snapped and was going to harm you. Not sure how he pulled it off."

"What'd you do?"

"Some Jason Bourne shit," I said.

"Sick."

The police rolled in on us like a rogue wave of confused authority. Thankfully, it was Huntington Beach PD and not Orange County Sheriff. I mostly told the truth, though I left out Brody Nash. Julian didn't even know about him, and it'd stay that way. It remained to be seen whether Graham manipulated Brody into killing Asher Nolan, or if he'd done it out of some funhouse view of his role in this thing. Maybe I was just tired of the gods deciding who lived and who died.

I said the unregistered Glock belonged to Holt and was probably a drop gun. That's what she got for duping me and stealing my laptop. I wouldn't admit until later that it'd been a solid move on her part. Something I'd have done.

An EMT saved me from the full brunt of questioning. She concluded that I'd likely suffered a concussion and needed to seek medical attention. They took me to Huntington Beach Hospital. Unfortunately, it meant that I wouldn't get to coach Julian through what to say to the authorities. At this point, I'd hoped he'd picked up enough from me by osmosis to keep his mouth shut. My biggest fear was him fingering the wrong person. Either out of ignorance or spite.

I texted Vivian Vaughn as accurate a summary as I could manage in the ambulance ride from Julian's.

37

I didn't wake until sometime in the late morning, and there was a Huntington Beach Police detective waiting for me when I did. The doctor got first go and said that I'd suffered cracked ribs, multiple contusions, and head trauma, though I had not been concussed. I was free to go and would be sent home with pain medication and should follow up with my primary care doctor in a few days. Good reminder that I should get one of those. The ER doc cleared me to speak with the detective.

Vivian Vaughn was there as well and said that I fully intended to cooperate, but told the detective about the situation with the OC Sheriff to explain why I'd be questioned in the presence of my attorney. As the two of them were discussing details about me, I casually reminded them both that I was in the room, hadn't eaten in close to twenty hours, and would like a drink of water.

Once the logistics were sorted, I told the cop everything that'd happened from the moment I left Vivian's office the afternoon before. I could tell by Vivian's facial expression that even she was surprised at how much trouble I could get into in such a short period of time. She did not hide her displeasure at my doing the exact opposite of what she told me to do.

I asked about Julian, and they said he was at home, resting, and that they had a squad car out front.

The detective stayed with me for about an hour. I told him about my work with EchoTrace, which should paint an effective trail from Silas Grey to Asher Nolan to Denis Kwan and, ultimately, to Graham Wexler. I also explained that courtesy of that bullshit arrest warrant and pending action on my PI license, my app access was currently suspended. EchoTrace has a law enforcement override, so they could access it once they produced a warrant. That would take some time to work out, however.

After the detective left, Vivian Vaughn had some rather pointed questions about why I ignored the advice of counsel and didn't, and I'm quoting her here, "stay the fuck out of Orange fucking County."

I informed her that was an excellent primer to our relationship.

They discharged me shortly after.

Vivian drove me home and, I have to tell you, if you ever get your ass kicked by a former spec ops guy and then further pummeled by an ex-cop, being driven home from the hospital in your attorney's Range Rover is the way to go.

Vivian said that she'd already had my Defender driven back to my place, and that she'd had the house cleaned up after the hurricane search from the warrant service. As we drove, Vivian tried to unravel as much of this Gordian knot of legal problems I'd created.

First, I clearly and knowingly violated the restraining order. But, thanks to the magic of government bureaucracy, there hadn't been the requisite hearing for a judge to issue it. Vivian expected the sheriff's department to lean on the District Attorney to make a case for intent, but she didn't think that would work. So, I *technically* hadn't violated anything because they hadn't gotten in front of a judge to make the case for it.

My entering Grant Matthews's home was another matter. That was felony crime scene tampering, and she did not see a way around that. Vivian hoped that she could use extenuating circumstances to get me out of jail time, but I would certainly lose my license. She also admonished me that if I wasn't going to follow the law, perhaps I shouldn't have a license to begin with.

She was absolutely correct.

Orange County dissolved into greater Los Angeles, the kind you saw at freeway speed. It was sun-bleached asphalt, crystalline blue sky, and rows upon rows of buildings stretching to the mountains.

The train of good news continued when I got home, because Jim, my landlord, was waiting. He said he'd been trying to reach me ever since the police notified him of the warrant. He politely asked that I find a new home. Can't say that I blamed him. About a year before, a Russian hit squad broke into the place looking for information they thought I had, and now this. And those weren't the only times work followed me home.

Vivian sharply told him that now wasn't the time and that I would comply with his request. Jim was a nice guy and a good landlord. I'd do as he asked. He was the kind of person that had to talk himself into a confrontation. Still, when he saw the shape I was in, it didn't flush him with empathy so much as solidify his decision. The kind of person who got into fights at work and needed to be driven home from the hospital by his attorney was not the kind of person he wanted as a tenant.

I asked him for a couple of days.

We got inside and, irrespective of the industrial-grade pain killers I was on, I really wanted a scotch. Then I remembered the sheriff's department confiscated it, so I asked Vivian about scorching them.

I'm not a fan of suing police departments over the misconduct of their members. Usually, the outcome is little more than fines, and that's a burden on the taxpayers rather than the organization. As a PI, it's also a great way to burn yourself with law enforcement writ large, whose help you will inevitably need. A civil suit against the sheriff, though, was something else. Vivian was convinced that these events would show a jury that the sheriff had allowed himself to be influenced by Nathaniel Crowder. Further, I had Vanessa Holt's statement about how Crowder had bought influence all over the county. While that in and of itself wouldn't be decisive, it would give us a jumping-off point for further investigation.

"LAPD is sending over two detectives to interview you tonight about Asher Nolan. They know it was Nash, but they need a statement from you anyway. I'm going to have Laura here just in case. I suspect they'll want to know how Nash knew about Nolan in the first place, which will help solidify the case against Graham Wexler. We'll spend a lot of time over the next couple days with Orange County Sheriff and Huntington Beach PD."

"What's going on with Wexler?"

"Nothing yet," Vaughn said heavily. "Perhaps ever. Unless you can make Silas Grey appear, there's no one around to testify that Wexler did anything."

Maybe letting Brody off the hook wasn't such a great idea.

"What about those records I found of him transferring funds to pay Silas Grey?"

"We need a digital forensics expert to weigh in. I know someone. The challenge will be proving that Wexler actually did it." Wexler had indeed gone to NOVA's HQ after leaving Julian's last night and locked his partner out of everything. He then called an emergency board meeting for this morning, conveniently while Julian was tied up with the police.

"That," I said softly, "is the reason I do this job."

Vivian didn't speak, instead she regarded me with a sad, knowing look. She nodded and stood, giving me a squeeze on my shoulder. As she left, she said, "I know."

My instinct about Nolan having video cameras inside his place proved to be correct. LAPD had footage of Brody Nash talking his way into Nolan's place. There wasn't accompanying audio, though the assumption was it was under the guise of them both working for Wexler. An unsuspecting Nolan turned around, and Nash shot him in the head. I showed up immediately after.

The LAPD detectives were gruffly appreciative of the details I'd filled in, but gave me the usual business of how I should've called them in when I found Nolan's body. It turned out that Holt didn't make a 911 call. The sirens I'd heard last night were totally unrelated to Nolan's murder. It made sense in retrospect that she wouldn't want police attention. By that point, Holt was just calling audibles.

The next morning, Vaughn told me that she'd deflected any further conversation with the Orange County Sheriff for a few days, but that they would be taking the investigation over from Huntington Beach.

By the end of the week, we learned that the Orange County DA empaneled a grand jury to sort this shit circus out.

Honestly, I was glad for the help.

38

Since my private investigator's license was currently suspended pending an investigation, the grand jury gave us the legal authority to reopen my Echo-Trace account. It took a few dances with their tech support and legal teams, but eventually they figured it out. I provided the entire contextual summary to the group and testified for hours on how I used the device to connect the various actors. Paired with the information I'd gotten from NOVA, I painted a picture of a comprehensive strategy to progressively undermine Julian Kessler's personal and professional reputation with the goal of forcing his ouster from the company. This was bolstered by Wexler's late-night panic run to the HQ to lock out Julian and his hastily scheduled board meeting. Julian and the other corporate officers testified as to the company's structure and why the strategy relied on his needing to be fired or being encouraged to quit. We made it clear that could only be orchestrated by someone with intimate knowledge of NOVA AI's governing rules and Julian's personal history.

In short, a business partner and close friend since college.

While in the thick of the investigation, there is a tendency to be caught up in the twisted logic of it. Unravelling the puzzle is like a mental drug, it drives you while demanding more and more again. It's easy to abstract the players and smooth over the human cost while you're in the middle of it.

Those are details, essential ones, but they amount to facts to add to the calculus. In the Agency, we were taught not to get too close to the assets we recruited, because we needed to act objectively and decisively. Being a PI isn't much different.

Experiencing the playback of that betrayal was heartbreaking to watch.

This was my first experience with a grand jury, and I was a bit confused by the entire process. I also understood this would not be the only one. These proceedings were intended to uncover whether there was sufficient evidence to bring charges against Graham Wexler. There was a prosecuting attorney, and they had sole discretion over the evidence introduced. There were no defense attorneys present. The prosecutor was the Orange County District Attorney, and I suspected we were going to be quite familiar.

During the proceedings, which I sat for every part of, Julian came across as a hopeful, if slightly awkward, dreamer who truly believed he could push society forward with this technology. He described how he approached Graham Wexler with a vision for his friend's struggling technology and, in that, NOVA AI was truly born.

It was the first time I'd heard this version of their shared story.

I'd hoped that the one he'd shared under oath was the truth, though if I'd learned anything on this case, it's that you couldn't be sure.

If Wexler's legal team coached him through how to testify, they should give him his money back. Wexler came across as calculating and manipulative. When he tried to explain his actions that night after leaving Julian's house, he gave a fumbling justification that he claimed was born out of fear that Julian was staging a coup. He ventured the theory that Julian hired me to fake the disclosures about him, painting some phantom threat that he'd use to seize control of the company. It sounded both outlandish and hastily concocted. From where I sat, Graham's testimony read like he didn't want to give Julian credit for transforming NOVA AI into a marketable product and wanted the jury to know that he was the brains behind the operation. Which, if you're being investigated for hiring a corporate hit man to set up your business partner, is not a good look. It was legitimately mind-boggling, and I could not fathom why his attorneys would advise him that way. Unless he just couldn't help himself.

Things turned south quickly when we reached Grant Matthews.

Brody Nash was the convenient scapegoat and became the avatar of either side's argument against the other. Graham accused Julian of hiring someone dangerously unstable for such a key role, clear evidence of his unsuitability to lead. Julian accused Graham of manipulating Nash into his scheme with dreams of wealth. The prosecutor painted him as a career special warrior that no longer understood the line between war and... not war.

It was sloppy jurisprudence, and never sat well with me. It felt reductive, if not manipulative. It was a convenient and easy excuse, a logical off-ramp to avoid more complex questions. The prosecutor argued that Nash learned Matthews sold Asher Nolan access to NOVA, and tried to confront him over it, which ended with Matthews getting into a one-way argument with a streetlight. Nash then turned his sights on Nolan. Here, the prosecutor showed that I'd recruited Nash to help surveil Nolan. During testimony, the prosecutor paused to emphasize the recurring theme that I should've involved the police at this point. Each time I testified, I reinforced the message that I'd tried damned hard to get the sheriff to take notice and they would not.

Wexler argued that I coaxed Nash into killing Nolan, though I could read the jurors' expressions—from blank to incredulous—that none of them bought it.

Nash was again named for that first shooting at the office park that resulted in the SWAT call and my arrest. Julian and I both testified that we believed this was Silas Grey's attempt to set up Nathaniel Crowder, thereby forcing his expulsion from the board of directors and removing Graham's primary challenger to control the company. I did my best to explain this was an elaborate and expertly crafted false flag operation engineered by Silas Grey to convince everyone Nathaniel Crowder was the mastermind. The fact that Crowder had his own off-the-books troubleshooting squad certainly bolstered that argument.

It was a confusing story, and I don't know how effectively I sold it.

I was forced to testify, under oath, that I'd entered Matthews's house under false pretenses and that I'd removed evidence from the scene. The sheriff's department did not look good for having missed it, and it was clear they had not investigated any of this thoroughly. The prosecutor, however, made absolutely sure that the jury knew I'd committed a pair of felonies.

Things really went sideways when we got to the speculations of drone surveillance.

I'd laid enough breadcrumbs, bolstered by Vanessa Holt's revelations that Crowder used his company's assets to illegally surveil me.

The DA called in representatives from the Departments of Justice, Defense, and Homeland Security and the FAA. Watching Crowder Dynamics lawyers try to tap dance around that was the most fun I'd had in weeks. Crowder was subpoenaed to testify and was not happy about it. I suspect it'd been a very long time since anyone told him where he had to be.

Crowder claimed not to have any knowledge that any of his drones had been deployed to surveil civilian targets, or that any they operated for LASD had been temporarily re-tasked. He similarly claimed no knowledge of the existence of private security officers operating through a Russian nesting doll of shell corporations. Vanessa Holt, as the head of corporate security, was made the convenient fall gal for this.

As with Nash, it was a convenient and expedient answer to give more powerful people a way to dodge accountability.

Her actions that final night did not go in her favor and, ultimately, her hastily assembled legal defense was no match for the white-shoe gladiators her boss brought into the ring. Holt knew she'd be called on to testify that Silas Grey tricked her into believing I was a threat to Julian and that she alone could save him. She did not expect to take the stand as a potential defendant, and was caught totally flat-footed.

It wasn't until then that I finally puzzled out Silas Grey's strategy. I'd been working on it slowly, methodically since the trial started. Hell, since I left Julian's that night in an ambulance. Brody created a convenient patsy for the violent parts of this, but it wasn't everything. Grey wanted me and Vanessa to fight each other. He forced that conflict for a reason. If I'd shot and killed her, it would look like a reprisal for her tricking me and stealing my evidence. Anything I did on this case would be immediately ques-tioned. If Vanessa killed me, I had no doubt Grey would somehow paint this as a maneuver by Crowder.

Instead of Brody Nash being our scapegoat, the blame would've rightly fallen on Grey. It wouldn't have mattered in the grand jury; it wasn't as if Grey was around to testify. As it stood, the jury largely discounted his existence as a fabrication, something dead men created to throw blame in another direction.

The prosecutor didn't believe Grey was real, because he did not issue a subpoena for him to appear, nor did he task the police to find him. Not that it'd have done them any good. The symbolism was clear.

I don't know why Silas Grey wasted his time in this line of work. He was the best gambler I'd ever seen. He should be making a fortune at cards.

The best bluffs have a long lead-up of meticulously curated details to sell them.

After the first week of testimony, I had a sense of where this was going to go. There was a better chance of me finding orbit without a rocket than there was of Nathaniel Crowder entering a courtroom.

That first weekend, I flew to Palo Alto to meet with Nate McKellar. This was not a conversation I wanted anywhere near a phone, and I wouldn't take the chance that there was a warrant authorizing my phone being tapped. Nate's last job in the CIA had been running a front company the Agency used to covertly invest in tech companies. As such, he'd dialed in to both the Silicon Valley scene and the Agency's acquisition process.

After explaining everything that happened on the case, Nate said, "By Monday, Crowder is going to be frozen out of any Intelligence Community contract until the sun goes black. Not even Graves can get him out of this."

"Thanks, Nate."

"If half of what you say is true, this is public service." Nate and I met in his home office, in a room surrounded by the innocuous-seeming mementos of a life lived undercover. Several of the items displayed, I'd given him. "You doing okay, kid?"

I considered that question for some time.

When I answered, I said truthfully, "Not even a little bit."

I'd gone up against some horrible people in my career, and gotten into plenty of near-death situations. This thing rattled me to my core in ways that I hadn't fully comprehended. The best answer that I could come up with was that I expected this kind of behavior from people in government.

The minds who believed they were shaping the world. Perhaps it was naïveté on my part, or ignorance, maybe both. I didn't think these people would be so cavalier with lives. Consequence didn't even factor into their calculations—not of the implications of what they built, or of the effect their power plays would have.

After leaving Nate's, I caught the BART into San Francisco and met another friend. Arnie Trahn was a writer for the *Chronicle* who covered government. We'd met on a case I had up here a few years ago, and I'd been a source for him ever since. We met at the 21st Amendment taproom not far from Oracle Park.

After the first round of beers and some catching up, I said, "So, technically I'm under an NDA and I'm not supposed to discuss anything related to the case."

"Deep background, I got it," he said. Arnie was an old-school newsman. He talked fast, thought faster, and had a way of seeing angles that even I missed. When you could channel that frenetic energy, it made for fascinating conversation.

"Nathaniel Crowder, head of Crowder Dynamics. Formerly on the board of NOVA AI. Crowder is secretly funding a group of…call them troubleshooters. They were run by a man named Lucious Kett. Not sure if that's an alias. Kett is dead. These are guys who make problems disappear. Look into a Kyle Haney."

"Kyle Haney, got it. Anything else?"

"Yeah. Crowder has also paid off nearly every politician in Orange County up through the congress. He gets preferential treatment, he gets access and, on occasion, he gets the Orange County Sheriff to look a little too closely at the wrong person."

Arnie chuckled. "I want to guess who?"

I just smiled and shook my head.

"You may also want to dig into NOVA AI. Just check out how the company is being run."

"Anything specific?"

"Let's just say they could use a little scrutiny. Anonymous tip."

This next one, I did by phone. I didn't care if a cop listened in. I called a friend in the FBI, Special Agent Katrina Danzig. She was currently riding a desk at FBI headquarters and contemplating how much longer she wanted to do that. But as long as I had a friend in Washington, I was sure to abuse the privilege.

"If you're calling me on a weekend, you have to be in jail."

"I am not," I said, indignant.

"Are you about to be in jail?"

"Not to my knowledge."

"Then, what's up, Matt?"

I told her about Crowder and the sheriff and about his squad of flying monkeys. "Any chance you can share this with the LA field office and see if their public corruption squad wants to take a crack?"

"I've got some friends down there. Let me see what I can do."

"I owe you."

"Yes. Yes you do," she said seriously, but I could hear the smirk in her voice.

When the grand jury wrapped after two exhausting weeks of testimony, it confirmed my suspicions. Even though the inquiry spawned multiple separate trials, none of them were going to bring any real justice.

They blamed Brody Nash for the deaths of Grant Matthews and Asher Nolan, and for shooting Vanessa Holt.

Holt was indicted on charges of industrial espionage and attempted murder—me. The police were never able to locate any members of Crowder's private security operation, and that office in the industrial park was vacant when investigated. Courthouse scuttlebutt was that it had been vacant for some time. That wasn't just a cover-up, it was a wash job so good it bordered on ritual.

For all the good it did, I testified in Holt's defense that I'd identified Lucious Kett and this team, that I'd seen Crowder talking to him, and that they'd attempted to scare me off the case with a beating.

Despite the evidence I'd produced linking Wexler with Silas Grey, because we couldn't produce the operative, Wexler walked. No doubt coached by his lawyer, Wexler alleged it was an alias Asher Nolan used. Without Silas Grey, there wasn't a tangible link between Wexler, Nolan, Grant Matthews, and the plot to destroy Julian.

The DA never brought Wexler or Crowder to trial. It was never clear enough to the jury that Wexler orchestrated this, let alone ordered it. The DA never subpoenaed Denis Kwan, the investor who introduced Wexler to Silas Grey.

I used every opportunity to discuss Crowder's influence with local authorities, which Holt spitefully amplified. Few messages land with working-class citizens like a rich guy can buy his way into or out of whatever he wants. They would eventually recommend a further inquiry into Crowder's businesses and his use of political influence to clear blockers. I didn't have a lot of hope that it'd be successful, but I loved that he'd burn time, money, and PR on this.

They indicted me on felony crime scene violation and evidence tampering.

In the end, the grand jury wasn't about truth. It was about the appearance of accountability, with all the substance of a hologram. And for the good people of Orange County, California, that would have to do.

Turns out the legal standard had shifted—beyond reasonable bullshit was the only bar they had to clear.

I caught Amara Singh walking out of the courtroom following her testimony on that last day. She looked tired and sad and haunted. She'd gotten into this not to change the world, but because it was a fascinating new technology with incredible problems to solve. Tech people, I found, were not unlike explorers. They wanted to see if it could be done, that was the thrill.

"You never told me how you learned about Denis Kwan," I said.

"No, I didn't," she agreed. Amara looked down the street, an unconscious tell that she wanted to be anywhere else. "Guess it doesn't matter now." Her shoulders lifted in the slightest hint of a shrug. "You know that Graham and I were involved." I nodded. "We agreed when I joined the company that we wouldn't start back up. It would just make things too complicated, and Julian tended to jump at shadows." Her eyes welled and flushed, she held the tears back through sheer force of will. Amara hugged herself. "We hooked up."

"Did Graham tell you about his plan?" If she knew and held this back, it'd just detonated two weeks of grand jury trial.

"No. He definitely hinted that he thought Julian was out and that he could do a better job. He wasn't exactly bragging, but, I don't know. It felt like he was testing the waters."

"How did you find out about Kwan?"

"I knew Denis. We were all at Google together. I knew they were back in touch, but I didn't make much of it. I always figured Graham told Denis to invest in NOVA because he thought it was a good bet. One night when we were together, I woke up to go to the bathroom and saw that Graham wasn't in bed. I went looking for him and walked in on him talking to someone. He didn't hear me. He was kind of yelling, asking why it was taking so long. Obviously, I couldn't hear both sides of the conversation, so I'm just piecing this together from what Graham said. He didn't 'want to be patient' and that he was going to take matters into his own hands. He complained that everything went sideways and that there was too much attention."

"When was this?"

"After we voted Crowder out."

"So, Grant Matthews had been killed. We had the SWAT situation."

Amara nodded. "That's right. I ran back to bed. Graham eventually came back. The next morning when Graham was in the shower, I checked his phone and saw he was talking to Denis."

"You don't think that was worth bringing up in there?"

Amara's face darkened with a flash of anger. "You saw what he did to Julian. What do you think he'd do to me? Or have this Silas Grey person do? And anyway, they didn't ask."

"I guess they didn't," I said.

"I don't know what that was, but it wasn't justice," I said. Vivian Vaughn waited until Amara was out of earshot before approaching.

"The DA is lazy. He doesn't think he can sell Silas Grey to a criminal jury, especially if they don't have him in custody. Or even prove that he exists." Her voice was even, almost clinical, like she was delivering a law school lecture. "So, instead, they just wipe him from the record and blame Nash and Asher Nolan."

"Nash killed one person, not three. And he didn't do it out of some twisted loyalty to the company. They're up there making him out to be Colonel Kurtz, when the real answer was Graham Wexler got in his head."

Vaughn did not argue.

"There's an offer on the table," she said, after we'd descended the steps.

I could feel what was coming, the way a plane crash is no longer a surprise once the engines go.

"DA wants to make a trade," I said.

The sheriff's department provided security at the courthouse, and I looked around to see if they were lurking like gargoyles, waiting to swoop in to arrest me. The grand jury delivered an indictment. The warrant was no doubt in process.

"This is not to be repeated," Vaughn said. We were outside now, and she scanned the sidewalk to confirm no one was within earshot. A thin crease appeared on her brow and her dark eyes narrowed in the squint; more lines appeared at the corners while she drew a pair of designer sunglasses out of her purse. "The DA knows Sheriff Reynolds has no defense. There will be phone records showing Crowder called him because this isn't the kind of thing he's leaving to someone like Holt. She's working on a plea deal of her own, and this has already come up. They'll withdraw the felony charges if you agree to withdraw your civil claim and shut up about the sheriff's office. Quiet exit for both sides."

"What does this mean about my license?"

"Without the felony charge, we have a fighting chance."

"As soon as I see confirmation that the charges are withdrawn, I'll do the same," I said.

Vaughn was already on her phone to call it in.

"You're doing the right thing, Matt."

The sick feeling lurking at the bottom of my stomach said otherwise.

Julian and Benjamin Blake wanted to take me out to celebrate.

The case cost me my PI license and my home, but yeah, let's go have a nice dinner.

Well, to be fair to my client, it was my handling of the case that cost me my license. I couldn't blame that on anyone but myself.

Still, I didn't want to be there.

Julian paid me before the grand jury investigation began. His legal team wanted there to be no doubt that our business had concluded and I wasn't technically an employee during any subsequent trials.

My rate structure tends to be whatever feels right in the moment, so I couldn't say by exactly how many orders of magnitude Julian exceeded my usual fees.

I'd never gotten a three-hundred-and-fifty-thousand-dollar check before.

He said he'd put something extra in there because of how badly I'd been injured and how many times I'd risked my life on his behalf. He wasn't wrong. It was still guilt money. If I were a more principled man, I might have turned it down. Or at least told him I'd only accept what I'd quoted him. Principles don't put a roof over your head, and Jim had given me until the end of the grand jury to find another place to live.

It was also orders of magnitude more than what Asher Nolan had stolen from me.

Eager to be out of Orange County, Julian and Blake selected an exclusive steakhouse in downtown LA. By "exclusive" I mean it was on the fortieth floor, and you needed to be on some kind of list just to know it existed. There weren't prices on the menu, and I imagined that when they ran the credit cards for the bill, lights somewhere dimmed.

"What happens to Graham now?" I asked as the wine was poured.

"He knows that he skated with the grand jury," Blake led off the conversation. I found that interesting. "He won't be so lucky in a civil trial."

Blake said little and yet, said everything.

It was clear to me that they'd already negotiated a deal with Wexler. I wondered if that's what this dinner was about. A trial would fully expose Wexler's scheme, his diabolical manipulation and amplification of his friend's past mistakes. It would take away any future he could hope to have, which was a prison all its own for someone like him.

"He needs to be held accountable for what he did. People are dead," I said.

"Do you have Silas Grey?" Julian asked acidly.

It was a rhetorical jab and a dirty one. Julian was projecting, but that didn't excuse it. Sure, he'd paid me three hundred thousand, that wasn't enough to take this out on me. After a few seconds of watching my face sour, Julian concluded that himself.

Julian had never seen Silas. He only knew of his existence because of me. I wouldn't be surprised to learn that his legal team latched onto the idea that Silas was a fabrication. They'd argue he was a creation of Crowder's people to give us a bogeyman to chase, or conjured up by me, to have someone to blame my failure on.

"I'm sorry, Matt. That wasn't fair."

"It's all right. You've been through a lot," I said, voice flat. I couldn't muster the emotion to buttress my words. It just wasn't there.

"I'll have full control of the company shortly, and I'll be selecting a new board. I'm considering making the company a nonprofit research corporation, just to ensure that our goal in furthering NOVA isn't guided by something other than the collective good." That was as rehearsed a delivery as I'd ever heard. Frankly, he was better on stage. "I will have a need for a new head of security, Matt." He and Blake traded a look. "I'd like to offer it to you. For what it's worth, NOVA endorsed you as well." He laughed softly because I guess that passed as a joke in his world.

"Matt, I know you can appreciate that Julian needs people around him that he can trust," Blake said. "Since no arrests were made, the safe assumption is that someone will try again. Nathaniel Crowder isn't one to quit lightly."

Even if he didn't make the company a nonprofit, that would still be more money than I'd ever seen in my life. Christ, I'd even have decent health insurance. Of course, in a job like that, I'd probably need it less than I did as a PI.

Which I couldn't be anymore.

Julian didn't need the world's most advanced computer to read my thoughts, though. It was dripping off my face.

"Don't tell me now," he said. "Take tonight."

"Julian, I don't know anything about corporate security or industrial espionage."

"You know everything about the real kind, though. Flipping Verala into an agent? That was badass. That's what we need."

"You should consider this, Matt," Blake said evenly, wisely.

They both wanted a spy, but for different reasons. Julian reveled in the cachet of having an ex-spook on the payroll, the same way he did an ex-SEAL. It wasn't about skills I had in this life, it was what I did in my past one. He wanted to believe someone was coming for him again and wanted a weapon equal to the threat his ego created.

Blake, for his part, wanted an actual spy. He knew Julian was erratic and volatile, he wanted someone he could trust to protect his investment. I suspected there was an amount of altruism buried in there, too. Give me something for all the trouble this caused me. And, perhaps, give me less reason to disclose the skeletons in Julian's closet.

Blake steered the conversation away from business, and I ate what I am sure was one of the finest meals of my life. I barely tasted it.

In the morning, I declined Julian's offer.

I'd probably never turn down that much money again.

It occurred to me, after I declined, that I never did learn which of the things Grey exposed were the manipulated truth and which were fabrications.

None of that mattered in the end. I was done with Julian Kessler and his vision and the people and things that orbited him like planets. He could change the world all he wanted, just not the part I was in.

Diana and I agreed not to see each other during the grand jury investigation. Wexler's lawyers certainly had someone following me and, if they saw us together, could use that to suggest my investigation was biased. I missed her presence. There hadn't been time to think about or process whatever was going on between us, but her absence felt like something had been taken from me.

When you're looking to impress someone in Santa Monica, you take them to Orla, a Mediterranean seafood restaurant in the Regent with the best view of the ocean that doesn't put sand in your toes. I took the art deco–style booth so that Diana could face the water at sunset. A slow fan toiled above us, and we were alone in the world. She chose the wine, a Spanish Tempranillo, and we ate one of the best meals of my life. This one, I fully enjoyed.

"Benjamin Blake called us all in today," she said, lifting her glass. "Except the general, of course. He's had enough of Los Angeles."

I laughed at her impression of him.

"He said Julian asked him to restructure the board. We were all dismissed." She shrugged with a gesture that was equal measures demure and dismissive. "After everything, we were all ready to be done."

"I think Julian would never be sure someone else wasn't in on it."

"The only thing I care about is what you think," she said.

"Graham Wexler had a massive inferiority complex and had played second fiddle to people all his life. Whatever he might tell you, whatever he's telling himself right now, he needed Julian to make NOVA a reality. Before Julian showed up, Wexler had an algorithm. Except, someone got in his head. An old colleague named Denis Kwan was whispering in his ear that he didn't need Julian, then Kwan introduced Wexler to Silas Grey. Kwan worked with Grey in the past. There are already too many people involved for this to stay a secret. I suspect that if there were any more co-conspirators, Grey wouldn't have taken the job. We'll never know for certain, but I suspect Kwan believed he could manipulate Graham." I leaned back into my seat, considering my next words carefully. I wouldn't say it if it wasn't true. Vanessa Holt tried to pin all of this on Diana, which confirmed that Crowder had been watching me. That all but assured me of her innocence. It was a strike delivered when I was most vulnerable, most in need of a lifeline.

I explained all of that to her, because I felt like she needed to know.

I remained silent while Diana contemplated what I'd said.

After a minute or so, she extended both hands across the table and took mine. She smiled. It was a little sad, a little wan, yet somehow still warm.

"That's not the reaction I was expecting," I said.

"No one's ever framed me before. This is a new experience for me."

"It's not unlike wine. You find you appreciate the really good ones, despite the damage it does," I said, smirking. And with that, the situation was disarmed.

Lifting her glass, Diana took it all in. Los Angeles, Julian and Wexler, NOVA AI, the other board casualties, Vanessa Holt framing her for no good reason. "I think I'm tired of California. I have an idea," she said slowly, playfully, as if teasing the words themselves.

"Yeah?"

"Why don't you come back to Lisbon with me?"

That was not what I'd expected her to say.

The next morning, we sat on my couch drinking coffee, warm sunlight coming in through the window. Diana wore one of my shirts and little else, her long legs draped across mine. For the first time I could remember, I felt whole.

"So," she said with a lilt, "what do you think? Coming with me to Lisbon?"

"That is absolutely what I want to do," I said.

Her face darkened.

"But you're not going to," she said, and I shook my head slowly, already wondering what in the hell I was doing.

"Because it would be too easy for me."

"Too easy for what?"

"To run and hide. Diana, if there's one thing I know how to do, it would be to disappear in that country. I could be fluent in your language in six months. I wouldn't even need to pretend to be an expat. I'd blend into the background, and no one would ever know. And that's why I won't do it. It's the easy way out."

"What do you have here? They took everything from you." She pulled her legs back and curled them beneath her body.

"There was a time when I needed someone like me and there was no one. That's why I do this job. And what would I even do? I won't leech off you. My case money eventually runs out."

"I make more money than I can possibly spend. I'd rather burn it *living*...with you."

That was the most compelling reason in the world for telling this place, this profession, to go to hell. Diana was everything that was missing from my life.

Except, maybe, one thing.

My eyes went from her to the boxes in the room. There hadn't even been time to rearrange things from the destruction the warrant service had wrought. Instead of putting things away, I just packed it.

"There is no one here you owe anything to. Just come with me."

"The DA dropped the charges against me, which means the state shouldn't have revoked my license. My attorney is filing a suit to get it back now. I need to see that through. And I'm not done with Crowder. Or Silas Grey."

Diana smiled sadly. "That sounds more like you."

It wasn't the truth, at least not the whole of it. But it was a truth that she would understand, and that would have to be enough.

I wouldn't run, now or ever. I wouldn't take the easy way out, a hasty escape even if it was as convenient as it was logical. Because that would mean admitting to myself that they'd won. That people like Crowder could run me out of the business if I caused them enough problems.

I didn't have a license when I started this. I only got one after Katrina Danzig convinced me to. This wasn't a mindset that would ever make sense to someone like Diana.

39

A few days later, I took Diana to the airport for her flight home. She never pressed me on my decision, only saying once as we moved through the goodbyes that she hoped I'd change my mind. We were both adult enough to know that offer had a shelf life.

That goodbye hurt as much as any wound I'd suffered. I never reconsidered my decision, though.

It was a fittingly cloudy day at the tail end of November.

I climbed back into the Defender and was leaving LAX, the full gloom settling in, recrimination riding shotgun.

My phone rang as I was clawing my way onto the cloverleaf to lead me out of the airport. I didn't look at the number because I was driving, and I was expecting a call from Vivian Vaughn.

It wasn't her.

"I'm glad I caught you, Matt."

Fingers gripped the wheel out of reflex, knuckles turning white. Couldn't escape the emphasis he put on "caught you" either.

I exhaled a silent breath to calm myself. Dialing back as much fury as I could, I said, "Good morning, Silas."

I let the words hang in the electric ether, that impossible space between our phones. He was going to work for this.

"I'd like to meet with you. Face-to-face."

"I'm a little booked up now. Call me in a year," I said.

"You can spare ten minutes. It's on your way back to Santa Monica anyway." That icy, flat delivery.

I was getting really tired of seemingly everyone in this thing knowing where I was all the time.

"I'm texting you an address," Grey said and hung up.

———

Seven minutes later, I walked into an old diner with a bad attitude. This place hadn't seen an interior decorator since the seventies. The thick smell of fried food hit me at the door, and the low din of a hundred background sounds blended into a single band of white noise. The place was half full, that space between the end of the breakfast rush and the start of the lunch one.

I spotted Silas right away. It takes a grim confidence to sit with your back to the door.

"Have a seat," he said, when I broke the plane of his peripheral. There was a pot of coffee and two cups on the table. His was half full.

I slid into the booth opposite him. "Why did you want to meet now?"

"Because the police have all of your guns."

"That's a big bet for someone in your shoes," I said.

"Coffee?"

"No."

"I didn't do anything to it," he said sourly. It was the most emotion I'd gotten from him.

"What do you want?"

Silas wore a gray suit, white shirt, and no tie. There was a pair of sunglasses folded on the table, different than the Clubmasters I'd seen him with earlier.

"I told Graham that Brody Nash was a mistake. He was erratic. Erratic people are irrational, and irrational people are dangerous."

"That what this is about? You wanting me to walk away from this believing you were right? Or that you were innocent?"

"Nothing so heavy as all that. I tried to talk Graham out of using him, but clients don't always do what you tell them to. I'm sure you can appreciate that."

I wasn't going to give Grey the satisfaction of an agreement.

"Wexler is out," I said. "You failed."

The negotiation between Wexler's attorneys and the company's didn't take long because Wexler knew what he was up against. It would take the two parties months to work out the details, change of control and intellectual property, but they'd reached an agreement in principle that would allow Wexler to walk away without a civil trial.

"*I* didn't fail. I did everything my client hired me to do. What I didn't count on was you. I expected you to throw pebbles at a window, not a rock through the glass."

"I do live to disappoint," I said. "You pulled Julian apart from the inside, ruined his reputation and caused harm he can never undo. There were a hundred ways Wexler could've gotten to this point, or a better one, without nearly destroying a man."

"All of that is true," Grey said and spread his hands. "But that's not my concern. It's up to my clients to work out the morality of their actions and their implications."

"Three men are dead because of you. Several more are ruined."

"I didn't kill anyone." Grey's voice wasn't *ruthless*, necessarily, just cold. He was devoid of any emotion. When I first met him, I attributed that to his being a bureaucrat. Now I knew he was just a sociopath.

"Who shot Vanessa Holt? It wasn't Nash."

"A contractor. That's all I'll say."

Details of Grey's background from the EchoTrace search flashed into memory. His formative years were working for a UK-based private security firm.

"SAS or Royal Marine Commando?"

"Commando," he replied in a flatline.

"Did you meet him when you were with FrontPoint or Aegis?"

"No," Grey said. *So, yes.* "In any regard, the thread isn't worth pulling, he's already out of the country."

I didn't care who killed Lucious Kett. I doubted anyone that wasn't the police did either, and I was done doing their legwork. I knew someone who might be interested in that, however. It confirmed my suspicion that Silas voice-cloned me, got Vanessa to that location, and called in the SWAT team.

"Fine. He's forgotten. Why? At that point, Grant Matthews is dead, there's no tangible link to your operation. It was also a...stretch."

"Oh, I admit it was a bit of a mousetrap. Many things had to fall into place for it to work. The intent was only to remove you from play for a while. I had faith even the Orange County Sheriff could figure out your gun wasn't a match."

He just didn't think a SWAT lieutenant wouldn't let that go, irrespective of the evidence.

"You wanted to finger Crowder. That's why we were in front of that warehouse his people used."

Grey nodded and pointed at the air across the table. The rest of his delivery was so cold, so mechanical, the gesture struck me as out of place. "Unfortunately, the authorities were so preoccupied with you that they failed to follow the breadcrumbs to Mr. Crowder. The result was largely the same, he was maneuvered off the board and was the voice loudest in Julian's ear. That also shifted your suspicions to another board member rather than to my client."

"Why did you have Matthews killed? That seemed unnecessary. The only name he had was Nolan."

"I didn't," Grey said with stone-tablet surety.

The only one left would have been Crowder's security team. "Crowder did it?" I ventured.

Grey nodded again. "Your instinct that it was a bump-and-run was correct. They hadn't intended to kill him, just scare him into revealing Asher." I didn't say anything further. I only gave Grey an ambivalent stare across the table. "Crowder rightly assumed that this was a corporate espionage op. His mistake was that he thought you were behind it. He was afraid to move against you directly at that point, but thought he could convince Matthews to flip on you."

"How'd you find that out?"

"One of Kett's people talked." Again, that icy ambivalence. I didn't want to consider the implication of that and let the subject drop.

"Now, it's my turn."

His expression soured. He hadn't called me here to tell me this. Grey styled himself a master magician, and he wasn't going to reveal how he set up the prestige before he performed it. The question was what he was leading up to. Grey waved his hand dismissively, indicating he would accede to my request.

"Why did you send Holt after me?"

I found it unnerving that he didn't pause to contemplate the answer. "If you killed Ms. Holt, it would appear that you lured her to Kessler's to ambush her. This discredits your entire operation. Julian would be ruined, and my client would win. If she killed you, the authorities would conclude she acted under Mr. Crowder's direction." He spoke with a reptilian conviction that sent a cold slither down my spine.

The level to which these people so cavalierly discussed human life disgusted me.

The final piece materialized.

"Then you posthumously add some electronic evidence suggesting Julian hired *you* and that this was all a false flag. Somehow it slips that I figured that out, and it's why we lured Holt to your place, to get my laptop and kill her. Julian goes down in disgrace, and Wexler takes over. You don't care about your name or reputation because the authorities all think you're a bogeyman anyway. Either outcome, Wexler takes the company."

Silas slow-clapped, and he was lucky the police had all my guns.

"When did you turn, exactly?"

"I could ask you the same question," he countered. "But, I'll answer. You mentioned FrontPoint. I'll tell you, Crowder's little gang has nothing on the Europeans. In the UK, they just call that 'business.' FrontPoint was just such a place. Oh, they colored it up with pretty packaging and called it 'risk mitigation,' but it was corporate espionage and preemptive damage control. Inconveniently for me, our hand in an operation was exposed, and I became the risk they needed to mitigate. I learned only too well that loyalty is a fungible commodity."

Felt like he was fishing for some kind of brothers-in-arms kind of camaraderie.

"This has been interesting, Silas," I said, making sure he knew he'd find no commonality in my tone. I slid to the end of the booth. He still hadn't told me why he'd called me here. Nothing he'd told me would've been worth the risk of exposure.

He lifted a finger. "One question, before you go."

I paused. "What?"

"What are your intentions?"

"You mean am I coming after you as soon as you leave this diner?"

"I've enjoyed our match, Matt. You're quite good. I imagine you were formidable in the Clandestine Service. When you could do that, of course." Couldn't help himself. "You and I played by a set of rules. Others did not."

"Crowder," I said evenly, and Grey nodded in reply.

"Were it not for his influence with the sheriff, this would have played out differently. I'd have won."

Crowder's people running Matthews off the road might or might not have worked out in Grey's favor. It cauterized any easy connection to Nolan. If Matthews was alive, I wouldn't have been able to get the phone, which ultimately led me to Grey. The sheriff would have kept me occupied after the swatting, but without Crowder trying to pin Matthews's murder on me, that would have faded quickly. There was no easy path for me to identify Grey and map that back to Wexler. Certainly not before the board falsely concluded Crowder orchestrated the plot. They'd remove Julian, and Wexler would "reluctantly" offer to take full control of the company.

To Grey, Crowder's interference was what cost him his victory.

Now he was looking for some get-back, and he wanted to know if he had to worry about me while he did it.

Curiously, I was the one who foiled the backup plan by not killing Holt and simply surviving the night. Grey's transactional view of loyalty seemed to play into this as well. That comment he made about the client not doing what he wanted. Wexler bringing Nash in created a variable Grey couldn't control. Nolan's murder meant the police were now involved in the investigation in a drastically more dedicated way, increasing the chances of it getting linked back to Grey. His cachet, his persona, his entire business proposition was predicated on his being a ghost. Now the authorities had Grey's name, and it was all because of his client.

I finally poured a cup of coffee from the pot. I'd spent a lot of time in parts of the world where that act was the surest sign of trust between two warring factions. I suspected that was the symbolism behind it.

Lifting the cup, I offered a subtle toast and drank. It was acrid and just this side of cold, about two hours past its prime. Seemed fitting.

"If there's nothing else," he said. Grey inclined his head in a single, purposeful nod. Then he slid out of the booth and stood.

He turned, but before he made a step, I said, "Be seeing you."

"Of that, Mr. Gage, I have no doubts."

Silas Grey left the diner.

I called Vanessa Holt from the Defender.

"I have some information you might find interesting," I said. "Check out a company called FrontPoint and look for some intersections between Silas Grey and an ex–Royal Marine Commando, probably someone sniper qualified."

"Thank you, Matt. I think I will."

In the weeks to come, I learned that the state dropped Vanessa Holt's charges on a technicality. Funny how that works.

She started a "security consultancy," and the first client was Evelyn Hawthorne's nonprofit. So at least I knew that Silas Grey wasn't motivated solely by revenge. He was giving Nathaniel Crowder a lot of problems to worry about. I didn't hold anything against Holt. We'd both been played by larger forces. Giving her the clue about who'd shot her was my way of saying we were even. If things had played out just a little differently, I could see us being partners.

Julian maintained control of the company but couldn't quite escape the gravity of those tumultuous few weeks. Finding a technical mind like

Wexler was not easy, and Julian found himself to be radioactive in many circles. You can put a fire out, but you never get the smoke out of your clothes. Grey's lingering ghost haunted NOVA AI. There was rumor out in the ether that Julian masterminded these events to oust Graham and seize control. Not many people believed it, but enough did. It slowed NOVA's pace for sure. They might eventually shape tomorrow, but they weren't doing it today.

Ortega saw me during the grand jury, though he didn't say anything. A few weeks after the dust settled, he called and offered a halfhearted apology for keeping me at arm's length during the case. Said he was glad that I made it out okay. I let him do it over a beer. Ortega was a good sort, a hard man trying to do a harder job and not let it eat his soul. I don't think either of us envied the other much.

Vivian Vaughn kept me employed as a freelance investigator while we fought with the state over my PI license. It wasn't exciting work, but it was a steady paycheck, which was something I hadn't seen in years. Anyway, I needed the money because I used my payout from Julian to buy the house from my landlord. Moving is a pain in the ass, and the house already had the safes that I needed. Plus, it was close to my office.

People who know can find me. And the ones that do don't care whether I've got a license.

That's the reason I didn't vanish with a woman who loved me. That was the work I still had to do.

If the system failed you and you need someone in your corner, you can call me. I'm usually in the back booth at Cosmic Ray's.

Firewall
Book 1 in The Firewall Spies

When a scientist at the world's top AI company is murdered, a covert CIA operative must recruit a former love interest to help uncover the killer.

With its genius CEO and breakthrough technology, the Silicon Valley-based Pax AI Corporation is one of the hottest companies in the sector. But when one of their top scientists is murdered at a prestigious tech conference, company executives and foreign spies are all on the suspect list.

In the aftermath of the killing, CIA officer Colt McShane has been assigned to a joint counterintelligence unit based in San Francisco. The unit's leadership believes that an international espionage ring has been stealing classified technology from Pax AI.

Now they want Colt to use his past relationship with Pax AI executive Ava Klein to penetrate the company's inner circle, and uncover the mole.

But as Colt learns more about Pax AI's classified programs, he discovers just how powerful—and dangerous—their new technology can be. As the struggle for AI dominance grows ever more competitive, the factions vying for power are becoming desperate to achieve victory.

In the fight for absolute power, there can be only one winner. Each side has their own spies and secrets.

Whose side will win? And what secrets will they reveal?

Get your copy today at
severnriverbooks.com

ACKNOWLEDGMENTS

This book marks the ninth that I've done with my editor, Randall Klein. I am forever grateful for the collaboration, the guidance and advice to follow my instincts. My books and my writing are better for it.

ABOUT THE AUTHOR

Dale M. Nelson grew up outside of Tampa, Florida. He graduated from the University of Florida's College of Journalism and Communications and went on to serve as an officer in the United States Air Force. Following his military service, Dale worked in the defense, technology and telecommunications sectors before starting his writing career. He currently lives in Washington D.C. with his wife and daughters.

**Sign up for the reader list at
severnriverbooks.com**

www.ingramcontent.com/pod-product-compliance
Lightning Source LLC
Chambersburg PA
CBHW010557310726
48969CB00009B/2461